CANDLE FLAME

CANDLE FLAME

Being the Thirteenth of the Sorrowful Mysteries of
Brother Athelstan

Paul Doherty

CRÈME de la CRIME

This first world edition published 2014
in Great Britain and the USA by
Crème de la Crime, an imprint of
SEVERN HOUSE PUBLISHERS LTD of
19 Cedar Road, Sutton, Surrey, England, SM2 5DA.
Trade paperback edition first published
in Great Britain and the USA 2014 by
SEVERN HOUSE PUBLISHERS LTD.

Doherty, P. C.
  Candle flame.
  1. Athelstan, Brother (Fictitious character)–Fiction.
  2. Murder–Investigation–England–London–Fiction.
  3. Great Britain–History–Richard II, 1377-1399–
  Fiction. 4. Detective and mystery stories.
  I. Title
  823.9'2-dc23

ISBN-13: 978-1-78029-060-7 (cased)
ISBN-13: 978-1-78029-545-9 (trade paper)

All Severn House titles are printed on acid-free paper.

Severn House Publishers support the Forest Stewardship Council™ [FSC™],
the leading international forest certification organisation. All our titles that
are printed on FSC certified paper carry the FSC logo.

Typeset by Palimpsest Book Production Ltd.,
Falkirk, Stirlingshire, Scotland.
Printed and bound in Great Britain by
TJ International, Padstow, Cornwall.

To Master Elliot Paul Bruce. All our love to our first grandson.

PROLOGUE

'Bloodletting': a technique to restore the humours.

The Guardian of Sin, that Creature of Dread from Hell, had certainly set its mark on London during the freezing month of February, the year of Our Lord 1381. Candlemas had been honoured with taper-light and candle-bright in all the city churches, but the hiss of Hell's adders and the venom of the ancient serpent, or so the chroniclers would have us believe, could be heard in the very air. The Demon of the Abyss had allegedly set up camp in the narrow spires of those same London churches. According to the monastic scribes, 'The demons who sheltered there peered out between the bells to seek their prey before tripping merrily along the narrow alleys of Southwark to kiss and caress their legion of followers.' Foul deeds were perpetrated, grievous sins committed and none more so than in the spacious Southwark tavern The Candle-Flame which lay along the riverside, a mere bow shot from the Church of St Mary Overy. The Candle-Flame was a majestic hostelry built, enlarged and developed on the profits of the recent war in France by Mine Host Simon Thorne, a former captain of hobelars who had served with such distinction under Sir Walter Manny. The Candle-Flame was certainly a house built on blood; nevertheless, it had prospered from the busy river trade and was established as a popular resting place for the constant pilgrimages to Canterbury, Glastonbury, Walsingham, the Holy Blood of Hailes and the Black Virgin of Willesden. The Fraternity of the Water Men, the Guild of Mudlarks who scavenged the banks, not to mention the Society for the Saving of Souls – former sailors prepared to go to help any craft in difficulty on the Thames – were all worthy covens that met at the tavern to discuss business and celebrate their achievements.

The Candle-Flame was a landmark in Southwark. The tavern's shiny, grey-tiled roof capped a soaring three-storey mansion fashioned in brick and timber and eked out with lathe and plaster, its brickwork a smart red, the plaster snow white, its timbers a glossy black. The hostelry's northern entrance facing the river consisted of a splendid water gate, a towered structure approached by a firmly embedded jetty which swept along to broad entrance steps. The southern side boasted a majestic battlemented gatehouse which led into an expansive cobbled stableyard bound by the tavern proper and on the other three sides a range of two-storey buildings comprising bake house, wash house, brew house, larder, stables, store-rooms and a well-furnished smithy. The Candle-Flame was famous for its grotesquely carved gable ends with the grinning faces of monkeys, satyrs, wodwoses and fish-men. Inside stretched a great taproom called the Dark Parlour because of its polished oaken pillars, rafters, panelling and other wood-work. It was a truly comfortable taproom with proper tables, a cushioned stool area and window seats. The thick rope matting across the floor was scrupulously cleaned at least once a week. The tavern windows were filled with horn and close-shuttered both within and without; a few of these were even glazed in fine glass delicately painted with heraldic insignia. On either side of the Dark Parlour, with its great fire roaring in the cunningly carved mantled hearth, ranged the kitchens, refectories, butteries, herb parlours and pantry stores. Bread was baked on the premises and the sweet, fresh smell of the pure manchet mingled with the cured hams and flitches of smoked bacon, as well as the dried vegetables and herbs all hanging in their snow-white string baskets from the Dark Parlour's polished beams. Above the ground floor stretched the middle chambers, as Mine Host proudly described them: well-furnished rooms with soft four-poster beds, warmed by dark-blue curtains and costly embroidered counterpanes. The rest of the furniture was handsomely carved and delicately inlaid. Pictures, triptychs and crucifixes, each covered with a gauze veil which could be pulled back, decorated the shiny cream plaster walls above gleaming wooden wainscoting. Candlesticks with a carved hand clasping the socket provided light. Wire-mesh braziers and silver chafing dishes exuded warmth whilst guests could use the elmwood coffers, aumbries and cypress chests to stow their belongings. On the floor above ranged less luxurious rooms and, just under the roof, lay the garrets and cocklofts with their truckle beds and meagre sticks of furniture.

However, The Candle-Flame was famous for more than its magnificent appearance, hot stews of venison and pike and delicious ale brewed on the premises or even its comfortable lodgings. The tavern also possessed the Barbican: a grey-stone, two-storey soaring tower which stood, solitary and forbidding in the Palisade, a broad stretch of wasteland to the east of the tavern. The Palisade still served as the execution ground for Southwark, the gallows and execution block being erected close to the Barbican. Gossips hotly debated this grim donjon's origins. Some argued that it had been built during the reign of the present king's great, great grandfather, when the Crown of England used the ancient wharves and quaysides of Southwark to provision war cogs ready to sail out and fight the galleys of France, which nosed like savage wolves into the Thames Estuary and along London's great river. Over the years the Barbican had ceased to be a weapon store or fighting tower. Mine Host Simon Thorne often hired it out to parties who might need seclusion, privacy or protection. On 13 February 1381, the eve of the Feast of St Valentine, Edmund Marsen, collector of the poll tax along with Mauclerc, his scribe, Hugh of Hornsey, a captain of archers, and five bowmen had arrived at The Candle-Flame and taken up lodgings in the Barbican. They could well need such a strongly fortified tower, with its heavy oaken door, latticed eyelet and solitary shuttered window on the second storey. Marsen was responsible for collecting the poll tax along the south bank of the Thames. He had been most ruthless in pursuit of what was due to his master, John of Gaunt, uncle to the boy king, Richard II, and self-styled Regent to the kingdom during the minority of his nephew. Marsen's name was hated, both high and low. A cruel, avaricious man, Marsen had squeezed the families and communities to the south of London in a grip as tight as any hunter's snare. No one dare oppose him, at least not yet. Marsen, full of

malicious glee at his achievement, had broken his journey at
The Candle-Flame to rest, take stock and plot even further
plundering on behalf of his royal master. Marsen was a land
pirate, the most feared of his kind. He had swept into the
hostelry demanding the very best for himself. Mine Host Simon
Thorne, tall and rubicund-faced, who acted the ever-smiling,
ever-merry tavern master, had been expecting him. The
Palisade, that stretch of rough, common ground which ran
down to the river bank, had been cleared and the Barbican
prepared for Marsen, Mauclerc and their military escort.
Marsen had demanded the very best food, so he dined on the
likes of charlet and pork with eggs, as well as roast capon in
a highly spiced black-pepper sauce, tansy cakes and other
delicious dishes, accompanied by tankards of The Candle-
Flame's famous ale brewed by Thorne himself and popular
all along the riverbank for its taste and potency.

Mooncalf, chief ostler and cleaner of the latrines and garde-
robes at the tavern, was the one to rouse Marsen after his
nights of gluttony, drunkenness and lechery. Early on the
morning of 17 February, Mooncalf reluctantly prepared to do
this. He wrapped a cloak about himself, gripped the lantern
horn more tightly in his ragged, mittened hand, using the other
to pull over the deep capuchon to protect his head against the
icy cold breeze which bit as sharp as a razor. For a while
Mooncalf stood in the tavern porch staring up at the clearing
sky. This had been a cruel, iron-hard winter. Would spring
ever come, but what then? Mooncalf was most fearful. London
seethed with unrest like oil in a fiery hot skillet. The king was
a child and his uncle, John of Gaunt, ruled with a mailed fist
from his magnificent palace of the Savoy. Gaunt was depicted
by his many enemies, and there were many, as the Prince of
Hell and his ministers the Minions of Darkness. Opposition
was growing like weeds on a dung hill. In the shires surrounding
London and now the great city itself, the poor, taxed and tied
to onerous burdens, had formed their own coven, the Great
Community of the Realm; its leaders, the Upright Men, were
feverishly plotting the Day of Swords, the Season of the Great
Slaughter. On that fateful day the poor would rise in rebellion.
They would create a new commonwealth free of any prince,

prelate and pontiff; it would be a time of blood, when deep-rooted grievances would be settled and the ground cleared so the New Jerusalem could arise along the muddy banks of the Thames. The doggerel chant of the Upright Men, 'When Adam delved and Eve span who was then the gentleman?' was proclaimed all over the city, spiked on church doors, the Great Cross at St Paul's, the Standard in Cheapside and even the splendid gateway to the Savoy palace. Gaunt retaliated with hangings, disembowellings and quarterings at the Elms in Smithfield, Tyburn and Cheapside. Severed heads, boiled, pickled and tarred, decorated the execution poles above the great gatehouse on London Bridge. Blood bred blood. The Upright Men fought savagely against the tightening, panther-like embrace of Gaunt, or so Mooncalf's master Mine Host Thorne described it, and the taverner was well versed in his horn-book. The Upright Men had only to bray their trumpets and they would summon up all the dark dwellers from the Halls of Shadows, London's squalid slums, be it Whitefriars or, Mooncalf shivered, here in Southwark. The Children of the Twilight, the Knights of the Knife, the Squires of the Sewer, the Pages of the Pit, all sharp as the tooth of any saw, waited impatiently for the black banner of anarchy to be raised. Hatred seeped the streets and alleyways of London like the curdling venom of a subtle serpent. The Upright Men encouraged, nourished and supported this, their envoys coursing through a London crowd like hungry pikes in a mere. The Earthworms, the horsemen of the Great Community of the Realm, all garbed to terrify, would appear abruptly in the city, pouring out of some alley mouth to clash with Gaunt's mounted retainers. They had recently captured one of the Regent's tax collectors, Owain Tabbard, in Cricklegate. The Earthworms had surrounded him, beat him, robbed and stripped him, then set him back on his mount with his face turned to the horse's rump, holding its tail between his hands instead of a bridle. The Earthworms had paraded Tabbard through the streets before cropping his ears and nose and throwing him into a filthy lay stall. Another collector had suffered even worse. He had been ambushed and decapitated, his severed head left in blood-filled wineskin close to the main gate of the Savoy.

Mooncalf's teeth chattered as he stared into the cold darkness. The ostler nourished his own secret plans to escape the impending conflagration. The Lollard, the heretic Sparwell, had been taken up and imprisoned in the Bocardo, Southwark's vile prison; Sparwell's arrest would warn others of the danger of belonging to any sect which disagreed with the Church. If Mooncalf's plans came to fruition, and last night's secret meeting was promising, then he would pack his belongings and move to more comfortable lodgings. In the meantime, the sky was lightening. Mooncalf dare not waken Marsen and his coven too early and so be greeted with foul curses and the slops of their night jars. Mooncalf, like his master, just wished the tax collector and coven would go: their very presence at The Candle-Flame was dangerous, whilst it provoked Mine Host's worries about continuing to stay and manage the tavern. The Great Revolt would surely come. Southwark was a hotbed of unrest. Did not some of the inhabitants of the nearby parish of St Erconwald's, men like Watkin the dung collector and Pike the ditcher, sit high in the councils of the Upright Men? What would happen to The Candle-Flame once the horror emerged? Would they, as Mine Host's pretty new wife, Eleanor, wailed, be murdered whilst the tavern was put to the torch? Mooncalf glanced again at the sky; the weak light was strengthening. He grasped the lantern horn and moved out, bracing himself against the freezing air. He crossed the frost-hardened gardens, through the wicket gate and into the Palisade, stumbling over the harsh, uneven, ice-bound ground, the pool of light thrown by the lantern horn dancing and jittering around him. Mooncalf paused at a grunting sound. He lifted his lantern horn. The Palisade was a stretch of common land and Don Pedro the Cruel, the tavern's huge boar pig, loved to browse there. The great pig had surprisingly spent the night out in the open. Mooncalf could glimpse the boar's sleek skin as it lay prostrate beneath a bush snoring and gasping. Mooncalf lifted the lantern, his curiosity now quickening. Don Pedro liked his comforts – usually he would return to his sty. So why had he settled down here? Mooncalf moved towards the pig, only to be distracted by the dying fire of Marsen's guard. Two of the Tower archers under their captain Hugh of Hornsey had set up camp outside the Barbican. Mooncalf wondered why this guard was not active; why had no challenge been issued? He peered through the murk and saw two bodies lay close to the flickering embers of the fire. A stomach-lurching dread seized the ostler: something was very wrong. A few yards away the Barbican loomed massive and sombre through the mist. The grey dawn-light was thinning. The breeze was cutting, yet it was the silence which frightened Mooncalf, as if some hell-born malevolence shifted in the shadows. Mooncalf glanced at the fire – nothing more than red-hot embers. The two archers were lying strange, not rolled in their cloaks. The ostler hurried over and stifled his scream. Both guards lay sprawled on the ground, open-eyed before their dying fire; the trickle of blood between their gaping lips had mingled with that from their noses, now frozen hard to form a hideous death mask. The weapons of both men, sword and dagger, lay close by but these had proved no defence against the harsh feathered bolts which had taken each of them deep in the chest. Mooncalf, moaning in terror, hand clutching his groin, stumbled over to the Barbican, which also lay quiet in all its stark bleakness. The ostler stared up at the donjon's only window: it looked shuttered from within and out. He placed the lantern horn down and tried the heavy oaken door. He pressed hard only to realize that the door was bolted at both top and bottom. Shaking with unspoken terrors, Mooncalf crouched down to peer through the large keyhole but this was blocked by the heavy key on the other side. Mooncalf beat the door, shouting and screaming, but his voice trailed away at the ominous silence which answered him. He glanced back at the dying campfire, those glassy-eyed corpses frozen in death. The ostler's courage gave way. He grabbed the lantern horn, stumbling across the Palisade and running blindly until he reached the tavern's postern door. He hurled himself through this and found himself in the hallway, feverish with terror. He unlocked the main door, grasped the bell rope in its casing and pulled as hard as he could, shouting as loud as his dry, cracked throat would allow.

'Harrow! Harrow!'

Mooncalf breathed out noisily. The hue and cry had been

raised. Above him doors and window shutters were flung open, footsteps clattered on the stairs. Mine Host Simon Thorne, burly-faced, his hair all a-tumble, arrived shouting and cursing, followed by his black-haired, pretty-faced wife Eleanor. The taverner seized Mooncalf.

'What is it, boy?'

Thorne's fierce eyes, red-rimmed with sleep, glared at the trembling ostler. Behind him mustered the servants armed with clubs, cudgels, ladles and anything they could snatch from the kitchen. Nightingale the candle boy even had a cooking pot on his head whilst Thomasinus the turnspit had snatched an ancient battleaxe from the wall.

'What is it, boy?' Thorne repeated. Mooncalf gabbled what he had seen. Mine Host's jaw sagged as he stared in disbelief at the ostler.

'It can't be,' he muttered, 'no, not here!' He shook off his wife's hand, bellowing orders as he struggled to put on the leggings and boots his wife brought. Once ready, Thorne led his horde of servants out of the tavern and into the Palisade. Pedro the Cruel, now recovering from its slumber, struggled to its feet, snuffling and snorting at the bitter cold breeze. Thorne, mindful of what Mooncalf had told him, ordered Porcus the pig boy to drive the boar back to its sty, well away from the corpses of the two archers. The morning light did nothing to lessen the horror. The cadavers of both archers were blood-soaked, their bearded faces whitened by the hoar frost, full of glassy-eyed terror at their sudden, violent death. Thorne strode towards the Barbican. Mooncalf watched intently as his master thundered against the heavy oaken door before stepping back to stare up at the square, shuttered window.

'We would need a battering ram to shatter the door,' he called over his shoulder, 'and we don't have a ladder high enough for that window.' The taverner pointed to a nearby tangle of carts, barrows and ladders under a heavy, dirt-encrusted tarpaulin. 'Pull that back and you'll find what we need. Mooncalf, Nightingale – swiftly now.' They hurried off with others and pushed back a handcart used to carry the filth from the pigsty on the far side of the Palisade. They positioned this under the window and brought a siege ladder, resting it secure so its hooks grasped the deep sill beneath the Barbican's only window. Thorne tested it was secure and climbed cautiously up. The cart provided an extra two yards in length to the ladder. Mooncalf stood holding the bottom rungs. Thorne was now at the top. He had drawn his dagger and pushed this between the gap in the shutters, trying to prise up the iron-hook clasp. Eventually he pulled back the shutters.

'I will have to cut the horn,' he shouted down. Mooncalf watched his master slit the horn and put his hand through to lift the latch. He pulled back the door window and began to hack at the inner shutter. At length this too gave way. Mine Host made to climb through but then thought again and stared down. 'I am too bulky, too fat. Mooncalf . . .' The taverner came down and Mooncalf reluctantly went up. He reached the top rung and clambered over the sill, pushing back both windows and shutters, and climbed into the horrors awaiting him. The candles had long guttered out, the great lantern on its table had been snuffed, but the grey morning light revealed a grotesque scene. Tables, stools and other sticks of furniture had been overturned, yet it was the four corpses which caught Mooncalf's terror-filled gaze. The two whores brought in by Marsen lay tumbled on the floor. One had suffered a thrust to the heart, her naked breasts now crusted with blood from the other's severed throat. She leaned drunkenly back over a stool, belly and breasts thrust up into the air, her slender throat gaping like another mouth. Marsen the tax collector lay against the wall, sword and dagger close to his lifeless fingers, his chest speared by a deep thrust. Nearby Mauclerc had suffered a savage belly wound which seemed to have drained his body of all fluid. Mooncalf could only stand and stare, his throat and mouth bone dry, his tongue thickening so he could hardly breathe.

'Why this?' he murmured, then remembered the iron-bound exchequer coffer, Marsen's pride and joy: it now stood on a footstool, the concave lid thrown back, empty as a spendthrift's purse. Mooncalf glanced back towards the window and noticed a square of vellum pinned to the inner shutter. Mooncalf, who had been instructed in his numbers and letters by his parish priest, went across and quietly mouthed the letters written there. In fact, as soon as he had whispered the first word he realized what it was. He had heard the chatter in the taproom about this quotation from the Bible. Mooncalf pointed out the letters to himself as he mouthed the words, recalling what Nightingale had told him, something about *'mene, mene'*. Mooncalf let his hand drop and stepped back. He would leave that to others. He walked towards the trapdoor, pulled back the bolts and lifted the great wooden slab. He clumsily scrambled down the ladder. The ground floor of the Barbican held fresh, gruesome sights. The three archers on guard lay soaking in thickening pools of blood, weapons not far from their hands. Mooncalf, mouth gaping, eyes blinking, could only shake his head. The Upright Men were performing all kinds of mischief, but how could all this be explained? Two archers lay dead outside with shafts to their hearts? And here in the Barbican, its window, entrance and trapdoor all bolted, locked and secured? Nevertheless, some misty messenger from Hell had swept through this tower and dealt out bloody judgement.

PART ONE

'Flesh-Shambles': butchers' yard.

'Oh City of Dreadful Night!' Athelstan whispered. The Dominican parish priest of St Erconwald's in Southwark, *secretarius atque clericus* – secretary and clerk to Sir John Cranston, Lord High Coroner in the City of London – could only close his eyes and pray. Once again he and Sir John were about to enter the treacherous mire of murder. The hunt for the sons and daughters of Cain would begin afresh; God only knew what sinister paths their pursuit would lead them down. Athelstan's olive-skinned face was sharp with stubble, his black-and-white gown not too clean, his sandals wrongly latched, whilst his empty belly grumbled noisily. The little friar, his dark eyes heavy with sleep, had been pulled from his cot bed by Cranston, who now stood behind him. The coroner had been most insistent. The Angel of Murder had swept The Candle-Flame tavern and brushed many with its killing wings. Edmund Marsen, his clerk, two whores and five Tower archers had been brutally murdered. The gold and silver, harvested south of the Thames and intended for the ever-yawning coffers of John of Gaunt had been stolen. Thibault, master of the Regent's secret chancery, had sent that raven of a henchman Lascelles to rouse Sir John to discover what had happened and, above all, recover the looted treasure.

Athelstan stood just within the wicket gate leading into the Palisade. He peered through the misty murk at the forbidding donjon, the Barbican, and, beyond it, the expanse of rough land which stretched down to the piggeries and slaughter pens.

'Lord,' Athelstan whispered, 'I am about to enter the domain of murder. If I become so busy as to forget you, do not thou forget me.' He crossed himself and turned to where Cranston stood in hushed conversation with the burly taverner Thorne.

Two great hulking men, though Mine Host was clean-shaven and more wiry than the generously proportioned coroner. Both men wore close-fitting beaver hats and heavy military cloaks. Cranston had whispered to his 'good friar', as he called Athelstan, how he and Thorne had both served in France under the Black Prince's banner. Thorne was a veteran, a captain of hobelars who had secured enough ransoms to make him a wealthy man and buy The Candle-Flame.

'Sir John,' Athelstan called, 'we should shelter from the cold and view this place of slaughter.' All three walked over to the remains of the campfire, where a few embers glowed and sparked. Athelstan crouched down, staring at the shifting heap of grey ash.

'A cold night,' he murmured. 'Yet this fire has not been fed for hours.' He rose and walked over to the corpses of the bowmen, knelt between them, closed his eyes and whispered the words of absolution. Opening the wallet on the cord around his waist, he pulled out the stoppered phial of holy oil and sketched a cross on the dead men's foreheads. Their skin was ice cold; the blood which they coughed up through their noses and mouths was as frozen as the congealed mess on their chests. Both men had been armed but there was little evidence that they had used the weapons lying beside them.

'They were killed. I am sorry.' Athelstan held up a hand. 'They were murdered, foully so, in the early hours. The fire has burnt low, their corpses are icy to the touch and their hot blood is frozen.' Athelstan pointed into the darkness. 'Their assassin crept very close.' Athelstan indicated the blackjacks drained of ale and a half-full waterskin lying near the corpses. 'These two unfortunates were crouching, warming themselves by the fire enjoying their drink. They would make easy targets against the flame light.' Athelstan sighed, sketched a blessing in the air and rose to his feet. He stared around at a bleak, stark stretch of land frozen hard by winter, the trees stripped of leaves, their empty branches twisted, dark shapes against the light and that Barbican, solitary and forbidding.

'Executions take place here, don't they?'

'Yes, Brother,' Thorne replied. 'By ancient charter the Palisade must serve, when required, as a gallows field.'

'It's certainly a field of blood,' Cranston declared, bringing out the miraculous wineskin from beneath his cloak and offering this to Thorne then Athelstan. Both refused. The friar stared at the larger-than-life coroner. Sir John stood legs apart, white hair, beard and moustache bristling, beaver hat pulled low, almost covering those large, bulbous blue eyes which could dance with glee, though Sir John was not so merry now. Athelstan could sense the shadow lying across his great friend's generous soul. London bubbled and crackled with unrest. The dirt and filth of the city's restless soul was being stirred. The monster within, the city mob, was honing its greedy appetite as well as its weapons. John of Gaunt was plotting a military expedition, a great *chevauchée* against the Scots. Cranston and others feared that once Gaunt left for the north the Great Community of the Realm would make its move. The Upright Men would raise their red and black banners of revolt and London would slide into bloody strife and turmoil. Cranston had already sent his buxom wife, the Lady Maude, together with the two poppets, their twin sons Stephen and Francis, into the country for shelter. Cranston's personal steward with the coroner's great wolfhounds, Gog and Magog, had followed, leaving Sir John alone. As for the future? Athelstan gnawed his lip. He agreed with Sir John: London would burn and he knew from chatter amongst his parishioners that Gaunt's palace of the Savoy would be the scene of a great riot. Athelstan had begged his portly friend that when this happened Cranston would seek sanctuary in the Tower. The coroner had gruffly agreed, as long as Athelstan joined him. Ah, well . . . The friar felt beneath his cloak to ensure his chancery satchel was secure.

'We should go,' Cranston called out, stamping his feet. 'Murder awaits us.' The taverner led them across to the Barbican with the white-faced, shivering Mooncalf trailing behind. Athelstan pushed against the heavy oaken door, stepped into the lower storey and stopped in shock at the slaughterhouse awaiting them. Fresh candles had been lit. Lantern horns flared, a flickering, eerie light which sent the shadows shifting. Athelstan blessed himself and walked across. He stopped to dig at the fresh rushes covering the floor and, despite the foul odours which polluted the air, caught the spring freshness of newly crushed herbs.

'There is no trapdoor to any cell below?' he asked. 'No secret passageway or tunnel?'

'None, Brother,' Thorne replied. 'The only entrance from outside is the door or the window on the second storey. There's a trapdoor to the upper chamber where you will find another which leads out on to the top of the tower.' Athelstan walked across to the ladder on the far side of the chamber. He carefully climbed up, pushed back the trapdoor and clambered into the upper storey. He immediately closed his eyes at the savagery awaiting him. Four corpses, two men and two women, lay tossed on the rope matting covering the floor. The candle-light dancing in the freezing breeze through the half-open window made the chamber even more of a nightmare. Athelstan opened his eyes. For a few heartbeats he had to fight the panic welling within him, a deep revulsion at seeing human flesh hacked and hewn, sword-split, gashed, their lifeblood thickening in dark-red, glistening puddles. '*Jesu Miserere*,' he whispered and climbed back down the ladder. Athelstan took a set of Ave beads from his wallet. He just wished the others would stop staring at him. He wanted to be away from here. This macabre tower reeked of blood; it was polluted by mortal sin. Demons gathered close, their wickedness souring the air. He wanted to flee; to be back in his little priest house sitting on a stool before a roaring fire with Bonaventure, the great one-eyed tomcat, nestling beside him. He needed to pray, to kneel in the sanctuary of St Erconwald's . . .

'Brother?' He glanced up. Cranston offered him the miraculous wineskin, his red, bewhiskered face all concerned, the beaver hat now pushed well back. Behind the coroner stood Thorne, one hand on Mooncalf's shoulder. The taverner shuffled his boots and stared around at the murderous mayhem. Athelstan smiled. He could feel his own panic easing. He refused the wineskin and sat down on a stool. He let his cloak slip and loosened the straps of the chancery satchel across his shoulder. He found it comforting as he took out a tablet of neatly cut vellum sheets and uncapped the inkhorn and quill from their case on the thick cord around his waist. He put this on a nearby stool and made himself comfortable. He felt better. So it begins, he thought. He stood in murder's own chamber. All was chaos and confusion within. He would, with God's own help and that of Sir John, impose order, some form of harmony. He must apply strict logic and close observation to achieve this.

'Very well, Sir John.' He looked up. 'Tell me, what have we seen?'

Cranston bowed mockingly as he now broke from his own mournful reverie. He recognized what his little friar was doing and he rejoiced in it. Murder was about to meet its match, mystery its master.

'Well, Sir John?'

'Two corpses outside,' the coroner declared, 'both killed by crossbow bolts. They were clear targets in the firelight. It would take no more than a few heartbeats. Three corpses in here,' Cranston intoned solemnly. 'All Tower bowmen; they were relaxing – boots off, leather jerkins untied. According to Mooncalf the front door was locked and bolted and so was that trapdoor from the other side. There is only this.' The coroner went across into the shadows. He opened a narrow door and peered into the shabby closet which served as the garderobe and housed the jake's pot. 'Definitely been used.' He came back wrinkling his nose.

'And that drains off where?' Athelstan glanced at Thorne.

'Into an old sewer deep beneath the ground,' Mine Host shrugged, 'not really big enough for a rat. The garderobe would serve all who would stay here.' Athelstan put down his writing tablet and went across to inspect. The garderobe was cold and stinking, the jake's hole built into the cracked wooden seat fairly narrow.

'Nothing,' Athelstan murmured to himself and smiled, 'could come out of there except for foul smells.' He walked back into the chamber studying the floor and walls. 'This is hard, close and secure,' he declared, 'as any dungeon in the most formidable castle. Who built it?'

'The present king's great, great grandfather,' Cranston replied. 'Such buildings will appear in my chronicle of the history of this city.'

'Why?' Athelstan asked. 'I mean, why a fortified tower like this?'

'It served as a guard post on the Thames, a place of refuge and a weapons store in case French galleys and war cogs appeared along the river. We could do with such defences now,' Cranston continued. 'Rumour has it that the French are mustering hulkes, even caravels, off Harfleur.' Athelstan thanked him and went over to inspect the corpses of the three archers. He had already decided on what he would do with the murder victims. Now he concentrated on learning all he could. The dead were of different ages though somewhat alike in looks: heads and faces closely shaved, skin weathered by the sun, they wore braces on their left wrists, leather jerkins over ragged fustian shirts, leggings of buckram and threadbare woollen stockings, and tawdry jewellery which glittered on their wrists and fingers. They had apparently drawn swords and daggers; these lay close by, tinged with blood. The weapons had proved no defence against their ferocious body wounds.

'Did you strike your assassin?' Athelstan murmured aloud. 'How could such veterans be so easily despatched?' Athelstan steeled himself against the agony of death which contorted their faces in a last hideous grimace as they fought for their final breath. The barrel tables and stools had been overturned. The corpses lay in different positions across the chamber, indications of an assassin who had managed to divide his opponents. Athelstan walked around the room tapping at the wall, stopping to inspect the chafing dish full of spent ash. The archer's cloaks and bundles of clothing had been spread out to form makeshift beds. He could tell by the creases and folds that they had been lying there when the assassin struck. Athelstan crouched and went quickly through their saddlebags and pouches. He found nothing untoward, just the paltry remnants of professional soldiers – men who had wandered far from their woodland villages to serve in the royal array then stayed to seal indentures for military service in this castle or that. He rose and continued his inspection. On a bench table near the wall empty platters were stacked, stained horn-spoons, a small tun of ale, still quite full, and bowls of dried fruit and congealed spiced capon. Athelstan stooped and sniffed the platters but could detect only the sharp tang of spices and herbs. Around the room lay tankards; he picked one of these up and observed the dregs, but he could smell nothing tainted. Meanwhile, Cranston and Thorne remained deep in conversation whilst Mooncalf stood rubbing his arms and stamping his feet. Athelstan called him over.

'Fetch a wash tub.' He smiled at the ostler's blank gaze. 'A wash tub,' he repeated. 'An empty one. I want you to collect the tankards, the ale-tun, bowls and platters and put them in it along with any scraps or dregs.' Athelstan dug into his purse and handed over one of his precious pennies. 'Do that,' he urged, 'and keep them safe. Collect the same from the camp outside and, once I have inspected it, the upper chamber. Do you understand?' Mooncalf nodded and hurried off, ignoring his own master's shouted questions.

'He has got work to do,' Athelstan called out. 'Now, Master Thorne, Sir John.' Athelstan paused, his gaze caught by a large bowl of water with ragged napkins beside it. He went across and stared down at the dirt-strewn water.

'The *lavarium*,' Thorne called out. 'The water was once clean and hot. Brother, what do you want me to do?'

'Master Thorne, Sir John?' Athelstan picked up a dagger and weighed it in his hands. 'You have fought in battles. Each of you is, I suppose, a master-at-arms. Have these weapons been used recently in a fight?' Cranston and Thorne needed no second bidding. Taking up some of the fallen blades they pointed to the scrapes, the streaks, the nicks on the steel and the flecks of blood around their hilts and handles. Athelstan nodded as Cranston explained his conclusion that the weapons had been used very recently. Athelstan shook his head in amazement.

'Why, Brother?' Cranston asked. 'Do you think all this,' he gestured around, 'is a mummer's play, some masque staged to mock and hide the truth?'

'It's just a thought,' Athelstan replied. 'But that's impossible. So, let us view the upper storey.' They climbed the ladder through the trapdoor into the more luxurious solar of the Barbican. The rounded walls were plastered white, rope matting covered the floor and there were cushioned stools,

candle holders and a triptych celebrating the Passion of St
Sebastian. Nonetheless, the chamber reeked of the same
hideous stench as the chamber below, whilst the ghastly sight
of four corpses, brutally cut and hacked, chilled the blood and
darkened the soul. Athelstan blessed the room before walking
around. He noted the wine jugs, goblets, tankards and platters
of congealed food; the tankards were clean, whilst the small
cask of ale stood untouched.

'Marsen cursed me,' Thorne declared. 'Said he did not want
my stinking ale, only the best Bordeaux out of Gascony.'

Athelstan heard Mooncalf busy below. He went to the
trapdoor and shouted that once the ostler was finished he
must join them. The friar then moved from corpse to corpse.
Thorne pointed out Marsen garbed in a costly gown. The tax
collector was sprawled against the wall drenched in his own
heart's blood, an ugly white-faced, red-haired man with a
thick moustache and straggly beard. He looked grotesque,
all twisted, squatting in his own dried blood. Mauclerc lay
on his back, fingers curled as if frozen in shock at the wounds
which sliced his flesh. The two whores, their scarlet wigs
askew, gaudy painted faces now hideous, had been despatched
into the dark with deep lacerating cuts. The two women were
unarmed. Mauclerc had drawn a dagger which lay near him,
but there was nothing to suggest that Marsen had time to
protect himself.

'The exchequer coffer.' Cranston pointed across to where
the chest, its concave lid thrown back, perched on a table stool.
'My Lord of Gaunt,' Cranston grumbled, 'will be furious, not
to mention Master Thibault.' Athelstan studied the coffer
closely. It was fashioned out of sturdy wood reinforced with
iron bands. He had seen similar in the exchequer and chancery
of his own mother house at Blackfriars. The chest was slightly
marked but sound, its heavy lid held secure by stout hinges:
it would be difficult to force when clasped shut by its three
locks, yet there was no sign this had happened.

'A key to each of them, yes, Sir John?' Athelstan queried.

'Undoubtedly. One would be carried by Marsen; Mauclerc
would hold the second.'

'And the third?'

'I would hazard a guess that would be Hugh of Hornsey, who seems to have disappeared.' The coroner clapped his gauntleted hands. 'Oh, Satan's tits! This is a filthy, bubbling pot. My Lord of Gaunt will want answers.'

'My Lord of Gaunt will have to learn patience.' Athelstan now stood near the window shutters. So far he had avoided this. He recalled what Mooncalf had told him: the only real evidence left by the killer was a piece of costly parchment cut in a neat square and pinned with a slender tack to the wood. The writing was clerkly, that of a professional scribe. The letters carefully formed, the message most threatening: '"*Mene, mene, teqel* and *parsin,*"' Athelstan murmured. 'The same warning carved on the walls of the King of Babylon's palace by the finger of God and translated by the prophet Daniel. 'I have numbered, I have weighed in the balance and I have found wanting.'

'Beowulf!'

Athelstan turned quickly.

'Beowulf!' the coroner grimly repeated. 'You have not heard of him, Brother?'

'Of course. The Saxon warrior hero, the keeper of the shield-ring, the slayer of the monster Grendel and its mother.'

'It's not that,' Thorne declared, 'is it, Sir John?'

Athelstan blinked and took the parchment down; it felt soft and yielding. 'I've heard something . . .'

'A skilled assassin,' Cranston explained, 'hired by, or certainly working for the Upright Men. He, she, they – whoever the demon is – has wreaked grievous damage.'

'Of course.' Athelstan breathed. 'Justice Folevile and an escort of three men-at-arms at Ospring on the road to Canterbury. They stayed at The Silver Harp. All four were brutally murdered.'

'Robert de Stokes,' Cranston took up the story, 'and his clerk collector of the poll tax in south Essex. Both were found dead, stripped naked in a filthy ditch.' Cranston waved his hand. 'And so on, and so on. A true will-o'-the-wisp, a sinister shape-shifter, a Hell-born wraith.' Cranston warmed to his theme. 'Beowulf being Saxon stands for the Great Community of the Realm against their Norman French masters. Gaunt, of

course, is the monster Grendel, and his mother the power
which spawned him.'

'And Beowulf was responsible for all this murderous
mayhem?' Athelstan shook his head in wonderment. 'Master
Thorne, I would be grateful if you would help Mooncalf. I
want every cup, platter and morsel heaped in that washtub.
Meanwhile . . .' Athelstan and Cranston searched the chamber
as well as the panniers and chancery satchels of the murdered
men. These were full of memoranda, billae, indentures and
rolls of greasy thumb-marked parchment. The more he searched
the more suspicious Athelstan became.

'Mauclerc was a skilled chancery scribe, Sir John?'

'One of the Master of Secrets' favourites, a veritable ferret
of a man. He was Thibault's spy, a henchman appointed to
watch Marsen. Why, little monk?'

'Friar, Sir John. I am a friar.'

Cranston grinned and took another sip from the miraculous
wineskin. 'Why, my little friar?'

'I am sure these panniers and saddlebags have been riffled.
Someone has gone through them. Certain items were taken,
just by the way the scrolls are piled together.' Athelstan paused.
'One other thing: have you noticed, Sir John, that none of the
victims have coins on them? They were killed and their bodies
robbed. Even the whores! From the little I know don't such
ladies of the night ask for coin before custom?'

'They certainly do, little friar, and look at this.' The coroner,
crouching down, had moved a stool. He now held up a gauntlet
and a piece of shiny, oiled chainmail. The gauntlet was an exquisite piece of craftsmanship: the velvet coat over the stiffened
Cordova leather was finely stitched in gold, with small pearls
along the finger furrows. Athelstan took both items over to the
squat, evil-smelling tallow candle and examined them carefully.
The chainmail was finely wrought. Athelstan suspected it was
the best, probably Milanese; the links were fine and shiny with
clasps on each corner. The gauntlet was also costly. Athelstan
noticed the fingertips were smudged with dry blood. He glanced
swiftly at the hands of the four murder victims: the two whores
would not wear such items, whilst the gauntlet would certainly
not fit the stout-fingered hands of Marsen or Mauclerc.

'The chainmail,' Cranston called out, 'probably served as a wristguard.'

Athelstan summoned Thorne, but the taverner could not recall Marsen or any of his group carrying such items.

'Both are the property of a knight,' Thorne declared, scratching his reddish face with stubby fingers. 'Surely such chainmail, a gauntlet . . . they might even belong to Beowulf?'

Athelstan turned back to Cranston. 'Sir John, does Beowulf always leave those verses with his victims?'

'Yes, Brother, he certainly does, and he is putting the fear of God into all of Gaunt's servants. Master Thibault's minions now go everywhere with a well-armed comitatus, be it in the cobbled square of some market town or the darkest greenwood. But how could it happen here?'

Athelstan held up a hand. 'Not now, Sir John, and not here. We are harvesting the grain of bloody murder. Once the harvest is in we shall grind it and,' he smiled, 'never forget, the Mills of God may grind exceedingly slow but they do grind exceedingly small. So.' Athelstan turned back to the window. There were shutters on both the inside and outside held together by large, sharp hooks which rested in clasps. Athelstan fully closed the shutters, scrutinized the gap and could see how a dagger could be inserted to lift the hooks. The window in between had a wooden frame with a horn covering that worked like a door with hinges and a latch on the inside. Thorne agreed that he had to rip the horn to lift the handle. Athelstan, mystified, could only stare, baffled at how the murderer came in and left. Both Thorne and Mooncalf were resolute in their assertion that the shutters were clasped shut and the window undisturbed. Athelstan walked around, sifting through the tumbled furniture, the blankets and sheets of the two cot beds. He was aware of Cranston lifting the rope matting. The taverner and Mooncalf were now collecting the last of the tankards, goblets and platters in a large iron-rimmed tub. Athelstan climbed the steep ladder, pushing open the trapdoor and carefully pulled himself up on to the top of the tower. A piercing cold wind buffeted him as he staggered across the thick shale to grasp a rusting iron bar which connected the ancient, moss-eaten crenellations. Athelstan took a deep breath

as he stared around. To the north glinted the river – he could
see the war cogs riding at anchor and a myriad of small boats,
barges and wherries. The sky was now brightening but the
day promised to remain freezing cold. The friar stared up at
the wisps of cloud, then down at the huddle of buildings
below. He turned. Somewhere to the south nestled his own
church; his parishioners would be stirring. Benedicta, the
beautiful dark-eyed woman would be in the church along with
Crim the altar boy and Mauger the bell clerk. Athelstan realized he would have to celebrate his Mass late. He was also
determined to meet his parish council so they could discuss
the events of the recent 'Love Day' which had gone disas-
trously wrong. He heard Cranston call his name and made
his way gingerly down. Cranston, Mooncalf and Thorne were
examining two crossbow bolts taken from a small pouch. The
coroner held them up. The steel barbs were blunted, their
flight feathers split.

'Apparently a trophy,' Cranston remarked. 'Mine Host
claims that on his journey here Marsen was attacked as he
crossed the small footbridge near Leveret Copse, a little to the
south. Both bolts missed. Marsen crowed in triumph like a
cock on its dunghill.'

'They are the same.' Athelstan studied both carefully.
'Identical, I think, to those used to kill the archers outside.
Ah, well, let's continue.' Athelstan went out into the bitter
cold morning, Cranston and the others trailing behind. The air
reeked of the nearby piggeries and trails of smoke from the
dying campfire. Athelstan walked to the ladder, still positioned
on the handcart. He made sure it was secure and carefully
climbed up to the window. He noticed how the ladder hooks
fixed securely under the sill. He pulled the shutters open,
ignoring Cranston's call to be careful and studied the wood-
work, split horn and the handle to the window. Satisfied, he
climbed back down.

'Sir John, I have seen enough.' He pointed to the door.
'My Lord Coroner, Flaxwith, your master bailiff, must arrange
for all the corpses to be removed to the death house at the
Guildhall. They should be blessed by the chaplain and examined by the best physician that can be hired. The washing tub

containing the tankards and the scraps and dregs must be taken down to one of those rat-infested dungeons beneath the Guildhall and spread out. The door is to be locked and guarded by the same Flaxwith, who must inform me about what happens next. Also, make sure the Barbican is sealed and guarded until all that is done. Sir John, you must, as soon as possible, issue an arrest warrant for Hugh of Hornsey, formerly Captain of the Tower archers. He is missing, fled. We have no sight of hide or hair of him. Now, Sir John, we truly should break our fast.'

They made their way across the Palisade, past the stiffening corpses of the two archers and into the tangy warmth of The Candle-Flame. Cranston shouted at Flaxwith and the other bailiffs, toasting themselves in front of the roaring fire in the Dark Parlour, to go out and guard the Barbican. Eleanor, Thorne's wife, her comely face all concerned, then served Athelstan and the rest in the small, pink-plastered parlour with its gleaming dark-wood table and cushioned stools which led off from the main taproom. The food served was piping hot and delicious: black porray, roo broth and small white freshly baked manchet loaves thickly buttered and sprinkled with garlic, together with stoups of light ale. Sir John, once he had taken out his large horn-spoon and polished it with a napkin, 'fell on the food' as he himself observed, 'like a hawk on a pigeon'. For a while no one spoke as platters were cleared and tankards emptied. Athelstan ate sparingly, complimenting Thorne on both the chamber and the food served. The taverner, crouched over his own dish, simply murmured how he wished to sell The Candle-Flame, adding that the turbulent times were not proving to be the best of seasons to host a tavern. Athelstan nodded understandingly; such sentiments were common amongst the tavern masters of Southwark. He also asked if Sir John's earlier instruction about the other guests had been served. Mistress Eleanor, standing on the threshold, agreed, saying they had left their chambers but were breaking their fast in the buttery refectory. Athelstan waited until Sir John had finished eating and tapped the table with his horn-spoon. He smiled down the table at Mooncalf, the young ostler had recovered from both his terrors and the biting cold. He now sat sleepy-eyed and red-cheeked next to his master.

'When did Marsen and his company arrive here?'

'Four days ago,' Thorne declared. 'He sent Hugh of Hornsey ahead of them.'

'When?'

'About a week ago. Hornsey insisted that the Barbican be given over entirely to his master.' Thorne pulled a face. 'There was no problem with that. They arrived just as the Vespers bell tolled. Marsen acted the arrogant pig; Mauclerc no better. He proclaimed how he had been attacked on the road but God had intervened. He showed me the bolts loosed at him and said that no such danger better threaten him here.' Thorne sniffed. 'The Barbican was all prepared thanks to Mooncalf.' Thorne patted the young man's shoulder. 'I told him to look after Marsen and his coven and he did, with great patience and good humour.'

'Why didn't Marsen cross London Bridge and shelter in the Tower?' Cranston asked.

'I suppose they had further business here in Southwark levying their devil tax, including what I owed.'

'You paid it?'

'Of course, Sir John. What choice do I, you or indeed anyone have?'

'Before last night,' Athelstan asked, 'did anything happen – any strangers appear, whatever their business?'

'You mean the Upright Men or their assassin, Beowulf?' Thorne spread his hands. 'Brother, this is a very busy tavern, not so much from the guests who stay but any who travel through Southwark. Of course, a gaggle of strange characters gathered; I'm sure some of these were despatched by the Upright Men who would have loved to take Marsen's ugly head.' He grinned. 'We even had some of your parishioners, Brother; Pike the Ditcher, Watkin the dung collector, golden-haired Cecily the courtesan and Moleskin the boatman.'

Athelstan sighed and put his face in his hands. If he questioned his parishioners they would blink like baby owls and murmur all innocence even though Athelstan knew that the likes of Watkin and Pike were high in the hierarchy of the Upright Men.

'But nothing untoward happened?' Athelstan took his hands away.

'No, Brother.' Thorne sipped from his tankard. 'Marsen would be up with the dawn. He and his coven would break their fast and go about their evil business, returning to the tavern at twilight after the market horn had sounded. They kept to themselves. Food and drink were served. Mauclerc went out to find whores for both himself and his master. They wallowed like pigs in their filthy muck. The Barbican became their sty.'

'And where were these whores from?'

'Oh, the stews of Southwark, a notorious brothel, a house of ill repute well known as the Golden Oliphant. It's under a very strict keeper; she calls herself the "Mistress of the Moppets". The two whores, I don't know their names . . .'

'We will find out,' Cranston broke in. 'I know the Mistress of the Moppets very well as she is widely advertised in the city. Despite their death wounds those two whores in life were very pretty young women. The mistress only hires the best but whether we get the truth from her is another matter.' He jabbed a finger at Athelstan. 'When we get the time we will give the mistress a visit.'

'Would that explain why they were not carrying money? Marsen would do business with their keeper?'

'Possibly, Brother,' Cranston replied. 'I suspect a man like Marsen got what he wanted free of any charge.'

'But they were carrying something,' Mooncalf broke in, surprising even his master.

'What's that, boy?' the taverner asked.

'One of the whores, she was carrying a leather bag and it clinked. I met her at the wicket gate and she stumbled. She could curse like the best of them but I heard it clink, the bag she was carrying.'

Cranston stared at Athelstan, who just shook his head. 'We found no such bag in the Barbican, Sir John.'

'Then the killer must have taken it,' Mooncalf insisted. 'I definitely saw it, I definitely heard it.'

'Apart from the whores, were there any other visitors?' Athelstan asked.

'Yes,' Thorne replied, 'a black-garbed fellow, hair of the same colour drawn tightly back and tied behind the head, harsh-featured with the unblinking stare of a hawk.'

'Lascelles,' Cranston broke in. 'Master Thibault's henchman. When did he come?'

'The night before last. He met Marsen in the Barbican then left. Sir John, I know nothing of their business.'

'And this morning?' Athelstan glanced at Mooncalf.

'As usual I went to wake them. I found the two archers as you did. I hurried across to the Barbican and hammered on the door.'

'Did you notice anything out of the ordinary, boy?' Cranston asked, helping himself to the miraculous wineskin.

'Anything at all?' Athelstan insisted.

'No. Pedro the cruel,' Mooncalf grimaced, 'the tavern boar, was sleeping outside his sty. Sometimes he does that. Anyway,' he shook his head, 'I became frightened and hurried back to the tavern to raise the alarm.'

Athelstan turned to Thorne.

'I came out with the others, all shaken from our sleep. You've seen the Barbican, Brother, it is built for defence. Apart from the heavy door the only way through is the window. There is no ladder long enough so I put the one we have on a handcart and climbed up. The outer shutter was still hooked. I inserted a blade and lifted that; the door window was clasped shut. I cut back the horn, put my hand through and lifted the latch. The inner shutter was easier; the hooks came up but,' he patted his stomach, 'too much baggage. I came back down and sent Mooncalf up.'

Athelstan glanced at the ostler.

'Brother, you saw what I did. The upper chamber was warm as the shutters had been closed all night. The brazier still glowed, as well as the chafing dishes.' Mooncalf screwed up his eyes. 'All of the candles had burnt out – they were extinguished.'

'And the trapdoors?'

'I remember the one to the roof was locked – yes, both were. The trapdoor to the lower chamber was also bolted.' Mooncalf paused at Cranston's loud snoring. The fat coroner, warmed and fed, was now relaxing in the comfort. Mooncalf stared at him then back at Athelstan in open-mouthed wonderment.

'Don't worry,' the friar reassured, 'Sir John can sleep with his eyes open and see when they are closed.'

'And the truth never escapes me.' The coroner opened his eyes and smacked his lips. 'The main door?' he asked.

'Bolted top and bottom, the key turned and still in the lock.' The ostler's reply created a profound stillness. Even the distant sounds of the tavern faded. Athelstan stared down at the table top. They were now approaching the true mystery of this murderous maze. Athelstan recalled his youth, working on his father's farm in the West Country. He and the other children would be clearing the furrows following the massive hogged-maned drays which pulled the sharp-toothed plough. Warm, sun-bright days but out to the west he'd glimpse sombre clouds massing, the heralds of a coming storm. Athelstan closed his eyes as other memories surfaced. He recalled sitting on the brow of a snow-covered hill staring down at the dark line of forestry certain that shadows would creep out of the blackness across the hard-packed snow. So it was here as the mystery unfurled. Athelstan opened his eyes. What was the sinister truth behind this heinous massacre? Nine souls had been ruth-lessly despatched along that mystical path stretching to God's judgement and their eternal destiny. How did it, how *could* it happen? Two able-bodied archers, surprised and summarily executed, and then the real mystery: the same blood-seeking wraith had swirled into the Barbican. The well-armed guard on the ground floor were slaughtered before the demon moved up to murder four others in the upper chamber. Once done, he had apparently pillaged a three-locked coffer without using the keys. Afterwards this killer had left just as mysteriously with the windows still shuttered, the main entrance and the two inside trapdoors all firmly locked.

'Brother?'

'My apologies, Sir John.' Athelstan sighed deeply. 'I have said this before but I shall do so again. I want the corpses taken to the death house at the Guildhall. The chaplain should anoint them. Afterwards, hire the most able physician, strip and search each corpse, scrutinize them carefully. The tub of platters and cups must be scraped; all the dregs and scraps placed in one of the Guildhall dungeons.' Athelstan blew his cheeks out. 'Of course, there is also Hugh of Hornsey, holder of the third key and captain of archers. Where is he? Dead? Alive? Innocent or guilty? Sir John, this assassin, Beowulf? How long has he been waging his secret, bloody war?'

'Oh, about two years.'

'And does he confine himself to the city?'

'The city and the shires around London, as far north as Colchester and as far south as Richmond.'

'And, when he strikes, is he always successful?'

'No, as with the attack on Marsen at Leveret Copse, sometimes he fails.'

'And are his victims always crown officials?' Athelstan held Cranston's gaze as the friar hid his own fears. Does that include you, my fat, faithful friend? Athelstan thought. Are you also, incorruptible though you are, marked with the sign of the beast, an intended victim for slaughter?

'No.' Cranston's beaming smile was eloquent enough. 'Beowulf hunts Gaunt's creatures, the minions of Master Thibault.'

'And who are the other guests, those who roomed here last night?' Athelstan hid his relief beneath his question to Thorne.

'Philip Scrope, the physician, Sir Robert Paston, a member of the Commons from the shire of Surrey, together with his daughter Martha and his clerk, William Foulkes.'

'I know Paston.' Cranston spoke up. 'Gaunt's most bitter enemy. A critic of the poll tax, Gaunt paid him back in equal coin. Sir Robert is a seasoned mariner who believes he should have been appointed as admiral of the king's ships from the mouth of the Thames along the east coast to the Scottish March. Instead, Gaunt appointed one of his own favourites. Paston constantly criticizes the lack of war cogs to protect English merchantmen. Paston should know. He makes his wealth out of wool. He would be no friend of Marsen.'

'Ah, Sir John, Brother Athelstan.' Thorne leaned forward. 'I am sorry, I should have told you this but it slipped my mind. Two nights ago, just after Marsen returned from collecting the

tax, the same evening Lascelles appeared here, Sir Robert and
Marsen met in the Dark Parlour. There was an angry exchange
of words, fingers falling to daggers.'

'Why?' Athelstan asked. 'What happened?'

'Sir Robert called Marsen a robber, a wolfshead, a vile
plunderer.'

'And Marsen?'

'He just jeered and jibed. He said he knew all about Sir
Robert and didn't care for him, though he would more than
welcome a visit during the night from Paston's daughter –
that's when fingers fell to daggers. I intervened. Marsen just
sauntered off, laughing over his shoulder.'

'What do you think Marsen meant when he said he knew
all about Sir Robert?'

'Brother Athelstan, you must ask Sir Robert yourself. I
suspect Marsen was quietly mocking Paston for not being
appointed as Admiral of the Eastern Seas. I know Sir Robert
was very sensitive on the issue.'

'And the rest of the guests?' Cranston asked. 'How were
they to Marsen?'

'I would say they were just as hostile but that's based on
tittle-tattle. There's Brother Roger, a Franciscan from their
house at Canterbury. I have mentioned the physician who
claims he has been on pilgrimage to Glastonbury. Finally,
there's a professional *chanteur*, minstrel or whatever else he
proclaims himself. I understand he enjoys quite a reputation
as a troubadour. He calls himself Ronseval. I cannot say
whether he was baptized as such; he claims he is against
anyone who fetters the human spirit.'

'In which case,' Athelstan retorted, 'he must champion most
of London. I presume they are all waiting for us in the
refectory?'

'Then come.' Cranston heaved himself up.

They left, crossing the Dark Parlour into the refectory. Five
people sat around the common table. Athelstan was aware of
hostile looks and bitter grimaces as introductions were made
and they took their seats. Mine Host and Mooncalf stood in
the doorway. Cranston asked if they wished for anything to
eat or drink but all he received were muttered refusals.

Athelstan sketched a blessing. Cranston then clapped his hands and moved swiftly to business.

He asked what each of them had done the previous evening and received the expected, perfunctory replies. All the chamber guests, as Thorne described them, had eaten supper, returned to their chambers and retired to bed. They had neither seen nor heard anything to report. Athelstan sensed they were lying. He was certain that the killer must be in this tavern, even though logic dictated the very strong possibility that last night's massacre was the work of a professional assassin despatched by the Upright Men. Athelstan studied the guests closely. He noticed the easy flow of conversation, the relaxed attitude between them all and concluded they liked each other.

Sir Robert was a wealthy wool merchant, a manor lord, a grey-haired, sharp-eyed man with ever-twitching lips as if there was something unpleasant in his mouth. He was clean-shaven and dressed most conservatively in a *houppelande*, a long gown fringed with lambswool, clasped at throat and wrist with silver studs. A former soldier and a mariner who had fought in France as well as in the constant sea battles between Dover and Calais, he was a rather sad man, Athelstan considered, a widower who apparently doted on his delicately faced, blue-eyed daughter Martha: she sat close to him dressed as soberly as a Benedictine nun in her white-starched wimple, dark-blue veil and unadorned gown of the same colour. She wore doe-skinned gloves studded with pearls, her only concession to fashion. Nevertheless, despite all her coyness, Athelstan noticed the fervent glances between the seemingly doe-like Martha and her father's clerk William Foulkes. Athelstan hid his smile; both young people were deeply in love, although Martha's father appeared blithely unaware of it. Foulkes acted all precise and courtly: vigilant and keen-witted, an observer rather than a talker, probably a graduate of the halls of Oxford or Cambridge. Foulkes was dressed in buckram and dark fustian, constantly fiddling with the chancery ring on his finger, apparently resentful at being detained and questioned, although he tried to hide it. Athelstan noticed that the two young lovers wore no religious insignia, be it a cross, medal or ring. Young women such as Martha often carried crystal Ave beads entwined between their fingers, more a service to fashion than prayer, but she did not. Nor had she or Foulkes crossed themselves when Athelstan first entered the refectory and, as was customary, sketched a blessing in the air. He was also intrigued that, as each of the guests described what they had done the previous evening, both young people glanced at Mooncalf, who stared warningly back, fingers twitching as if the ostler was trying to communicate some secret message to them. Athelstan wondered why all three seemed so uncomfortable.

The same applied to Philip Scrope the physician. He sat cross-legged, his costly slashed robes gathered about his scrawny frame. An arrogant man with harsh dry features and heavy-lidded eyes, Physician Scrope apparently regarded himself as superior to those around him. He kept scratching his thinning hair, lips twisted in a sardonic grimace, tapping the table as if impatient to be gone. Ronseval, the wandering minstrel, troubadour and whatever else he claimed to be, exuded the same arrogance. Ronseval was dressed in a sky-blue jerkin, tight black hose and costly, ankle-high leather boots. His reddish hair was neatly coiffed and crimped, his smooth, swarthy face generously rubbed with perfumed oil. He slouched at the table, fingers smoothing its surface. Now and again he'd touch the hand-held harp lying nearby, a delicately carved instrument with finely taut strings. Despite Ronseval's confident stare and poise, Athelstan detected a nervousness which expressed itself in what the friar could only judge as slightly feminine gestures of his mouth and eyes, the nervous twitching of long, well-manicured fingers and the way he kept touching his hair and glancing up at the ceiling. Brother Roger in contrast sat upright, still as a statue, his raw, high-boned face and slightly slanted eyes cold and impassive. A wiry man, the Franciscan was dressed in the clay-coloured robes of his order with stout sandals on his feet and the white cord around his waist displaying the three knots symbolizing his vows of poverty, chastity and obedience. He held Athelstan's gaze, staring coldly back as he chewed the corner of his lip. Then he relaxed, smiled and winked quickly, as if he and the Dominican were conspirators and all this was some elaborate masque.

'*Pax et Bonum*, Frater.' The Franciscan's voice was strong
and carrying. 'You ask what we did last night when the great
sinner Marsen was sent to Hell. Thanks be to God, the Eternal
Lord, that I lived to see this day. Now,' he continued brusquely,
'we have told you what we did. You have your business, I
have mine.'

'Which is?' Athelstan asked.

'Alms to collect. Brothers to meet at Greyfriars. Sermons
to compose. Preaching to prepare. Shrivings and blessings to
administer so that souls can be saved. Our business is not this
fierce hostility, this murder lust between men.'

'Did you try to save Marsen's soul?'

'No, Brother,' Friar Roger grinned, white teeth bared like
that of a mastiff, 'isn't it wonderful to recount how, in his
magnanimity, the master of all things would allow the soul of
such a man to wander in delight before judgement is imposed.
I know Marsen and his ilk. They milk the poor of every last
penny. They grind God's people beneath the boot.' The
Franciscan gestured around. 'No one here grieves for Marsen
and his coven. Most of us, if not all, rejoice that such a
malefactor has been sent to judgement but it does not mean
we sent him there.' Friar Roger's words were greeted with
grunts of approval. Ronseval, in a high-pitched voice, started
to chant popular verses about the brotherhood of man. Paston
delivered a diatribe as if he was gathered with the Commons
in St Stephen's Chapel at Westminster. Cranston, however,
banged on the table imposing silence. Athelstan noticed how
young Martha and Master William exchanged secret glances
and furtive smiles, as if the issue was of no concern to them.

'When did you all arrive here?' Athelstan asked. Both the
physician and Father Roger declared they had done so after
Marsen and his coven had taken up residence in the Barbican.
Sir Robert Paston said they had been at The Candle-Flame for
at least a week because he had to attend the Westminster
parliament. Ronseval declared he had arrived the same day as
Marsen.

'Have any of you,' Athelstan persisted, 'stayed at any other
tavern when Marsen was there?' Everyone shook their heads
with cries of denial, except the minstrel, who kept weaving

his fingers together. Athelstan recalled the gauntlet found in the Barbican. He had established that it did not fit any of the murder victims in the upper chamber but, glancing quickly at the fingers of the guests, Athelstan wondered if the gauntlet might belong to Ronseval, Physician Scrope or even Sir Robert Paston.

'Master troubadour?' Athelstan asked, 'can you explain the coincidence that you arrived here the same day as Marsen?'

'I was deliberately following Marsen,' Ronseval replied slowly, not meeting Athelstan's gaze. 'I am composing a ballad against him which I hope to have copied by the scriveners along Paternoster Row. I can show you it if you wish.' He picked up the chancery bag lying between his feet, opened it and drew out a scroll which he passed to Athelstan. The parchment was soft, cream-coloured, the writing clean and distinct though not at all like the proclamation left by Beowulf. Athelstan read the opening line about 'Wolves being sent out amongst lambs, hawks roosting in a dovecote'. He smiled and handed it back.

'Very good, Master Ronseval but,' Athelstan pointed at the bag, 'we may have to search that,' he gestured around, 'and all your property.' Athelstan knew it was an empty threat; he suspected anything incriminating would be already hidden away if not destroyed.

'This is not,' Paston bellowed, half-rising to his feet, 'acceptable.'

'Treason.' Cranston's thunderous retort silenced everyone. 'Treason,' the coroner repeated. 'Marsen, whatever he might have been, was a royal official foully murdered for collecting the king's taxes, and those same taxes have been stolen. Now the lawyers can argue whether this is petty treason or misprision of treason, but treason it still is. We are searching for stolen royal treasure.'

'And this is relevant to it.' Athelstan opened his own chancery bag and passed round the gauntlet, the piece of chainmail and Beowulf's proclamation. He found it difficult to judge their individual response to each item. Martha and young Foulkes simply passed these on, though Sir Robert appeared agitated. Athelstan could not decide whether the items were

the cause of Sir Robert's resentment at being detained here
for questioning. Friar Roger, however, read the proclamation
and laughed quietly to himself.

'Marsen,' he glanced down the table at Athelstan, 'was
truly found wanting.' He crossed himself swiftly. 'Though
who found him so is a mystery.'

Athelstan nodded in agreement.

'If there is nothing else,' the Franciscan rose to his feet,
'search my chamber if you wish – there is little to find. I have
business in the city, Brother . . .?'

Athelstan nodded at Cranston.

'You may all go,' the coroner declared. 'But you must return.
No one is to leave this tavern without my written permission.
By all means go about your business but this is your place of
residence until these matters are resolved. If you disobey I
shall have you put to the horn as a wolfshead, an outlaw.'

The guests rose and left, followed by Thorne, his wife and
Mooncalf, who had been standing on the threshold. Once they
had left the refectory, Athelstan collected the items he had
distributed.

'Sir John, what do you think?' Athelstan closed the door
and rested against a metal milk churn.

'They have, all of them, a tale to tell and a truth to hide.
However, one thing unites them all: they hated Marsen.'

Athelstan, lost in own thoughts, absent-mindedly agreed.
Cranston said he would supervise the removal of the corpses
and everything else and bustled out. Athelstan sat down at the
table, staring at the painted cloth pinned to the far wall
depicting a Catherine wheel, surmounted by a cross and
crowned with lighted candles, which held off the darkness in
which murky-faced demons could be glimpsed.

'Come, kindly light,' Athelstan whispered. He took a deep
breath, closed his eyes and recited the 'Lavabo' psalm, '"I
will wash my hands among the innocent and encompass thy
altar O Lord . . ."'

Athelstan dozed for a while and started awake at a heart-
cutting shriek which echoed through the tavern. He jumped
to his feet and entered the sweet-smelling Dark Parlour, where
Thorne, standing on a barrel, was busy hanging fresh herbs

and flitches of bacon from the smoke-stained rafters. He just
stood gaping; the shriek was repeated and the taverner swiftly
clambered down. He and Athelstan hurried out into the main
hallway and up the stairs into the gallery. They pushed their
way through the slatterns and servants milling about. Thorne
shouted at them to be quiet. He and Athelstan strode down
the gallery which ran past chambers on either side to another
narrow stairwell at the far end. Eleanor Thorne stood stricken
outside one of the chambers. She glanced up, her face white
as snow, pointing at the blood seeping out from beneath the
chamber door.

'Scrope's chamber,' Thorne whispered, gathering his wife
in his arms, comforting her and pushing her gently back down
the gallery to the waiting maids. Athelstan tried the door but
it was locked. He hammered on the dark oaken wood but
realized it was futile. Thorne took a ring of keys from his
apron pocket and tried to insert the master key but failed.

'The lock's turned on the other side.' Thorne, his craggy
face now sweat-soaked, tried to push back the eyelet high in
the door, a small square of wood hinged on the inside, but
this was firmly closed. Other doors in the gallery opened, faces
peered out. Athelstan glimpsed Father Roger's fearful and
wary face just before Cranston came pounding up the stairs
shouting at everyone to stand aside or keep to their chambers.
The coroner stared at the thick bloody plume still spreading
out from beneath the door.

'The window is open!' Mooncalf shouted as he threw
himself up the other set of stairs. 'The shutters are pulled back,
it would be easy to enter from the stableyard.'

'Off and up you go lad,' Cranston shouted, twirling a penny
at the ostler, who deftly caught it. Athelstan turned and tried
the latch on the door to the chamber facing Scrope's.

'Empty,' Thorne murmured. The taverner inserted a key and
opened it. Athelstan went in. The room was neat and tidy, the
window opened to air it. Everything was in order. The four-
poster bed was made up, its curtains drawn back. There was
a high-back chair, two stools, tables and an open aumbry for
clothes, although the pole between the uprights had been taken
down. Athelstan shivered at the draught created by the open

door and hastily retreated back into the warmth of the gallery. He heard movement in Scrope's chamber. Mooncalf's exclamation followed by gasps and cries. The bolts on top and bottom were pulled back and the key turned. The door swung open. Cranston immediately ordered the white-faced ostler to stand with his master in the gallery as he and Athelstan stepped over the physician's body into the chamber. Athelstan glanced quickly around. The room was very similar to the one he had just visited, though the physician's clothing and possessions lay scattered about. In order to open the door Scrope's corpse had been pulled back and rolled on to one side. Athelstan crossed himself and pulled the corpse further into the room, turning it over so they could see the crossbow quarrel embedded deep in Scrope's chest. The dead physician's pallid face, twisted in agony, was caked with the blood which had erupted through his nose and mouth. Athelstan felt the corpse's hand: it was still slightly warm.

'He was murdered very recently,' Athelstan murmured. 'Sir John, a moment, please.'

Athelstan took out the holy oils and anointed the corpse, reciting the absolution, followed by the final prayer for the departed. Once he had finished, Athelstan scrutinized the chamber door but could detect no interference with the bolts, lock and eyelet. He walked to the window, which was very similar to the one in the Barbican, with shutters on either side of a horn-covered door window. Athelstan pushed this back and stared down. The stableyard below was busy: yard servants and customers were staring open-mouthed up at the chamber. Athelstan asked one of them to remove the ladder Mooncalf had used.

'Did you see anything?' he shouted. A chorus of denials answered his question.

'Obviously not,' Athelstan murmured, turning away. Anyone trying to climb into Scrope's chamber would have been noticed. Athelstan went to the corpse and knelt by it, half-listening to Cranston's theories. He noticed a manuscript, a small book, its pages tightly bound together by red twine. It had been opened and lay half-hidden by Scrope's robes. He held this up.

'Brother?'

'A *vademecum*, Sir John.' Athelstan leafed through the
bloodstained pages. 'A pilgrim's book listing all the great relics
at Glastonbury Abbey: Arthur's tomb, Joseph of Arimathea's
staff. The Stella Cristi, the Star of Christ, a beautiful ruby.
The Holy Thorn and other items. Scrope must have been
clutching this when he died. I wonder why.' Athelstan rose as
Cranston opened the door and began to question others outside.
The friar quickly sifted through the dead physician's possessions: clothing, most of it very costly, two purses containing
silver and gold coins, a set of spurs and a war belt finely
stitched with gold thread. He emptied Scrope's chancery bag
on to the bed and sifted through the billae, memoranda, lists
of herbs and other medicines as well as letters of attestation
from different universities. He opened a bronze chancery
cylinder, shook out a small roll of documents and went through
these. His exclamations of surprise brought Cranston back in
from the gallery. Athelstan handed over what he had found.

'True bills, Sir John, drawn up by a notary in Coggeshall,
Scrope's home town. They contain a confession of one Alain
Taillour, housebreaker. Apparently, about ten years ago, around
the Feast of Michaelmas, Scrope's house in Coggeshall was
burgled and ransacked. Scrope was attending a guild meeting
in town. On his return he found his house a place of mayhem
and murder. Scrope's wife and their manservant had been
brutally slain. During the first week of Advent last, Taillour
was caught red-handed breaking into a warehouse. He turned
king's approver; applying for a pardon he named all his confederates in his life of robbery.' Athelstan drew a deep breath.
'He clearly accused Edmund Marsen as the person responsible
for the murder of Scrope's wife and manservant. Taillour swore
this on oath before a local justice providing the names of other
witnesses. Apparently Scrope made his pilgrimage to
Glastonbury in grateful thanks and as well as to seek divine
help . . .'

'To indict Marsen,' the coroner interrupted. 'Of course,'
Cranston whispered, 'Marsen is, or was, a royal official. Scrope
was planning to appear before the Court of King's Bench in
Westminster Hall. He would swear out a true indictment which

Marsen would have to answer before a jury and three royal justices.' Cranston sat down on a stool, cradling the miraculous wineskin. 'Now both are dead,' he continued, 'sent to appear before Christ's Assize. But how was Scrope murdered? Who was responsible and how? Friar Roger claims he was sure he heard a loud knocking on Scrope's door and that this was repeated, but that is all. Father Roger opened his door but could see nobody. The assassin could not have entered by the window as the entire tavern would have seen him. So how could the assassin enter this room, kill Scrope then leave, locking and bolting the door behind him?' He pointed to the corpse. 'The same quarrels were used in the Barbican, loosed from a hand-held arbalest.' Cranston got to his feet. 'Brother, what is the matter – what are you staring at?'

'Go back outside, Sir John. Ask Thorne, Mooncalf and the rest what our learned physician did after he arrived here two days ago. Did he go out? Were his boots cleaned? Please, Sir John.' Athelstan smiled at the coroner who shrugged and left, shouting for Thorne. Athelstan knelt by the lantern horn, standing on a small stool. The copper casing was mud-stained around the base, the horn covering was dirt-splattered and the squat tallow candle had burnt low. Athelstan then scrutinized the heavy cloak hanging from a wall peg. It was pure wool dyed a deep green but its silver-threaded hem was splattered with crusts of mud. The expensive Spanish riding boots standing nearby were also marked; their leggings were polished but the sole, heel and toe were caked in drying dirt. He glanced up as Cranston re-entered the chamber.

'Brother, according to what I've heard, Scrope remained in his own chamber, probably preparing that indictment. Mooncalf and others polished his boots to a gleam after he arrived.'

'Nevertheless, he did go out.' Athelstan gestured at the cloak and boots. 'That's what caught my attention. According to reports our fastidious physician remained closeted in this chamber, never going out, making sure the likes of Mooncalf cleaned his boots. Yet Scrope's cloak and boots are muddied, as is the lantern horn where it's been put down, whilst its candle must have burnt for some time. Look, Sir John, at the mud drying on your boots – it's similar in colour and texture to this. I suspect our physician went out last night. The mud is fairly recent. I believe he entered the Palisade and approached the Barbican.'

'Is he the killer?'

'No, but I suspect Scrope might have glimpsed the assassin or nursed deep suspicions about who he really is. That is why he was murdered, to silence him.' Athelstan rose to his feet, stretched and crossed himself. 'Sir John, have Scrope's corpse join the rest at the Guildhall then seal this chamber with the signet of the Lord High Coroner.'

'Brother?'

'Yes, Sir John?'

'Marsen was hated. He was Thibault's creature, a vile, ruthless tax collector, yet he moved with impunity. Surely the Upright Men must have heard about his depredations as well as his stay here? You seem to be implying that they are not responsible, but why shouldn't they spring a trap and snatch Marsen's nasty soul from his filthy body?'

'Perhaps they did, Sir John.'

'So this is the work of the Upright Men?'

'Umm.' Athelstan pulled his cowl up, a sign to Cranston that he wanted to retreat and meditate in some quiet corner. 'Truly, Sir John, I don't know. This could be the doing of the Upright Men or it might not be. Perhaps they left all this to their assassin, Beowulf, and yet . . .' Athelstan shook his head, blessed the corpse once more and left the chamber. He walked to the top of the stairs and paused at the clatter of hooves, shouts and the rattle of steel from the stableyard. By the time he reached there the horsemen who had entered, all wearing the blue, scarlet and gold livery of the royal household, were milling about, swords drawn, shouting orders at Thorne and Mooncalf to close the gates and to allow no one in or out until they were gone. Lascelles was in charge, dressed as usual in black leather and his helmet off, his harsh, pointed face twisted into a scowl. Mine Host Thorne crossed the yard and angry words were exchanged between the two. Lascelles dismounted as Thorne ordered the gates to remain open. Fearful of an ugly confrontation, Athelstan hastened across, relieved to see Cranston also come striding out. Calm was restored, Lascelles nodding at Cranston's whispered advice.

'Very good, Master Taverner.' Lascelles smirked at Thorne. 'Go about your business even though your tavern is now the haven of murder, felony and treason. I need to view the corpses.'

Cranston objected, pointing out that all the dead had been sheeted in mort cloths and were being removed. Lascelles, peeling off his black leather gloves, again nodded understandingly, his glittering dark eyes never leaving Athelstan's face. 'It does not matter,' Lascelles wetted his lips. 'The money is gone, yes? Cannot be found? Yes? Well, well. My business here, Sir John, is you and Brother Athelstan. His Grace My Lord of Gaunt and Master Thibault want to know what happened here and discover what you will do to remedy it. They also want to have words with you on other matters.' He pointed across at the tavern stables. 'Get two horses saddled. I want to be out of here as soon as possible.' He frowned at Cranston's loudly whispered curse. 'My Lord High Coroner of London, the hour is passing, my business is pressing. We must be gone – now!' Athelstan caught Cranston's gaze, warning him with his eyes to be careful. Cranston strolled off, shouting for Mooncalf to saddle two horses. Ronseval sauntered out and stayed in the porch to watch proceedings. Athelstan looked past the troubadour and glimpsed Paston, his daughter and Foulkes deep in conversation at a table in the Dark Parlour. Lascelles, holding the reins of his horse, beckoned Athelstan closer and asked what had happened. The friar replied in short, blunt sentences.

Lascelles, that raven of a man, listened intently, the arrogance draining from his face at the litany of bloody destruction. 'Master Thibault,' he whispered, 'will not be pleased, such a vast sum stolen. Beowulf the assassin must be in the city. Who is he hunting, Brother?'

Athelstan sensed the deep anxiety of Thibault's principal henchman. That same cloying, creeping fear which was spreading through the city like some invisible mist, thickening and curling its way around the men of power. The day of judgement was approaching. Only God's good grace could divert the bloody confrontation between the lords and the seething masses thcy ruled. The seed had been sown for generations, now harvest time was due. The wine press of God's anger was about to be turned. No one would be safe. Lascelles could swagger about in his black leather garb, silver spurs clinking on his riding boots, cloak swirling back to reveal his heavy leather war belt, but what real protection could they offer against the silent knife thrust or the swift sling shot? Athelstan left Lascelles to his thoughts as Cranston led across the saddled horses. Athelstan made sure he had all his possessions and was about to swing himself up when he heard a piping voice.

'Master Lascelles, Master Lascelles?' A ragged boy, face all dirty, his tunic no more than a discarded flour sack with holes cut for head and arms and tied around the waist with a dirty rope, caught Athelstan's attention. He came running into the yard yelling Lascelles' name, which he stumbled over as he held up the scrap of parchment in his grubby hand. Athelstan felt a cold, prickling premonition. The stableyard was busy. Local traders, tinkers and craftsmen were drifting in to break their fast. Slatterns and scullions hurried across. Doors slammed. Windows were unshuttered. Slops were being emptied, horses led in and out. The smith had begun his clanging. Thorne stood in the doorway shouting orders at a washer woman. Athelstan, however, watched that beggar boy. Lascelles was approaching him. The urchin handed over the scrap of parchment and fled like the wind through the main gate. Lascelles uncurled the parchment; he glanced up as Athelstan hurried towards him.

'Brother, what is this?' Athelstan lunged forward, knocking Lascelles away from his horse, which reared, hooves flailing as a crossbow bolt whipped the air between it and its rider. Athelstan crouched even as Lascelles tried to calm his horse, turning it to use a shield. Cries of 'Harrow!' were raised. The stableyard erupted in uproar as another bolt whistled through the air, smacking into the wall of an outhouse. Women screamed and grabbed their frightened children. Dogs snarled, racing about, agitating the horses further. Lascelles' escort hurriedly grabbed kite-shaped shields from their saddle horns

to form a protective ring around their master and Athelstan.
For a while both men just sheltered. Athelstan closed his eyes
and murmured the Jesus prayer whilst Lascelles cursed a litany
of filth. Athelstan thanked God he could not understand it. At
last, order was imposed. Cranston shouted how the mysterious
bowman must have disappeared. The shield wall broke up.
Lascelles grasped Athelstan's hand, squeezing it, thanking him
with his eyes before screaming a spate of abuse at his escort.

'He's gone!' Cranston declared.

'Where, Sir John, where was he?' Athelstan asked.

'Brother, God only knows! A window or somewhere here
in the tavern yard, or did Beowulf – and I think it was our
mutual friend – simply slip in from the street? The tavern is
thronged with every rogue under the sun, the usual beauties,
the school of Tyburn scholars and Newgate nuns.' Athelstan
walked over and picked up the deadly message. This time the
parchment was faded and grease-marked, the scrawling hand
uncouth, but the message was the same in all its stark menace.

'Our assassin changes his hand,' Athelstan remarked. 'Sir
John, we should be gone.' People were now emerging from
the tavern, all busy and inquisitive. Cranston had a word with
Lascelles and the order was given to mount. They were joined
by a smiling Father Roger, who asked if he could join their
comitatus. Lascelles shrugged and the friar pushed his sorry-
looking mount alongside Athelstan. They left the tavern yard
and made their way towards the battlemented gatehouse and
walls of London Bridge. Athelstan immediately experienced
the inner panic that washed over him whenever he entered the
turbulent, frenetic streets of Southwark. He became acutely
aware of what he glimpsed, as if he was studying scenes from
a stained-glass window or the intricate details of one of the
Hangman of Rochester's wall paintings at St Erconwald's.
Friar Roger was chattering like a sparrow on a twig, but
Athelstan was distracted by the swirling images which surged
out towards him on that brisk, cold February morning. Church
bells clanged, marking the end of morning Mass and the
beginning of the eleventh hour. Market horns brayed. Whores
screamed and cursed as they were led down to the thews to
the sound of blaring bagpipes. Traders, tinkers, fripperers and

geegaw-sellers set up stalls and booths, ringing the air with their shouted offers of mousetraps, ratkillers, bird cages, bottles, ribbons, collops of meat and fresh fruit. Itinerant cooks, dressed in rotten, stinking weeds, pushed their battered barrows with portable stoves; around the cooks' unwashed necks hung strips of ancient but heavily salted meat ready for grilling. An enterprising water-seller with a tub on his back trailed behind these offering 'the freshest water from St Mary's spring' to slake, salted throats. The crowd pushed backwards and forwards, thronging down the narrow lanes where the grotesquely carved gables of shops and houses jutted out above dark and dingy chambers. Slops were being emptied into the already fetid, crammed sewers. Space was narrow; people had to step aside for Lascelles' cavalcade. Curses and threats were hurled and, on a few occasions, slops from upper chambers narrowly missed them as night jars were emptied. Southwark, however, was different from the city, where resentments rankled deeper. In Southwark the dog-leeches, sow-gelders, rumagates, runaways, jingle-brains, tooth-drawers, broom men and a multitude of lowlife were hotly against any titled authority. All these denizens from their 'ruffians' hall', as Cranston described them, wandered the streets looking for mischief or anything which might brighten their lives.

Justice was also busy. The Carnifex, the Southwark execu-tioner, was performing his grisly trade on the approaches to the bridge. A moveable three-armed scaffold was being pushed along the riverside with a strangled, purple-faced malefactor hanging from each branch of the gallows; notices pinned to their filthy nightshirts proclaimed how these criminals were guilty of committing arson in the royal dockyards. A failed magician, who'd tricked people out of their coins for nothing in return and aptly rejoiced in the name of 'Littlebit' was being fastened in the stocks. Former customers had gathered, picking up rotting rubbish and even filth from the sewer running down the centre of the lane, intent on pelting him. A mad woman, her hair painted purple and garbed in rabbit skins, stood on a broken barrel. She proclaimed how once upon a time she had been a luxuriously adorned maiden who used to sit in a hazel grove until Satan had appeared in the guise of a bird-catcher and snared her soul. Next to her, three whores, whose grey, grimy naked buttocks had been soundly birched, were being fastened in the pillary for 'lechery beyond their threshold'. Athelstan noticed with grim amusement the placards hanging around their clamped necks; these declared how the two younger ones were *'Mea Culpa'* and *'Mea Culpa'*–'my fault' and 'my fault', whilst the third, their mother, was named *'Maxima Culpa'* – 'my most grievous fault'.

On the corner of the lane a preacher and his travelling troupe had rented the Eyrie, a plot of ground reserved for mummers and their plays. The preacher – Athelstan could not decide if he was acting or genuine – was garbed in horsehide, his sun-darkened face almost hidden by lank hair through which his eyes gleamed feverishly. He had attracted a good crowd. Athelstan, with a start, noticed a fellow Dominican garbed in the black-and-white robes of his order, standing a little forward of the crowd, fascinated by what was being enacted. The crowd was noisy. The air reeked with a fug of odours which mingled with the ever-present stench of stale, salted fish, rotting vegetables and human sweat. Nevertheless, the Dominican, tall and rugged, his black hair neatly tonsured, seemed impervious to his surroundings but listened intently to the rant of the preacher's most scathing diatribe against the Church. Behind the preacher, the rest of his troupe was assembling cleverly painted panels, each depicting a message. On one a fiend jeeringly pulled the ropes of a prayer bell torturing a damned, fiery-red soul who served as the bell's clapper. Below that on the same panel, a rat-headed demon was throttling a banker whilst another stabbed a goldsmith with a candle prick. On the second panel, a hare carrying a hunting horn, game-bag and a deer-spear was striding towards a castle with a wench slung by her feet to the spear. At the castle gate, a thorn-beaked lizard devil, dressed as an abbess, waited to welcome them. The third panel depicted the Prince of Hell, Lord Satan, with a gigantic sparrow hawk's head and a spindle-shank thin body. The master of demons was busy devouring a damned spirit, whose perjured red-hot soul slipped from the Devil's anus in the form of a swarm of ravens.

Lascelles stopped his cavalcade here. One of his lackies

dismounted, pushed through the crowd and whispered to the Dominican; he reluctantly nodded and followed the man back, hoisting himself into the saddle of a spare horse. Athelstan caught his breath; he was sure he recognized that round, serene face from his days in the novitiate at Blackfriars. Athelstan stared again. He noted the sharp eyes, full lips, skin burnt brown by the sun and rather delicate hand gestures and how fastidiously clean this fellow friar appeared to be.

'Brother Marcel.' Friar Roger had been watching just as closely. 'Don't you recognize him, Athelstan, a man much loved by your order? Some say he will become Minister General of the Dominicans. Brother Marcel of St Sardos – the Papal Inquisitor from our Holy Father in Rome.'

Athelstan closed his eyes. He certainly remembered Marcel, the son of Anglo-Gascon parents born in English-held Bordeaux, a brilliant canon lawyer who particularly excelled in the disputation, the sharp cut and thrust of question and answer so popular in the halls of Oxford and Cambridge. What on earth was he doing in London? Athelstan glanced back at the mummers as Lascelles urged his cavalcade on. Such dramatic presentations were certainly not orthodox and, if what he recalled about Marcel was correct, would certainly be frowned on by the Papal Inquisitor.

At last they reached London Bridge. A firedrake was performing magic tricks with a torch he had inveigled from the keeper of the gatehouse, Robert Burden, that diminutive dresser of the severed heads of traitors which hung like black balls on their poles against the lightening sky. Burden, dressed in the usual blood-red taffeta, had assembled his large brood of offspring to watch the fire-swallower. Athelstan called out a greeting but Burden, engrossed in the spectacle, simply raised a hand in reply. They entered the lane which cut through the houses and shops which ranged either side of the bridge. As usual, Athelstan found such a journey frightening, literally crossing between heaven and earth. The sights and sounds always disturbed him. The clatter of nearby windmills, the stench from the tanneries, the stink of the lay stalls and that ever-crashing thunder as the river poured through the bridge's twenty arches, pounding the lozenge-shaped starlings protecting the pillars below. Nevertheless, this was also a busy market-place where everything was sold: Baltic furs, Muscovite leather, Paris linen, lace from Lieges and cloth from Arras. An apprentice ran up to offer a laver, a tripod pitcher with a nipped-in neck and spinous spout which ended in a dragon's head. Athelstan examined the inscription around the bowl, 'I am called a laver because I serve with love.' In his other hand, the lad offered a shining bronze aquamanile from Lubeck carved in the shape of a naked man riding a roaring lion. Athelstan smilingly refused, though he quietly promised to remember both items as possible purchases by the parish council. He just wished they could just cross London Bridge, but they had to pause for a while as one of the lay stalls, heaped to fullness with smoking-hot filth, had collapsed to the merriment of some and the disgust of many, for the reeking stench crawled like a poisonous snake along the bridge.

Eventually they passed through the towered structures on the bridge's northern side and made their way up into the city. The reaction to Gaunt's party became more hostile. Oaths and curses followed them and, at one point, the escort had to draw swords against the flurry of flung filth. They passed under the shadow of high-towered St Paul's, which, despite its spire being crammed with relics, had been recently struck by light-ning. At last they reached the broad trading thoroughfare of Cheape. On either side elaborately hung stalls, shops and booths offered fabrics, precious metals, foodstuffs, footwear and weaponry of every kind. Here the court fops, resplendent in their elaborate headgear, brocaded short jackets, tight leggings, protuberant codpieces and fantastical long-toed shoes, brushed shoulders with the poor from the midden-heap manors and the dank, dark cellars of Whitefriars. The air was rich with a mixture of cooking smells from bakeries and pastry shops. Here also gathered Cranston's 'beloved parishioners', the underworld of London: the Pages of the Pit, the Brotherhood of the Knife, the Squires of the Sewer, the nips and the foists, the glimmerers and the gold-droppers as well as whores both male and female. These surged about like dirt through water, all intent on seeking their prey: a heavy-bellied merchant's pouch, a drunk's half-open wallet, a young lady with an untied satchel or some distracted stall-owner. Cranston recognized them all, shouting out their names so everyone else would be wary: Spindleshank the foist, Short-pot the pickpocket, Shoulder-sham the counterfeit, Poison-pate the snatcher and Needle-point the sharper. Most of these disappeared like snow under the sun. Nevertheless, as they passed the great water conduit, the prison cage on its top crammed with more of Cranston's 'parishioners', Athelstan sensed true danger. Mischief was being plotted. The crowd around was growing openly hostile.

A cart abruptly appeared and it stopped just near The Holy Lamb of God tavern. On it stood a puppet booth, narrow and curtained with a small stage on which gloved puppets shouted shrilly. One glance at these told everything. The central puppet had golden hair and a crown, the second was a plump cleric and the third, a mitred bishop, a clear allusion to Gaunt, Master Thibault and the hated Archbishop of Canterbury, Simon Sudbury. A fourth suddenly appeared, dressed in the mud-coloured garb of a peasant, who promptly began to beat the other three figures with a club, much to the merriment of the fast-gathering crowd. Lascelles' party was noticed and the mob around them hemmed tighter. A hunting horn brayed and the puppetry immediately ceased. Cranston, swearing loudly, drew his sword. Out of the side streets debouched clusters of horsemen. Faces blackened, they all carried red cowhide shields, spears and clubs. Their hair was heavily greased and rolled up to resemble the horns of a goat.

'Earthworms!' Cranston shouted. 'The Upright Men!' The horsemen forced their way into the throng whilst the few footmen who followed opened the necks of the bulging grain sacks they carried to release an entire warren of rabbits loose in the crowd. Chaos and confusion immediately descended. Dogs snarled and broke free to pursue the rabbits, as did the horde of beggars who saw them as free fresh meat for the pot. The legion of ragged urchins who always frequented the market joined in the mad hunt. Horses skittered. Stalls overturned. Carts and barrows crashed on to their side. Apprentices tried to defend their masters' goods from wholesale pilfering; others tried to rescue themselves from the cutting press. The real danger to Athelstan's party were the fearsome Earthworms. Cranston, who had now taken over the cavalcade, ordered shields up and swords out but fresh danger emerged: more horsemen were spilling out of the side streets on the far side of Cheapside. Cranston urged the cavalcade forward. The Earthworms drew closer. One hurled his spear, which bounced off a raised shield; another followed, narrowly missing Lascelles, shattering against the helmet of one of his escort. Friar Roger snatched a club from an apprentice and grinned at Athelstan.

'Let us go forth!' he shouted. 'Furnished with fire and sword to fight as long as the World Candle shines.' Athelstan was about to follow suit, leaning down to grasp a staff, when trumpets shrilled and the crowd before them abruptly broke. A schiltrom of pikemen, kite shields locked in the testudo formation, long-axe spears jutting out, were advancing down the centre of Cheapside under the flowing banners of the royal standard. The mail-garbed, shield-protected footmen were fearsome enough. However, the real threat was the billowing royal banner. Anyone carrying arms in a hostile fashion when this standard was unfurled were traitors to be punished with summary but gruesome execution. The schiltrom reached Lascelles' cavalcade and parted to gather them into its steel protection. They paused, turned and advanced back. A short while later they passed under the yawning, arched gateway of the Guildhall into the great bailey which stretched beneath the entrance portico dominated by the towering statues of Justice, Prudence and Truth. The schiltrom now broke up. Lascelles led them across the frozen cobbled yard, the air savoury with the mouth-watering smells from a nearby bakery. Friar Roger made his hasty farewells and left. Athelstan followed the rest as they were ushered up steps across floors, shiny mosaics of black, white and red lozenge-shaped tiles. Walls covered in oak panelling reflected the light from a myriad of candles glowing in alabaster jars of different colours. Beautifully embroidered tapestries proclaimed the history and glory of London city since its foundation by King Brutus. They reached a small buttery, where Lascelles told them to wait. White wines and waffle cakes were served. Only then could they relax after the hurly-burly of their journey. Athelstan waited until the servants had left and then walked over to Marcel to exchange the kiss of peace. Marcel grabbed Athelstan close before standing back.

'Time is the Emperor of Life,' he declared. 'Yet you, Athelstan, have not changed.'

'And you, Brother, look as studious as ever, but what are you doing here? I heard you were assigned to the Papal court, the Holy Father's personal adviser?'

'I am very busy in France, Athelstan, rooting out the weeds of heresy.'

'So why are you here? The Inquisition has no power in England.'

'I am here to observe, Athelstan, as a hawk does a field. You have your heretics, Wycliffe the Leicestershire parson and the Lollards, who object to the power of us priests.'

'And mummers who perform near London Bridge!'

Marcel laughed deep and throatily. 'I have been in London for about ten days, Athelstan. I have visited the Tower and all along the riverside. I watch and I listen.' Marcel dropped all pretence of merriment. 'Don't you find such weeds in that little seedy parish of yours? Don't you swim against a tide of heretical filth and radical aspiration?'

'Marcel,' Athelstan retorted, 'I serve in a parish which is as poor as Nazareth, where a carpenter called Crispin tries to raise his family free of the tyranny of Herod.' Marcel's face turned harsh, mouth twisted in objection. 'I work with poor people, Marcel, the lowest of the low. Yet, perhaps in the eyes of Christ, they are princes. Do you remember our vows Marcel, the vision of our founder? How Christ can be found amongst the poor? Marcel, you are a brilliant scholar, I recall your disputations. Don't you remember arguing how Christ seemed happiest when he and others met for a meal with the outcasts of society?'

'True, true,' Marcel's eyes softened, 'but we have all grown older. Life turns colder. Christ's banqueting hall has to be defended against the wild dogs which would invade it.' The conversation was cut off by Lascelles entering, indicating that Athelstan and Cranston follow him out along the gallery into a warm, wood-panelled chancery office deep in the Guildhall. Two people sat at the long polished table. John of Gaunt, Regent and uncle of the king, slouched in a throne-like chair. Gaunt always reminded Athelstan of an artist's depiction of Lucifer before he fell, golden-haired, steely blue eyes and perfectly formed features slightly kissed by the sun. In all things Gaunt was so elegant, be it his neatly cropped hair, moustache and beard or the high-collared gold and scarlet jerkin over the purest cambric shirt. Around Gaunt's neck hung the SS collar of Lancaster. On his fingers dazzled rings, whilst the wall behind him proclaimed the banners of kingdoms Gaunt lay claim to: Portugal, Castile and Aragon. Thibault, sitting on Gaunt's right, was dressed in the dark robes of a monk, though these were of the costliest wool, whilst the sapphire on his chancery ring glowed like a miniature candle. Thibault, with his corn-coloured hair and smooth round face, looked as cherubic as any novice sworn to God. Athelstan knew different. Thibault, despite his innocent appearance, was a highly dangerous man, totally dedicated to his dread master. Athelstan and Cranston bowed. Lascelles directed them to the stools at the far end of the table and sat with them. For a while there was silence. Athelstan watched the candlelight gleam and shift in the waxed, polished wood around him.

'So,' Thibault whispered, 'Brother Athelstan, Sir John, what say you? What has happened?' He pulled a face. 'I am sorry that your journey here, how can I say it, was eventful.'

'Yes, you can say,' Athelstan retorted. 'Very eventful.'

'My henchman,' Thibault smiled at Lascelles, 'has informed us about your quick thinking and courage at The Candle-Flame. My grateful thanks.' His smile faded. 'Beowulf shall hang at Smithfield. I shall be there to see his body ripped open, his entrails plucked out and his severed head balanced on a pole. Then we shall discover who has been found wanting.'

'What do you know of him?' Athelstan asked.

'A traitor.' Gaunt took his hand away from his mouth – even that was a delicate, studied movement. The Regent just sat staring at Athelstan with those strange blue eyes, as if he was trying to break into the friar's very soul.

'Your Grace,' Athelstan leaned forward, 'Beowulf's origins
. . . Who gave him that name?'

'He assumed it himself,' Thibault snapped, 'at his very first
murder. He left a message, "From Beowulf to Grendel, his
enemy". I suppose this Beowulf sees himself as a mixture of
the pagan and the Christian, an Anglo-Saxon hero who can
quote the sombre verses of the prophet Daniel from the Old
Testament.'

'Very good, very good,' Athelstan mused.

'What is, Brother?' Gaunt snapped.

'Well, Beowulf is a man who bestrides two traditions.'

'He is a contagion, a pestilence.' Gaunt's voice thrilled with
hatred. 'He and his damnable proclamation appear here and
there, as far north as Colchester and as far south as Richmond.'
Gaunt's eyes slid to Thibault. 'So far he has evaded capture.
You, Brother, you and Sir John will trap him. Once you have,
I shall kill him. So, what have you learnt?'

Athelstan faithfully reported all that happened: the mysterious murders, the locked entrances, the plundered exchequer
chest, the disappearance of Hugh of Hornsey and the murder
of Scrope. He conceded that all the killings defied logic and
explanation. Now and again he would turn to Cranston for
confirmation. The coroner sat, eyes half-closed, calm and
confident. Athelstan quietly prayed that he would remain so.
There was bad blood between Gaunt and the Lord High
Coroner of London stretching back years, when Sir John had
been the Black Prince's bannerman, body and soul. Cranston
had resisted all approaches from Gaunt, be it through fear or
favour. Sir John openly distrusted the Regent. On one occasion, deep in his cups, Cranston had confided to Athelstan
how he suspected Gaunt secretly cherished and nursed dreams
of seizing the crown. Sometimes the coroner feared for the
safety and welfare of the young king.

Once Athelstan had finished, Gaunt and Thibault questioned
them closely. The friar remained firm in his conclusion. He
had as yet no explanation or evidence even to speculate on
the murders at The Candle-Flame. Cranston added that he
would issue writs immediately all over the city for the arrest
of Hugh of Hornsey, if he was still alive.

'My officials, royal archers, have been brutally murdered.'
Gaunt's words hissed like the serpent he was. 'My treasure,'
he beat his breast, 'my treasure has been stolen. My name
besmirched. My reputation ridiculed.' He brought his fist down
on the table. 'For that, Sir John, Brother Athelstan, someone
is going to die, and only after he has experienced the full
horrors of Hell. Now there is more. Master Thibault show
them.' Thibault rose and opened a chancery pouch on a side
table beneath an arras depicting the execution of England's
first martyr, St. Alban. Bearing in mind Gaunt's threat,
Athelstan was amused at the gory and gruesome picture, which
reflected all the hidden menace of the Regent's threat. Sir John
had now closed his eyes, softly snoring, so Athelstan kicked
him gently. The coroner sighed and pulled himself up. Thibault
slid two pieces of parchment on to the table. The first was
water-stained, the ink had run, the letters blurred. The second,
on the costliest chancery parchment, was clerkly and clearly
inscribed. It provided a list of stores, military impedimenta,
siege machinery and war carts being brought to the Tower;
also an estimate of the garrison there, the number of troops
around London, river defences, the condition of the bridge
and a list of the war cogs, caravels and hulkes being gathered
in the estuary and further up river, their tonnage, armaments
and what crews they carried. At the top of the costly sheet of
vellum were the words, 'To the Lord High Constable', and at
the bottom, 'I reside at The Candle-Flame, 16 February.'

'What is this?' Athelstan asked.

'A report from a spy,' Thibault replied, going back to his
seat. 'Yesterday afternoon Ruat, a sailor from the *Rose of
Picardy*, a Hainault merchantman bound for Dordrecht, was
returning to his ship at Queenhithe when he was attacked,
robbed and killed. Ruat's two assailants were caught red-
handed by the wharf master, their plunder seized. Both were
hanged immediately on the river gallows. The wharf master
looked at that document, now water-soaked. He could not
make sense of the cipher.' Athelstan picked it up and studied
it; the words appeared to be pure nonsense.

'Now,' Thibault continued, 'all port officials have been
alerted against spying. The wharf master was suspicious; he

passed the document to the sheriff, who of course delivered it to me. The document is stained, badly so because the sailor in question was thrown into the water.'

'But he was only a messenger?' Cranston asked.

'Ruat carried a report written in a Latin cipher where the vowels AEIOU were replaced by five random numbers. In this case A is six, E is nine and so on. I broke the cipher and transcribed it. The report must be from a very high-ranking spy as he relates directly to the High Constable of France, Oliver de Clisson. More importantly, it gives us some clue to the identity and whereabouts of the spy. The last line in the cipher in clear Latin reads as follows, if I remember it correctly: *"Apud Candelae Flammam XVI Febr, Resideo*, I reside at The Candle-Flame, sixteenth of February."' Athelstan looked at both the stained manuscript and the clear Latin translation and nodded in agreement.

'The sixteenth of February was yesterday,' Thibault continued. 'Consequently, is someone at that tavern not only an assassin but a traitor?' Thibault held Athelstan's gaze. 'Is it the same individual or two different persons? I don't know. I cannot say except the spy must be learned and skilled. He is also very good. He was only stopped, thanks be to God, by mere accident from supplying his masters in the Secret Chancery at the Louvre with a very detailed description of our river defences from the estuary to the Tower. Look again at the translation, Brother Athelstan.' He waited until the friar did so. 'You see the names of ships and other information but notice that enigmatic phrase which I have transcribed.' Athelstan did. *"Et intra urbem et extra urbem populi ira crescit"* – both within the city and outside,' Athelstan translated, 'the anger of the people grows.' The friar kept a still tongue in his head even though he was inclined to agree with the spy's sentiments. Cranston just coughed rather noisily, fumbled for his miraculous wineskin then thought otherwise.

'We believe,' Thibault continued, 'the French are planning a landing along the Thames, a true *chevauchée*, a great assault on our city. They hope to break our defences and count on the unrest you have witnessed to render these defences even weaker.'

'Why admit he was residing at The Candle-Flame?' Cranston queried.

'Perhaps,' Thibault replied slowly, 'he expected a reply as well as to assure his masters that he had entered the city . . .'

'Or The Candle-Flame may be part of his task,' Athelstan declared. Gaunt, who had remained passive throughout, leaned forward, rapping his fingers on the table. Athelstan listened to the silence abruptly broken by the piping voice of a young girl in an adjoining chamber. Thibault's smooth, well-oiled face creased into a genuine smile. Athelstan recalled how this ambitious clerk, before taking minor orders, had fathered a child, a young girl, Isabella, who was the veritable apple of his eye.

'Brother Athelstan,' Gaunt demanded, 'explain.'

'Your Grace, if French galleys pierce the Thames they can go no further than London Bridge. True?'

'Of course.'

'And the north bank of the Thames is, and can be, heavily fortified and defended.'

Gaunt grunted his agreement.

'Now, The Candle-Flame overlooks the river; it stands opposite the Tower and close to the approaches to London Bridge. The French might be plotting to control the southern bank whilst they direct attacks against the quaysides of the city. The Candle-Flame would be an excellent place to set up camp.'

'Brother Athelstan,' Gaunt jibed, 'you should have been a soldier.'

'Like you, Your Grace?'

Gaunt's smile faded.

'Brother Athelstan may be correct,' Cranston intervened swiftly. 'The Candle-Flame can be fortified, the Barbican easily defended, and it would also be an excellent location to survey both the river and all approaches to the bridge.'

'Find him then!' Gaunt snapped. 'This business, Sir John, is the king's matter. It cannot be set aside for anything else.'

'There is something else,' Athelstan declared. 'We have told you about the murder of Scrope. Master Thibault, did you know that Marsen was a housebreaker in Coggeshall, the murderer of an innocent woman and manservant?'

Thibault shook his head.

'I would be the first to concede,' Gaunt declared, 'that not all royal officials are angels in disguise.'

'They may well be demons!' Athelstan retorted. 'The murder of Marsen and the others could be the work of Beowulf, or even this spy. I also concede that the assassin and the spy might be the same person or . . .' Athelstan paused.

'Or what?' Thibault asked.

'There may be a number of strands here.' Athelstan counted them out on his fingers. 'The Upright Men, the spy, Beowulf or someone quite distinct with his or her own motive.'

'Sir Robert Paston is one of the guests.' Gaunt's mouth creased into a fake smile. 'He is my enemy – this could be his revenge.'

'Brother Athelstan, Sir John,' Thibault declared hastily, 'we have no information to give you, no further assistance.' He pointed to the two sheets of parchment. 'Take them, study them. Is there anything else you need?' Athelstan put the parchments into his chancery satchel then explained about the corpses being brought to the Guildhall. Thibault agreed, saying Lascelles would assist Flaxwith in hiring the finest physician in Cheapside, the cadavers would be scrutinized and Athelstan informed of his conclusions. Thibault then signalled to Lascelles, who left and returned with Brother Marcel.

'I believe,' Thibault smiled expansively, 'that you and Marcel know each other. We are pleased to welcome the Pope's legate, a member of the Holy Inquisition, here to London.'

'What for?' Athelstan demanded.

'Heresy does flourish, Brother, whatever the soil.' Marcel bowed to Gaunt and Thibault before sitting down on the chair pulled back by Lascelles. 'We have spoken already, Your Grace,' Marcel continued, 'about the teaching of the Leicestershire priest John Wycliffe and the beliefs of the Lollard sect, who do not accept the authority of our Church or the Holy Father's interpretation of scripture. They apparently do not understand the divinely revealed truths—'

'That is because,' Athelstan interrupted hastily, 'most of them can't read. They are just too poor, too hungry, too tired and too oppressed.' Athelstan bit his tongue as Cranston kicked his ankle.

'The Inquisition has no authority in England,' the coroner offered. 'Our Archdeacon's court is weighty and powerful enough.'

'Sir John, Sir John,' Marcel winked at Athelstan as he held his hands up in a gesture of peace, 'I am not here to interfere or probe. The Holy Father simply wishes to learn more about a kingdom where the papacy itself, the Blessed Gregory, sent its own apostle Augustine to convert and preach.'

Athelstan nodded understandingly though he strongly suspected the truth was that John of Gaunt was looking for papal support, and if licence issued to the Inquisition to meddle and interfere in the English Church brought him favour at the papal court, then so be it.

'Brother Marcel had been in the city,' Thibault explained. 'Now he wishes to move to Southwark and what better place than a fellow Dominican's parish at St Erconwald's?'

Athelstan coughed to hide his surprise.

'Do not worry, Brother,' Marcel asserted, 'I will not trouble you or yours or even lodge in your little house. I shall hire a chamber at The Candle-Flame, even though, unfortunately, that tavern seems to be the setting for murder and treason.'

'We approve of that,' Thibault added. 'Brother Marcel may discover, see or learn something of interest to us as well as the Holy Father.'

'Of course,' Athelstan retorted. He paused. 'Your Grace, Master Thibault, one more question.' He gestured at Marcel. 'What I have to say will, I am sure, be only of passing interest to the Papal Inquisitor. I speak in confidence which I know he will respect.' Athelstan paused as Marcel agreed to what he'd said; the friar did not wish to alienate his visitor by asking him to leave.

'Your question?' Gaunt insisted.

'How much, at a swift reckoning, was Marsen carrying in that exchequer coffer? You must know,' Athelstan insisted. 'You sent Lascelles here to visit him the night before his murder?' The friar glanced at the henchman who just smirked and stared at his master.

'Yes, Lascelles was sent to The Candle-Flame. He was under strict instruction to check on all monies. Marsen gave a proper accounting, as he would at the Exchequer of Receipt at Westminster.'

'There is something else,' Athelstan chose his words carefully, 'Master Thibault, I would like the truth. Marsen collected taxes. I suspect Mauclerc was there to watch Marsen, a man with a highly unsavoury history and a malignant soul.'

'You use the cruellest mastiff, Brother, to bring down a bear.'

'I believe Mauclerc had other duties, didn't he?' Athelstan glimpsed the surprise in Thibault's eyes.

'What duties, Brother?'

'Information, any information he could collect on the Great Community of the Realm and the Upright Men.' Athelstan kept his voice steady. He believed certain records had been taken from Mauclerc's chancery satchel but what he was saying was really a wild guess. 'Indeed,' he continued, 'Mauclerc would have lists of possible sympathizers, rumours and gossip about who might be involved with the Upright Men?'

Thibault looked as if he was going to object. Brother Marcel now had his head down.

'I also suspect . . .' Athelstan realized this truly was a game of hazard, yet he had nothing to lose.

'What else do you suspect, Brother?'

'Well,' Athelstan sighed, 'if the Pope's own Inquisitor is in London what better way of helping him than by providing him with a list of people tainted by the teaching of Wycliffe or even members of the Lollard sect?'

'Very good,' Thibault breathed, 'very shrewd indeed, Brother. Yes, Mauclerc did have a list and yes, that list has probably gone but more than that we cannot say.'

'And the money?' Athelstan persisted. 'Marsen must have boasted about what he had collected. He would be ever so proud of squeezing so much money out of those he taxed.'

'Very proud, Brother,' Lascelles replied. 'When I visited him, he opened the coffer and it was crammed with gold and silver coins.'

'How much?' Cranston barked.

'A king's fortune. At least two thousand pounds sterling in the finest coin of the realm.'

Athelstan whistled in surprise.

'Such a sum! Tell me now,' Athelstan continued, ignoring Gaunt's gesture of impatience, 'Mauclerc and Marsen not only collected taxes but information which would be useful to you. Sir Robert Paston, as you have conceded, Your Grace, was – is – not your friend. Were this precious pair collecting titbits of gossip, slander about Paston and his family to, how can I say . . .?'

'Blackmail him,' Thibault interrupted. 'Let us move to the arrow point, Brother. The answer is yes. I would not call it blackmail but the push and shove of fierce debate. Paston portrays himself as a protector of the people, a partisan of the truth, a merchant who gives to good causes, a master mariner cheated out of his dues.' Thibault sneered and waved a hand. 'Paston is no more a saint than I am. If he is going to climb into the pulpit to preach then perhaps he should make sure his own hands are clean.'

'And are they?'

Thibault just twisted his mouth and stared away.

'But that's another reason why you despatched Lascelles to The Candle-Flame, isn't it?' Athelstan insisted. 'You were impatient to find out what had been discovered about our worthy member of the Commons?'

'Marsen said we would have to wait, that he hadn't yet finished, whilst Mauclerc dare not oppose him,' Lascelles replied.

'And did Marsen know that Physician Scrope was hunting him, demanding justice?'

'I suspect so.' Thibault shrugged. 'Marsen's past was, as you say, highly unsavoury. He had applied to Chancery for a King's Pardon for all past crimes and felonies. I told him that I might support this depending on the success he achieved in collecting the king's taxes. On the night they met, Marsen informed Lascelles that I would be very pleased about what he had learnt.'

'And Hugh of Hornsey?'

'Most surprising, Brother. Hugh of Hornsey was a

mercenary, a good captain of archers who kept to himself. I suspect he is dead. I cannot see him as an assassin. He is shrewd enough to know that flight is perhaps not the best protection. But,' Thibault smiled falsely, 'we all have our little secrets, Brother, only some of us are more successful at protecting those secrets than others . . .'

PART TWO

'Via Dolorosa': the way of anguish.

The Vault of Hell was a much decayed though magnificently constructed tavern at the heart of the deepest darkness around Whitefriars. Here one of the most notorious captains of the slums, a true Knight of the Knife, a Lord of the Dunghill, Humphrey Wasp, held court on behalf of even more sinister overlords. Sharp as a tooth on a finely honed saw was Humphrey Wasp. He usually sat enthroned on a velvet-draped throne chair, formerly a bishop's but appropriated during a recent riot in Norwich and despatched south for Humphrey's use. Indeed, most of the costly goods stolen from the shops and stalls along Cheapside and elsewhere were brought to the Vault of Hell – the finest plunder: rolls of velvet and damask from Venice, lace from Lille, leather from Castile, wood and furs from Cracow. Here the most elegant pieces of art and craftsmanship, filched from their owners, were offered for sale: leather caskets cleverly embossed with symbols brought to vivid life by incised scrollwork, ivory tablet covers from Paris, delicate bone caskets from Cologne carved at the seams with the legend of Tristram and Isolde. All these were offered for sale along with jewel-studded brooches with inscriptions such as 'You have my heart' or 'Love conquers all'. Humphrey was particularly keen to collect mazers fashioned in Flanders from a rare speckled wood known as Bird's Eye Maple and set on a silver-gilt stand. Naturally such plunder glowed as fierce as any beacon light, attracting in all the rogues: the children of the horn-thumb, the trillibubs, the cackling cheats, cock-pimps, tart-dames and other land pirates, the Fraternity of the Filch and the Foist, not to mention the Brethren of the Block, who rejoiced in names such as Blow Blood, Tickle Pitcher and Jack Pudding. They all assembled at the Vault of Hell to eat and drink the finest food, wine and ale stolen from the best establishments.

A sumptuous banquet had been laid out along the common table of the great taproom called the Hall of Darkness, even though it was brightly lit by a myriad of pure beeswax candles stolen from churches the length and breadth of the city. The chamber was warmed by a great roaring fire in the massive hearth carved like a cathedral porch, as well as by clusters of braziers which crackled as merrily as the coals of Hell. However, on the night of 17 February, the eve of the feast of the Blessed Simeon bishop and martyr, there was a difference. Humphrey Wasp's herald, the red-haired Chanticleer, had brayed for silence and no one dare disobey. The Earthworms had appeared, at least two score of them, dressed in dark leather and with their faces blackened, their hair dyed red and stiffened into plaits which stood up from their heads like devil's horns. They were well armed with rounded shields, bows, clubs and arrows, and led by captains known as the Rook, the Jackdaw, Magpie, Hawk and Falcon. Fearsome in appearance, ruthless in reputation, the Earthworms were the envoys from the leaders of the Upright Men: Simon Grindcobb, Jack Straw, Wat Tyler and others. They had soon brought the midnight revelry at the Vault of Hell to an abrupt close. Their leader, the Crow, now stood on the dais next to a drunken Humphrey Wasp and drew out from a bucket of red wine the severed head of Grapeseed, former rope-dancer and mountebank, well-known for his drunken boasts that he had no fear of the Upright Men. The Crow just stood there grasping the roughly cut head whilst his companions around the Hall of Darkness nocked their bows.

'Listen Ye!' the Crow proclaimed. 'Marsen's death at The Candle-Flame is now well known, despatched to Hell as he deserves.' He paused at the stifled cheer. 'The plunder Marsen carried, the fruit of his wickedness has disappeared. Look on Grapeseed's head and be warned. The Upright Men will not be trifled with. The treasure Marsen was taking to his satanic master Gaunt belongs to the people and the Upright Men are the true and only guardians of the people. Such treasure is ours and should be, must be, handed over.' The Crow shook the severed head. 'Know Ye also that Hugh of Hornsey, former captain of archers at the Tower and Marsen's erstwhile help-mate in wickedness, has fled. Information about the stolen treasure, good, sound information, will earn you the protection of the Upright Men and five gold pieces. The apprehension of Hugh of Hornsey alive will bring you firmly within the love of the Upright Men as well as a reward of seven gold pieces. I have left with your self-proclaimed squire, Master Wasp, a description of the fugitive.' He dropped the severed head to splash noisily into the bucket of bloody wine, wiped his hands and held them up. 'I have now chanted my own vespers. I leave you our peace until the next time . . .'

oOoOo

Brother Athelstan left through the devil's door built into the north wall of St Erconwald's. He stood in the freezing dark-ness and peered up at the night sky swarming with stars – faint stars, bright stars, a maze of stars. The heavens sparkled bril-liantly but, in the cemetery of St Erconwald's, deep shadows clustered around the outlines of the winter-bound trees. Athelstan gazed up again.

'I promise you, Brother,' he murmured, 'when spring erupts green, lovely and lush, I shall climb to the top of this tower and study those stars most closely, all to the glory of God. And will you join me, Bonaventure?' Athelstan stared down at the one-eyed, fierce-looking tomcat who had adopted Athelstan and become his companion during the lonely watches of the night. 'Holy cat, Catholic cat,' Athelstan whispered. Bonaventure just glared imperiously back. 'Many thanks for joining me.' The cat had been his sole companion in church. Even the Hangman of Rochester who lived in the ankerhold Athelstan had constructed along one of the transepts was absent. The anchorite had joined the rest of Athelstan's wayward flock in The Piebald tavern, where, after eating hot, juicy, pies from Merrylegs' cookshop, they would be downing tankards of ale as they set the world to rights. Athelstan chewed the corner of his lip. The Hangman of Rochester had been a tragic figure when he arrived at St Erconwald's. He had earned his name whilst serving as one of England's finest hangmen after losing his wife and child to outlaws. The Hangman, who had been baptized Giles of Sempringham, had also proved to be a truly talented painter who had begun to sketch out a series of eye-catching tableaux, some of which troubled Athelstan with their stark message. The friar closed his eyes. 'Giles of Sempringham,' he murmured, recalling the Hangman's long, yellow, straw-like hair framing that tragic, cadaverous face, 'I am glad you have become a member of our community.' He opened his eyes and stared down at Bonaventure, who gazed hungrily back. 'I just pray my flock don't draw you into their nefarious schemes.'

Athelstan crossed himself swiftly. He had arrived back in his parish just as the vesper bells tolled to find all in order. The church had been used during the day by the different guilds, fraternities and brotherhoods. The sacristy and sanctuary had been tidied – Benedicta and Crim had seen to that. Nevertheless, Athelstan had walked every inch of his church to ensure all was as it should be; it was not unknown for Watkin and Pike to set up shop in the nave to sell certain goods they'd found 'lying about'. Athelstan stared across God's Acre at the old death house now converted into a comfortable dwelling for the beggar Godbless, who had adopted Thaddeus, the omnivorous parish goat. 'At least you control Thaddeus,' Athelstan whispered, watching the candlelight dance at the shuttered window. Other animal keepers were not so successful. Ursula the pig woman's extraordinary fat sow, which accompanied her everywhere, even to Mass, was the bane of Athelstan's life, or rather that of his small garden. Athelstan felt a spurt of pleasure. The garden was now coming into its own. The friar wondered if Crispin the carpenter had finished the 'Hermitage' as Athelstan called it, a comfortable box for the large hedgehog which had taken up residence in Athelstan's herb plot and been given the name of Hubert the Monk. Athelstan pulled his cloak tighter about him.

'Are you well, Godbless,' he called out, 'on this freezing cold night?'

'Godbless you too, Father,' came the reply. 'Thaddeus and I are as warm and crisp as a Christmas pie. Not even the ghosts who swarm like buzzing bees around us disturb our humours. Cream-faced they are, black-eyed, but they are wary of Thaddeus.'

Athelstan smiled. Godbless was as mad as a box of frogs; he claimed to be related to Oberon, king of the fairies; even so, Athelstan had insisted that he take up residence as Guardian of God's Acre. Godbless had proved to be a sure defence against the warlocks and wizards who prowled city cemeteries at the dead of night to practise their abominable rites. Athelstan had recently heard of such an incident at the nearby Church of St Mary Overy, where a coven of witches and warlocks had assembled to sacrifice black cockerels to the demon lords of the air. They had fashioned oils and salves from their sacrifices, mixing them with worms, dead men's teeth, the garments of suicides and many other heinous ingredients, all boiled together over an oak fire in the severed skull of a beheaded felon. Athelstan recalled the Inquisitor Brother Marcel and smiled grimly. If his fellow friar looked hard enough, Southwark would provide him with a glut of heresies and a veritable litany of evil practices. Something about Marcel deeply disturbed him, something not quite right. To calm himself Athelstan went and checked on the old warhorse Philomel sleeping in his stable before moving across into the priest's house. Athelstan had scrubbed it clean the previous day and he was proud of what he had achieved. The flagstone kitchen floor gleamed, the bed loft was neatly ordered, whilst all the cooking utensils and platters shimmered in the light of the banked hearth fire. He busily lit candles and the lantern on the table, which served both for eating and study. Once satisfied Athelstan stoked up the fire, used the bellows on the braziers then locked and bolted the door for the night. Benedicta had left one of Merryleg's pies in the small oven built next to the hearth. Athelstan poured a stoup of ale, polished his horn-spoon on a napkin, blessed himself and Bonaventure and began to eat, his every mouthful being watched by Bonaventure, who had lapped his milk in the twinkling of his one good eye.

'This is excellent!' Athelstan murmured. 'I will leave you some juicy venison, Bonaventure. I do wonder how Merrylegs obtained such good meat in the depth of winter.' He leaned over and stroked the cat's head. 'On second thoughts, perhaps it's best not to ask.' Athelstan put the platter down near the fire beside Bonaventure. He opened his chancery casket and took out sheets of vellum, a clasped ink horn and fresh quill pen all courtesy of Sir John. He then emptied his satchel and made himself ready by intoning the *'Veni Creator Spiritus'*, asking for divine help with the murderous mystery confronting him. Certain matters had already been clarified. Earlier in the evening a Guildhall courier had brought him information on how all the corpses taken from The Candle-Flame had been examined by no lesser person than Bertrand de Troyes, a royal physician. He declared how he could detect no trace of poison or any other potion except ale and wine. All victims had died brutally of their wounds. The same physician had been with Lascelles when the scraps and dregs served in the Barbican had been examined. They could discover very little. A horde of rats had devoured the lot but with no ill effect. Lascelles had even called in the services of the Guildhall rat-catcher, who searched about but concluded there was nothing amiss which a gaggle of ferrets could not resolve. So, Athelstan wondered, how had all those murders been perpetrated so mysteriously?

'*Primo*, Bonaventure.' The friar spoke as he wrote. Occasionally he would glance up; the great cat had demolished what was left of the venison and now squatted on the table watching Athelstan expectantly. '*Primo*, Bonaventure,' he repeated, 'those two archers killed by the campfire were tired and cold. The flames would illuminate them as clear targets for the assassin. In a matter of a few heartbeats, crossbow bolts struck one and then the other. *Secundo*, how did the assassin, or assassins, enter that Barbican? The solitary window was locked, closed and shuttered firmly on both sides. Apparently the tavern has no ladder long enough to reach it; moreover, Marsen and the rest would surely have killed any intruder attempting to break in? The door? Mooncalf, and I believe him, swears that it was locked and bolted. More mysteriously, so was the trapdoor which governs access to and from the second storey. Both entrance and flight from the roof is nigh impossible. *Tertio*,' Athelstan paused to dip his quill in ink, 'the assassin must be a skilled master-at-arms to slay seasoned archers, veterans, not to mention Marsen and Mauclerc who would surely resist. More mysterious still, why hadn't those on the upper storey who heard the swordplay below be warned and gone to their help or, if the assassin abruptly appeared in the upper storey, though only God knows how, surely those on the ground floor would have been alerted? *Quarto*, the exchequer coffer. How was that opened and plundered? It had three locks. When Marsen and Mauclerc's corpses had been stripped in the death house at the Guildhall, a key had been found on chains around each of their necks. The third must be held by Hugh of Hornsey, who has disappeared. So, how had the exchequer chest been opened and riffled so easily? *Quinto*, how did that assassin leave carrying the treasure without using window or door?' Athelstan paused as Bonaventure padded closer, head going out to Athelstan's tankard. 'Judas cat!' the friar whispered. 'You act all humble but in truth you are hungry. Let us continue.' Athelstan smoothed the parchment in front of him. '*Sexto*, Hugh of Hornsey. Victim or perpetrator? Did that elegant gauntlet and the chainmail wristguard belong to him? Was the captain of archers dead or alive? If the former, why hasn't his corpse been found like the rest? If alive, why the flight, which obviously casts him as the murderer? *Septimo*, which is seventh to you, cat.' Athelstan ruffled the fur between Bonaventure's scarred ears, battle trophies of the cat's ferocious fights along the alleyways of Southwark. 'Was that mysterious assassin, Beowulf, the secret friend and ally of the Upright Men, responsible? Was Beowulf a stranger or someone at the tavern? *Octavo*, had Beowulf also been responsible for physician Scrope's murder, and if so why? The physician was Marsen's implacable foe, preparing to indict him before the Court of King's Bench. So why should Beowulf risk killing him and so mysteriously? Again, how did the murderer enter and leave a locked chamber without hurt or hindrance? He must have come through that door as the only window overlooked a busy stableyard. Friar Roger claimed to have heard knocking on Scrope's door, yet when he looked out, the Franciscan could see no one in the gallery.' Athelstan paused to take a sip of ale and, as Bonaventure edged closer, abruptly rose to his feet. If a cat could smile it did at the success of its strategy. The little friar, as usual, went across to the buttery and brought back the milk jug to fill Bonventure's bowl in front of the fire. The cat leapt down and nestled in the warmth to tongue the milk and revel in his achievement.

Athelstan studied what he had written. '*Nono*, Physician Scrope was fastidiously clean. According to witnesses he had been closeted in his chamber, yet his costly boots and cloak were splattered with blood. The same is true of the lantern horn, whilst the candle inside had burnt low. Scrope must have gone out on the night of the murder and didn't have time to get the mud cleaned off his clothing. He must have, or might have, seen or heard something suspicious, so he was silenced. *Decimo*, the attack on Lascelles? Undoubtedly Beowulf, but was he also responsible for the other murders? *Postremo*.' Athelstan paused. 'Finally, the spy who declares he is residing at The Candle-Flame . . . is he only a spy or an assassin?' Athelstan pulled across the sheets of parchment given to him by Thibault. 'So many questions, Friar,' he muttered, 'and I am so tired.' Athelstan kept reading but his eyes grew heavy and, putting his head on his arms, he slipped into a deep sleep.

oOoOo

Cranston had risen very early in the principal bedchamber of his now empty, rather desolate house. He'd stoutly resisted the temptation to mope and mourn the absence of the Lady Maude and the two poppets. Instead, he had washed thoroughly and clipped his hair, moustache and beard using an enamel-backed mirror, a Twelfth Night gift from the Lady Maude. Once satisfied, Cranston had dressed in one of his finest lawn shirts, a sea-green woollen hose, a blue jerkin and a dark-red mantle. He donned his silver chain of office, rubbed perfumed oil on to his face, collected his boots, cloak and sword then paused by the front door to recite a short prayer for his loved ones. He crossed himself, opened the door and went out to brave the freezing night mist which still cloaked Cheapside.

Cranston strolled down the thoroughfare until he reached the Church of St Mary-le-Bow. He entered its incensed-hallowed darkness, which was lit fitfully by golden tongues of candle flame before the Lady altar. Cranston genuflected and entered the Chantry Chapel of St Alphege, where the Jesus Mass of the day was about to begin. Afterwards Cranston ambled across to what he called 'his other chapel' – The Holy Lamb of God – to be soothed by the tender ministrations of the land-lady. Cranston dined on *cormarie*, a dish of the house: pork roasted in red wine, cloves, garlic and black pepper, served with freshly baked white bread. Cranston gave thanks to her and God as he ate and drank lustfully. Of course, within a heartbeat of entering the tavern the coroner was joined by two beggars, the constant bane of Cranston's life: Leif the One-Legged and his comrade Rawbum, a former cook who, under the influence, had sat down on a pan of bubbling oil. Cranston was able to fend them off with a few pennies and so they left, shouting their praise and thanks.

At peace with God and man, Sir John then adjourned to his judgement chamber in the Guildhall where his two acolytes, Osbert the plump-faced clerk and Simon the meagre-featured scrivener had prepared the agreed schedule. The coroner ruefully conceded that the business of the day had begun. He listened to both men even though he was distracted by memories of what he had seen and heard the previous day. The murders at The Candle-Flame were truly baffling. Athelstan had left early in the evening equally mysti-fied. Cranston had reviewed and scrutinized all he had learnt and wondered if Athelstan had reached the same conclusion as he had, a rather minor solution yet still interesting. Cranston had not bothered about Beowulf or the possible spy. He had been fascinated by the costly blue gauntlet and the expensive chainmail wristguard. Had these been deliber-ately left by the assassin, who had excelled himself in the deadly skill of his murderous enterprise? If the killer had been wearing these, and Cranston accepted Athelstan's theory that neither item fitted any of the corpses in the Barbican, surely the killer would have noticed they were missing? He would have searched for them. Moreover, both items were quite difficult to take off, especially the wristguard. And why take one off and not both gauntlets and wristguards? If the items had been deliberately, left, for what purpose? The killer would not incriminate himself, so who was he trying to blame? Moreover, if those items belonged to an innocent party, how did the killer obtain them and why leave them in that murder chamber? Cranston was also intrigued by what they had found on the physician's corpse. Why was Scrope clutching that *vademecum*, the pilgrim book about the wonders of Glastonbury? The book had been open at a certain page stained with the dead man's blood. Was it a mere accident, a coincidence? Had the physician been reminiscing about his pilgrimage?

Cranston was roused from his reflections by Oswald and Simon who, helped by Flaxwith and his bailiffs, had now assembled the usual litany of offences with their perpetrators. Mooncurser, who believed demons, disguised as a gang of sparrows, were massing in the eaves of houses ready to strike. He and his comrade Hugh the Howlet, who believed he was Master of the Owls, had noisily proclaimed with trumpet and bagpipe such a message along the entire length of Cheapside well after the chimes of midnight. Eventually they had been arrested by the bailiffs, given a good thrashing and lodged in the cage on the tun. Cranston bellowed at them and let both go. Make-bait and Duck-legs appeared next, accused of drunkenness. They had the charges quashed in return for providing valuable information about the jakemen who issued counterfeit licences to the glimmers so the latter could go begging the length and breadth of the city. Cranston took careful note of these as he did the Queen of the Night, who claimed she ran a family of love in a chamber above a tavern in Dowgate. Cranston declared that she was a bawd supervising a brothel. He fined her as such and bound her over to keep the peace. Cranston sat as the whole sorry gaggle of petty malefactors appeared and disappeared before him as he issued his judgements. The market horn was braying for the start of business along Cheapside when Cranston noticed Muckworm, one of his most trusted informants, slide into the judgement chamber to stand statue-like in his long brown robe until the room emptied. Once it had, Muckworm, his bald head and girlish face all glistening with perfumed oil, sidled forward.

'My Lord Coroner . . .'

'Two shillings,' Cranston retorted. 'Four shillings if the information is useful.'

'The business at The Candle-Flame?

'What of it?'

'None of the plunder has appeared on the streets. No one is saying anything. Rumour claims the Upright Men, though rejoicing in Marsen's death, had no part in it.'

'And?'

'They have issued the ban against anyone who tries to profit from the stolen treasure. Any information about the murders and robbery must be conveyed to them. They have also issued their own warrant and posted a reward for the capture of Hugh of Hornsey.'

'Have they now?' Cranston breathed, stirring in his chair. 'In other words, the Upright Men do not know what happened at The Candle-Flame. They had no part in it, which brings us back to the original question. Who did? Ah, well, Muckworm, see Osbert and collect three shillings.'

Muckworm bowed and left the chamber. Cranston sighed and pulled across a copy of an indictment: how Thomas Elan in Farringdon ward feloniously entered the close and house of Margaret Perman of the same ward, attempted to rape her feloniously, and feloniously bit the said Margaret with his teeth so that he ripped off the said Margaret's nose with that bite and broke three of her ribs so that four days later the said Margaret died because of infection and pain of that bite . . . 'Satan's tits!' Cranston swore quietly and immediately took a slurp from the miraculous wineskin. He grasped a quill and scribbled across the indictment that Elan be arraigned before the justices of oyer and terminer at Westminster.

'Sir John?' He glanced up. Oswald and Simon stood in the doorway, both looking highly anxious. Cranston felt a pang of pity. These two faithful servants of his court were always ready to tease him, but not today. The coroner realized how that rising tide of fear creeping through the city was beginning to lap along the corridors of the Guildhall. Horrors like Thomas Elan could be dealt with but the appearance of the Earthworms yesterday, erupting into the heart of the city, audacious enough to attack crown officials, heightened the tension. These two men were terrified. Yesterday royal troops had invaded Cheapside but when the revolt came these would be pulled back to defend Westminster and the Tower. And what then?

'Gentlemen.' Cranston smiled. 'You have family?'

'Yes, Sir John,' they chorused.

'Get them out of this city as soon as possible.'

'Where, Sir John?' Oswald pleaded.

'They can join the Lady Maude in a well-fortified manor deep in the countryside, your wives, your children and the rest of your households. I will leave you the details but mark my words, they should be gone by tomorrow's vesper's bell. Also,' Cranston gestured around, 'start stripping my chambers here. Have all the tapestries and other moveables chested away. Any weapons and monies must be hidden. The coroner's rolls and all other documents should be locked in the war chests in the cellars. Oh, by the way, have those corpses from The Candle-Flame been moved to St Mary-le-Bow yet?'

'Yes, Sir John,' they chorused.

'Good, now do what I say.'

'Of course, Sir John.' The relief of both officials was obvious.

'By the way,' Simon piped up, 'Sir John, you have two visitors who wish to speak to you urgently, the taverner Master Thorne and Sir Robert Paston . . .'

A short while later both men were ushered up into the chamber, Oswald closing the door as Cranston waved his visitors to the cushioned window seat. Refreshments were offered and refused. Thorne, his hard-favoured face slightly red, eyes constantly blinking, came swiftly to the point.

'Sir John, we have information for you. Sir Robert here has discussed it with me. We thought it best to come to you.'

'On the night of the murders,' Paston broke in, 'I heard a disagreement, a fairly violent one as I walked down the gallery and passed Ronseval's chamber. Voices were raised. Ronseval was challenging Hugh of Hornsey. I recognized the captain's Yorkshire burr; he apparently hails from Pontefract.'

'This disagreement?' Cranston asked.

'I could only hear catches of their conversation. Ronseval was accusing Hornsey of cowardice, of being too frightened to confront Marsen. I passed on and returned to my chamber.'

'When was this?'

'I would guess about an hour before midnight. But listen, Sir John, I am sure that Hornsey left that chamber. I heard the door open and close. However, I am equally certain that sometime later he returned. I am sure I heard a knock. Again, I went out on to the gallery. I heard raised voices, a scuffle. I hid in the shadows. The door was thrown open and Hornsey stormed out.'

'So.' Cranston paused. 'What you are saying is that Hugh of Hornsey left his post at the campfire at least twice to quarrel with Ronseval? But why him? Why should a captain of archers consort with a wandering minstrel?'

'All I can say,' Thorne replied, 'is that both have stayed at The Candle-Flame. There is more. Yesterday, after you left, the tavern fell silent. Your bailiff Flaxwith and the others carted away the corpses and what remained of the food and drink. On his way out Flaxwith removed your seals and declared the Barbican could now be used, that is correct?'

Cranston nodded.

'As I said, everything quietened down. Everyone was stricken by what had happened. My wife Eleanor is sorely aggrieved.' He paused to catch his breath. 'Mooncalf, just before twilight set in, glimpsed Ronseval out on the Palisade. He seemed to be searching for something. Mooncalf decided to hide and watch.'

'And?' Cranston leaned forward.

'Mooncalf saw Ronseval pick up a dagger and hurry back into the tavern. Now, I left The Candle-Flame in the early evening; everything remained quiet. Sir Robert will attest to that. You had instructed myself and all the guests to remain until you issued licence to leave.'

Cranston grunted his agreement.

'Well, between vespers and compline bell, sometime before

the curfew sounded and the steeple lights were lit, Ronseval fled the tavern.'

'What!'

'Sir John, I was not there. Mooncalf met Ronseval in the Dark Parlour, preparing to leave. Mooncalf had words with him about that. Ronseval said he was leaving for a short while and would return. He never did. This morning a Dominican, the Papal Inquisitor, Brother Marcel, arrived to lodge at the tavern. I gave him the Lombard chamber, spacious and comfortable, next door to the minstrel's. I had been expecting him for days.' He sniffed. 'Whilst doing so I could hear no sound from Ronseval's room. I unlocked the door but he and all his baggage were gone. He had left the chamber tidy enough, though I detected blood smatterings on the rope matting and turkey rug. It looked as if Ronseval had tried to wash it off and failed. I asked Sir Thomas to come and witness what I had discovered. He did. Sir John, Ronseval has disappeared; he has fled.'

'Why?' Cranston asked himself loudly. 'No, I don't expect you to answer that but what actually happened at your tavern, Master Thorne, during those dark hours of the night?'

oOoOo

Brother Athelstan was wondering about the same problem as he took his seat in the sanctuary chair, moved specially through the rood screen so he could meet and converse with his parish council, who were now sitting on three long benches before him. They had all turned up for the Jesus Mass. Athelstan had been waiting for them; the candles had been lit and the braziers fired so St Erconwald's lost some of its misty chill. Athelstan glanced at Mauger the bell clerk, who sat hunched over his small chancery table taking notes. Athelstan was pleased they had covered a great deal of business including the collapse of the recent Love Day, so carefully prepared by Athelstan. Relationships amongst some of the parishioners had soured and Athelstan had hoped that a Love Day would soothe all these problems. There had been a Mass followed by a solemn exchange of singing bread and the kiss of peace with revelry planned in the nave. At first everything had gone smoothly, until Pike's game of Hodman's Bluff descended into Hot Cockles: a lewd, bawdy ritual where participants blindfolded each other then tried to slap their opponent's buttocks. Of course, Pike had cheated. He immediately spied on Cecily the courtesan's beautiful round bottom and, drunkenly lecherous, led the rest in hot pursuit, provoking the dire wrath of their wives, Pike's Imelda in particular.

This morning's parish council meeting had restored peace and harmony, and Athelstan and his little flock were moving swiftly down a list of outstanding business. They had agreed to the creation of new paintings on the south side of the church. The Hangman of Rochester, now smiling beatifically to himself, had described in great detail the story of Elijah and the Prophets of Hell. The Hangman also solemnly vowed that no one from the parish would recognize themselves in the painting. A new lid for the baptismal font had been decided. Purple candles had been ordered for Lent. The time and liturgy for the distribution of ashes on Ash Wednesday were fixed, whilst the cleansing of the mort-pall used to cover the parish funeral bier was also agreed. Judith, once a mummer, a former player in the Straw Men acting troupe, had been studying Athelstan's precious book of plays. She had announced how the mystery play at Easter would centre around the betrayal of Christ. Judith had asked for volunteers for the difficult roles: Pilate, Herod, the two high priests, Judas, Pilate's wife and Pilate's daughter. Athelstan had never heard of the latter but he thought it more prudent not to comment. Judith's announcement had distracted everyone and of course stirred the latent rivalry amongst the parishioners. Once Judith had finished, Athelstan revealed his cherished plan. On Good Friday, during the celebration of Christ's Passion, he hoped to arrange a three-voice choir to sing the '*Ecce Lignum Crucis*' and the '*Christus factus est*' – 'Behold the wood of the Cross' and 'Christ made himself obedient'. Athelstan was determined on this. He would personally teach them the Latin phrases, easy to memorize as well as recite. This, as planned, had deeply flattered his flock, who would be very eager to show off their newfound learning – Latin no less, in all the taverns of Southwark. The parishioners discussed this heatedly amongst

themselves before falling strangely quiet. Athelstan's heart
sank. The council sat staring at him. All remained silent, even
Ranulf the rat-catcher's two ferrets, Ferox and Audax, who
crouched placidly in the cage between their master's feet,
whilst Ursula the pig woman's massive sow sprawled docilely
on the floor. Athelstan recalled Pedro the Cruel at The Candle-
Flame. Perhaps, Athelstan smiled to himself, the two pigs
should be introduced to one another! Only Thaddeus the goat
moved, trying as usual to chew his master's ragged cloak.
Athelstan glanced at the lovely face of Benedicta but she
seemed totally distracted by her hood, lined with squirrel hair.
Athelstan waited patiently. The council members were now
turning on their benches to peer at Watkin and Pike. The friar
suspected what was about to happen.

'Father?' Pike shot to his feet. 'Father?'

'Yes, Pike.'

'Father we heard about what happened at The
Candle-Flame.'

'I am sure you have, as you would about the attack by the
Earthworms in Cheapside.' Athelstan paused, the winter light
pouring through the lancet windows seemed to dim, the
shadows creeping closer.

'Father,' Pike blurted out, 'we are worried about you. I
mean, when the time comes . . .'

'When God's time comes, Pike, when my time comes . . .'
Athelstan rose to his feet, fighting back tears of sheer frustration as he studied the faces of these men and women whom
he truly loved and cared for. They could infuriate him beyond
belief, and heaven knows they did, but they were funny, kind
and generous with a deep mocking humour, a love of the
ridiculous, even if they themselves were often the brunt of
such comedy. He baptized their children. He schooled, whenever he could, the older ones in their horn-book. He visited
them in their homes and celebrated the much-loved rhythms
of both the year and the Church's liturgy. These poor people
shuffled through life; now they were all stumbling towards
disaster. Athelstan felt his temper break. 'I have preached on
this before,' he thundered, 'and I will do so again. The Lord
Jesus sees all men and women equal in the sight of God.

Christ, I assure you, weeps bitter tears at the greed and power of the great ones of the soil. God does interfere through the grace he sends to change the way things are to the way things should be. The only obstacle to God's grace is the stubborn, obdurate and evil self-centeredness of those who block God's plan. Nevertheless, God will achieve what he wants. The community of this realm is growing stronger. The good will flower. The seed, however, lies deep, the soil is hard yet still the seed grows. Bondage to the master is being broken. The Commons sit to question the Crown and its lackies—'

'And still we starve.' Pike had, as he could so often do, dropped his usual foolish antics, showing that sharp leadership which had made him so favoured amongst the Upright Men.

'Yes Pike, sometimes we starve but violence will not put food on your children's platters. The revolt will come, I know that. I pray against the day because Sion will not come to Southwark. The new Jerusalem will not rise in Cheapside. The great ones will mass their armed men to the north, south, east and west. It will be a time of great slaughter . . .'

'When even the strongholds fall.'

Athelstan whirled round at the voice behind him. Brother Marcel appeared through the door of the rood screen and walked quietly into the nave. He held out his arms to his fellow Dominican.

'Frater,' he whispered. '*Pax et Bonum.* I did not mean to startle you. I wanted to visit your church. I walked its precincts and saw the sacristy door open, so I came in.' Athelstan embraced the Inquisitor, exchanging the kiss of peace on each cheek. For all his surprise Athelstan was amused by his colleague. Marcel, as he had been in the novitiate, was extremely fastidious: his face was smoothly shaven and smelt fragrantly of perfumed oil, his hands were gloved in soft deerskin, whilst his black-and-white robe was of the purest lambswool and fresh as the day.

'You are most welcome, Brother.' Athelstan stood back and gestured at his parishioners. 'We were discussing matters close to our hearts.'

'So I heard, so I heard.' Marcel turned to the council, who immediately fell to their knees as the Inquisitor raised his hand to deliver a solemn blessing. Once finished, the council resumed their seats, whilst Marcel took the stool next to Athelstan.

'Brother,' he declared, 'I heard what you said. I wonder if I could have a word with your parishioners?'

Athelstan agreed, introducing Marcel as a visitor from the Holy Father who wished to learn more about the state of affairs in England.

'We can tell him a tale or two,' Pike muttered but loud enough to provoke muted laughter.

'I am interested,' declared Marcel blithely, 'in what you think of the state of Christ's Church in this kingdom.'

'You mean the one founded by the Carpenter of Nazareth?' Crispin challenged. 'The man who worked with wood, who blessed the poor and warned the rich and powerful?'

Athelstan just stared down at the floor.

'But the Church,' Marcel persisted, 'the Holy Father, your Bishop—'

'Don't know them!' Pike shouted back. 'Athelstan's our pope and our bishop.'

Pernel the Fleming began to croon one of her madcap songs whilst she threaded her orange-dyed hair between her fingers. Ursula's sow promptly clambered to its feet, trotters skittering on the paving stones.

'Will you join the revolt?' Marcel's stark question imposed silence. 'I ask you as a guest in your parish about something which will profoundly change your lives.'

Athelstan, alarmed, rose to his feet. He did not want any of his parishioners to convict themselves out of their own mouths. Thibault's spies swarmed everywhere, even here. Athelstan had not forgotten Huddle, their former painter. Huddle, because of his gambling debts, had been forced to act as Thibault's spy and paid for his mistake with his life. Athelstan sighed with relief when the corpse door leading to the cemetery quietly opened and two cowled figures walked into the nave. One of these pulled back the deep capuchon to reveal the harsh features and cynical eyes of Brother Roger. The Franciscan extended his hands, whilst his companion, still hooded, quickly side-stepped Athelstan. He almost ran into the sanctuary, up the steps to the mercy enclave on the right side of the altar. As he passed this he grasped a corner, the usual gesture of someone claiming sanctuary. Only when he reached the mercy enclave did the figure turn and pull back his hood to reveal a hard-bitten face, pock-marked, the high cheekbones rawed by wind and rain, thin lips and narrow eyes. The man's head was completely shaven, though his face was stubbled, dirty and drawn. Athelstan could see the man was clearly exhausted.

'Sit down.' Athelstan noticed the brace on the man's left wrist, whilst the two forefingers of his right hand were slightly curved and calloused. 'You are Hugh of Hornsey, aren't you?'

'Yes, captain of the archers at the Tower. I claim sanctuary here. I invoke all the protection of Holy Mother Church.'

'And you shall have it as long as you observe canon law,' Athelstan replied. 'You cannot leave here. You cannot receive visitors and you cannot bear arms. In forty days' time you must either surrender to the sheriff or abjure this realm.' Hugh of Hornsey, however, had slumped down on the mercy chair, face in hands. Athelstan, hearing the growing tumult behind him, walked back into the nave. The parish council were now grouped around the Inquisitor, questioning him closely. They had taken Marcel over to show him the wall painting depicting St Peter, the patron saint of Moleskin's boatmen. Crim was describing one of the ships as a caravel, but Marcel gently corrected him as he explained the difference between a hulke, a cog and a galley. Marcel acted all charming, ruffling the lad's hair whilst chatting to members of the parish council.

'Like Herod dancing amongst the innocents,' Athelstan whispered to himself. Pike, Watkin and Ranulf the rat-catcher, however, stood apart in a place where they could peer through the door of the rood screen at the fugitive hiding in the sanctuary. Athelstan did not like the look on their faces and, calling Mauger and Benedicta over, urged them to clear the church. He then turned and walked over to where Brother Roger was admiring a wall painting in the chantry chapel of St Erconwald's.

'Father!' Athelstan whirled round. Pike, Watkin and Ranulf were standing behind him.

'Yes?'

'Father, we want to know, I mean about Hugh of Hornsey . . .'

'Why, Pike,' Athelstan walked forward, 'how do you know our captain of archers?'

'Just,' Pike pulled a face, 'why did he flee to here of all places? I mean, we've all heard about The Candle-Flame murders . . .'

'Have you now?' Friar Roger came over. He winked quickly at Athelstan. 'Well, I'm very thirsty. After I've talked to your parish priest, perhaps you could buy a poor friar a tankard of The Piebald's splendid ale; it would slake the thirst and certainly soothe my humours.'

Pike and the others beamed with pleasure, saying they would wait for him outside. Athelstan watched them go. 'Be careful, Brother,' he warned. 'I do not betray any secrets, but that unholy trinity sit high in the councils of the Upright Men. They'll be very interested to hear of Marsen's death.'

'As I am in St Erconwald's.'

'Are you?' Athelstan exclaimed.

'A great Bishop of London, surely?' And the Franciscan insisted on informing Athelstan about all he'd learnt of St Erconwald. How the saintly Bishop of London had been of the royal line; he had founded religious houses at Barking and Chertsey, so holy even Erconwald's horse litter was now regarded as a sacred relic. Friar Roger paused as Marcel shouted his farewells and left.

'Your fellow Dominican is rather strange.'

'Aren't we all?' Athelstan retorted. 'Brother Roger, welcome to my church. By all means study this parish consecrated to St Erconwald. But how on earth did you meet Hugh of Hornsey and why did you bring him here?'

'Oh, I had words with him in the tavern before the murders occurred – the usual courtesies.' Brother Roger's voice fell to a whisper. 'I am not my brother's keeper but Hugh of Hornsey thought differently. Early this morning he presented himself before the pauper's gate at Greyfriars, joining the others begging for bread and a bowl of pottage. He informed the almoner that he needed sanctuary and asked for me. According to our charter Greyfriars cannot provide such refuge, though

Hornsey himself was already insisting that he lodge with you. He claims to be innocent of any crime, yet he is being hunted both by the law and the minions of the gang leaders in London. What could I do? I disguised him in a Franciscan robe and hurried him here. More than that, Brother, I cannot say.' The Franciscan exchanged the kiss of peace with Athelstan and left saying he would relish his visit to The Piebald.

For a while Athelstan busied himself with the fugitive bringing him all the necessaries: a wash bowl, napkin, jug, as well as food and drink. Hugh of Hornsey remained taciturn, especially when members of the parish such as Mauger the bell clerk and Benedicta came into the sacristy with items donated by the parish: pies from Merryleg's cook shop and a small tun of ale from The Piebald. Benedicta plucked at Athelstan's sleeve and led him back into the sacristy.

'Father, be careful,' she pleaded. 'Ranulf told me how your sanctuary man is not only being hunted by Sir John but scurriers despatched by the Upright Men. They have posted rich rewards on his head.'

'So there you are, my lovely.'

'Sir John!' Athelstan exclaimed and hurried back into the sanctuary. Cranston stood just within the rood screen along with Flaxwith, who, of course, had brought his mastiff Samson with him, a dog Athelstan secretly considered to be the ugliest animal created by God.

'Sir John!' Hornsey warned. 'I have been given sanctuary.'

'And you are welcome to it. Brother Athelstan, a word.'

The coroner took the friar over to the privacy of the chantry chapel. Resting against the shrine of St Erconwald, Cranston swiftly summarized his suspicions about both the gauntlet and the chainmail wristguard found in the Barbican. He relayed what Paston had told him. He also warned Athelstan what the friar already knew: how the Upright Men were hunting Hornsey and might not give a fig about sanctuary. 'Thibault,' Cranston murmured, 'will also learn what has happened. Lascelles and his bully boys will certainly pay you a visit, so I best leave some of my bailiffs here. Now I must go. Ronseval has fled and remains so . . .' Cranston raised a hand and strolled off, shouting at Flaxwith and his bailiffs to mount guard outside.

Athelstan watched them leave. He agreed with Cranston's suspicions about the gauntlet and wristguard: they weren't dropped accidently, so why were they left? More importantly, why was Hornsey so reluctant to talk? The friar closed his eyes. He just wished he could gather every item he'd learnt about the swirling mysteries confronting him. He must impose order on them, analyse them with logic, form a conclusion and test them against all the available evidence, but, he thought as he opened his eyes, that would have to wait.

Athelstan went back into the sanctuary. Hugh of Hornsey squatted on the ground. He had eaten all the food and drained his tankard; now he was sleepy. Athelstan stared around. The church lay silent. He was fairly confident that no one would dare accost the fugitive. Sanctuary was a sacred, inviolable right; anyone who broke it faced the full rigour of the law, both secular and religious. Holy Mother Church was jealous of such a privilege and protected it with bell, book and candle as well as the most fearsome sentence of immediate excommunication in this life and eternal damnation in the next. The only person who could accost the fugitive was himself. He certainly had questions for his unexpected guest but they would have to wait. Athelstan went into the sacristy. He ensured the outside door was unlocked so Hornsey could, when he wished, use the jakes built into an ancient but crude garderobe in the corner of one of the bulwarks next to the leper squint. Athelstan stared at the bolts on the door and recalled those in Scrope's chamber. How had that physician been murdered, and why?

Athelstan shook his head, unlocked the parish chest, took out his chancery satchel and found the blood-stained *vademecum*, the pilgrim's book of Glastonbury. The source of the information it contained was the Magna Tabula, the great wooden boards hanging in Glastonbury Abbey church. Each of these was covered in parchment which listed the fabulous relics of that ancient Benedictine house. Athelstan had visited it himself and studied both the lists and the treasures themselves: Arthur's tomb, Merlin's cave, the Holy Grail, St Joseph of Arimathea's staff planted miraculously so it bloomed every year. Glastonbury also owned the relics of St Patrick and St

David, both of whom, the Benedictines claimed, were buried in their sacred precincts . . . Athelstan noticed how Scrope's blood was at its thickest on the two pages describing Joseph of Arimathea's visit to the site of the abbey after Christ's resurrection.

'Why?' Athelstan murmured. He glanced up and stared at the bleak holy rood nailed to the far wall. 'Why were you reading this, holding it when your assassin struck?' Athelstan started as the door was flung open and Hugh of Hornsey limped through. He bowed at Athelstan and, clutching the points on his hose, hurried through the outside door. He came back a short while later and, under Athelstan's direction, he washed his hands at the great wooden *lavarium*.

'Sit down.' Athelstan pulled a stool closer. 'You are safe here,' he reassured this most fearful man, 'but, Master Hugh, I have to question you. However, I must also make you secure.' He pointed to the sacristy door leading into the cemetery. 'Once you return from the privy you can bolt and lock that from the inside. Open it only for me. At night, be careful. If you have to, relieve yourself and do so swiftly. Take great care, however, that no one approaches you in sanctuary apart from myself.'

The archer grunted his agreement.

'Look at the outside door, Master Hugh. Study the eyelet high in the wood. Always use that if you hear anyone stirring about in the cemetery or there's a knock on the door. Follow my instructions and you will be safe.'

'What about the church?' the archer replied. 'They could creep up the nave and enter through the rood screen.'

'No, no.' Athelstan shook his head. 'Those doors will be locked and bolted and, I suspect, closely watched by a number of people. Inside the church lives an anchorite, the Hangman of Rochester.' Athelstan glanced away. The fugitive might not know it but, if he was captured, tried and sentenced, the same Hangman would despatch him either here in Southwark or on some gibbet in the city. Now,' Athelstan continued, 'the key? You hold the third key to Marsen's exchequer coffer, yes?' Hornsey undid the clasp on his filthy grey shirt, clutched the piece of cord around his neck which held a small key, snapped this and handed it to Athelstan.

'Much good that was,' Hornsey slurred.

'Why?'

'Oh, Marsen made sure the coffer was firmly locked during the day but at night when we rested secure,' he pulled a face, 'or so he thought, Marsen always made me unlock the third clasp. The tax collector loved the sight of gold and silver, his plunder, his glory or so he called it. He and Mauclerc would push the lid back and venerate their ill-gotten gains as any monk would a sacred relic.' Hornsey drew a deep breath. 'Marsen loved that display.'

'Did he help himself?'

'I don't know, Brother. I don't think so. Mauclerc was there to watch him. The scribe was Thibault's man. Moreover, during our journey along the south bank of the Thames, Lascelles would occasionally meet us to ensure all was well.'

'As he did at The Candle-Flame?'

'Yes, Brother. Just as twilight deepened and the gloom thickened, Lascelles came. There was not much love lost between him and Marsen. Anyway, what does it matter? Apparently Lascelles was assured all was well. By then I was on watch outside the Barbican. I unlocked the third clasp; Marsen probably undid the other two to impress Lascelles.'

'So what happened on the night of the murders?'

'Very little, Brother. We arrived back at The Candle-Flame. Marsen made himself comfortable in the Barbican as a hog does in its sty. I was instructed to set the usual watch: three guards outside including myself and three in the lower chamber of the Barbican. Marsen then relaxed, as he described it, after the rigours of the day. Marsen was a toper, a tosspot, he loved his ale and food, wine and sweetmeats: he instructed the taverner to send the best across whilst Mauclerc was despatched to find two whores to amuse himself and his master.'

'So nothing out of the ordinary happened that night?'

'No. We returned from levying taxes. The horses were stabled, our watch was set. Food and drink were ordered. Whores brought in. The two archers outside, Adam and Breakspear, lit a campfire . . .' His voice trailed off.

'But something did happen?' Athelstan insisted. 'We know you visited the troubadour Ronseval at least twice in his chamber. You and he had an argument, blood was spilt. The following day Ronseval was seen searching the Palisade and found what he was probably looking for – a dagger.' Hugh of Hornsey sat staring at Athelstan then lowered his head. 'So what did happen?' the friar insisted quietly. 'Witnesses talk of raised voices. Why was Ronseval searching for a dagger? Why was blood found on the rug in his chamber? Master Hugh, in forty days' time you will probably surrender to the king's justices and the same questions will be asked. What was – is – your relationship with Ronseval? Why did you flee your post?' The archer shifted on the stool, hands clasped, fingers weaved together. 'You are a veteran soldier,' Athelstan continued remorselessly. 'Why are you so nervous? Tell me!'

'We had been collecting the tax,' Hornsey replied, not lifting his head. 'We returned to The Candle-Flame at twilight. Marsen was full of himself. He unlocked the exchequer coffer as if he was revelling in the Holy Grail.' Hornsey took a deep breath. 'Ronseval had been following us, though Marsen dismissed him as a fool, a poet who was composing a ballad. Of course, Marsen was secretly flattered. Anyway, once the festivities had begun, Ronseval met me in the shadows of the tavern. He bitterly criticized my allegiance to such a man and such a cause. I resented what he said; his words rankled with me so I went to his chamber late at night.'

'When?'

'Brother Athelstan, I don't know, perhaps midnight. And why not? Everything was quiet. I wanted to explain. True, there was an argument. Ronseval drew his dagger; he was deep in his cups and cut me but only slightly.' Hornsey pulled back the ragged sleeve of his jerkin to display a fresh cut high on his forearm.

'So you must have had your jacket off?' Athelstan declared. Hornsey blinked, wetting his lips.

'I don't know,' he stuttered. 'All I remember is that I seized the dagger and left. I went back on to the Palisade where my comrades were on guard.' Hornsey was now damp with sweat, his chest heaving. He kept his head down, refusing to meet

Athelstan's gaze. 'I found both of my comrades slain. I dropped Ronseval's dagger. I lost it in the grass. I was frightened, Brother. You see, despite the deaths everything lay quiet. I ran to the Barbican and pounded on the door. There was no answer. I realized something was very wrong. I admit I was terrified. I had left my post and two of my archers had been slain. I might even be accused of their murder. Either way I would hang. I slipped back into the tavern and told Ronseval what had happened. He tried to reason with me. Again we argued and I fled. I thought of reaching Dover or one of the Cinque Ports.' He shook his head. 'It was useless. Cranston,' he now met Athelstan's gaze, 'the Lord Coroner's people were searching for me as was every rogue in London. I decided to seek sanctuary, I sought out Brother Roger and he brought me here.'

'Did you see anything to explain the death of your comrades or what you must now know as the massacre in the Barbican?'

'Brother, I never saw the corpses there. True, the news is all over the city.' He rubbed his sweaty hands on his hose. 'Of course, at the time I realized something was wrong. The Barbican lay so silent. Brother, more than that I cannot say.'

'More than that you can!' Athelstan countered. 'Hugh of Hornsey, look at me!' The archer did. 'You are lying,' Athelstan accused. 'You are too glib. What are you hiding? What do you mean you saw nothing? Why should you and Ronseval argue about Marsen to the point of daggers being drawn? Why didn't you stay and raise the alarm? You are guilty of something.'

The archer arose abruptly to his feet. 'I am in sanctuary,' he whispered hoarsely. 'I am protected by God's own angel. I need to be.' He walked to the door into the sanctuary then turned. 'Brother, whatever you believe, whatever you think, I killed no one that night. I had no hand in that bloody business, though I am pleased Marsen has been despatched to Hell.' He shrugged. 'I am tired. I must sleep.'

Athelstan watched him go and heard him lock and bolt the door on the other side. Athelstan sat for a while and decided he must return to The Candle-Flame. He needed to search the Barbican again. Something might prick his mind or jog his memory. He knocked on the door; the eyelet was opened and

Hornsey let him into the sanctuary. Athelstan quietly thanked him and watched him lock and bolt the door again. Athelstan walked down the steps and stopped for a while by the rood screen door, reciting a few Aves under his breath. He crossed himself, turned and stared down the nave. The day was beginning to fade, the light weakening. He glanced over his shoulder. Hugh of Hornsey slouched in the mercy enclave beneath the crimson-red sanctuary lamp, which kept constant vigil besides the pyx in its silken tassled coping. Athelstan walked into the nave. The murk was deepening. A river mist was sifting beneath the door and the shuttered windows. Athelstan listened to the silence. For a brief spurt he felt guilty at not going out to visit the sick, the aged and the housebound. 'God forgive me,' Athelstan prayed, 'but you will have to wait.' He knew what he had to do. He truly believed this was God's work. In the Bible, after Adam and Eve fell, the first sin perpetrated was Cain slaying his brother Abel. God had hunted Cain down and branded him as a murderer, the wicked slayer of an innocent. Now Athelstan had to do the same; not for Gaunt or Thibault but because it was the right thing to do.

Athelstan lit a taper before the Lady altar, prayed for guidance and prepared to leave. He went out through the main door; his parishioners had long gone but he glimpsed different individuals seemingly going about their business: a hawker with his tray of goods, a fruiterer with his barrow, three wandering beggars roped together their clacking dishes out before them, and close by two tinkers stood offering ribbons and baubles. Athelstan glanced away; he was certain some of these were envoys or spies from the Upright Men. Flaxwith and his bailiffs also stood about, though Athelstan wondered how many of them were sober. He hooked the straps of his chancery satchel over his shoulder, pulled his cloak about him and strode into the tangle of alleyways which surrounded his church. He walked purposefully, stepping around midden heaps, piles of rubbish and deep puddles of frozen filth. He kept his head down as he passed through what he secretly called 'the underworld of his parish': strumpets stood brazenly in doorways, their fiery red wigs beacons of lust; cunning men nestled in crooks and crannies, ever vigilant for the opportunity to exploit; rifflers and roisterers, young men armed with cudgels and blades, grouped at the mouth of alleyways. Athelstan was safe from these. Pike and Watkin had spread the message that an attack on Athelstan was an attack on them and the Upright Men. Now and again the friar would glimpse one of his parishioners, those he defined as 'Gospel Greeters' – he would raise a hand and pass swiftly on.

The dismal world of Southwark engulfed him: the drunks pilloried in the stocks, hands and feet tightly clasped; the young whore, skirt thrown back, being lashed by a beadle; two drunken women roped together and paid to fist fight. Nearby, a relic-seller fresh from Canterbury touted relics from Becket's shrine. People shrieked from open windows. Dogs fought and chased the cats that burrowed for vermin in the muck heaps. Half-naked children danced around a pole or chased an inflated pig's bladder. A legion of food sellers shouted for trade, their trays displaying items filched from stalls and the public ovens. Above him, the crumbling tenements leaned over to block the sky and turn the alley below into a perpetually dark tunnel where all forms of nightlife scuffled. Athelstan passed doorways locked shut to hide the wickedness within; windows boarded up so those who passed could not witness what was happening inside. The friar dodged carts, barrows and sleds. He paused to bless a corpse covered with a filthy mort cloth being taken down to the corpse cottage at St Mary Overy. Eerie sounds assailed his ears. The excited cries of a woman were drowned by the curses of a man, whilst a chorister stood on a barrow and sang the opening lines of a psalm: 'I lift my eyes to the hills from where my salvation comes.' Prisoners were being led down to the Bocardo, Southwark's filthy compter, clink or prison. Acrobats and jugglers tried to entice the crowd. Faces, hooded and cowled, pinched white or turned red raw from the wind and rain, peered out at him. Athelstan was pleased to leave the thoroughfare with all its macabre sights and sounds and hasten along Pepper Alley into the warmth of The Candle-Flame.

Mine Host was busy in the Dark Parlour adjusting a shutter, helped by Mooncalf. The taverner was short and curt: he informed Athelstan that the guests were about their business and he was busy with his, though the friar was welcome to wander around. Athelstan thanked him and walked out across the wasteland on to the Palisade. He paused at the remains of the camp where the archers had been slain, and recalled his conversation with Hugh of Horsey. He was sure the captain of archers was lying, withholding the truth of what truly happened. Yet that truth may have nothing to do with the gruesome murders. Athelstan believed Hornsey was innocent of those killings but what was he really hiding? Allegiance to Marsen? 'Nonsense,' Athelstan whispered to himself. 'Hornsey is a professional soldier, a mercenary who has seen battle against the French and done his fair share of killing. So why should he have scruples about escorting the likes of Marsen?' Athelstan fell silent and glanced around. He could hear snatches of conversation on the breeze. He was sure of it, but in this desolate place? The Palisade stretched bleak and stark around him. Ghosts hovered here, the stricken souls of those so brutally slain. A raven, sleek and as black as the night, floated across to perch on a hummock of grass, its raucous cawing shrill and harsh. The day was dying. The breeze from the river brought the stench of rich mud, dried fish and a heavy saltiness. The raven took flight, feathery wings extended, flying up to wheel above the Barbican, which rose sinister and forbidding, a fitting monument to the horrors perpetrated within. Athelstan walked towards it; the door hung open and again he heard those snatches of conversation. Shading his eyes, Athelstan stared up and glimpsed figures against the battlemented walls at the top of the tower. He hurried into the Barbican and climbed the ladder to the upper storey. Now the corpses and baggage had been removed both chambers were neat and tidy, yet this made them seem even more macabre, a silent witness to the murders committed there. He climbed the next ladder leading to the top. He could hear Sir Robert Paston and the harsh carrying voice of Brother Marcel. The conversation died as Athelstan clambered through the trapdoor and, braving the buffeting wind, carefully walked across the shale-covered floor to stand with them against the crenellations. Athelstan greeted them all. Brother Marcel and Sir Robert had apparently come here to enjoy the view of the river, which was not yet cloaked in mist, whilst Martha and Foulkes clustered together, more interested in each other than anything else. Marcel edged closer.

'Brother Athelstan, Sir Robert was describing the different craft. Splendid sight, is it not?'

Athelstan, who always felt a little giddy on the top of any tower, nodded in agreement. The river was still clear, bustling with a frenetic busyness; Picard whelk boats, fishing craft, fighting hulkes, cogs of war, galleys, caravels, barges, bumboats and wherries moved majestically or scudded across the choppy water like water beetles. Banners, standards and flags fluttered their gorgeous colours in the snapping breeze. Sails of every shape and colour billowed vigorously or ruffled as they were drawn in. The very air was rich with all the pungent smells of the river craft.

'You served against the French, Sir Robert?' Athelstan asked more to make conversation than anything else.

'I certainly did, and little reward it brought me,' Paston replied hotly. 'I know these waters and the entire coastline north to the Scottish march. I have written to Gaunt – My Lord of Gaunt,' he added hastily, 'for the construction of better ships. You see,' Paston pointed down at the river, 'as I told Brother Marcel, not all of those ships are seaworthy . . .' His voice trailed off as Martha came hurrying over.

'Father!' she grasped Sir Robert's arm, 'I am sure the good brother does not need your homily on the king's ships. You have lectured us long and hard about the fleet, or lack of it, and the weakness of our river defences. It's growing dark and cold – we should go down.'

'I certainly must go,' Marcel replied. 'Sir Robert, I will accept your invitation to dine with you after the vesper's bell. First, I must finish my office and change my robes. Look, they've become dirty.' The ever-fastidious Inquisitor made his farewells and carefully walked back to the ladder, followed by Paston's group. Athelstan stayed. He ensured the trapdoor remained open and stood staring across the river, recalling all he had seen and heard. A deep unease welled up within him. Athelstan felt so agitated he tried to compose himself by searching for the emerging evening star. He watched fascinated as the twilight deepened, the birdsong died and the world prepared itself for the deep hush of night. He knelt down, protected by the battlements, and tried to recite a psalm, but stumbled over phrases such as 'The wicked brace their bow, who will oppose them?' He kept thinking about Hugh of Hornsey's passionate quarrel with Ronseval.

'You are lying,' Athelstan whispered. 'You couldn't give a fig for Marsen.' Athelstan recalled Ronseval's rather girlish gestures. 'Yes, the only logical explanation is that Paston overheard a lover's quarrel.' Athelstan crouched for a while as the darkness deepened and the air grew colder. He heard sounds below and realized it was time he was gone. He crept towards the trapdoor and went gratefully down the ladder. The upper storey felt strangely warm and Athelstan paused. He could smell smoke. He hurried to the trapdoor leading down to the storey below but the trapdoor was bolted shut from the other side and the ring-handle was hot to the touch. Athelstan, damp with fear, stared around. Tendrils of smoke curled up between the floorboards and an eerie crackling noise grew louder. A tongue of flame appeared against the far wall, followed by another. The floorboards, thick, oaken planks, were becoming hotter. Grey smoke curled like angry wraiths. Someone had bolted the trapdoor from below and started this conflagration. Athelstan recalled the dry furnishings and bedding. The swift leaping flames would be fanned by the draught through the open door, as they would by the window on the upper storey. Athelstan hurried across, clutching his chancery satchel. He pulled back the shutters, pushed open the window door and propped himself over the ledge, peering down. There was no ladder and the drop was steep and highly dangerous. If he jumped broken limbs would be the least he might suffer. Athelstan fought against the welling panic. These first flames would soon become a roaring fire; the trapdoor was sealed, the walls of thick stone. The only escape was the window. Athelstan glimpsed the iron ring beneath one of the shutters, some relict of when the barbican was a weapon store. He threw his chancery satchel out, took off his cloak and hurried across to the bed, pulling off the linen sheets and blankets. He tied these together, coughing at the smoke now billowing around him. He used his cloak as the last strand, tied one end of the makeshift rope to the iron ring and threaded the rest through the open window. He hauled himself up, turning to clasp the long cord he had fashioned and lowered himself carefully. He brushed the wall, now hot to the touch. Gasping and praying, Athelstan carefully slipped down, resisting the temptation to hurry. He realized the makeshift rope stopped at least a yard from the ground. Athelstan was preparing to jump, only to feel strong hands grasp him. Brother Roger had dragged across a barrel and used this to catch Athelstan. The Franciscan whispered that he was safe, he was there.

They clambered gingerly off the barrel. Athelstan crouched on the rain-soaked ground, head down and gasping for breath as he tried to recite a prayer of thanksgiving. He stared up. Flames now licked the window, whilst the surging plumes of grey smoke had already alerted the tavern. A toscin sounded. Voices carried. Athelstan heard footsteps; hands helped him up. Thorne was shouting at his grooms, servants and scullions to stand back and allow the fire to burn as it was too strong to fight. Athelstan, swaying on his feet, accepted a cloak from Mooncalf, found his chancery satchel and staggered back towards the tavern. In the Dark Parlour he washed himself at the *lavarium*, tending to the cuts and bruises on his hands, arms and legs. Mistress Eleanor served him a bowl of steaming hot pottage and a deep goblet of Bordeaux. Others came in and gathered round. Thorne, full of apologies which Athelstan gently acknowledged, muttered about candles or lanterns left glowing – some form of terrible accident. Athelstan kept his own counsel: that trapdoor had been deliberately locked, whilst the speed of the fire could only be explained by arson. Friar Roger came over.

'I decided to visit the riverside,' he remarked. 'I smelt the smoke and saw you at the window. I admit, I hesitated. I was once a mariner. I served at sea. I hate fire. I have a secret dread of it but each man carries own his own special fear deep inside him. I wondered if I should seek help and find a ladder.' He grinned. 'But you were as nimble as any squirrel. You escaped the dragon's breath. Now come, Friar, rejoice you were not fried.' Athelstan grinned at the pun on his calling. The Franciscan lifted his cup in a toast. Brother Marcel appeared all washed and finely attired for the evening meal. He went back to his chamber and returned with a heavy cloak of the purest wool dyed a deep black.

'Have this, Brother,' Marcel offered. 'I travel with a good wardrobe and a clean one. Our founder the blessed Dominic always maintained that dirt,' he winked at Athelstan, 'does not mean the same as holiness.' Athelstan thanked him and the rest and slowly sipped the wine. The shock was now receding. He felt embarrassed and was highly relieved when Cranston bustled into the Dark Parlour, clapping his gloved hands and rubbing his arms against the cold.

'I went to St Erconwald's,' he bellowed. 'Those rogues you call parishioners said you might be here, as did Flaxwith.' He paused, his eyes blinking as he caught Athelstan's glance. 'You had best come,' he added quietly. 'Gentlemen, lady. Come,' he repeated. Athelstan needed no further bidding. He thanked everyone and followed Sir John out of the tavern, almost running beside him as the coroner strode along the lanes down to the nearby quayside. Moored alongside the wharf was a high-prowed barge lit by torches fixed in their sconces along the deck; brilliantly glowing lantern horns hung just below the standards on both prow and stern. These rippling banners displayed the heraldic device of that eerie harvester of the Thames, the Fisher of Men, an eye-catching insignia displaying a silver corpse, hands extended in greeting, rising from a golden sea.

'I do wonder,' Athelstan whispered, 'why our path and that of the Fisher of Men constantly cross.'

'Because, my dear friar, murderers in London have what they think is a great disguise, a subtle device at their fingertips, a moving deep pit to hide their nefarious handiwork: Old Father Thames. We and the Fisher of Men know different. The river always gives up its dead. In this case Ronseval.' Athelstan didn't reply; he felt slightly sick, distracted at how close Death had brushed him with its cold, feathery wings.

'You don't have to tell me but I know something happened, little friar.' The coroner grabbed Athelstan's arm. 'I glimpsed smoke rising above the Palisade as I approached the tavern, whilst the smell of burning curled everywhere. So, little friar, tell me in your own good time.' He tightened his grip. 'I should really take you into an alehouse and have you drink some of Cranston's holy water, but I don't think this will wait.' Athelstan, comforted, followed Sir John along the windswept wharf to the waiting barge, where the six oarsmen, garbed in their black-and-gold livery, greeted Cranston and the friar like old friends. Athelstan recognized them all: Maggot, Taffety-Head and the rest, the Fisher of Men's coven, grotesques and outcasts rejected even by the poor of Southwark because of their repellent injuries. None of these, however, were as strange as the captain of the barge, Icthus, the Fisher's leading henchman. Dressed in a night-black tunic, Icthus had a distinctive appearance, hence his name, the Greek word for fish. Icthus was completely devoid of any facial hair, be it eyelids or brows, whilst his bald head, bulging eyes, snub nose and protuberant cod-mouth in a completely oval-shaped face made him look extremely fish-like. In fact, he could swim like a porpoise whatever the mood of the river, which Icthus knew like the palm of his slightly webbed hands. The henchman bowed in welcome and waved them aboard to sit on the comfortable cushioned seats under the canopied stern. Once they were settled, Icthus in his eerie, high-pitched voice gave the order to cast off. The oarsmen pulled away in unison, chanting their favourite hymn, taught to them by Athelstan, 'Ave Maris Stella', Hail Star of the Sea. The barge rocked and swayed, sometimes pitching dangerously. Athelstan closed his eyes and murmured a prayer to St Christopher. The barge surged on, battling the water. Lanterns on other boats glowed through the murk. Icthus, sitting in the prow, pulled at the bell rope, warning others of their approach. Most barges and wherries were only too eager to pull away from the Fisher of Men's barque, well known along the river for its grisly work, paid for by the city council to scavenge the Thames for the corpses of those who'd drowned, committed suicide or, as in this case, 'been feloniously slain'. Cranston was correct, Athelstan mused: London truly was a city of murder, and many of its victims were hidden beneath the rushing waters of this river.

Nevertheless, murder will out and corpses regularly surfaced in the sludge, shallows or reed banks of the Thames.

'Well, little friar?' Cranston offered him the miraculous wineskin. Athelstan shook his head. Cranston took a generous slurp, sighed noisily and made to share it with Icthus and the rowers. These all chorused back a polite refusal. Icthus added, shouting over his shoulder, how the Fisher of Men would never permit any of them to drink whilst they navigated the Thames.

'Wise man,' Cranston murmured. 'Now, little friar, tell me what happened or I will bore you to death with an account of my history of this waterway.'

'Terror indeed!' Athelstan exclaimed. He then told the coroner exactly what had happened in the Barbican.

'No accident!' Cranston's anger was as palpable as the strong breeze. 'A murderous soul plotted that fire. He, she or they recognized your skill, little friar. Beowulf, or whoever slaughtered Marsen and the others, plotted a very devious and subtle design, certainly one which would baffle myself, my bailiffs, the sheriff and his people but not you, little friar, hopping around like some bright-eyed sparrow. This child of Cain recognized a true adversary, and what better way to silence you than trap the sparrow and kill it?'

'Some sparrow, Sir John.'

'Aye, and much faster than the hawk, Athelstan,' Cranston squeezed his companion's arm, 'but for God's sweet sake and mine, be careful.'

Any further conversation was frustrated by the cries of Icthus and the oarsmen. The barge shuddered as it turned swiftly on the swell and came along a quayside just past La Reole. The wharf looked deserted except for the moving shadows which leapt out of the dancing pools of light thrown by the flaring torches lashed to poles. Cranston and Athelstan disembarked. From the shadows, hooded, cowled figures clustered silently around and escorted them towards the grey-bricked, red-tiled house of the dead called a variety of names: 'The Barque of St Peter', 'The Chapel of the Drowned Man' or 'The Mortuary of the Seas'. This building stood a little further back on the quayside, flanked by the wattle and daub cottages of the Fisher of Men and what he called 'his beloved disciples'. On the

right side of the mortuary door hung the great nets, stretched
out like massive cobwebs, used by the Fisher of Men to harvest
the deep. To the left of the door the usual proclamation, finely
inscribed, listed the fees for the recovery of the corpse of a
loved one or relative. Athelstan noticed how the price of a
murder victim had risen steeply to three shillings. The Fisher
of Men himself came outside to greet them. The Fisher's bald
head and skeletal face were framed by a shiny leather black
cowl edged with lambswool; a heavy military coat, made of
the purest wool, hid his body, hanging down to elegantly
spurred, high-heeled riding boots. He clasped their hands and,
as usual, asked Athelstan to deliver his most solemn blessing.
Icthus sounded the horn to summon all the Fisher's beloved
disciples to gather on the cobbles. Once the eerie congregation
was assembled, Athelstan intoned St Francis of Assisi's
blessing followed by the *'Salve Regina'* – Hail Holy Queen.

Once vespers were over, the Fisher of Men led Cranston
and Athelstan into the Sanctuary of Souls, a long rectangular
chamber scrubbed with lime mixed with vinegar. On a dais at
the far end stood an altar draped with a purple cloth; above
it a huge crucifix. The Fisher's guests, as he called the corpses,
lay on trestle tables, covered by funeral cloths drenched in
bitter pine juice. Despite this the stench of death and decay
hung heavy. The Fisher gave them each a pomander soaked
in rose water, whilst two of his grotesques, swinging thuribles,
perfumed the air with sweet incense smoke. The Fisher took
them over to one of the tables and pulled back the cloth to
reveal the liverish face and bloated corpse of the minstrel
Ronseval.

'We heard about what happened at The Candle-Flame.' The
Fisher's voice was pleasant, his Norman French as cultivated
as any clerk in chancery. 'I wondered if the waters there might
bear fruit. Sir John, I know you have issued warrants for certain
individuals who've apparently fled. My spies at the Standard
in Cheapside and around the Cross at St Paul's keep me
informed. Anyway, late this morning, Icthus and my beloveds
discovered this corpse floating in the reeds of Southwark side,
not far from The Candle-Flame.' Athelstan handed the
pomander to Sir John, took out the phial of holy oil and

anointed the corpse, bestowing absolution for any sins of a soul which may not yet have travelled to judgement. He did so swiftly, trying to ignore all the gruesome effects of violent, harrowing death: the staring eyes; the blood-encrusted, purple-hued face; the body almost swollen to bursting with stinking river water; and the cause of Ronseval's death, the hard-quilled crossbow bolt driven so deeply into his chest. Athelstan suspected it had shattered the man's heart. The friar stood back and scrutinized the corpse.

'Killed instantly,' he declared. 'And that is stating the obvious. The corpse is river-swilled. How long would you say it was in the water?'

'At least a night. We have washed away some of the dirt but, apart from that, made little preparation.'

'Notice the dagger,' Athelstan declared, 'still in its sheath, the cap buttoned, the money purse still on the belt. See how deep the arrow bolt is embedded. Ronseval was killed at very close quarters. He left yesterday evening going out in the dark. He was not the victim of a robbery. Ronseval met someone he trusted down on the river bank, a lonely, secluded place. He allowed his killer to draw very close. He suspected nothing. He didn't even unclasp the strap on his dagger sheath.' Athelstan peered closer. 'The same barb was used against those two archers.'

'We also found this.' The Fisher crouched, drew a water-soaked chancery satchel from under the table and placed it on a nearby stool. Athelstan recognized it as Ronseval's. He took it and shook out the contents: clothing, baubles, a knife, Ave beads, a purse and scrolls of parchment, most of these damaged by water. Whilst Cranston and Fisher discussed the situation in the city, Athelstan attempted to decipher some of the writings but decided he would have to wait until the parchment was dry. Nevertheless, his eye was caught by one scrap of parchment in which Ronseval had attempted the newly structured sonnet coming out of Italy. This piece of parchment had escaped relatively unscathed. Athelstan read it carefully: the poetry, both rhythm and rhyme, were uneven but the content was thought provoking, a love poem from one man to another.

'Sir John?' he called out. 'The Fisher of Men has a claim

on all such property, but I need this.' He held up the scroll of parchment. The Fisher of Men shrugged his acceptance even as Cranston beckoned the friar over.

'Brother, our friend here has some rather interesting information about our honourable Member of the Commons, Sir Robert Paston.'

'Not here,' the Fisher declared. 'Brother Athelstan, are you finished?'

The friar said he was. Arrangements were agreed about the burial of Ronseval's corpse and the disposal of his effects, and the Fisher of Men led them into his solar, a comfortable chamber off the Sanctuary of Souls with a mantled hearth and quilted chairs. Hot spiced posset was served, the Fisher toasting Cranston and Athelstan with his goblet.

'If you use the river as we do,' he said, smacking bloodless lips, 'as a way of life, you observe many things.'

'Be brief, my friend,' Cranston intervened. 'Darkness is falling. Night approaches and we must be gone.'

'Sir Robert Paston is a wool merchant,' the Fisher declared. 'He owns *The Five Wounds*, a handsome, deep-bellied cog which takes his wool to Flanders.'

'And?' Cranston insisted.

'*The Five Wounds* empties its cargo then sails down the west coast of France to Bordeaux.'

'To collect wine and import it,' Athelstan agreed, 'a prosperous and very lawful trade.'

'Sir Robert,' the Fisher countered, 'seems very inquisitive about other cogs. We often see him in a special barge hired at a La Reole. He stops at certain ships.'

'Which ships?'

'Brother, you name any standard and I'm sure Sir Robert knows it. He often goes aboard to confer with their masters.'

'And?'

'He is not so keen on others being as equally curious about his own cog, *The Five Wounds,* when it berths at quaysides on either side of the river: wherries, tilt boats and barges are warned off whilst on shore, its master Coghill maintains a strong watch over the boarding plank.' The Fisher paused and held his hand out. Cranston sighed, dug into his purse and counted enough silver to cover the fee for Ronseval's corpse as well as extra for this information. 'Thank you, Sir John. More posset – no? In a word, My Lord Coroner, Sir Robert Paston is not the perfect gentle knight but a grubby merchant with dirty fingers in many filthy pots.'

'Such as?'

'He is a bosom friend of the Mistress of the Moppets at The Golden Oliphant. I just wonder, Sir John, if Paston exports more than wool.'

'You mean young women for the flesh markets of Flanders?'

'And beyond. The settlements along the Rhine are garrisoned by soldiers. Buxom young wenches can demand a high price – it's just a suspicion. Sir Robert is a very skilled mariner and his knowledge of the sea and the English coast is second to none.' The Fisher smiled. 'All the attributes for a king's admiral as well as those of a professional smuggler.'

'And Master Simon Thorne?' Athelstan asked.

'Strange man. Former soldier. Married again after the death of his first wife. Mistress Eleanor is the daughter of a taverner who owns a hostelry on the Canterbury road. Apparently she is not just a pretty face but has a good business head and keeps careful ledgers, or so I understand. I have also heard rumours that Thorne would like to deepen the waters along that lonely quayside which serves his tavern. Again, a man who knows the river.'

'And the murders there?' Cranston asked.

'I know nothing, Sir John,' the Fisher whispered, 'except Satan's own misty messenger certainly visited that place.'

oOoOo

Mine Host Simon Thorne had prepared a sumptuous meal. The taverner had proclaimed how he wished his guests to be feasted like any king at court. Mooncalf's empty belly strained at the savoury smells and mouth-watering odours curling out of both kitchen and buttery. The tavern refectory had been especially prepared. Fresh greenery had been brought in to bedeck the woodwork, along with pots of winter roses and jars of crushed spices and herbs. The sweetness of a summer garden mingled with that from the slender beeswax candles in their spigots along a table, covered by a silver samite cloth, with the tavern's gold-encrusted nef standing in pride of place at the centre. The best pewter platters and silver-chased goblets had been brought up from the arca in the tavern's strongrooms below ground. Snow-white napkins had been laid out for every guest and the best jugs gleamed, all brimming with water fresh from the spring, the richest reds of Bordeaux as well as tongue-tingling white wine, Lepe and Osey from Castile as well as that from the Rhineland. The gilt-edged maple-wood mazers were filled, and the chamber guests could look forward to an appetizing array of dishes from the cooks: roast chicken in jelly, goose with sauce and onions, venison in black crushed pepper, aloes of highly spiced beef and other mouth-watering dishes. Mine Host had invited the Pastons and Master Foulkes, Brother Roger and the Inquisitor Marcel together with himself and Mistress Eleanor. The taverner had declared that, despite the heinous slayings, this was a banquet of reparation for the inconvenience, as Master Thorne so tactfully put it, 'caused by the dead on the living'. Now Thorne, with his comely wife sitting on his right, welcomed them all to feast on this cold February evening, with the winter's wind still beating against the shutters and a fire leaping as merrily as it did in mid-winter.

Mooncalf, Nightingale, Thomasinus and all the other tavern servants could only gape in mouth-watering envy as the guests cut, sliced and feasted on the delicious dishes. Mooncalf kept staring at Mistress Martha and William Foulkes. He wondered when that inquisitive friar would discover that all had not been as quiet as it should be on the night of the murders. Worse – and Mooncalf forgot his hunger – what if Athelstan stumbled on the truth? The ostler, Martha and Foulkes couldn't look for help from Sir Robert: if the whispers were true, he also had a great deal to explain. Mooncalf just wished it was all over. He felt like a guard dog, constantly alert, and, even as he stood there, he abruptly realized something was wrong. So lost in his own hunger and personal worries, Mooncalf became acutely aware of how all the noise from the adjoining taproom had faded. The Dark Parlour was sealed off from this select

refectory by a thick oaken door. Nevertheless, all the usual
chatter and laughter of a busy taproom had died completely.
Something was very amiss. He tried to catch his master's eye
but failed. Mine Host was listening most attentively to his
guests' description of what they thought might have happened
on the night of the great slaughter. Brother Marcel, who had
made himself very much at home at The Candle-Flame, was
now sitting very close to Sir Robert Paston. Mooncalf noticed
how the two were often in deep conversation. The ostler drew
a deep breath then started at a rapping on the door to the
taproom. Due to all the merry noise no one else heard it.
Intrigued, Mooncalf decided to settle all his doubts. He quietly
opened the door and slid into the taproom, closing the door
behind him. He immediately stood, mouth gaping in surprise.
Despite the mysterious knocking the Dark Parlour was
completely empty. Candles glowed, lantern horns flared,
shadows fluttered and merged with the other slivers of darkness, but all the customers had gone. Half-filled tankards and
food-strewn platters remained on the tables. The fire-eater, the
snake-conjurer, the relic-seller recently returned from Nazareth,
the bargemen, the tinkers, the tanners from London Bridge
and the fishermen from Billingsgate had disappeared. Mooncalf
shivered. The fire still glowed, as did the charcoal turning
crimson in the braziers. He glanced towards the door on the
other side of the parlour but, in the poor light, that seemed
closed. Mooncalf felt the tremblings, as he called them, return.
The Dark Parlour lay ominously silent and yet, Mooncalf
blinked, there was movement. He was sure someone was there.
He caught the sound of heavy breathing, a floorboard creaking,
a shutter rattling and the drip-drip of an overturned tankard.
A rat scuttled out of the darkness, slithering across a ring of
candlelight. Mooncalf moaned quietly. He would have turned
and fled back into the refectory but he could only stand trans-
fixed as the shadows shifted. First one, then others merged
into the meagre light. They moved soundlessly, boots wrapped
in rags, the round oxhide shields they carried daubed a blood
red. Swords and axes glittered. Mooncalf felt a blade point
prick the side of his neck. He glanced sharply to his right at
the nightmare figure, face visored by an ugly crow mask

fashioned out of black feathers. The spectre's hair, stiffened with grease, stood up in long tufts, which gave him the appearance of a frightful demon.

'Mooncalf, Mooncalf.' The voice was soft, pleasant. 'Peace, Brother. It's not your blood we want, or that of any of your customers or comrades, which is why they have fled.'

Mooncalf swallowed hard. The Dark Parlour now seemed full of these nightmare wraiths. He realized what had happened. The Earthworms had appeared and quietly persuaded everyone to disappear, not that they would need much encouragement.

'Who is in the refectory?' the voice whispered.

'Master Thorne.'

'Ah, Thibault's creature.' Mooncalf was so astonished he turned, gaping. 'Oh, yes, Mooncalf. Thorne sells taproom tittle-tattle, tavern chatter and ale gossip to Thibault and his brood of vipers. We know that. Don't be surprised – most of London is now in our pay. Who else is there?'

Mooncalf told him.

'Now, master ostler,' the voice continued, 'the Council of the Upright Men has received good information that the money Marsen stole from others and then had taken from him still lies here. Where?'

'The angels be my—'

'Oh, I know!' the voice replied. 'You may have no knowledge of it, but there again, you have no knowledge of us either, eh, Master Mooncalf? Why is that now? Do you have your own secrets, eh?' The voice had turned ugly. 'Not of this world, Mooncalf, but of the next. You are a follower of Wycliffe, aren't you? A member of the Lollard sect. You meet them out on the wastelands, even here along the Palisade?'

Mooncalf could feel the sweat break out on him.

'There are no secrets from the Upright Men or their riders, the Earthworms. However, our present business is Marsen's gold. It would be difficult to carry away, which is why my comrades and I believe it still lies hidden here.'

'You were told this?' Mooncalf stuttered. 'Who informed you about that?'

'Never mind,' the voice hissed. He paused as a burst of

laughter from Friar Roger echoed through the stillness. Mooncalf could only stand and tremble. He was no longer nervous about the Upright Men, just shocked that they knew his secret. How many others knew? Would he be denounced before the Archdeacon's court or even to that fearsome Inquisitor?

'Come now,' the voice urged. 'Time is passing. Announce us.' Mooncalf opened the door and was pushed into the refectory, followed by the Earthworms, their grotesque bird masks covering blackened faces. A sudden silence fell, shattered by Martha's scream as she jumped to her feet in a clatter of plates and goblets. Foulkes half-rose, a platter in his hand. Thorne cursed and seized a carving knife from the saucery. Sir Robert sat like a toper, eyes glazed, mouth half-open, whilst the two friars could only protest. The commotion was silenced by the Crow raising his heavy arbalest and loosing a whirring quarrel to smash into a painted cloth hanging on the far wall.

'Sit down,' the Crow ordered. 'Peace be with you all. Master Thorne, we have business with you. Your customers have gone.' He paused at sounds from the gallery above. 'In fact, our business has already begun. We will search this tavern.' He walked round the table and pressed the now-loaded arbalest against Eleanor's forehead. She quivered in fear, whispering under her breath. Master Thorne would have lunged forward, but the Raven menaced him with an arbalest and he sat down.

'If you cooperate,' the Crow's voice was almost a drawl, 'nothing will happen. If you do not . . .' He let the threat hang.

'We are priests,' Marcel spoke up, 'clerics with benefit of clergy.'

'It makes no difference, does it?' Brother Roger shouted, face all flushed. The Franciscan grasped a goblet as if he wished to throw it at his tormentors. 'To you we are . . .'

'The oppressors, good brother?' the Crow quipped. 'As the Bible says, those who aren't with us are against us. So hush now and let us do what we came for.'

Mooncalf could only stand, trying to hide his fear. He wanted to catch the eye of Foulkes and Mistress Martha, but that was futile. Both young people were more concerned in comforting each other. The noise and clattering in the tavern was now loud and continuous. The Earthworms demanded and seized the key to each and every chamber including the strongrooms in the cellar. Thorne objected but the Earthworms threatened the terrified Eleanor, whilst assuring Thorne that his property was safe. Marcel intoned a psalm, whilst Brother Roger sat tapping his sandaled feet against the floor. The evening drew on. Mooncalf tried to make signs to Martha but she was imprisoned deep in her fears. The search continued and the Earthworms grew more aggressive, threatening Thorne with torture. At this Marcel sprung to his feet.

'I am a cleric!'

'You will be a dead one!' the Raven retorted.

'You—' He broke off as one of the Earthworms burst into the refectory and whispered in his ear. Mooncalf felt a chill; the danger was deepening. The Raven walked to the door and shouted a question. The response he received silenced all clamour. Royal troops were fast approaching the tavern.

PART THREE

'Lollard': old Dutch word for a mutterer or stammerer.

A thelstan and Cranston had just finished their deliberations with the Fisher of Men when a breathless Grubcatcher, courier for his master, came slipping and slithering across the quayside. War barges were on the river, crammed with soldiery, all heading across to the deserted quayside near The Candle-Flame. Athelstan and Cranston hurried down to the Fisher of Men's barge. Icthus agreed to transport them swiftly across the swell and they cast off. A mist had billowed in, thick and curling. Nevertheless, Athelstan glimpsed the war barges surging before them, all despatched from the Tower quayside and displaying the blue, scarlet and gold of the royal household. Trumpets bellowed and horns brayed, telling other craft to swiftly pull away. Athelstan sat under the awning and wondered what was happening.

'You are well named,' he whispered. 'Candle-Flame – you certainly draw in all the moths of murder.'

Cranston, half asleep, stirred and asked him what he said. 'Just a prayer, Sir John; as the pot stirs, this mess of trouble thickens.'

They disembarked at the quayside to find the royal standard had been set up on a war cart with Thibault, Lascelles and officers from the Tower. They all stood about in half armour beneath floating standards and fiercely burning torches.

'Sir John,' Thibault greeted them, 'Brother Athelstan, we have the Earthworms trapped.'

'How?' Athelstan asked. 'Why?'

'I received information that the Upright Men were plotting to visit The Candle-Flame after dark to search for Marsen's looted treasure.'

'Who gave that to you?' Athelstan turned his head against the stiffening breeze.

'Does it matter? A written message left at the Guildhall. It was well scripted, the message stark and simple.'

'I suppose,' Athelstan declared, 'it was delivered by a ragged urchin who promptly disappeared?'

Thibault made a face and turned away.

'You have Hugh of Hornsey at St Erconwald's?' Lascelles declared. 'If we cannot seize him . . .'

'And you will not!' Athelstan intervened sharply, half-listening to the sounds drifting across the Palisade; peering through the darkness he could make out the sinister outline of the Barbican.

'We could at least question him,' Lascelles insisted.

'No, I shall do that,' Athelstan retorted. 'The law of sanctuary is quite explicit. No officer, and that includes Sir John, can approach the fugitive in sanctuary after the felon has grasped the horn of the altar. I, as the priest, however—' Athelstan broke off at the clatter of armour. A serjeant-at-arms, face almost hidden by the broad nose guard of his helmet, came hurrying out of the gloom.

'Master Thibault,' he gasped, 'we have despatched archers and men-at-arms but the enemy command all approaches to the tavern. We could attack or encircle them but, I suspect, their defence will be fierce.'

'Or,' Lascelles snapped, 'we could wait for those troops crossing the bridge to approach the south side and seal it off.'

'They will have to thread their way through the needle-thin lanes of Southwark,' Cranston declared. 'They will not be able to move swiftly.'

'Try and encircle them now,' Thibault ordered.

'They will resist fiercely,' Cranston urged. 'They will know what you plan and be prepared.'

'Sir John, I hear what you say but time is passing and we should attack now.'

The serjeant glanced at Cranston, who just turned away. The officer hurried back to his post. Thibault, Lascelles and their escort followed. Cranston seized Athelstan's arm.

'The Earthworms are more cunning than Thibault thinks.

The south side of the tavern looks out over a maze of alleyways; it could take hours before reinforcements arrive. The Earthworms will plot to break out. All they have to do is run a few yards deep into the protection of a dark Southwark night. There will be . . .' Cranston's words were drowned by screams of pain shrilling through the night. Both Athelstan and Cranston hurried across the Palisade, past the Barbican to the place of battle. Thibault's men had lit fires. Cranston cursed this as a mistake as they only provided light for the Earthworms hiding behind the different windows of the tavern; their archers had already loosed a shower of shafts and bolts. Many of the Earthworms were master bowmen who had served in the royal arrays in France and elsewhere. They rarely missed their mark. Already corpses littered the ground. The screams of the wounded echoed through the night; these did nothing to hide the deadly sound of arrows and quarrels whirling through the darkness. Thibault's officers tried to rush a door only to be beaten back, whilst their attempt to encircle the tavern had been reduced to a creeping crawl. The rain of arrows increased, their speed and accuracy frightening. Cranston and Athelstan hid behind a cart, watching the deadly hail fall time and again.

'They are going to break out,' Cranston murmured. 'They have increased the intensity to numb us. An old trick which rarely fails.' The volleys of arrows abruptly ceased. Lascelles shouted the order to advance. A few hapless souls did only to be immediately cut down. Again the death-bearing silence, only this time Thibault's men remained hidden, the cries of their wounded comrades pitiful to hear. Athelstan tried to crawl to the nearest stricken man but Cranston pulled him back.

'For God's sake, wait,' he urged. The silence lengthened, broken only by the fading moans of wounded and dying men. A door to the tavern was suddenly flung open. Thorne, a white cloth in one hand, a crucifix in the other, came tentatively out.

'They are gone!' he cried. Thibault's men rose, hurried into the tavern and out through the main doorway. There was no one. Cranston and Athelstan followed. Thorne explained how the Earthworms had begun to slip away whilst the others had gathered at certain windows in an ever-diminishing mass.

'You are correct, Sir John. The enemy will now be deep in

the warren of streets beyond,' Lascelles muttered. 'The reinforcements will not be needed.'

Athelstan wondered whether he should go back to minister to the wounded and the dying. He just felt so tired, bleakly exhausted, drained by the fury of battle which had closed about him like a veil. Voices shouted, pleaded and cried. Armour clattered. Torches flared. Thibault was shouting for a search to be made. The smell of fire smoke, horse dung and sweat heightened Athelstan's awareness of those spiritual odours: hate, fear, pain and desperation. Thibault was furiously deep in conversation. Lascelles made to walk away when Athelstan heard the angry whirr of a crossbow bolt. Lascelles stopped, hands reaching out; one shoulder slightly drooped. He walked towards Athelstan, entering a pool of light. He was blinking then he gagged, swaying on his feet, staring down in surprise at the crossbow bolt embedded deep in the right side of his chest. Lascelles walked forward again only to stagger sideways and, in doing so, intercepted a second quarrel aimed for his master but now shielded by himself. The quarrel smashed Lascelles' skull and he tipped forward. Athelstan, ignoring Cranston's cries and the clash of kite shields as a ring of steel was thrown around Thibault, hurried to the fallen man. Lascelles, however, was past all caring, his face a mottled mask of bloody froth, red skin and broken bone. He lay twitching and trembling as Athelstan tried to give him what spiritual comfort he could. The friar tried to calm his pitching stomach, the evening cold freezing the sweat on his body, the stinking muck of the yard and, above all, his curdling rage as the sheer futility of it all racked both mind and body. Horsemen appeared, hooves clattering, their leader shouting about how he had taken two prisoners, captured them, hooded and visored, as they tried to hide in a nearby alleyway. Thibault, screaming at his men to find the archer who killed Lascelles, abruptly fell silent. Athelstan rose wearily to his feet. Cranston's hissed curse warned him. He glanced to his right; the two prisoners, arms bound tightly, staggered into the light. Athelstan stared in horror as Pike and Watkin, their faces blackened, scraps of the masks still tangled in their greasy hair, were pushed forward to fall on their knees. Thibault swept through his escort and, before he could be stopped, punched both prisoners viciously in the face. He pointed to the poles jutting out above the entrance to the tavern.

'Hang them!' he screamed. 'They have been taken in arms against the crown. Hang them now!' Thibault's bully boys hurried both prisoners over to the tavern entrance. Athelstan could only watch. Ropes were produced, nooses fashioned and slung round the prisoners' necks. Watkin shouted Athelstan's name before he was hustled over to stand beneath one of the poles. Thibault's men moved swiftly. Looping the rope over, they pulled and Watkin, gargling and choking, legs kicking, was hoisted off the ground. Athelstan recovered from his shock and lunged towards him. Cranston, with a speed that belied his size, swept forward, his sword creasing the air to slice the rope. Watkin crashed to the ground, coughing and spluttering.

'Due process!' Cranston yelled, turning round and drawing his dagger with his other hand. 'Master Thibault, I am the king's Lord High Coroner. I will not be a witness to summary murder.'

Thibault, his usual cherubic face glinting with sweat, his chest heaving and his lips twitching with rage, glared at Cranston.

'Your brain is nimble as a clerk's pen. Think, Master Thibault,' Cranston warned. 'If you hang them,' he lifted both sword and dagger, 'I will arrest you for murder. Both these men should be interrogated, indicted, tried and, if found guilty, hanged, but only then.' The clamour of battle was fading. Brothers Marcel and Roger appeared in the tavern porch. Messengers approached but stood back, aware of this dangerous confrontation. Thibault was talking to himself; now and again he would glance at Lascelles' corpse, then the two prisoners.

'Take them away,' the Master of Secrets barked. 'Drag them, kick them and throw them into the Bocardo. They live in Southwark, they can rot in Southwark and, when I have my way, they will hang in Southwark.'

'Wait.' Athelstan walked over to the two prisoners. 'God protect you,' he whispered. 'I will tell your families.'

Pike and Watkin, however, seemed different, no longer the two jesters of the parish but hard, solemn men, former soldiers, peasants who'd confronted all the cruelty of life. They didn't seem interested in him but glared at Thibault. Athelstan caught the real hatred simmering there. He felt guilty at under-estimating the fierce resentment which curdled these men's souls and now threatened their very lives. Athelstan turned away to hide his own bitter tears.

'I had better minister to the wounded,' he murmured, 'see to the dying and the dead.'

'No need to,' Cranston declared. 'Brother Marcel, Brother Roger, you will help?' Both men agreed. Pike and Watkin were dragged away. Athelstan just stood, arms crossed, staring down at the ground half-listening to Thibault's officers report to their master how they had swept the tavern and found nothing. Thibault nodded and walked over to kneel in the mud beside Lascelles' corpse. He took out his Ave beads and, eyes closed, began to loudly recite one Ave after another. Eleanor's sobbing and that of Martha could now be heard, followed by the gruff voices of their menfolk trying to give comfort.

Cranston walked over to Athelstan and grasped his shoulder. 'Little friar, come.'

'No, Sir John.' Athelstan gently prised himself loose. 'Thank you for what you did, but I need to go home.' Athelstan walked out into the warren of streets leading back to St Erconwald's. By the time he reached the church the news had already arrived and families clustered anxiously in the nave. Athelstan gave whatever comfort he could to Watkin and Pike's families, reassuring them, though he knew the truth of it, that all would be well and their menfolk released.

'I hear what you say, Father,' Pike's wife Imelda declared, her hard eyes brimming with tears, 'but Pike knows, you know and I know the way of the world.'

Athelstan could only sketch a blessing in the air above her head. The Bocardo was a rat-infested, stinking, foul prison down near the river. Cranston believed it was worse than Newgate or the Fleet, a living Hell where corrupt turnkeys, beadles and keepers ruled underground cells which would have disgraced a filthy hog pen.

The church eventually emptied, Athelstan's reassurances ringing hollow along the nave. Once they were gone the friar slumped down at the base of a pillar and stared at the rood screen. Beyond it Hugh of Hornsey sheltered in sanctuary but Athelstan could not go there, not yet. He simply did not have the strength for more interrogation, more lies and sly evasions. Perhaps he should go across to the priest's house and open that flask of wine Cranston had given him as a Yuletide gift. He would drink the rich red juice until sleep swallowed him.

'Father?'

He glanced up. Benedicta was standing just behind him. 'I thought you had left with the rest?'

'You look tired, Father. Why not go to your house? I have left you a stew, rich and brown, the meat soft and minced, or you could eat at my house. I have wine?' Athelstan held her gaze. 'We could talk, plot what to do for poor Pike and Watkin.'

'An invitation which cannot be resisted,' Athelstan replied, clambering to his feet. 'I am tired, I am lonely and I am angry.'

'Father!' Ranulf the rat-catcher came hurrying up the nave, banging the door behind him. 'Father, I have to do a great ratting tonight in the cellars of a merchant's house. He has offered me good silver. I need . . .' The rat-catcher paused at the look on Athelstan's face and glanced at Benedicta. 'I am sorry,' he muttered. Athelstan studied his peaked-white face peeping out of the stiffened tarred hood. Once again the friar was struck by the likeness between Ranulf and his two ferrets, Ferox and Audax. He abruptly leaned forward and pulled back the rat-catcher's hood, studying his scrawny scalp and lined cheeks. 'Father, what have I done?'

'Nothing,' Athelstan smiled, 'except remind me that I am your priest. Ranulf, Benedicta, angels come in many forms. Now, Benedicta, fetch the holy water stoup from the sacristy. Let's give Ferox and Audax the holiest of blessings.' The widow woman hurried away. Athelstan stepped closer. 'You are not really here about the ferrets, God save them, are you, Ranulf?' The rat-catcher glared unblinkingly back. 'You were there tonight, weren't you, disguised as an Earthworm?' Athelstan pointed to Ranulf's head. 'I can see the remains of the mask. What where you? The Jackdaw, the Magpie? Sir

John has told me all about the Earthworms and their eerie disguises.'

'Father, I have no idea . . .'

'Of course you don't, but you want to ask me what is going to happen to those other two birds of a feather, Watkin and Pike. Yes? Well, let me tell you the truth. They will hang within the week unless God or Sir John Cranston intervenes.'

'And you, Father?'

Athelstan bit back his tart reply as Benedicta, all flustered, hurried back. To ease the tension Athelstan grasped the Asperges rod and intoned the blessing.

'May the Lord turn his face to you and smile . . .' Athelstan sprinkled the cages, 'and may God make you what he always intended you to be, the finest ferrets ever.' Ranulf, embarrassed by this little priest's mood, grabbed the cages and left. Benedicta made to follow. Athelstan called her back. He grasped her hand and smiled.

'Benedicta,' he kissed her softly on the forehead and cheeks, 'some angels are more welcome than others.' He squeezed her hands. 'Goodnight and God bless you for your kindness.'

She stepped back. 'You will be all right, Father?'

'Knowing that I have your love, Benedicta, of course.' He watched her go, fighting the overwhelming urge to call her back. He closed his eyes and said a prayer before going round the church to lock and bolt the different doors. The Hangman of Rochester was fast asleep in his ankerhold, or at least pretending to be, and the friar wondered what role, if any, the enigmatic recluse had played in the dire events of that evening. Athelstan paused by the chantry chapel. In truth he was deeply worried about Pike and Watkin. Thibault's justice would be swift and brutal. The two prisoners would appear before the justices of oyer and terminer: if found guilty, and Athelstan believed they would be, they'd hang. He knew about Thibault's macabre sense of humour: the Hangman of Rochester might well be hired to carry out the execution, which could take place just outside St Erconwald's for all to see. Would the Upright Men allow that? And what about these mysteries? Athelstan walked into the centre of the nave and stared down at the paving slabs, row upon row of oblong stone. He walked carefully along, putting one foot in front of the other. What happens, he wondered, if the mysteries which confronted him were all tangled but with one root, like some shrub in God's Acre? He conceded to himself this was the direction he was tempted to follow: to dig deep, find that root and pull it up. But what if it was otherwise, like these paving stones? Three lines which ran parallel but never crossed. It would be easy to argue that Beowulf was both the spy and the murderer. But perhaps he should keep them separate? Should he accept that he was in fact hunting three people, not one? Athelstan paused at the thought. 'I'll do that,' he murmured, 'when I have the time, energy and peace. I am going to sit and think.' Already memories and images floated through his mind, but he considered them to be like leaves on the wind – nothing substantial: a phrase here, a remark there.

'I said the Candle-Flame attracted the moths of murder,' Athelstan murmured. 'I should really go back there.' He crossed himself, went through the rood screen and up into the sanctuary. Hugh of Hornsey was dozing in the mercy enclave. Athelstan took a stool and sat down close to him. Hornsey woke, blinking his eyes and rubbing his face.

'Brother Athelstan, the hour is late.' He pointed to the heavy-lidded jake pot. 'My apologies, I have used that, the smell . . .?'

'Incense covers a multitude of sins,' Athelstan smiled, 'but, Master Hugh, I have dire news. Ronseval lies dead – murdered. His corpse has been taken from—' Athelstan broke off at Hornsey's cry of disbelief. The archer, mouth half-open, rocked backwards and forwards, hands half-raised in supplication.

'God assoil him,' Athelstan continued gently. 'God loves him as did you, didn't you? You share that love which David had for Jonathon in the Old Testament, the love which surpasses that of a man for any woman?' Athelstan's remark calmed some of Hornsey's obvious grief. He lowered his hands and sobbed, head down, a heart-rending sound which provoked Athelstan's compassion. He stretched out and placed his hand on the archer's head, quietly reciting a blessing.

'He has gone to God, Master Hugh. I have prayed over him and I will do so again. Tomorrow morning,' Athelstan turned to the altar, 'I will offer the Jesus Mass for Ronseval's long journey into the light so that when the accuser, the adversary, presents his challenge, Christ's blood will answer it. But now, you must tell me the truth and I shall help you.' Athelstan paused, listening to the profound silence which hung deep throughout the church. The stillness was broken only by Hornsey's quiet sobbing, like that of a child, and the scrape of the sanctuary stool as the former archer shifted in his grief.

'Tell me, Master Hugh, the truth for the love of God and the saving of all our souls.' Hornsey stopped rocking backwards and forwards; he took his hands away from his face.

'Ronseval,' he began tentatively, 'the troubadour did not follow Marsen because of any ballad or poem.' Hornsey lifted his head, breathing in deeply. 'I am, Father, what you see: a soldier, a bowman, a captain of archers. I met Ronseval years ago when we both served in the royal array. From my youth I have never felt any love or urge for a woman. I have tried but,' he shrugged and glanced away, 'in his youth Ronseval was beautiful. He and I became brothers in soul, heart-clasped, two comrades. We knew the danger of such a love. If we had been caught in the act, we could have been burnt or impaled on stakes. Life swept us apart. I met him again here in Southwark. There are places, taverns, alehouses.' He half-smiled. 'I am sure Sir John and his law officers will have a list of such establishments.' Hornsey paused. Athelstan sensed the fugitive was thinking swiftly, like a ship preparing to trim its sails against the shifting wind. 'Oh, by the way,' Hornsey indicated with his head, 'I heard the clamour, the snatches of words about men being taken up by Thibault and his coven?'

'Lascelles is dead,' Athelstan replied and he described in a few pithy sentences what had happened. 'Anyway,' Athelstan concluded, 'this does not resolve the mysteries confronting me. You and Ronseval were lovers but these murders . . .?'

'Bless me, Father, for I have sinned.'

'No!' Athelstan almost shouted. 'I will not shrive you. I will not hear your confession. I know what you want. Once you have told me under the seal I cannot discuss it. This is not the time for games but for the truth. Moreover, such a confession would be invalid.'

Hornsey's eyes shifted, glancing down the church as if he feared someone lurking in the darkness. He opened and shut his mouth.

'The truth?' Athelstan insisted.

'Marsen was hated,' Hornsey replied slowly. 'But that is stating the obvious. We all knew he had a violent past. There must have been many who would have loved to take his head. Indeed, on the night he died, the entire tavern seemed to be as busy as a rabbit warren in spring. Sir Robert Paston was up along the galleries. He saw me, I saw him. He looked worried, anxious. A young woman visited him.'

'His daughter?'

'No, a whore, a well-cut and prosperous one but still a whore. She knocked on Paston's door and went in. She must have left some time later. There were others walking about. I am talking about very late in the evening.'

'Who?'

'Paston's daughter, Martha, and her lovelorn clerk, Foulkes. I saw them together with that gormless-looking ostler Mooncalf in the Dark Parlour.'

'And Brother Roger?'

'I never saw him. He must have been in his chamber and stayed there.'

'And Scrope the physician?'

'Oh, he was wandering about slightly drunk, unsteady on his feet. I saw him come from outside. He was carrying a lantern horn. He said he wanted to visit Marsen.'

'And Master Thorne, Mine Host?'

'Busy in the taproom and out in the stableyard.'

'And finally the killer?'

Hornsey just stared, his lower lip jutting out. Athelstan caught a mere shift in the man's eyes. This sharp-witted captain of archers was keeping his own counsel. Athelstan quietly considered the possibilities. Hornsey was finished as a royal retainer. He might be innocent of murder and theft but he had left his post without good reason and there was every possibility that he could be exposed, tried and punished, not only as a deserter but as a self-confessed sodomite. Hornsey himself must have accepted that. So was he planning for the future?

A vast amount of money had been stolen. Had Hornsey seen the killer? Or could he prove who it was? Was Hornsey hoping that he might escape and use his knowledge to acquire a share of the plunder, a small fortune to set himself up as a prosperous peasant farmer, merchant or trader far beyond this city? Hornsey would not be the first to assume a new name, an identity, a fresh start to a different life.

'Brother, do you have more questions?'

'Oh, of course I do but I am not too sure if they will be answered truthfully. I suspect, Master Hornsey, that you know more than you have told me.'

'Brother,' Hornsey held a hand up, 'I have told you the truth.'

'But not the full truth.' Athelstan tried to curb his welling temper. 'Tell me now: why did Marsen choose The Candle-Flame? I have asked the others the same question but I would like to hear it from you.'

'I suspect it was chosen for him. Master Thorne is probably in the pay of Thibault. The tavern has many entrances by land and by river. The Barbican is a strong, fortified tower, ideal for Marsen, or so he thought, to protect himself and his treasure.'

Athelstan nodded in agreement. Hornsey's assertion was logical. Most of London's taverners worked for Thibault, be it out of fear or favour or both. Athelstan decided to take another direction.

'Marsen,' he declared, 'collected taxes. He was good at it, yes?'

'Yes. He took to it like a rat gnawing cheese.'

'But he collected information as well, didn't he?'

'Of course. Marsen sifted all the gossip and—'

'No,' Athelstan interrupted. 'Marsen was just not a snapper-up of mere trifles, he was hunting, wasn't he? In fact,' Athelstan jabbed a finger, 'he was hunting people like yourself because that was Marsen's nature, so he could control, bully and blackmail. That was the cause of your quarrel with Ronseval, wasn't it?'

'True.' Hornsey rubbed his face. 'Ronseval and I used to meet. On that day late in the evening he invited me to his chamber. He wanted me to relax with him. I told him that was far too dangerous. We argued and we sulked, sometimes we whispered and on one occasion we just sat silently. Ronseval didn't realize how evil Marsen truly was.'

'Do you think Marsen suspected your secret?'

'It's possible. I was adamant in protecting it. Yes, there was a quarrel. I drew my knife and a little blood was spilt, but only a cut. I eventually left and returned to my post.'

'And?' Athelstan intervened.

'The two archers were dead. I was still carrying Ronseval's dagger. I was so shocked I dropped it. I was fearful—'

'No, stop.' Athelstan held a hand up. 'You left Ronseval's chamber, yes? The tavern lay quiet, yes? So when you entered the Palisade what did you actually see?'

'The campfire had burnt down. My two comrades lay sprawled, crossbow quarrels deep in their chest. Apart from that there was a deathly silence. I could not see nor hear anything untoward.'

'How along had you been away – the truth?'

'By the time candle in Ronseval's chamber about three hours.'

'Paston said you appeared around midnight.'

'No, that was pretence. I had in fact been there for some time. I didn't want anyone to realize that. So I went outside the chamber and knocked on the door, pretending to have just arrived.'

'Your comrades, I mean, if they had survived?'

'Brother, I was their captain. I told them I was going to patrol the tavern and the surrounding streets – that was part of the quarrel. I wanted Ronseval to leave his chamber,' he flailed a hand, 'to walk with me, to go elsewhere. He refused to acknowledge how dangerous Marsen truly was.' Hornsey picked up the tankard beside him and drained it. 'As I said, I found both men dead. I immediately ran to the Barbican and knocked. No one answered. I could hear no sound. It was obvious a hideous mischief had been perpetrated. By then I was so terrified I staggered away to be sick. Once I'd recovered, I returned to Ronseval. I told him what I had seen. He asked for his dagger. I told him I had dropped it. We quarrelled. He wanted me to stay but I begged him to flee with me.' He shook his head. 'On reflection it was stupid, but I was terrified more than on any battle day. I had deserted my post and my comrades lay slain – the man I was supposed to protect probably so as well.'

'These two archers . . . before you left them, how were they?'

'Oh, they were good men, tired and weary after a day's work, resentful at being given such an onerous watch. But they had fire and food. They said they had eaten well. Thorne's meal was hot and spicy. They tried to entice me with what they had left but I couldn't eat. I said I wasn't hungry. In fact, I was too nervous.'

'So they had eaten and drank before you left?'

'Oh, yes, and with no ill effects.'

'And Marsen had instructed you to unlock the third clasp of the exchequer chest?'

Hornsey nodded in agreement.

'So,' Athelstan mused, 'what happened? Did Marsen and Mauclerc unlock the other two?'

'Brother, I cannot say.'

'And the two whores?'

'Mere shadows. I saw them slip into the Barbican.'

'Had Marsen visited The Golden Oliphant, the brothel run by the Mistress of the Moppets?'

'Of course. Marsen swept in there like Gaunt himself demanding this and that. He would know a few of her secrets as well.'

'Ah, yes.' Athelstan stirred on the stool, fighting a deep exhaustion which wearied him. 'Marsen collected information, knowledge. Was he searching for anything specific?'

'Certainly,' Hornsey replied, 'I heard about what happened in Cheapside, the attack by the Earthworms. Haven't you or Cranston ever wondered how the Earthworms can suddenly appear on horses in deep disguise all weaponed for war?'

'What do you mean?'

'Oh, horses can be stabled all over the city but those shields and spears, the masks – where can they be stored? How can a throng of armed men abruptly emerge in the heart of the city? How could they bring in such weaponry without being

noticed? Marsen was searching for where those arms were
bought, where they could be stored and how they could be
transported hither and thither with impunity.'

Athelstan sat silent. Again what Hornsey said was logical.
Horses could be stabled at alehouses or taverns, but there were
at least forty Earthworms involved with that affray in Cheapside
– all those spears, swords and clubs?

'You see, Brother, the Upright Men have learnt their lesson.
A year ago they stored such weapons in taverns, brothels,
alehouses, even cemeteries and crypts. They could dig pits but
these could be found. Thibault's searchers were hot in pursuit
so now the Upright Men have moved on. Marsen had more
than a passing interest in discovering just where these weapons
were bought, where they were kept and how they were moved
about. Before you ask, Marsen discovered nothing. He was
furious. I suspect that's why Lascelles visited him just for a
short while on the evening before the murders. Thibault wanted
the taxes but information can be just as precious.'

'Anything else?' Athelstan demanded.

'You told me about Lascelles being killed. Brother, I give
this to you in gratitude for what you have done for me. You
do realize Thibault was tricked and trapped tonight?'

'By the Upright Men?'

'No, by Beowulf the assassin. Somehow or other,' Hornsey
smiled grimly, 'that murderous will-o'-the-wisp brought Thibault
and the Upright Men together. He pedalled information to the
Upright Men, enticed them into The Candle-Flame, then gave
similar information to Master Thibault. He knew there would
be a confrontation. What better time to hide and wait for the
opportunity to destroy Thibault and his henchman?'

Athelstan sat still, surprised. He had suspicions about what
had truly caused the confrontation at The Candle-Flame.
Hornsey's explanation was logical. Marsen's treasure, heavy
to carry, could well be buried or hidden somewhere in The
Candle-Flame or the land around it. The Upright Men would
be keen to seize it – they had proclaimed as much. On the
other hand, Thibault would grasp any opportunity to inflict
bloody damage on his enemy. Hornsey was right. Thibault
and Lascelles had rushed into Beowulf's ambush. Lascelles

had been killed and it was only by sheer chance that Thibault had narrowly escaped a similar fate. Athelstan rose to stand beneath the pyx. Mentally he beat his breast and confessed his arrogance. Hugh of Hornsey was not just a simple soldier. He was more cunning and subtle than Athelstan had judged. He was an archer who had risen through the ranks, stood in the line of battle and survived on his wits, whilst hiding his own dangerous secrets. Was he also cunning enough to plot that massacre at the Barbican? The former captain of archers was steadily climbing what Athelstan called 'the Devil's staircase'. True, he had fled The Candle-Flame and taken sanctuary. However, at the same time he was taking one step away from the disaster which had nearly engulfed him. He was climbing away from both the truth and his own mistakes. Hornsey had seen something but he was determined to keep this to himself, to use further up the Devil's staircase. Athelstan closed his eyes and prayed. It would be futile to continue the questioning, to pursue this any further. He crossed himself, opened his eyes and pointed to the door to the sacristy.

'Master Hugh, bolt and lock that after me. The same for the door in the rood screen. Once you have done that no one can enter from the nave. Use the jakes pot and do not go out. If anyone tries to come through the sacristy they will have to knock on the outside door. Make sure that's bolted as well. Use the eyelet to determine friend or foe. I trust you consider me, Benedicta, Crim or the Hangman amongst the former.' He extended a hand for Hornsey to clasp. 'Goodnight, Master Hugh.'

Athelstan wearily left the church. He heard Hornsey bolt the doors behind him and plodded back through the dark to his house. He unlocked the door; the kitchen was cold, the fire had burnt low. Athelstan felt so tired he didn't care. He slumped down at the table and fell fast asleep. He was given a rude awakening by a pounding on his door just after dawn. He jumped to his feet, his heart a-flutter and his flesh tingling cold. The fire and brazier had burnt out; the candles were no more than stubs. Grey dawn light peeked through the shutters and tendrils of mist curled beneath the door. Athelstan stared around. Bonaventure was nowhere to be seen. 'I don't blame you, cat, this is not a place of rest.' Again the pounding at the door. Athelstan hastily unlocked and unbolted it. The Hangman, together with Benedicta and Crim, stood gasping in the bleak dawn light.

'Father, quickly! It's the fugitive!'

Athelstan followed them out, slipping and slithering on the icy rutted trackway up the steps, through the porch and into the church. It was freezing cold. The Hangman muttered something but Athelstan already had a premonition which proved true. Hugh of Hornsey lay dead in the sacristy almost as if he was floating on a wide, shimmering pool of dark red blood. He had been killed with a crossbow bolt loosed deep into his chest, almost the same way as his lover, Ronseval. He laid tangled and twisted, eyes staring blindly, blood-encrusted lips parted.

'I think you paid for what you saw,' Athelstan whispered, 'and so you were marked down for slaughter.' Athelstan blessed the corpse and glanced over his shoulder at the Hangman. 'You were here all night? You never left?'

'Father, I heard you leave, then the fugitive bolting all three doors. After that, nothing.'

'I came in to prepare for Mass,' Benedicta spoke up. 'The doors to the nave were all locked. That door,' she pointed to the one which sealed the sanctuary from the sacristy, 'that door,' she repeated, 'was wide open, as was the door from the sacristy to the cemetery. The fugitive was lying as you found him. He must have been killed when he opened the door to use the garderobe.'

'No.' Athelstan shook his head. 'I told him not to do that.' He went over to the mercy enclave and inspected the covered jakes pot. He hastily resealed it, wrinkling his nose, and returned to stand over the corpse. 'He had no need to go out. Not only did I warn him but Hornsey was an experienced soldier; he would be wary of leaving the safety of the sanctuary. Moreover, if that did happen it would mean his killer might have had to wait for hours in the freezing cold. No,' Athelstan paused, 'once more the paradox. Hornsey must have truly trusted his assassin.' Athelstan walked into the sacristy to inspect the door to the outside. 'Look, the eyelet hatch is down. Hornsey must have lowered it, looked out, recognized his killer, but felt safe enough to unlock the door. The bolts and locks,' Athelstan crouched down, 'are unmarked. No sign of force. Yes, yes,' Athelstan continued, 'it must have been so. Somehow the killer deceived Hornsey, who actually scrutinized his would-be assassin and utterly trusted him.'

'True,' Benedicta followed him over, 'the killer must have struck swiftly, not tarrying outside in the freezing night.'

'Precisely,' Athelstan agreed. 'So who was it? Why did Hornsey trust him so much?' He smiled absent-mindedly at Benedicta and walked back to the corpse. He administered the last rites then knelt on the bottom altar step, whilst the Hangman and Benedicta fetched the bailiffs, a shambling, drink-sodden group of men, bitterly complaining about the cold. They were shocked by what had happened, gazing fearfully at the corpse. All raised their hands and swore in the presence of the Blessed Sacrament that during the previous night they had seen no one approach the church nor heard anything to alarm them. Athelstan wondered how alert they had been but, as he whispered to himself, '*Alea iacta* – the dice is thrown.' He instructed them to remove Hornsey's corpse to the new parish death house. Benedicta promised that she would help Beadle Bladdersmith, Godbless and the Hangman of Rochester prepare the cadaver for burial. They discussed the cleansing of the church and the need to inform the bishop. Athelstan declared he would not celebrate his daily Mass or meet any of his parishioners. By now Benedicta and the Hangman had been joined by the bell clerk, Judith and Ranulf; they all assured Athelstan that they would look after the church, its precincts and, once he had gone, the priest's house.

Athelstan left and hurried across to the house, having despatched Crim to rouse Sir John. Once inside Athelstan locked the door. For a while he just sat feeding the meagre fire, allowing the tears of sheer frustration and despondency to well up, even as he murmured lines from the psalms asking for divine help. When Bonaventure scratched at the door to be let in, Athelstan crossed himself and smiled at the crucifix nailed to the wall. 'So that's your response,' he murmured. 'You have sent Bonaventure to help.' He allowed the cat in and for a while fussed over him, feeding him morsels from the buttery. At last, feeling more composed, Athelstan stripped, washed and shaved, donning new linen underwear and taking fresh robes from the clothes chest. He rubbed oil into his hands and face, took a deep breath and wondered what he would do. 'Distraction,' he whispered to a sleeping Bonaventure lounging across the hearth, 'is good for the soul.'

Athelstan began to walk up and down the kitchen, reciting, as he would a litany, the questions and problems which prevented him from unlocking the mysteries challenging him. Athelstan had been taught the technique by Brother Siward, Master of Logic at Blackfriars. 'Siward!' Athelstan exclaimed. 'A Saxon name. He was always so very proud of his Saxon ancestors. He loved to quote their poem about the Battle at Maldon and of course his precious Beowulf. He always had a soft spot for me, Bonaventure, because I bore the name of the great Saxon king. I wonder if Siward would loan me his manuscripts. Anyway . . .' Athelstan continued walking up and down, watched curiously by a bemused Bonaventure, who was fascinated by this little priest who shared his home and food with him. 'Now,' Athelstan sketched a blessing in Bonaventure's direction, 'we have Marsen and his company arrive at The Candle-Flame. They chose it because of the Barbican, a safe and secure refuge, or so they thought. A prosperous tavern, its master is probably in Thibault's pay. Marsen was a great sinner against the Lord like Ahab in the Old Testament, given to double-dealing in everything he did. He collected taxes as well as every scrap of information, either for own nefarious use or that of his master. Marsen loved his task, Bonaventure; he seemed to relish making enemies. He insulted Paston but there is little evidence of any relationship between him and the other chamber guests. The only exception is Physician Scrope, Marsen's secret enemy, who was preparing an indictment against him for previous crimes.' Athelstan paused. 'Marsen sets up the outside watch under Hornsey. They camp on the Palisade, where they are given food and drink by Thorne. In the Barbican's lower chamber is the internal watch, three archers who lock and bolt the door behind them. Marsen believes he can relax, he has food and drink and the company of two whores. One of them arrives with a bag which clinked. Was it money, Bonaventure, or was it that chainmail wristguard? If it was, why was it brought to the Barbican by a whore and, more importantly, why was it left?' Athelstan stared down at the cat. 'I must apologize to my congregation, even though it is only you, Bonaventure. You also have your needs.'

Athelstan went into the buttery, poured himself a stoup of ale and filled Bonaventure's bowl with some of the milk Benedicta had brought. The friar watched the cat hungrily lap his morning drink. 'Good,' Athelstan continued. 'Then there is the exchequer chest. Had it been opened, and why? Marsen and Mauclerc would be careful, especially with two whores in the chamber. Yet, even if it was partially locked, why would the other two keys still be left on cords hanging round their owners' neck? Apparently the killer-thief did not need them.' Athelstan sipped at his ale. 'No potion or poison could be traced in the food or drink. So, Bonaventure, we move to the heart of this mystery. Two archers were slain by the campfire. Three more in the lower chamber, four souls in the one above, yet both window and door were locked and bolted, whilst the trapdoor to Marsen's chamber was clasped shut from the upper side. How could a killer inflict such damage, provoke no real resistance and open a locked exchequer chest, even if the third clasp had been released, then remove the treasure and leave, passing as it were through sheer stone?'

Athelstan stopped to listen to the sounds echoing from outside, shouts and cries as Hornsey's corpse was removed. 'Yet another mystery, Bonaventure. Hornsey's murderer could have only entered our church by the door to the sacristy. Hornsey first peered through the eyelet and then, all trusting, opened the door and was immediately killed. The same, Bonaventure,' Athelstan started his pacing again, 'yes, just like Physician Scrope, only his death is even more mysterious. He was killed in a locked, bolted chamber. Wait now.' Athelstan's fingers flew to his lips as he recalled Lascelles being struck the previous evening. He must, he promised himself, truly reflect on what he'd seen last night, but, for the moment, he was too tired; it would have to wait. 'Why, oh why, Bonaventure, was Scrope killed in such a way? What did he see when he went out? Why was he clutching that pilgrim book on Glastonbury?' Athelstan, sipping his ale, crouched by the hearth, using a poker to shatter the crumbling, flame-flickering ash. 'As for the spy, well, Master Thibault will have to wait. And Beowulf – a silent, skilled killer, like you, Bonaventure? He has undoubtedly struck twice: at Lascelles that morning in the stableyard and more successfully last night. This time, he killed Lascelles and nearly did the same to Thibault. I wonder.' Athelstan put the poker down; a thought had occurred to him. Was Beowulf sheltering at The Candle-Flame or was he simply using the tavern as a shield? Athelstan got to his feet. 'And there are other strands to this mystery, Bonaventure. I must have a word with Mooncalf, Martha and Master Foulkes. Where were they going on the night those murders occurred? And why did a young whore visit Paston? Questions, questions, Bonaventure! Those two lovers Ronseval and Hornsey executed in the same way, the killer very close. Both men undoubtedly trusted that son of Cain. And why did Ronseval leave the tavern . . .?' Athelstan paused in his self-lecture at a pounding at the door. He hurriedly unlocked it, drew the bolts and stood back as Cranston swept in, his cloak billowing out as if he was the herald of God Almighty.

'I heard what happened, Athelstan. Hornsey's slain, the fool!' Cranston paused as Bonaventure, who seemed to adore the coroner, padded across to brush himself against Sir John's boots, his one eye staring up in mute admiration. 'God's teeth, I can't stand cats!'

'He certainly likes you.' Athelstan shooed Bonaventure away and made Sir John sit and listen to what he had learnt from Hornsey. Once he had finished, Cranston, threading his beaver hat through his hands, stared bleakly at Athelstan.

'Do you think we will ever solve this, Brother?'

'Sir John, I do not know.'

'Thibault is furious. He regarded Lascelles as kith and kin. He visited me at the Guildhall and told me that was Beowulf's work last night. Master Thorne found Beowulf's usual message pinned to a newel post on the tavern staircase. He sent it immediately to the Guildhall. Brother Athelstan,

I do fear for Pike and Watkin. Thibault may well make an example of them. I have used all the influence I can to delay their arraignment before the justices. Now, Brother,' Cranston got to his feet, 'let's go deeper into this maze. We must visit The Golden Oliphant and the Mistress of the Moppets. Let us see what that madam has to say for herself. Brother, what is it?'

'Just a thought, Sir John, but isn't it rather strange? The Upright Men invade The Candle-Flame. I could understand why they would not lift a hand against Brother Marcel or Roger, as they are priests. Violence against clerics incurs spiritual penalties and, whatever the Upright Men may boast, old habits die hard. What is remarkable is that no violence was offered to Sir Robert Paston, a manor lord, a natural enemy of the Upright Men, or even to Thorne or his own household.'

'Whom they probably regard as in Thibault's pay.'

'The Upright Men,' Athelstan declared, 'would be angry. They apparently searched and found no treasure, yet they didn't turn on their hostages.'

'Which they certainly can do,' Cranston added quickly. 'One of my spies informed me how the Upright Men executed Grapeseed, who mocked them. They used his severed head as a public display of their power. Yes, it's an interesting thought.' Cranston chewed the corner of his lip. 'But we must not be too hasty. Remember, the Upright Men were disturbed in their search by the arrival of Thibault and his soldiers. God knows what they would have done if that hadn't happened. But come, Brother, let me broaden your experience of this world.'

They left the precincts of St Erconwald's. Athelstan, head down, hood pulled over, did not wish to converse with parishioners all agog with the news of Pike and Watkin being taken up and Hornsey slain in sanctuary. The exception was Benedicta, whom he called over. He opened his wallet and took out a seal of the Dominican order with a cross on one side and a crowned lily on the other.

'Take this to Brother Siward at Blackfriars, would you, please? I appreciate the weather is harsh but this is important . . .'

'I was planning to visit Cheapside,' she replied, 'and remember, Brother, I have been to Blackfriars before on your behalf. I've met Brother Siward.'

'Yes, yes, so you have,' Athelstan conceded. 'Siward may be old but he is still partial to a fair face. Anyway, give him the seal. Ask him if I can borrow the library copy of a poem known as *Beowulf*.' He made Benedicta repeat the message. 'Take the Hangman of Rochester with you as a guard. He frightens the footpads as much as Sir John.' Benedicta, eyes closed, repeated the word 'Beowulf' until she knew it by heart. Cranston gave her a hug and kiss and she hurried off. Athelstan and Cranston strode on into the mesh of narrow squalid streets of Southwark, which ran like a tangled web, reeking of poverty and all kinds of wickedness. The day was iron-hard cold, the ground under foot still frozen solid, the filth strewn there turning to rock to score the foot and trip the boot. Shutters flew open above them. Doors slammed. Children chased dogs or guided the family pig with a whipping cane. Carts, barrows and tumbrils rumbled and rattled, pushed by sweaty labourers or pulled by spare-ribbed street nags. The legion of tinkers and traders, trays hanging around their necks, offered a range of goods from strips of hard cooked meat to crude sharp knives to cut it. A wild-eyed preacher had commandeered a broken wheeled cart on the corner of Hairlip Lane; his powerful voice bellowed how long hair was a sign of pride and the banner of Hell, and how the world was full of such banners, especially London ale. According to the preacher, this was Satan's own drink, making men yield to the temptations of fleshly women who bore in their person the marks of the great enemy of man. Athelstan couldn't make sense of what the preacher was talking about, although he agreed with the man's constant refrain of how London had become the seat of the Great Beast and idolatry peeked out of every corner.

In truth, the friar was so distracted by the hurly-burly of recent events that he almost forgot where he was. Cranston had to pull him around a funeral party, all drunk and trying to get a coffin out through a narrow door; its thin wooden side had split and a skeletal arm hung out to the distress of the tipsy mourners. They left Hairlip Lane and paused as a group of flagellantes proceeded by, their heads and faces hidden by bright yellow hoods and red masks. The tops of their gowns, both the men and women, were pulled down to expose them to the lashes of those behind, a ceaseless reign of cutting blows which ruptured the skin and sprayed the air with flicking blood. The flagellantes, swinging from foot to foot, lost in a trance, rhythmically chanted '*Miserere, Miserere, Kyrie Eleison*' – 'Have mercy, have mercy, Lord, have mercy on us.' A few city urchins, encouraged by the layabouts standing in the crumbling doorways of shabby alehouses, threw refuse at the penitents. Cranston doffed his beaver hat and bellowed at the top of his voice until the miscreants fled. The coroner was about to move on when he caught sight of a well-known pickpocket, Bird-brain, and shouted a warning for the felon to spread his wings and fly.

They reached The Golden Oliphant, standing at the end of an alleyway with walls of sheer red brick ranging either side. The tavern boasted a magnificent doorway smartly painted in black and gilt; the same colours were reflected in its broad sign and the rest of the tavern frontage. Two oafs dressed in black-and-gold livery stood on guard. Once Cranston announced himself they threw open the door and escorted them into the sweet-smelling parlour, just off the well-scrubbed paving stone floor leading down to the Golden Hall, as one of the guards grandly called the taproom. The parlour reminded Athelstan of a rather luxurious monastic cell with its gleaming oaken furniture, lancet windows filled with painted glass, thick turkey floor rugs and slender candles burning under bright copper caps. Cranston and Athelstan sat down on quilted, leather-back chairs before a brilliantly polished elmwood table; at its centre was a three-branched candelabra next to a blue and gold mazer full of freshly crushed herbs mixed in rosewater. The guards left. A short while later Elizabeth Sheyne, the Mistress of the Moppets, came in accompanied by her maid, a slender but buxom young lady, dressed as discreetly as any novice in a well-heeled convent. Introductions were made, refreshments offered and tactfully refused. Cranston and Athelstan retook their seats and the two women perched on chairs opposite as demurely as any city matrons. The Mistress of the Moppets, however, was a brazen-faced, hard-eyed woman with knowing eyes and a rat-trap mouth. The maid, Joycelina, as she introduced herself, looked no better – a pale, rather peaked face with hostile eyes, her disdain at meeting them barely hidden.

'You are most welcome, Sir John.'

'No, I am not!' Cranston barked. 'You,' he pointed at the mistress, 'run a brothel, a whorehouse, and I am an officer of the law.'

'Sir John, I have powerful protectors.'

'I couldn't give a fig if all the Pope's cardinals are upstairs with your ladies. Your business is not mine but if you lie I will make your business my business. I shall leave, but return with a warrant to search and a summons to court. Rest assured, I will be escorted by the burliest bailiffs who have ever graced a brothel.'

The mistress fluttered her eyes, laced her fingers together and forced a smile.

'What do you want, Sir John?'

'Marsen,' Cranston used his fingers to emphasize his points, 'Mauclerc, Sir Robert Paston and not to forget two dead whores. Be attentive to my questions. Answer them truthfully and you are safe; lie and I will have you in the stocks for a week, the public pillory down near the bridge. I am sure the wives of some of Southwark's leading gentlemen would love to see you there.'

Athelstan steeled himself against the fear he could sense in both women. They had lost their false demure attitude and were now becoming increasingly flustered. Apparently they had never done business with Cranston and were being given a rough schooling.

'I don't—' the mistress began.

'Oh, by Satan's tits!' Cranston thundered jabbing a finger at the maid. 'On the evening of the murders, and you know what I am talking about, you met Sir Robert Paston at The Candle-Flame – why? Look, accept my apologies,' the coroner persisted. 'In many ways I am a knight and a gentleman, but I am also a coroner. Hideous murder has been, and still is being, perpetrated. I don't want to sit here and parry words with you. I have no desire to convict you of anything. I just want information.'

'Sir John, Sir John,' the mistress lifted long, snow-white hands, 'I will tell the truth. What does it matter? We live in the rough world of men. I have no choice but to be subject to their iron-hard temper.'

'I will be fair and just,' Cranston intervened. 'I am here to do what is right, that is all. Help me and, if and when I can, I will assist you.'

'Marsen was a demon,' the mistress spoke quickly, 'a blood-drinker, a soul-crusher and, above all, a blackmailer. He loved to bully defenceless women. Oh, he was a guest here but not an invited one. He took what he wanted and never paid for anything, be it food, drink or a wench. He accused me of having secret dealings with the Upright Men.'

'Do you?'

The mistress just stared back.

'Everybody does, don't they, Elizabeth?' Athelstan said gently. She nodded.

'We help where we can,' she murmured. 'In return, we have guarantees that when the days dissolve into fire, The Golden Oliphant will be safe.' She ignored Cranston's mocking laugh.

'Do you store their weapons?'

'No, Sir John, that would be stupid. You know that. Someone like Marsen would soon find out.'

'What else did he want?' Athelstan asked, staring at the maid. 'Why did you go to The Candle-Flame? Why did one of your sisters who was slain carry a bag which clinked? Did it contain, and I think it did, a blue expensive gauntlet and a chainmail wristguard?'

The mistress drew a sharp breath, rubbed her face and twiched the folds of her dark-green, samite gown.

'Marsen knew,' she replied. 'One of the sisters told him how Sir Robert Paston is the most regular visitor here. After all, he is a widower and he has,' she fluttered her eyelids, 'his own needs. When he came here Sir Robert liked . . .' She pulled a face. 'Father, you are a priest?'

'You would be very surprised, Elizabeth, at what I hear in confession. Some of my parishioners are most forthcoming about what happens in establishments such as this. I under-stand,' Athelstan continued blithely, 'that some men like to watch, others require two or more girls together, and others like to be beaten.' The mistress stared at him in surprise. 'Elizabeth,' Athelstan smiled, 'we are all sinners. We do what we are good at, which is sinning. I always think men who knock on a brothel door are searching for God. Now, Sir Robert?'

'He likes to be playful.'

'You mean rough?'

'Yes, Father. He asks the girls to act like damsels in distress, to be taken by force by a rough soldier after her castle has fallen.'

'And her drawbridge forced?'

The maid abruptly added, glaring at Athelstan, 'Some men like that. What do you like, Father?'

'Women,' the friar replied before Cranston could intervene. 'I do love a beautiful woman; in my eyes one of God's greatest creations. I like to watch their eyes fill with laughter and admire their hair, long and lovely. It must be very easy to fall in love and so glorious for such a being to love you back. So, I have answered your question, lady. Now,' Athelstan's smile faded, 'answer mine. Sir Robert liked to wear gauntlets, chainmail wristguards – they made him feel fierce, yes?' The maid nodded, taken aback by this passionate little friar who seemed to be searching her soul.

'Sir Robert left such items here, didn't he? Marsen learnt about it and forced you, mistress,' Athelstan pointed at the older woman, 'to hand them over, or at least certain ones. He was going to publicly ridicule Paston, perhaps blackmail him or just pass such information on with the proof to Master Thibault.' Athelstan paused. 'I am correct?' Both women nodded in agreement. 'However, Sir Robert is a goodly man; he supports you, so you sent her,' Athelstan gestured at the maid, 'to The Candle-Flame to warn Sir Robert?' Both women murmured their agreement. Athelstan sat, letting the silence deepen. He glanced at Cranston, who was staring in surprise. Athelstan winked at him before turning back to the two ladies. 'And how did Sir Roger take the news?'

'He seemed slightly relieved,' the maid replied. 'I had the impression he was, yes, relieved. All he said was, "Is that all?"'

'Is that all,' Athelstan repeated. 'Why should he say that?'

'I do not know.'

'Does Sir Robert's cog, *The Five Wounds*,' Cranston asked, 'have anything to do with your trade, my lovelies?'

'No,' the mistress replied. 'Sir Robert is a very generous and kind patron but no more than that.'

'And Marsen hired two of your beauties?' Cranston demanded.

'Yes. Merrybum and Lovelorn.'

Cranston burst out laughing and swiftly apologized as Athelstan nudged him sharply.

'They also died,' Athelstan conceded. 'Brutally murdered. But listen, on his visit here, did Marsen say anything significant?'

The mistress undid the exquisitely embroidered purse on the silver cincture around her slim waist and took out two silver coins.

'Father,' she leaned over, 'if you could celebrate a requiem for my two girls.'

Athelstan gently pushed her hand back. 'I blessed their corpses,' he replied. 'I will say the Mass.'

For the briefest of moments the mistress's hard face relaxed. She sat, head down.

'Beowulf!'

'What?' Athelstan exclaimed.

'Beowulf, Brother,' the mistress repeated. 'I know about him. We have heard the stories. When he came here, Marsen grew deep in his cups. He boasted how he had survived an attack by Beowulf at Leveret Copse. He said Beowulf was a wolf in sheep's clothing. Marsen swore he would trap and kill this wolf as sure and as certain as that of Guttio.'

'Guttio? What does that mean? Where is it?'

'Brother, I don't know and I don't really care. Marsen was arrogant. He said it was just a matter of time, how he had to be prudent, careful. He would do it his way.' She spread her hands. 'More than that I cannot say.'

'When you visited Sir Robert,' Athelstan asked the maid, 'did you notice anything suspicious?'

'There was a darkness in that tavern,' the maid replied,

'more of the spirit than a lack of candlelight. A disturbance of the humours. The tavern was busy but everybody knew Marsen was there. It was like sitting in a woodland glade, peaceful and pleasant, but you knew some ferocious animal lurks deep in the darkness. You could almost feel his malign influence – you just knew he was there. People were fearful.' She paused, lost in her own thoughts. Once again, Athelstan mentally struck his breast as he sat, fascinated. This young woman, despite her appearance and occupation, was sharp of wit and keen of mind.

'Joycelina,' he said quietly, 'you did see something, didn't you?'

'Just a glimpse. The ostler, Mooncalf, he was in the garden with Paston's daughter, Martha, and that clerk who follows her everywhere. All three were in deep conversation, but about what I cannot say.'

'Apart from that, anything else?'

'No.' The maid shook her head. 'Ah,' she raised a hand, 'except in the Dark Parlour. The customers were hosting a drinking dirge to that Hainault seaman who had been attacked and knifed earlier in the day at Queenhithe. I think his name was Ruat.'

'Sir John,' Athelstan turned to Cranston, 'wasn't that the name of the courier carrying the list Master Thibault seized?'

'Yes, yes, I think it was.'

Athelstan rose from his chair and walked over to the latticed window. He stared down at the light rain splashing the puddles. Was the business of the spy as simple as that? he wondered. Was the Hainault sailor the spy? He glanced over his shoulder. 'Surely, if they were hosting a drinking dirge to a foreign sailor they must have known him?'

'I cannot say. According to the gossip he had visited St Mary Overy, where there is a special shrine for Hainault sailors, the Virgin of the Narrow Seas. He had lit a taper there and visited The Candle-Flame for a celebratory drink. Apparently his purse was heavy and he was generous in buying ale for customers. They felt sorry about what later happened to him.'

'Of course they would,' Athelstan agreed, 'a story as old as the hills. Some poor seaman, his purse well lined with silver, goes into a tavern and attracts the wrong kind of attention. I suppose he was followed from Southwark to Queenhithe. An easy victim, his belly full of ale and his purse full of coins.' Athelstan turned back to the window. He was tempted to leave the identity of the spy as that Hainaulter, but that would be wrong. The sailor had a berth on his own ship, which was ready to sail on the next tide, yet the document Thibault seized claimed the spy would be residing at The Candle-Flame on 16 February when the Hainaulter and his ship would be long gone. Athelstan ran a finger round his lips. And what did Mooncalf, Mistress Martha and William Foulkes have so much in common? He recalled meeting the two lovebirds in the refectory the morning after the murders. He was sure he had noticed something amiss.

'Brother?' Cranston called. The friar walked back to his seat.

'You are sure of that?' Athelstan asked the maid. He hid a spasm of excitement. All these mysteries were perhaps not so tangled; matters were drifting apart. Perhaps he could find a path through them.

'Sure of what, Brother?'

'The Hainaulter, Ruat?'

'Of course I am. I went up into the gallery to meet Sir Robert. I'd told Master Thorne I had a message for him. When I came down the taverner asked me if I wanted refreshment.' She glanced swiftly at her mistress. 'We have a good relationship with Master Thorne.'

'You mean he sends you custom?' Cranston asked.

'You could say that. Anyway, I joined the drinking dirge. Of course, everyone was talking about the man we were mourning for.'

Athelstan sat, nodding his head. Did the sailor come to The Candle-Flame, he wondered, to meet someone? The friar mentally listed all those who had been at The Candle-Flame that day . . .

'Sir John, Brother Athelstan, are we finished here?'

'Yes, yes,' Athelstan replied absent-mindedly. 'We certainly are. I thank you.'

They left The Golden Oliphant, tramping back through the

damp day. Athelstan, concerned about Pike and Watkin, insisted they visit the Bocardo prison to ensure all was as well as it could be. He also needed to question his two wayward parishioners on certain matters. They entered the grimy, dark heart of Southwark's slums, making their way down arrow-thin runnels called Nosegay, across small enclosures known as Pillory Place or the Whipping Post. All along the way the makeshift stalls and booths set up in any available space offered a wide range of paltry goods and putrid food probably stolen from elsewhere in Southwark or beyond. The tenements, on either side, their wood and plaster walls held up by heavy wooden crutches, teetered close over their heads. Brothels and whorehouses of every kind did a flourishing business, offering services not to be found elsewhere in the city. Athelstan glimpsed the well fed and richly cloaked, the would-be customers of such establishments, slipping in and out of door-ways. This part of Southwark was different from St Erconwald's – that was a parish where everybody knew each other, but this was the world's thoroughfare, where names were forged, no questions asked, and certainly no answers given. Everyone looked after their own. It was a place to pass through but not to stay. Wandering minstrels, chanteurs, troubadours, jesters and magicians offered entertainment. One group, the Brotherhood of the Bear, their faces plastered a thick white, their teeth deliberately blackened, had brought their tame bear to dance for pennies. Apparently the animal loved London ale; it had drunk too much and had promptly fallen asleep, a great huddle of slumbering fur almost blocking the lane. A dispute had broken out between the Brotherhood and a tinker selling powders and philtres. He was being accused of slipping a sleeping potion into the tankard the bear had drunk from, an allegation the tinker hotly disputed.

'Where is the proof?' the gap-toothed trader shrieked.

'Such a potion leaves no trace!' one of the Brotherhood screamed back.

Athelstan and Cranston passed on, dodging a high-backed execution cart painted a garish red and attended by three men dressed in devil's masks. They had been clearing the gallows of the cadavers of the hanged who had been displayed and gibbeted; these now sprawled under a dirty canvas sheet, ready for the common burial pit. Such macabre squalor was swiftly swept aside by the delightful carolling of three altar boys from St Mary Overy who were escorting a funeral bier down to the church. Athelstan stopped and pulled back his hood to listen to the exquisite refrain, '*In paradisum te seraphi portent* – may the Seraphim carry you into paradise'. The boys' faces were angelic, an impression heightened by the surplices which had miraculously escaped being stained by the grime and floating filth of the streets. The three boys led the funeral cortege down the alleyway. Merriment was caused by a St Anthony's pig following a mourner who had given it something to eat; such generosity is never forgotten by a pig, and this one now resolutely pursued its benefactor. Athelstan studied the scene and recalled the sleeping bear, Ursula's great sow and the lumbering mass of Pedro the Cruel being roused from its slumbers on the Palisade at The Candle-Flame. So lost in his thoughts was he that Cranston had to pull Athelstan aside as the window door above them was opened and the contents of a night jar tossed into the air.

Eventually they reached the lane stretching down to the dark, sinister mass of the black-stoned Bocardo prison, with iron bars over its arrow-thin windows and a massive reinforced main door. On either side of the entrance rose a two-branched gibbet. From each arm dangled a corpse sheeted in tarred black cloth. Deliberately beneath the dangling corpse stood the stocks with a prisoner held fast, a crude placard slung around their necks proclaiming their offence. The broad steps sweeping up to the main door were guarded by mail-shirted turnkeys armed with morning stars. Cranston showed his warrants. The two guards didn't move swift enough, so the coroner drew his sword and, fiddling with his cloak, let his badge of office boasting the royal arms be clearly seen.

'I will ask you again,' he growled. 'If you try to dilly-dally I am off to the Guildhall, where I will swear out warrants for your arrest on charges of treason. So open that door and get me Blanchard or—'

The door hastily swung open. Athelstan stepped into what Cranston called 'the black heart of the darkest hell'. A stark, whitewashed chamber stood to the right – the keeper's room, where he kept a faithful record in his *Book of Crimes*. The room opposite was a cell sealed by a thick, iron-studded door. Cranston whispered how freshly arrived prisoners were detained there to be stripped and searched.

'And worse,' Cranston murmured, 'if you are pretty.' Both chambers flanked a long, murky tunnel which ran steeply down into the gloomy bowels of the prison. The air was rancid with foul smells blown up from the 'pits', as the dungeons were called. A man dressed in a white gown came out of the keeper's room. He just stood on the threshold, hands hanging by his side. For a few heartbeats Cranston ignored him as if fascinated with something further down the passageway. At last he turned.

'Master Blanchard.' Cranston threw his hands in the air. 'What a pleasure . . .' The keeper's deep-set eyes in his furrowed face glowed with a suppressed rage. Athelstan recalled Cranston speaking of this official as a man who did more to shatter the king's peace than any Cheapside cunning man, a prison official who had more than a close relationship with many of the leading gangs of the city, a corrupt servant of the Crown who, Cranston had publicly vowed, he'd watch being strangled at Tyburn. In turn Blanchard nurtured and nourished a deep resentment, even hatred for the coroner. A malignant soul, Athelstan considered, with his shaven pate, beaked nose, yellow-skinned face and sour, twisted mouth.

'Sir John, Brother Athelstan, welcome to my kingdom.'

'And welcome to mine, Blanchard.' Cranston took a step closer. 'I represent the king. I exercise royal power here. I will see what I want. I will go where I want. I will do what I want . . .' He paused as a soul-wrenching scream rang along the cavernous passageway.

'Richard Sparwell,' Blanchard jeered, 'heretic, Lollard, follower of Wycliffe, condemned to be burnt alive at noon at Smithfield. The sheriff's men will be arriving soon.'

'Why the scream?' Athelstan asked. 'Is he being tortured?'

'Oh, no, no, no,' Blanchard lisped mockingly. 'We wouldn't do that here, would we, Sir John? Richard Sparwell mourns because he is going to die alone, bereft of any spiritual consolation. No priest would tolerate being seen with a convicted

Lollard. Now, Sir John, it is truly lovely to see you.' Blanchard forced a smile. 'I am sure you are here to visit Pike the ditcher and Watkin the dung collector, two birds being primed to have their necks twisted at the Crown's earliest convenience.'

'After their trial,' Cranston snapped, 'and they have yet to be convicted. I want to see them now.' Blanchard shrugged and, taking a set of keys from a hook on the wall, led them down into what he called his 'underworld'. Athelstan blessed himself. He felt as if he was walking through a truly wicked place; a malignant evil hung here, nourished by the breath of crushed spirits, tortured souls and torn bodies. The atmosphere seemed to seep from the very stones. The Bocardo's deep, perpetual night of murk and gloom were lit by evil-smelling tallow candles and fiercely burning cressets, their flames leaping like demons in the sharp draught. The Bocardo was not far from the river and the prison was soaked in a constantly dripping, foul-smelling dampness. Rats and other vermin criss-crossed the ground in front of them. Lice and other filth crackled under their feet. Hard-rending shouts and cries echoed eerily like the mourning of some lost ghost. Now and again they would pass through open chambers where the turnkeys squatted and lounged around barrel tables, or busied themselves at the moveable grills, cooking food which looked as disgusting as it smelt: fat wedges of pork roasted in skillets bubbling with dirty oil. Other open chambers were reserved for the interrogation of prisoners, heavy with chains. Blanchard pointed out the Lollard Richard Sparwell; the convicted heretic sat chained in a hand barrow being fed sips of water from a bucket. The prisoner would gulp then stretch out his hands for more. He jolted around as Cranston and Athelstan entered, peering through the gloom.

'A friar!' he shouted. 'Father, help me, some consolation.' Athelstan stared pityingly at the bruised, dirty face of the prisoner, his hair and his beard thick with greasy dirt and dried blood, eyes frenetic with the fear of death. 'Please,' the prisoner whispered hoarsely. 'For the love of God, to burn is hideous, but to die uncomforted is even worse.'

'You have been judged a heretic.' Athelstan hated his own

reply even as the words slipped from his lips. 'What need do you have for the rites of Holy Mother Church?'

'I am not asking for them.' Sparwell jerked back in the barrow as Blanchard struck him full in the face.

'Do that again . . .' Cranston warned, lifting his sword. 'Come, Brother.'

'I shall return,' Athelstan called. 'I promise you.' Blanchard led them deeper into the darkness, the foul vapours thickening, the squeak and scamper of rodents constant. Athelstan stopped and smiled as he heard a hymn, the one practised in his parish, being chanted by two deep carrying voices, *'Christus factus obediens usque ad mortem, mortem autem crucis* – Christ was obedient unto death, even death on the cross.' Watkin and Pike!

'They have been singing since their arrival,' Blanchard grumbled.

'And I want them singing on their release,' Athelstan retorted. The keeper stopped at a great wedge of a door. He unlocked this and beckoned Cranston and Athelstan inside; the cell was a filthy box, the mush of straw on the floor ankle-deep. Cranston demanded candles be brought. Athelstan approached the two men, weighted in clattering gyves, sitting on a rotting sack mattress which served as a bed.

'Father?' One of the figures half-rose in a jangle of chains.

'Pike, Watkin. It's good to see you, though not here. I am glad you are in fine voice.'

'Father, we expected you.' Athelstan took the stool Blanchard fetched, indicating that the two prisoners remain seated on the bed. The keeper also brought in candles and a cresset torch which provided meagre light. The two prisoners were garbed only in their tunics and, as the flames strengthened, Athelstan saw the bruises on the two men's faces and along their arms. Their legs and feet were caked with prison dirt.

'Give Master Blanchard some coins.' Athelstan spoke over his shoulder to Cranston. 'Once we go, these prisoners must have rushlights, good food and strong ale: their possessions must be returned, bruises and cuts tended to, their persons kept safe. If not, I will go to Westminster and go down on my knees before the king. His Grace Richard of Bordeaux once swore that he would grant any request of mine. In the meantime,' Athelstan continued evenly, 'you and I will be alone with these men. Master Blanchard will step outside and be busy on what I ask or, as God lives, by vespers he will be in a worse state than these.' Athelstan's soft but menacing tone even alarmed Sir John. He bundled Blanchard out of the cell, spitting out promises that this little friar was as good as his word. The coroner came back, slamming the door shut and standing behind Athelstan.

'Very well,' the friar began, 'Pike, Watkin, let us begin. First, your families are well but fearful. Secondly, Sir John and I will do what we can, though at the moment that will not be much.' Athelstan paused as a fearful cry rang through the prison.

'Sparwell,' Watkin grunted. 'The poor bastard is for the fire.'

'And poor Watkin,' Athelstan countered, 'is being prepared for the noose. Now look, we do not want to know the secrets of the Upright Men, but I do require certain information and I do not want to perform a May Day dance to learn it. Do you understand?' Both men gave their agreement. 'The night you visited The Candle-Flame with the likes of Cecily, you were hunting Marsen, weren't you?'

'Yes. We wanted to spy out both him and his escort.'

'The Upright Men were plotting to kill him?'

'Our leaders,' Pike replied, 'Grindcobb and Tyler had been assured by Beowulf that he would execute Marsen.'

'How were they informed?'

'We don't know.'

'But Marsen escaped at Leveret Copse?'

'Yes.'

'And, because of that, the Upright Men were planning their own assault when the murders took place?'

'That is true, Father.' Pike wiped the sweaty dirt from his face. 'The Upright Men were as puzzled as anyone else. There is a feeling that the massacre in the Barbican was not the work of Beowulf even though, well,' Pike coughed, 'as we know from our friends at the Guildhall, the usual message was left.'

'This Beowulf,' Cranston demanded, 'he works independently of the Upright Men yet he supports their cause. He marks down for death Thibault's minions, particularly his tax collectors. That is a fact. I just wonder how the Upright Men first became acquainted with him.'

'Sir John,' Watkin scoffed, 'as scripture says, "Those who are not against us are with us." We heard about Beowulf's bloody handiwork in the shires around London. We rejoiced at the news. His reputation grew – it was only a matter of time. Our leaders are well known even though they are in hiding. Eventually Beowulf and the council exchanged good wishes.'

'Surely,' Athelstan insisted, 'there must be speculation about his identity?'

'Father,' Pike retorted, 'we will not betray the cause. We will say nothing to weaken the work of the Great Community but surely it is obvious. Beowulf is schooled. He must have experience in war as well as the means to move from one place to another. He is not like us, tied like a dog to its post.'

'And the night you were captured, the attack on The Candle-Flame, you were searching for Marsen's treasure?'

Watkin and Pike glanced at each other. Athelstan's heart skipped a beat – he was always fascinated by how intelligent his little flock could be when they wanted, these two worthies in particular.

'Watkin, Pike,' Athelstan held his hand up as if swearing an oath, 'I vow solemnly as your priest that I will regard what you say here, and so will Sir John, as if told under the seal of confession. Now, we know Master Thorne at The Candle-Flame is in Thibault's pay.'

'And in ours,' Watkin smirked. 'Oh, Father, don't look so surprised. All the worthies of London, both high and low, are taking surety against the evil day.'

'You hide weapons there, food, stores?'

Watkin snorted with laughter.

'He makes a contribution towards the cause, doesn't he?' Cranston asked. 'Like scores of others the length and breadth of this city?'

'Which is why,' Athelstan added, 'no harm was done to Thorne or his people – I understand that. But Sir Robert Paston?'

'We would have eventually,' Watkin blurted out, but Athelstan caught a shift in Pike's eyes.

'So you have no business with Sir Robert?'

'Why should we? He criticizes Gaunt so we leave him be.'

'And his daughter?'

'A mere child.'

'And Master William Foulkes?' Athelstan glimpsed Pike's hand brushing that of Watkin's, a sign to be wary. 'Ah, well. Let's go back to my previous questions. Who told you that Marsen's treasure was there?'

'Oh, Beowulf.' Pike seemed relieved at the change in direction the questioning had taken. Sounds from the passageway drifted in. Cranston went outside to have words with Blanchard, who was hurriedly trying to comply with Athelstan's earlier demands on behalf of the prisoners. Athelstan waited until he returned.

'Well?' he continued. 'How did Beowulf inform you? In God's name,' Athelstan's voice turned hard, 'I am trying to save you from being strangled over Tyburn stream or the cattle market at Smithfield.'

'Letters were left,' Pike confessed. He glanced at Watkin. 'What does it matter? Scraps of parchment,' he continued, 'pushed under my door and that of Watkin's. They were written in a clerkly hand like yours, Father.'

'Liar!' Athelstan accused. 'Neither you nor Watkin can truly read. But the Hangman of Rochester can.'

'As does Mauger the bell clerk,' Pike added a little too hastily, eager to spread the doubt about who had read the letters for them.

'Giles of Sempringham,' Athelstan declared, 'also known as the Hangman of Rochester, is a trained scribe. Let us say he read both messages for you.'

'Very simple,' Pike screwed his eyes up, 'the message was something like this: "Marsen's treasure is still held deep, protected by the candle's flame." Pike opened his red-rimmed eyes and scratched at the suppurating ulcer on his arm. 'We know what it meant, Father. That is all I can and will tell you.'

'But why that particular evening?' Cranston asked. 'First, let me tell you something, gentlemen. Beowulf must have kept you under close watch. He was waiting for you to take action.

He would see you leave your houses and deduce that you and your confederates were assembling. Once convinced, he sent a second message to Thibault at the Guildhall. Hence the delay in Gaunt's troops arriving—' Cranston broke off at the protests of denial from the two prisoners.

'No, no, listen,' Athelstan intervened. 'Beowulf did not betray you. He just used you. He wanted to lure Thibault and Lascelles out of the fastness of the Guildhall. He created the opportunity for both to emerge as clear targets for his crossbow. This time he was successful: Lascelles was killed.'

'May the Devil welcome him into Hell,' Pike retorted.

'For that both of you might hang,' Cranston rasped.

'Enough of that!' Athelstan did not want Sir John to be so harsh. He needed such information as he slowly edged his way through this maze of murder. He was determined to discover something so that he could barter with the Crown for the lives of these two parishioners.

'I am your priest.' Athelstan pulled the stool closer. 'I walk those needle-thin runnels and no one accosts me. True?' He didn't wait for an answer. 'Footpads, felons and foists swarm there as plentiful as the rats. They keep a sharp eye on any likely prey as Ranulf's ferrets do vermin. And, of course, there is the Upright Men, who have their legion of watchmen, isn't that what you call them?' Pike grunted his agreement. 'And yet you say this Beowulf was an educated, prosperous man, certainly a stranger to St Erconwald's? So how could he slip along Hogpen Alley to you, Pike, or Muffin Lane to you, Watkin, without being noticed, because that is what he did.'

'The messages were delivered after dark,' Watkin grumbled. 'We took them down to The Piebald.'

'Oh, I am sure you did,' Athelstan snapped.

'But the problem still remains.' Despite the deep shadows which cloaked the prisoners as well as their own guarded concern, Athelstan sensed both men were as baffled as he was.

'How were you captured?' Cranston asked.

'We stopped at an alehouse,' Pike replied, 'and became separated from the rest. Father, we are sorry. Sorry for you, sorry for our families . . .'

'The parish will do what it can. I, we, will do what we can.'

'I have moved a writ in the courts,' Cranston leaned down to study both prisoners, 'you will not be arraigned before the justices immediately. I just hope,' he added menacingly, 'your comrades amongst the Upright Men do not attempt a rescue. Believe me, this time you might not escape unscathed.'

Athelstan gave a few final words of comfort, blessed both prisoners and stepped outside. Cranston emphasized with the turnkeys that the prisoners were to be well treated. They left the cell, Pike and Watkin's good wishes ringing clear, followed by more song, which faded as Cranston and Athelstan walked back up that long, gloomy tunnel. They reached the open chamber where Sparwell was being prepared for his gruesome death. The sheriff's men, garbed in the city livery of blue and murrey, had stripped the prisoner and were now pulling a piece of coarse sacking over him to use as a tunic. On the ground lay a long hurdle with leather straps on each of the four jutting poles. Sparwell, crying and protesting, was forced to lie down face up. When the hurdle was dragged across the frozen, rutted streets his back would only be protected by the leather sheet covering the main body of the hurdle. The prisoner struggled and kicked until a reign of blows forced him to comply. He was stretched out, wrists and ankles being tightly clasped in the leather straps. Sparwell begged for a drink and one of the sheriff's men unloosened the points of his hose, preparing to urinate on the condemned man's face. Athelstan, horrified, sprang forward. He knocked the man away. The would-be tormentor stumbled and fell and, ugly face snarling, he drew both sword and dagger and lurched forward, only to be sent spinning by Cranston's punch to the face. Uproar ensued. Athelstan staggered to kneel over the prisoner. Swords and daggers were drawn in a clatter of steel. Cranston, cloak thrown back, unsheathed both his weapons; he stood at a half-crouch, turning to the left and right. The sheriff's men edged closer.

'Think, my lovelies!' the coroner bellowed. 'I am Jack Cranston, Lord High Coroner. You have assaulted a priest, a cleric and now me. This man,' Cranston pointed his sword at Sparwell, 'has been sentenced to die according to due process. He is not to be used as a pisspot. So be good lads and reflect on what I have said. Lower your swords and, when we reach

The Candle-Flame, it will be a blackjack of ale for each and every one of you, courtesy of Jack Cranston.' The coroner's words sounded like a bell around that yawning chamber where the flames leapt, shadows danced and Sparwell's groans mixed with the laboured breathing of the sheriff's comitatus. Athelstan struggled to his feet.

'In God's name,' he shouted, 'we are men, not animals!' One of the sheriff's men sheathed his weapon and the rest followed. Cranston did the same before moving amongst the escort, clapping shoulders in infectious bonhomie. Harmony was restored, although the macabre ritual of execution continued. Athelstan, crouching by the hurdle, mopped Sparwell's face with a rag and fed him sips of water. The executioners arrived. The principal Carnifex and four apprentices, their faces covered with grotesque demon masks painted red and black with twisting yellow horns. All of them were garbed in black sleeveless jerkins and thick leather hoses, their boots soled in layers as protection against the flames and hot ash. They brought with them all the dreadful necessaries for Sparwell's burning: a barrel with its top and bottom removed, to be looped over the great pole and Sparwell placed in it. Bundles of kindling, faggots and brushwood were being fastened to long sledges which would be pulled by the Carnifex and his assistants. Athelstan tried to distract the prisoner by offering to shrive him and administer the last rites.

'Father,' Sparwell gasped, 'I am condemned because I refused in the bishop's court to accept the power of the Pope, his priests and their sacraments. I believe solely in the scripture – that is God's word. Everything else is of human fashioning.' He licked cracked lips. 'What I ask of you, Father, is that you accompany me, pray with me and for me, nothing more. No priest, no cleric will do it, that's why I am begging you.'

'I will go with you, but wait.' Athelstan rose, walked over to Cranston and informed him of his decision. The coroner, who had been in deep conversation with the Carnifex, gripped Athelstan's shoulder and led him away.

'My apologies for any harsh treatment of those two madcaps Pike and Watkin, but what you propose is even more foolish. Heresy is like a plague. The Church believes such infection spreads swiftly. Suspicion will fall on you, a preacher, a priest who works amongst the poor. They will drag you in for questioning and, in their eyes, that's guilt enough. They will trap you—'

'Sir John, I assure you, they may well question me but they will not trap me. No priest will help Sparwell because he fears he will lose all hope of preferment and be doomed to some paltry benefice. Now tell me, Sir John,' Athelstan grinned, 'where could they send me? They regard St Erconwald's as punishment enough.'

'Very well, Brother, but I will stay with you. The Carnifex has already despatched more of his assistants to the Palisade, Southwark's old execution ground. I wager Thorne will make a good profit from the crowds. We will make our way through the streets and take the riverside path on to the Palisade. Brother, this will be heinous. The Carnifex has informed me how the bishop's court has ruled *mors sine misericordia* – death without mercy.'

'Death without mercy. For God's sake, Sir John, that is obvious enough.' Cranston drew Athelstan closer.

'Oh no, Brother, worse than that. Sparwell will have green wood stacked close around him so the flames will be slow burning. The Carnifex has been instructed not to offer the mercy of a swift strangulation or, even better, a pouch of gunpowder around his neck. Sparwell will die slowly. Remember that.' Athelstan gazed pitifully at Sparwell, now lying moaning on the hurdle. He squeezed Cranston's hand and walked back to kneel by the prisoner.

'I shall stay with you,' he promised. 'But Master Sparwell, what brought you to this? I know the Papal Inquisitor Brother Marcel has come to hunt the likes of you.'

'Oh, we know he has arrived in England.' Sparwell turned his face towards Athelstan, leaning forward as much as he could. His lips were dry and his tongue swollen, so Athelstan fetched more water, which he fed to him in small sips. The chamber was now filling with other guards and a small party from the Bishop of London's court. One of these, a high-browed, pale-faced cleric, approached Athelstan, his mouth all twitching: the friar rose to meet him.

'Brother!' he whispered hoarsely. 'We understand that you will accompany the prisoner, a condemned heretic?'

'A soul,' Athelstan retorted fiercely. 'A human being in his last extremities, a very frightened man, bruised and injured. He is alone. He has no family?'

'None that we know of. A tailor who thought he could dabble in theology, a follower of the damnable Wycliffe. Brother, the bishop will not be pleased.'

'Jesus might be.' Athelstan grinned at the shock in the cleric's face. 'Who knows, I might even convert Sparwell. The bishop would not object to that would he, Master . . .?'

'Master Tuddenham.'

'Well, Master Tuddenham, you deal with your business and leave me to deal with God's.'

The cleric spun on his heel and, bony body all twitching, scurried across to gossip in a huddle with the rest of his party.

Athelstan shrugged and took a fresh stoup of water to Sparwell. Once he drank, Athelstan leaned down.

'The Inquisitor, is this his handiwork?'

'Brother, as I said, we knew about his arrival in England. We were terrified but so far he has posed no threat to our conventicles, our meetings.' He spluttered through bloodied lips. 'I trust you, Brother. True, *cacullus non facit monachum* – the cowl doesn't make the monk – but in your case it does. You have a good heart, so I will tell you what brought me here. Our conventicles meet beyond the city walls, desolate places such as Moorfields or parts of Southwark where it is easy to escape the bishop's spies. Our beliefs are well known. Pope and priest mean nothing to us. We will have nothing to do with superstitious geegaws, putrid relics, gaily painted statues or other religious baubles.'

'But how were you captured?' Athelstan insisted, his curiosity now roused.

'I am tailor, a good one. Enemies, rivals must have denounced me. In truth it wouldn't be hard. I stopped attending Sunday Mass, I did not observe the holy days. I did not pay my tithes.'

'Do you,' Athelstan sighed, 'did you, want to die my friend? You certainly raised the banner which would attract the attention of those who mattered. Tell me, is Sir Robert Paston one of yours?'

'No, no.' The answer came so swiftly Athelstan wondered if Sparwell was defending the manor lord. Any further conversation was hampered by shouts and cries. The great prison door had been opened. A cold breeze swept the chamber with all the smells of Southwark. The execution was about to begin. Athelstan had to stand aside as the sledges and hurdle were secured and dragged by the Carnifex and his coven out of the chamber and down the passageway to the yard outside. Athelstan and Cranston followed close behind. The friar opened his chancery satchel and looped the purple-hued stole around his neck. Outside all the midnight folk of Southwark had assembled, a sea of hard-pinched faces: whores in their flame-coloured garb surrounded by their hooded pimps; the capuchoned counterfeits and cranks; the ill-witted and the sharp-eyed; and all the predators from the slums. Athelstan recalled what Cranston often said, that the only person who could safely walk unarmed through the streets of Southwark were friars such as himself. This horde of rifflers shouted and cursed. Mud and other filth rained down on Sparwell as his hurdle was harnessed to a massive dray horse caparisoned in a black-and-white sheet, its mane all hogged and festooned with red ribbons, its thick tail decorated with scraps of scarlet cloth. The hurdle was fastened tight, the Bishop of London's people assembled at the front and the macabre procession moved off.

Athelstan walked slowly behind the hurdle as Sparwell began his journey along what was known as the 'path of thorns', dragged across the cobbles, ruts and sharp-edged potholes of Southwark. Athelstan deliberately kept as close as he could so the filth-pelters might think twice before hurling refuse which might hit a priest they recognized. Cranston's presence was also a help; curses and threats were hurled at him but his large, swaggering figure and gleaming drawn sword deterred any real mischief. Athelstan tried not to look at Sparwell, jerking and twisting in searing pain, as the hurdle bounced across the ground. The friar recited the Mercy Psalm but found he could not get past the opening line: 'Have mercy on us O God in thy kindness; in thy infinite compassion blot out our offence.' *What kindness, what compassion?* Athelstan thought bitterly, walking through this charnel house of broken souls, twisted spirits and bruised bodies. Athelstan could only recall a poem he'd learnt as a young soldier in France: 'The moon is pretty on the wave, the blossoms of the sky bright as lights.' Athelstan crossed himself. He glanced at the crowd, catching glimpses of those thronging around but held back by the burly sheriff's men. Two workers from the tanneries at the Tower were offering homemade pomanders as protection against the smell. A beggar-monk stood holding a skull, all white and bony, as if it was some precious vessel. A woman clasped a frightened child close to her face. A painted doxy, drunk and raucous, screamed abuse as the thick paste covering her poxed face began to run in the persistent drizzle which had begun to fall. A fire-eater, dressed in the garish red and green costume of a salamander, held a candle as he intoned a prayer, whilst a pickpocket with clipped ears and a mangled nose tried to open the fire-eater's purse. The reeking smells of the streets billowed sometimes, hidden by the gusts of incense from the thurible carried by the Bishop of London's party. Eventually they turned, leaving the crumbling tenements behind them, going down an incline on to the path which ran along the riverbank. The rain stopped falling. Athelstan noticed Cranston had disappeared. The friar curbed his own anxiety and returned to reciting snatches of psalms, trying to keep calm amidst the raucous noise, foul smells and the sheer horror of what was happening.

PART FOUR

'Mattachin': a mimed battle dance.

The execution cortege moved more swiftly as they approached the Palisade. Athelstan realized that this was the first time he had entered The Candle-Flame from this direction. It was a lonely place, a long line of mudbanks, desolate and windswept, littered with rubbish washed up by the tide: stacks of peeling driftwood, shattered barrels and the crumbling skeletons of former river craft. Gulls swept backwards and forwards, swooping up and down, their constant strident calls buffeted by the wind. Athelstan stared along the river bank. He noticed the clumps of reeds and wild, straggling bushes which sprouted over mud-caked pools.

'This is where you died, Ronseval,' Athelstan whispered to himself. 'You were lured here, but how and by whom?' Athelstan stared down at Sparwell, who, thankfully, had lapsed into unconsciousness. Athelstan returned to his prayers as the grim cortège, sledges and hurdle rattling and bouncing, made their way up a slight rise on to the Palisade. The crowd thronging here were as dense and noisy as at any summer fair at Smithfield, a restless and unruly mob eager to watch this macabre spectacle unfold. The execution place was on a piece of raised ground opposite the Barbican. Athelstan glanced at that fire-scarred donjon. He recalled battling for his own life against the inferno which had almost engulfed him. The friar grimly promised himself to revisit that dark tower. He would pluck its macabre secrets. For the moment, however, Athelstan decided to concentrate on the present. Sparwell was about to be executed. The clamour of the crowd, the press of sweaty bodies and the smell of such a throng had brought the usually desolate Palisade to gruesome life. All the villains and mountebanks had swarmed here together with the different guilds and fraternities dedicated to offering some consolation to those executed by the Crown. Not that they could, or really wanted to, achieve anything practical. Cranston was correct – heresy was an infection. A mere kindness towards someone like Sparwell might provoke the interest of the Church. Undoubtedly the Bishop of London's spies would be slinking through the crowd, eyes and ears sharp for any sympathizer.

The Carnifex and his assistants became busy leaping about like imps from Hell. Sparwell, his body one open wound, was unstrapped from the hurdle and dragged to the soaring execution stake driven into a steep hummock of piled earth. Athelstan followed and started with surprise as Cranston strode out of the crowd, his chain of office clear to see, the miraculous wineskin in one hand and a pewter cup in the other. He winked at Athelstan as he planted himself firmly in front of the executioners.

'A drink?' Cranston filled the deep bowled cup. One of the bishop's party rushed forward to object but Cranston bellowed he didn't give a piece of dried snot what he thought. The coroner was supported by the sheriff's men, who hadn't forgotten Cranston's promise of a free blackjack of ale. Sir John filled the cup to the brim and virtually forced it down Sparwell's throat. The prisoner drank greedily, coughing and spluttering. Cranston stepped back and the spectacle continued. The executioners had already slipped the barrel over the pole. They now seized Sparwell, bound hand and foot, and lowered him into the barrel. A herald of the bishop's court read out the *billa mortis* – the bill of death. How Sparwell 'was a sinner, obdurate and recalcitrant, steeped in his hellish ways and so deserving of death by the secular arm'. Athelstan had followed Sparwell to the execution stake, but had to step back as the Carnifex and his assistants heaped the brushwood and stacked the bundles of faggots. Athelstan studied these. Cranston was correct. A great deal of the wood was green to the point of suppleness.

'*Homo lupus homini* – man is truly a wolf to man,' Athelstan whispered to himself. He stared over the crowd, now pressing in against the cordon of soldiery: a mass of faces, a babble of voices. Some cursed and yelled; others chanted songs of mourning or hymns for the departed. Athelstan glimpsed members of his parish clustered around Mauger the bell clerk. What caught his attention, however, was Paston's daughter Martha standing close to the ever-faithful Foulkes. Both young people were markedly different from the crowd on either side. They stood so quietly, staring at the grisly ritual as if memorizing every detail.

'Let it begin!' the herald shouted. Athelstan blinked and stared around. The hurdle, sledges and great dray horse were being pulled away. The execution pyre was ready. Oil-drenched branches were fired from a bowl of glowing coals. The air grew thick with the stench of grey-black smoke. The flames on the fire-fed torches leapt up, almost exuding the horror they were about to inflict on this freezing February afternoon under a lowering winter sky. Athelstan glanced at the stake. Sparwell had fallen very silent. In fact, he just lolled against the barrel as if deeply asleep.

'Fire the wood!' the herald shouted. The executioners raced forward, torches held out, thrusting them into the kindling. Smoke and flame erupted, though the fire seemed to find the faggots stacked closer to the condemned man more difficult to burn. The smoke plumed up and billowed out, almost hiding that pathetic, lolling figure. The crowd strained to watch. The smoke grew thicker, forcing the sheriff's men and the executioners further back, leaving the execution ground to that great, fearsome cloud lit by darting flames, which seemed to just thrust itself up from the earth. The crowd had now fallen silent as if straining to listen to the cries and shrieks of the condemned man. There was nothing.

'He's gone,' Cranston whispered, coming up beside Athelstan. 'When I left you, Brother, I visited an apothecary and bought the strongest juice of the poppy.'

'The wine?' Athelstan asked.

'Oh yes, Brother. It was in the wine or rather the cup. Sparwell was already exhausted. Such a potion would have put him into a sleep very close to death.'

'Sleep is the brother of death,' Athelstan retorted. He forced a smile. 'Or so a Greek poet wrote. Sir John, I cannot stay here.' Athelstan raised his hand and blessed the air in the direction of the execution pyre. The smell of smoke was now tinged with something else: a foul odour like fat being left to burn. The flames had reached Sparwell! Athelstan took off his stole and walked away. One of the bishop's men tried to catch him by the sleeve but Athelstan ignored it and, pushing through the crowd, walked quickly towards The Candle-Flame.

'Brother Athelstan?' He turned. Master Tuddenham, face as white as a ghost, strode towards him. The man was deeply agitated, all a tremble.

'What is it?' Athelstan walked back to meet him. Tuddenham stopped, crossed himself and went down on one knee.

'Bless me, Father,' he intoned, 'for I have sinned.'

'I bless you indeed,' Athelstan declared, 'even though I am very surprised. Get to your feet, man. What is the matter?'

Tuddenham glanced over his shoulder at that great pillar of smoke rising against the sky. The reek was now truly offensive, and the crowd, disgusted at the stench, was already breaking up. 'That was my first burning of a heretic, Brother, and, by God's good favour, it will be my last. You see,' Tuddenham tweaked the sleeve of the friar's robe, indicating that they walk on, 'I am a canon lawyer, a notary. For me, heresy is a blot on the soul of the Church.' He blessed himself again. 'Today I found out different. I was shocked by what you did but,' he stopped to stare straight at Athelstan, 'I admired it. Sparwell was pathetic. A poor tailor who had certain ideas and could not give them up. Stupid but . . .'

'If stupidity was a burning offence?' Athelstan retorted. 'We'd all be living torches, yes, my friend?' Athelstan stared at this confused cleric. A good man, the friar reflected, who had just realized that heresy was not just a matter of belief but the arbiter of a very gruesome death.

'I never realized what it would entail.' Tuddenham shrugged. 'The Bocardo, the sheriff's men, Blanchard, who really should decorate a gibbet, the crowd baying for poor Sparwell's blood . . .' Tuddenham's voice faltered, tears in his eyes. 'Sir John?' he asked.

'The Lord High Coroner gave Sparwell wine laced with a strong potion which dulled the prisoner, a true act of compassion. I assure you, Master Tuddenham, for doing less a mercy many a soul will surely enter Heaven. But tell me,' Athelstan indicated they walk on. 'Sparwell was denounced?'

'No.' Tuddenham's voice was harsh. 'That is the other reason I have approached you, Brother. Sparwell was not denounced, he was betrayed. There is a traitor in his conventicle, as the Lollards call it.'

'Who?'

'We don't know but, Brother Athelstan, it makes me fearful. Sparwell's execution might be the first of many such horrors.'

'Did Sparwell know of this traitor?'

'Of course not. It was kept hidden lest, somehow, Sparwell communicated to other members of his conventicle. He was simply informed that he had been denounced.' Tuddenham pulled a face. 'Of course, he then convicted himself out of his own mouth. In the end we had no need for witnesses or proof.'

'And the traitor?'

'We know very little. He recently appeared in the shriving chair at St Mary-le-Bow. He was protected by the mercy screen. Let me hasten to add he made no confession, just gave Sparwell's name, his trade and where he lived, then added that there would be more.'

'Any indication of his identity?' Athelstan glanced over Tuddenham's shoulder; the smoke was thinning, the crowd clearing. He gestured for Tuddenham to follow him away from the throng now intent on slaking their thirst in the Dark Parlour. They walked over to a small enclosure shrouded by bushes.

'We know nothing,' Tuddenham replied. 'The priest reported the spy had a coarse voice, how he'd caught the odour of the farmyard. Whoever he was, his information proved correct.'

'And the Papal Inquisitor, Brother Marcel?'

'What of him?'

'He has talked to you?'

'He knows of us. Of course, he presented his credentials to the bishop's curia but apart from that little else. You know how it is, Brother: no bishop likes interference in his own diocese, whilst there are deep differences between religious and secular clergy.' Athelstan nodded in agreement: papal and diocesan, foreign and domestic, religious and secular, the different rivalries between clerics were infamous.

'You agree?' Tuddenham asked.

'I recall that quotation from the Book of Proverbs: "Brothers united are as a fortress." It's certainly doesn't apply to us priests, does it? So you have had little to do with our visitor from the Holy Father?'

'No. He has left us truly alone.' Tuddenham stretched out a hand. 'Athelstan, the day is going and so must I. Farewell.'

Athelstan clasped his hand. 'What will you do?'

'Seek a fresh benefice. Who knows?' Tuddenham smiled. 'I might even go to Blackfriars and become a Dominican.'

Athelstan laughed and watched Tuddenham stride away.

The friar remained where he was. He glimpsed Cranston leading the sheriff's men into the tavern, bellowing at the top of his voice about the virtues of Thorne's ale. Athelstan silently sketched a blessing in the coroner's direction. Cranston would be deeply disturbed by Sparwell's horrid death. The coroner had a good heart and he would hide his true feelings behind his usual exuberant bonhomie. Athelstan continued to wait. Now calm and composed he recited the 'De Profundis' and other prayers for the dead. Athelstan's mind drifted back to the execution and the glimpses which had caught his eye and quickened his curiosity. He left the shelter and made his way back over the Palisade. Twilight time, the hour of the bat. The light drizzle had begun again. The execution ground was empty. The crowd had dispersed. All that remained of the burning was a mound of smouldering grey-white ash blown about by the breeze and an occasional spark breaking free to rise and vanish in the air. Athelstan murmured a prayer and stared around; there was no one. Strange, he thought, that despite the clamour and the busyness of so many to see a man burn, once he had people became highly fearful of the very place they had fought so hard to occupy only a short while beforehand. Were they frightened of his vengeful ghost or the powerful spirits such a violent death summoned into the affairs of men?

Athelstan, whispering the words of a psalm, walked towards the Barbican. He'd noticed earlier how the door hung off its latch. The fire had certainly ravaged that thick wedge of oak, blackening the wood, searing it deep with ash-filled gouges.

The door hung drunkenly on its remaining heavy hinges. Athelstan found it difficult to push back but eventually he did and stepped into the lower chamber. The inside of the Barbican had been truly devastated by the fire. Nothing more than a stone cell, all the woodwork on both stories had simply disintegrated, with the occasional piece left hanging. 'I was almost murdered here,' Athelstan whispered to himself. 'And God knows what evidence that inferno destroyed.' Thorne had already begun to clear away the rubbish. Athelstan peered around; the light was murky but he noticed the deep, black stain on the far wall where refuse was still piled. The place, Athelstan reasoned, where the fire had probably started. He carefully made his way across and, taking a stick, began to sift amongst the rubbish. Athelstan paused at the clear stench of oil. He crouched, poked again and caught the same odour. He dropped the stick in surprise, rubbing his hands together to clear the dust. 'I wonder,' he declared. 'I truly do but let us wait and see.' A sound from outside alerted him. He rose and quietly turned to stand in the shadow of the main doorway. He looked out and, despite the deepening twilight, glimpsed two people, a man and a woman, both cloaked against the cold, digging and scraping around the execution stake. They worked feverishly and, once they were finished, hurried off into the darkness. Athelstan watched them go and followed them, pausing now and again so that he entered the tavern by himself.

Cranston was in the Dark Parlour roistering with the sheriff's men, regaling them with stories about his military service in France. Athelstan raised a hand in greeting and moved around the tavern, noting where everything was. Servants bustled by, now used to his presence and constant curiosity. Athelstan entered the spacious, cobbled tavern yard with its different buildings: smithy, stables, storerooms and wash house. As he passed the latter, a door was flung open and a woman bustled out with a tub of dirty water, which she tipped on to the cobbles.

'Good evening, Father,' she called out. 'So many guests, so much to wash.' She made to go back. 'Oh, by the way, Father, are all you monks the same?'

'I beg your pardon, mistress, but I am a friar.'

'Just like the other one,' the woman replied.

'Brother Marcel?'

'Yes, that's him. Ever so clean, he is. Fresh robes every day and of the purest wool.' She gestured at Athelstan's dirt-stained robe. 'Not like yours. But you see, pure wool is difficult to wash. Not that I am complaining . . .' And the woman promptly disappeared back into the wash house. Athelstan was about to walk on when he remembered his conversation with the maid at The Golden Oliphant. He hastened back into the Dark Parlour, nodding at Roger and Marcel, who were closeted together in a window seat. At another table, Sir Robert Paston, Martha and Foulkes were deep in conversation. The friar tried to catch Cranston's eye but failed. Sir John was now lecturing the sheriff's men on the Black Prince's campaign in Spain. Athelstan felt a touch on his arm. Eleanor, Thorne's wife, beckoned at him pleadingly. Athelstan followed her out of the taproom into the small, well-furnished buttery, where her husband sat at the top of the table with Mooncalf beside him. Athelstan took a stool.

'Master Thorne, mistress, what can I do? Why do you—?'

'This.' Thorne undid his wallet and placed six miniature caltrops on the table, very small but cruelly spiked barbs no bigger than polished pebbles. Athelstan picked one up and scrutinized it carefully. Once he had, he sent Mooncalf into the taproom to ask Sir John to join them urgently. He waited until the coroner swaggered in, face all red, lips smacking, in one hand a piece of capon pie, in the other a blackjack of ale. Cranston sat at the far end of the table toasting them all until he glimpsed the caltrops.

'Satan's tits,' he breathed, putting down both food and drink. 'It's a long time since I've clapped eyes on such vicious instruments. Where did you find them?'

'Let me explain.' Eleanor Thorne, despite all her pretty ways, was now cold and determined. 'On the night of the murders, my husband left our bed.'

'Why?' Athelstan asked.

'I . . .'

'Simon.' Eleanor indicated that she would answer for him. 'Well, we were both concerned about the goings and comings in our tavern. Earlier in the evening Mooncalf had glimpsed someone slip out of the stables.'

'A mere shadow,' the ostler added. Athelstan studied Mooncalf's pocked and shaven face, his rough voice and leather garb all splattered with mud. The friar had promised himself to have close words with Mooncalf, though not now – that would have to wait.

'A mere shadow?' Athelstan repeated.

'Mooncalf informed me.' Thorne wiped his hands on a napkin and picked at the minced chicken on the platter before him. 'I went down to the stableyard but I could not find anything wrong, yet you know how it is, Sir John. Like it was in the fields of Normandy when you can see or hear no enemy but you know they are close by. I was uneasy. I checked the horses but could discover nothing. After I retired, what with Marsen and his coven carousing and others moving about the tavern, I still remained agitated about the stables. I couldn't rest.' He waved a hand. 'I went down again. I was away some time but I truly searched, yet all remained quiet. The horses were having their evening feed, saddles and harnesses were hung drying after the day's rain. I found this close by.' Thorne tossed across a pouch. Athelstan examined it, battered and empty, the ragged neck pulled tight by a filthy cord. 'I wondered why it was lying there and who had dropped it. I continued my search but I eventually gave up. What with the hideous murders, the deaths here, I didn't give it a second thought until this morning. I was preparing to send back Marsen and Mauclerc's possessions to Master Thibault. I decided to clean the harnesses of their horses. I brought the saddles down from their rests and discovered these caltrops embedded deep in the woollen underbelly of both Marsen and Mauclerc's saddles.'

'I have seen the likes before,' Athelstan spoke up.

'An evil trick,' Cranston declared. 'The saddle is thrown over the horse's back, the girths and stirrups are fastened. These sharp pebbles might graze the horse and cause some petty discomfort . . .'

'But when the rider mounts,' Athelstan picked up where Sir John had left off, 'his full weight in the saddle drives the spikes down into the horse, which will rear in agony, certainly throwing its rider.' Athelstan rolled a spiked ball from one hand to the other. It was sharp to the touch. He recalled the mysterious attack on Lascelles the morning after the murders. 'I wonder,' he murmured, 'if these belong to our good friend, Beowulf, a plot which never came to fruition? Can you imagine . . .' He broke off. 'Never mind, it certainly proves one thing.'

'Which is?' Thorne asked anxiously.

'Nothing for the moment, Mine Host, but I have a question for you. On the afternoon before the murders took place, a Hainault sailor Ruat came into The Candle-Flame. He claimed to have visited a shrine much loved by his fellow countrymen, the Virgin of the Narrow Seas at St Mary Overy. Do you remember him?'

'Oh, yes,' Thorne replied. 'I remember him well, replete with good humour and even better silver. He was about to join his ship at Queenhithe. He drank and drank again, then left.'

'Did anyone accost him here?'

'No, the company was jovial.'

'And what was he talking about?'

Thorne pulled a face. 'Like all sailors, he was looking forward to going home. He seemed very pleased with himself, like a gambler who has won at hazard or a merchant who has made a good profit from his trade.'

'Or a man,' Athelstan asked, 'who has just been paid for carrying out a task?'

'Certainly, Brother; as I said, he had a heavy purse. I suspect he had just acquired it because he talked about his family and what he would like to buy them, but that would have to wait until he reached home because his ship was leaving on the evening tide.'

'Can you remember anyone leaving with him at the same time?'

'No.'

'Did he meet anyone here, anyone in particular?'

'Brother, I assure you he did not. He came in here, ate and drank, grew very jovial then left.'

'As must we.' Athelstan caught at Sir John's sleeve. 'Darkness is falling and our day's work is not yet done . . .'

'What were you going to say in there?' Cranston asked once they were free of the tavern, striding through the wet evening.

'Very simple, Sir John. Thorne was correct,' Athelstan declared. 'Someone stole into those stables that evening. They placed those spikes into the woollen flock beneath the saddles – mere pebbles, very difficult to detect. I suspect it was Beowulf. Can you imagine what would have happened the following morning? Marsen and Mauclerc swinging themselves into the saddle, their horses rearing violently, throwing their riders, who could be injured, perhaps even killed, and, just to make sure, somewhere close by is Beowulf with his crossbow all primed. Our two tax collectors would be an easy target. Two of Thibault's creatures humiliated then killed. Which means,' Athelstan paused and stared up at the night sky, 'if Beowulf was already planning his murders, those which took place at the Barbican were, despite that note, not his work. Beowulf was waiting for the morning. Of course Mauclerc and Marsen were killed, but Beowulf wouldn't let an opportunity slip. Lascelles appeared and Beowulf struck.'

'I agree, little friar. But who is this mysterious assassin?'

'I don't know. Our killer may have already been murdered or indeed one of those slain might have been an accomplice who had to be disposed of. But, I am making progress, Sir John. God help me, but I am. Now, let's visit the nearby quayside where Sir Robert Paston's cog, *The Five Wounds,* lies berthed in splendid isolation.'

The Southwark quayside was deserted when they reached it. The long wharf shone in the light of bonfires torched to burn the day's rubbish as well as provide warmth for the beggars and ragamuffins who haunted that place. These stood, dark shapes in their tattered clothes, warming themselves or trying to roast scraps of meat collected earlier in the day. Athelstan's stomach lurched at the smell, which brought back memories of poor Sparwell's burning. *The Five Wounds* was also illuminated by these fires as well as by the torches fixed either side of the gangplank, guarded by three fully armed men. The ship itself was handsome; it's raised prow and stern brilliantly painted, the two masts, fore and main, gilded brightly amidst all the cordage and reefed-white canvas sails.

There was a cabin under the stern and the deep-bellied hold
meant the cog was both a fighting ship and a merchantman.
Cranston strode straight towards the gangplank and, when
one of the guards tried to block his path, the coroner drew
his sword whilst pulling down the rim of his heavy cloak to
display his chain of office.

'Jack Cranston, Lord High Coroner!' he bawled. 'And you
must be Coghill, master of this craft?'

'Yes, yes I am,' the man spluttered, pulling back his hood
to reveal a bearded, weathered face. 'And I am responsible
for the watch on this ship.' He threw his own cloak back to
display the war belt strapped around his waist.

'Now I wouldn't do that, my friend.' Cranston's voice was
almost a whisper. 'Not against a royal official, surely, who is
visiting your craft on royal business? Now get out of my way!'
Cranston shoved the man aside and strode up the gangplank,
Athelstan following behind. Once on deck, dark shapes
emerged from the gloom. Athelstan caught the glimpse of
sword and dagger.

'Peace! Peace' Peace!' Cranston bawled, raising his own
sword. 'Brother?' he whispered hotly. 'What are we doing
here?'

'Inspecting its cargo.'

Cranston relayed this to the master and crew now coming
up from the hold or their resting places in the shadowy gulleys
beneath the taffrail. Coghill, a hard-faced, sober-sided man,
realized he had no choice, though Athelstan glimpsed the
young boy despatched down the gangplank, probably a
messenger hurrying to inform Sir Robert Paston about what
was happening. Cranston sheathed his sword and Coghill led
him reluctantly down into the hold, which reeked of tar, fish
and the sharp tang of saltpetre, used to fumigate it whilst it
was in port. Coghill, carrying a powerful lantern, explained
how *The Five Wounds*' hold, crammed with barrels, had recently
returned from Bordeaux with wine and other goods. Athelstan
hid his disappointment as he forced his way through the narrow
gaps between the cargo. Cranston followed, checking seals on
barrels, tapping the wood and, on one occasion, tipping a cask
so he could hear the wine within swirl back and forth. Athelstan

searched for any apparent concealment or deception. There appeared to be nothing wrong, yet why was such a close guard kept? He could understand the master wanting to protect his cargo but the crew also seemed eager to challenge and impede him. Athelstan glimpsed the padlock on the inbuilt cupboard built beneath what must be the master's cabin on the deck above.

'What's in there?' he asked.

'Our weapons store,' Coghill grated. 'We are a fighting ship as well. Corsairs, pirates and French warships prowl the Narrow Seas. We carry what is necessary to protect ourselves.'

'Open it,' Athelstan urged. Coghill seemed reluctant, but then he shrugged and squeezed between the casks, boxes and barrels and undid the padlock. Athelstan followed and asked for the lantern. This was handed over and the friar entered the musty darkness. He raised the lantern. The dancing light revealed the spears, swords and rounded shields stacked there. He studied the red-painted oxhide covering over a shield close to the door and smiled. He had at least solved one problem.

oOoOo

At the Bocardo prison, keeper Blanchard was intent on enjoying himself: two buxom young whores had been caught soliciting beyond Taplash alley, the prescribed limit. Both prostitutes had been seized by the bailiffs who were paid by Blanchard for making such arrests and bringing these street-walkers here for his own delectation and delight. Blanchard now sat on his cushioned stool in the waiting cell just within the main doorway opposite his chancery office. He still seethed with fury at being humiliated by Cranston and that little ferret of a friar. This was his kingdom. This was where Blanchard ruled and now he was being made to dance to the tune of a dung collector and ditcher. Blanchard's rage bubbled like filthy water in a pot. He would not forget such humiliation! Many of his turnkeys were still absent at the heretic's burning. Blanchard knew they would be laughing at him behind their hands – he would show them! Blanchard never prayed. He had given that up during his years as a wandering mercenary in France. But now he was tempted to. Blanchard knew all about Lascelles' death during the affray at The Candle-Flame. There was always the chance that Thibault, in his frustration and fury, would ignore the court's writs and arraignments and have those two felons dragged off and hanged out of hand. Blanchard sipped the tankard and watched as one whore began to undress the other. If Thibault didn't act, perhaps he could? Many prisoners died in the Bocardo of one cause or another. Blanchard grinned to himself. Prisoners fell down stairs. A few committed suicide; some were even killed whilst trying to escape. It was just a matter of choice. Those two peasants might luxuriate in the so-called protection of Cranston and their parish priest but they might be in for a very nasty surprise. In the meantime, these two delicious young wenches could strip each other and he would sport with both of them on the nearby bed. Blanchard cradled his blackjack as he watched one whore undo the buttons and clasps of the other's gown. The young prostitute prettily protested but started in genuine fear at the hammering and shouting from outside.

'Master Blanchard! Master Blanchard, we have visitors. We have . . .' The keeper cursed. He slammed the tankard down on the nearby overturned barrel, lifted a finger to his lips as a sign for silence from his 'two guests' and slipped out of the cell, locking the door behind him. Three turnkeys stood gathered around the grille high in the main door. Blanchard pushed them away, looked out and groaned. He reckoned there were five men, all wearing the black-and-white robes of the Dominican order.

'Master Blanchard?' The leading friar pressed up his face against the grill. 'I am Brother Marcel of the preaching order of St Dominic, Papal Inquisitor, despatched by no less a person than our Holy Father. I am his *legatus a latere* – accredited emissary and envoy of Holy Mother Church. I have sought an audience with Master Thibault and His Grace, the Bishop of London.' The friar withdrew his face and pressed a warrant against the grill so as to display the scarlet wax seals; this was then withdrawn.

'What do you want?' Blanchard slurred.

'The bodies of two traitors: Watkin the so-called

dung-collector and Pike the self-proclaimed ditcher. We have good evidence that these are not only traitors but self-professed heretics, followers of the accursed Wycliffe, sinners who have infected others with their foul contagion. They are to be surrendered into our custody. We hope that you will help us in putting them to the question.'

'Alleluia! Alleluia!' Blanchard slurred, indicating to his turnkeys to open the door. The friars slipped through, pulling their hoods close against the freezing cold in the passageway. The leader, Brother Marcel, grasped Blanchard's hand and pushed two silver coins into his palm.

'We need your help, Master Blanchard. Those two malignants have the names of others and we must break them swiftly.'

'But Cranston, his friar?'

'The coroner is simply a lackey of the secular arm. Brother Athelstan has acted *ultra vires* – beyond his powers. He is a simple parish priest and should not interfere in matters which are in *manus ordinarii* – in the hands of the bishop – in accordance with section seven of the Codex Juris Canonici – the Code of Canon Law. Now, the prisoner.'

Blanchard was delighted. He slipped the silver into his purse, collected the keyring from his chancery and, with three turnkeys carrying torches, led the Dominicans down the passageway to the prisoners' cell. He unlocked the door, swung it open and knocked aside the makeshift stool with its tankards and platters.

'Release them,' the Dominican demanded. 'Then, Brother, we shall need two of your men as an escort. The two prisoners are to be taken to the Tower to be questioned until they confess.'

'What are you doing?' Pike screamed, scrambling to his feet in a clatter of chains only to receive Blanchard's punch to his face. Pike stood swaying, staring at the Dominicans, mouthing protest. Watkin, face between his hands, rocked backwards and forwards, crying like a child.

'You are traitors and you are also heretics,' the Dominican's voice thundered. 'At the Tower you will be rigorously interrogated. Master Blanchard will assist us.' The threats continued to roll out as Blanchard unlocked the gyves. The keeper grinned at Watkin, pulling away the dung collector's fingers, only then did Blanchard's fuddled brain sense something amiss. Watkin had not been crying but laughing, his eyes bright with merriment. There was something wrong. If the Dominicans were from the Tower where was their escort? What did that warrant actually say? Blanchard's hand fell to his dagger but it was too late. The leading Dominican yanked back the keeper's head and sliced his throat in one deep, clean cut from ear to ear, whilst the others turned on the turnkeys and despatched them with swift dagger thrusts. Pike watched all four men quiver and jerk as they died, their blood spluttering out on to the filthy straw. He smiled and clasped the hands of Simon Grindcobb, Wat Tyler, Jack Straw and the two other leaders of the Upright Men.

'We borrowed the robes and shaved our faces,' Tyler murmured. 'We could not leave our friends here. Thibault and Blanchard cannot be trusted.'

'And we have always wanted to visit Master Blanchard.' Jack Straw kicked the dead keeper's body. 'We had more than a few scores to settle with him.'

'And now?' Watkin asked. 'Where do we hide?'

'Oh, you are not hiding.' Grindcobb laughed. 'We have the safest place in Southwark for you.'

oOoOo

Athelstan and Cranston knew fresh drama was awaiting them as soon as they turned into the narrow twisting alleyway leading up to St Erconwald's. The Piebald tavern stood eerily deserted. Merryleg's pie shop, which, with his large brood of children to assist, usually stayed open until the early hours of the morning, was all shuttered. The Fraternity of Free Love, a group of colourful characters who used St Erconwald's for their meetings, came hastily up behind them. They wouldn't even stop to answer Athelstan's questions but merely shouted that something was happening at the church.

'God knows that's true,' Athelstan groaned. 'The question is what mischief is brewing now?' They reached the enclosure before the church to find virtually all the parish had turned out. Gathering in groups, they were shouting at Mauger the bell clerk standing on top of the church steps. Athelstan heard the names Pike and Watkin mentioned. Mauger was shaking his head, throwing his hands in the air and, when he glimpsed Athelstan, cried shrilly as a cockerel greeting the dawn. The bell clerk virtually skipped down the steps, dragging Benedicta with him. He pushed his way through the crowd, almost colliding with Athelstan.

'Pike and Watkin!' he gasped, pointing at the open church door. 'Pike and Watkin!' he repeated. 'The Upright Men took them out of the Bocardo. Keeper Blanchard and three of his turnkeys lie slain. Pike and Watkin escaped; they fled here seeking sanctuary.'

Athelstan bit back his angry retort, brushed by Mauger and hastened up the steps into the church; the nave was freezing cold and black as pitch. The Hangman of Rochester had set up guard on the door through the rood screen. Athelstan pushed by him and strode up the sanctuary steps. The two miscreants crouched in the mercy enclave, warming themselves over a bowl of charcoal and sharing a pot of ale and a platter of diced meat, courtesy probably of the Hangman who dolefully followed Cranston into the sanctuary.

'Ye angels of heaven!' Athelstan exclaimed. 'What in the name of all that is holy?'

'Nothing to do with us, Father,' Pike brazenly declared. 'The Bocardo was attacked by the Upright Men disguised as Dominicans.'

'Dominicans!'

'Yes, Father, we thought they had been sent by you.' Pike's grin widened. 'It just goes to show you, doesn't it, that you cannot trust anyone. They slipped into the prison, executed Blanchard and his turnkeys for their many crimes against our community. The doors were left open and so we fled here for sanctuary.'

'Don't feed me your dish of lies!' Athelstan snapped, but at the same time the friar felt deeply relieved. Thibault was in a dangerous mood, whilst Athelstan could not forget the real sense of evil from the now dead Blanchard. Pike and Watkin were free of him, close to their families and parish, a clever, subtle move . . .

'Sir John?' a voice called. Athelstan turned. Flaxwith, cloak dripping, stood at the entrance to the rood screen, his ugly mastiff Samson as close to his muddy boots as any dog could get.

'Hell's teeth!' Cranston exclaimed. 'The scripture is correct: no rest for the wicked!'

Athelstan had a few admonitory words for his two fugitives and followed Cranston and Flaxwith into the nave, telling the Hangman to go and help Mauger and Benedicta. Once he had gone, the chief bailiff gave a pithy summary on what had happened at the Bocardo, interspersed by Cranston's quiet curses and Athelstan's exclamations of surprise.

'How do you know all this?' Cranston asked.

'From two young whores Blanchard had locked in the waiting cell. They won't be having the pleasure of him. Anyway, they heard the conversation, Pike and Watkin's exclamations and realized what had happened. Blanchard was tricked by Dominicans.'

'Dominicans.' Athelstan shook his head. 'I wonder where they got the robes from – but, there again, I am sure the Upright Men have chests full of what they need.' He laughed quietly to himself. 'Prior Anslem will have a great deal to say in Chapter, whilst Brother Marcel must be feeling highly embarrassed.'

'Very clever,' Cranston declared as Flaxwith let Samson out through the corpse door so the mastiff could run in the cemetery. Athelstan just prayed that Bonaventure and the dog did not meet, for the one-eyed tomcat nursed a passionate hatred for Samson which the mastiff replied in good measure.

'Very clever,' the coroner repeated. 'The Upright Men have taken Pike and Watkin out of the murderous clutches of both Blanchard and Thibault. Brother, I did not wish you to brood, but the Bocardo enjoyed the most sinister reputation. Blanchard was equally notorious for his senseless cruelty. In the meantime, no one will dare accost those rascals here, not in sanctuary at their parish church with its priest Athelstan a friend and colleague of the Lord High Coroner. No, no, they will be safe here, close to you, close to their family, and, if the worst happens, they can always swear to abjure the realm. The

Upright Men would give then safe escort to the nearest port. Brother, I will drink to them.' Sir John took a generous swig from the miraculous wineskin even as he quietly promised himself that he would have a hand in Blanchard's replacement. He glanced quickly at the friar. Athelstan seemed perplexed; he had turned away, staring through the open door of the rood screen as if trying to memorize every detail of what he was studying.

'Brother?' Cranston asked. There was no reply, so Cranston wandered over to examine one of the Hangman of Rochester's fresh paintings on the north wall. Sir John smiled. The scene described a story from the Acts of the Apostles about Peter being freed by an angel from Herod's prison. In the background was a river with what was probably Peter's barque, his fishing boat, though it looked more like a war cog on the Thames. Cranston narrowed his eyes. He knew what Athelstan had found and discovered on board *The Five Wounds*. Sir John had promised Athelstan he would not yet interfere, though the coroner had already instructed Flaxwith to approach Sir Robert and give him two warnings under pain of high treason. First, *The Five Wounds* must stay in its berth. Nothing must be unloaded from it. Secondly, Paston and his family were to reside at The Candle-Flame. If they left without his permission all three would be put to the horn as outlaws. Cranston now wondered what path Athelstan was following.

The friar was thinking the same himself as he stared across the sanctuary, his mind twisting and turning with snatches and glimpses of what he had seen and heard. Different voices echoed like the trailing verses of half-heard songs. Athelstan conceded to himself that he was now deep in the maze. He was certain of that. All he had collected, garnered and stored needed to be winnowed, sifted, crushed and milled to produce the truth. The reality of what happened was out there, that was logical. All he had to do was fit the pieces together, to reject what was false and to grasp what was real. The wine press was now ready, the grapes of God's wrath full to bursting. The dreadful sin of murder had been committed. Now the press would be turned. It was just a matter of time before it produced the juice of justice. Athelstan glanced over his shoulder.

'Sir John, we should go. But first, follow me whilst I preach the gospel, as it is, and as it shall be, to our two fugitives.' Athelstan then walked into the nave and called Benedicta and the bell clerk to join him. Once they had, he re-entered the sanctuary and lectured Watkin and Pike on what they could and couldn't do. He promised that Benedicta and Mauger, assisted by the Hangman, would bring them food, light and whatever else was needed for their comfort. Athelstan, however, had a few worries; the parish should protect this precious pair, whilst representatives of the Upright Men would soon take up position ever so cleverly around the church. What happened to Hugh of Hornsey would certainly not happen again. Athelstan then walked Cranston outside, where he immediately glimpsed a number of shadowy figures move in and out of the meagre pools of light. He was correct. The envoys of the Upright Men had already arrived. Thibault, on the other hand, would not be so hasty in coming here after the bloody affray at The Candle-Flame.

'You have questions, little friar? I can tell that from your face.'

'Of course, Sir John; it's the answers which elude me. Nevertheless, the mills of God are grinding, slowly but surely. Now look, Sir John, I need a guard, a good one. Men who will protect me and my house.'

'I will arrange that.'

'I also need a courier, the best you have, someone whom I can send into the city to fetch this and that.'

'Such as?' Cranston asked.

'Never mind, Sir John, just a good one. A veritable greyhound who can sally forth whenever I wish to parry out the truth.'

'Tiptoft,' Cranston replied. 'Tiptoft is the best. I will summon him tomorrow and despatch him to you. Oh, by the way, as you may know, the Pastons, their clerk and their cog will be going nowhere.'

Athelstan thanked him, absent-mindedly commenting on how brilliant the stars looked, blessed the coroner and ambled back to the priest's house. Benedicta was waiting for him inside. The kitchen, cleaned and scrubbed, glowed with warmth; the fire leapt merrily and the braziers crackled away. A bowl of pottage was warming in the small fireside oven and a jug of ale with Athelstan's finest pewter goblet stood on the table under a crisp, white napkin. Athelstan noticed the leather box beside it. Benedicta informed him how old Siward at Blackfriars had duly complied with Athelstan's request but begged his former student to take great care of the manuscript. Athelstan washed his hands at the *lavarium*, nodding his agreement. Bonaventure appeared, tail whipping the air, whiskers all a quiver, one eye glaring for his food. Benedicta chatted on about doings in the parish. Athelstan, now enjoying both the pottage and ale, half-listened. Once she had left, Athelstan wiped his hands, opened the leather case and took out the copy of *Beowulf*. He sat reading the Latin translation and abruptly his sleepy concentration sharpened. Athelstan had studied the poem during his novitiate; he also recalled it being read in the refectory during meals. Certain phrases and sentences, especially about the hero's battle exploits, made Athelstan tense with excitement.

'By their fruits ye shall know them.' He whispered a line from the scriptures as he stared into the fire. The Greek word for fruit was *karpos*; it could also mean how a man's inner spirit, for good or bad, would express itself in words and action. Athelstan sat for a while, applying this to the mysteries challenging him. He cut strips of parchment and began to list the images and memories of all that he had seen, heard and felt. He picked up his quill pen and wrote swiftly. The list would be fragmented. He would impose logic and order much later.

Item: The Candle-Flame on the night of the murders; Thorne going down to check the stables and discovering that battered wallet. Beowulf had been there. He'd planned for Marsen and Mauclerc's horses to rear and throw their riders the following morning, when he'd probably intended to strike both of them down. On that same fateful night, Sir Robert Paston went out into the gallery. He was met by that maid despatched by the Mistress of the Moppets to warn him how Marsen knew of

Paston's secret preferences when he visited The Golden Oliphant. Meanwhile, Hugh of Hornsey was closeted with his lover, Ronseval. They quarrelled. Hornsey was deeply concerned that Marsen did not discover the true nature of their relationship. Eventually Hugh of Hornsey left but came hurrying back when he discovered his two comrades were slain and the Barbican sealed and eerily silent. Others in the tavern were just as busy. The ostler Mooncalf met with Martha Paston and William Foulkes in the Dark Parlour and then outside. What did he want with them? Where were they going? On that same night Brother Marcel was definitely not at The Candle-Flame, he was elsewhere, whilst Brother Roger remained in his own chamber, apparently impervious to all that was happening around him.

Item: Inside the Barbican the window, its shutters and door were all sealed, locked and bolted, as was even the trapdoor to the upper chamber. Nevertheless, a killer, as deadly and as silently as a viper, had slithered into that forbidding tower and taken seven lives, seven souls brutally despatched to judgement. Who was responsible for that? How and why? The exchequer coffer was robbed. There was no sign of it being forced, whilst the keys to its three locks remained with their holders. So how could that happen?

Item: The following morning just before dawn, Mooncalf makes his grisly discovery. He goes out to find the two archers slain. Pedro the Cruel, the huge tavern boar, lies fast asleep in the mud; he is roused and wanders off. Mooncalf raises the alarm. Mine Host Thorne goes out to investigate. He has no ladder long enough, so one is placed on a handcart and fixed on that shallow sill. If Athelstan remembered it correctly, the handcart provided considerable length to the ladder. Mine Host climbs up, opens the outer and inner shutters, cuts through the horn covering in the door window and loosens that. However, due to his size, Thorne decides that Mooncalf should make the entry. The taverner comes down, the ostler climbs up and the gruesome discovery is made.

Item: The meeting in The Candle-Flame when he and Cranston made their first acquaintance with the guests. How did they react? What did he see, hear and perceive there?

Item: The discovery of the gauntlet and chainmail wrist-guard. The origins and ownership of these two items were now well established. Marsen was going to use them against Paston. What did that say, if anything, about the identity of the killer?

Item: The murder of Physician Scrope. What was the origin of that mysterious knocking on his door? Nobody was seen in the gallery. The physician had eventually opened it and, in doing so, sealed his own fate. A short while later, he was discovered murdered in his own locked and bolted chamber; his corpse slumped close to the door. Scrope died clutching a pilgrim's book on Glastonbury, open on the page listing some of the abbey's famous relics. How was he murdered? Why was he clutching that manuscript?

Athelstan recalled Lascelles being struck by the first crossbow bolt, and how he reacted before being hit by a final killing blow.

Item: Ronseval. Why did he slip out of The Candle-Flame? Whom did he meet? Certainly someone he trusted so much his killer could draw very close to him. And why was he killed? Did he know something? Yet, according to all the evidence, he never left his chamber that night.

Item: Hugh of Hornsey. Undoubtedly he panicked and fled. Nevertheless, Hornsey must have seen something which he kept to himself as he waited for better days. But what? And, like his lover, why had he trusted his killer so much he opened that heavy sacristy door?

Athelstan paused to allow Bonaventure out before returning to his list.

Item: The food and drink found in the Barbican were free of any taint or evil potion. Nothing illicit had been detected.

Item: On the morning they had left The Candle-Flame to visit Thibault at the Guildhall, Beowulf launched his attack on Lascelles. The stableyard was thronged and busy. Who had been there? Who was missing? Afterwards they had ridden through Cheapside. The Earthworms had sprung their ambush. How did everyone react?

Item: Those two shadowy figures who had returned to the execution ground to dig and scrape, undoubtedly Martha Paston and William Foulkes. And why the strange signs between them and Mooncalf? How significant was Tuddenham's remark about the Lollards sheltering a traitor close to their hearts?

Item: Sir Robert and what was stored in his cog. There were also the conversations and apparent friendship struck up between Paston and the Papal Inquisitor. Was Marcel hunting along the same path as he was? Did he suspect Paston might not be as orthodox in his religious beliefs as he should be?

Item: The rescue of Pike and Watkin by the Upright Men disguised as Dominicans, a most astute move. It certainly proved Cranston's remark to be correct. Friars, be it Dominican or Franciscan, could walk anywhere with impunity . . .

Athelstan paused in his writing at a scratching on the door. He opened it to let Bonaventure slip into the room, heading straight for his usual resting place in front of the hearth. Athelstan hurried to the buttery and prepared both milk and the remains of the pie, which Bonaventure deigned to eat before flopping back on the hearth.

'Thank God,' Athelstan murmured, 'you did not meet Samson.' Athelstan sat closely watching the sleeping cat as he mentally reviewed all he had learnt before returning to *Beowulf*, reading out loud the occasional line as if to memorize it.

'*Falsus in uno, falsus in omnibus* – false in one thing, false in all things,' Athelstan murmured. 'But that will have to wait a little longer.' He now turned to all the other manuscripts accumulated during his investigation. The memoranda drawn up in the Barbican; the warnings left by Beowulf the assassin; the *vademecum* from Glastonbury; the paltry poetry of Ronseval; and, finally, the lists of ships written by that enigmatic spy and carried by Ruat. Athelstan ignored the transcription, fixing his attention on the original. He stretched this out on the table, putting small weights on each corner. He opened his coffer and took out one glass of a precious pair of eye glasses, a gift from a brother at Blackfriars. Athelstan used these to scrutinize the manuscript. He found it clearer than before, the light was better and the manuscript had fully dried out. The actual letters emerged more distinct. Using the glass Athelstan studied the last few lines on both that and the transcript. He gasped in surprise. The document had been written in clerkly Latin but using the many abbreviations of the chancery: '*filius* – son' became 'fs'; '*apud* – at' became 'apd'; '*nostra* – ours' became 'nra'. Thibault had made two mistakes and Athelstan was astounded at the implications. 'I wonder.' He breathed. 'I truly do.' He was so excited he rose and paced the kitchen backwards and forwards, his mind racing about the possibilities and probable conclusions. 'Very well.' He sighed, staring at the crucifix nailed to the wall. 'Very well, let us say there are three, not two or even one.' Athelstan returned to his strips of parchment, writing a name at the top and listing all the evidence available. He stopped to eat and drink; only then did he realize how tiredness had caught up with him. He banked the fire, doused most of the taper lights and retired heavy-eyed to his bed loft. He tried to recite the night office from memory, only to drift off into the deepest sleep.

Bonaventure woke him just before dawn. Athelstan sleepily tended to him before building the fire and using the small bellows on the braziers. Eventually he broke from his half-sleep. He stripped, washed and shaved using water boiled over the fire. He took out new undergarments and his robe, dressed, drank a little water and left, making his way across to the church. Of course, the entire parish had assembled for the Jesus Mass, pressing into the sanctuary to catch a glimpse of the two fugitives openly regarded as heroes of the parish. Athelstan, now fully awake, just glared at the two miscreants, refusing to be drawn. He celebrated Mass and afterwards summoned the parish council into the sacristy. He told them he did not wish to be questioned or troubled and duly apportioned tasks for the day. Naturally, these included the care of Watkin and Pike. Athelstan repeated his short, sharp lecture on what the two fugitives could and could not do. Mauger, Benedicta, the solemn-faced Hangman and a nose-twitching Ranulf were left in charge. Flaxwith and his bailiffs appeared from their lodgings to announce four men-at-arms from the Guildhall would patrol the precincts to protect both church and house. Athelstan was pleased; the brutal attempt to burn him alive in the Barbican revealed the deeply sinful malice of the murderer he was hunting. Such a soul might plot fresh villainy. Athelstan returned to his house and broke his fast. A short while later Tiptoft appeared, slender as a reed and dressed completely in green with fiery red hair, with sharp blue eyes in a white, freckled face. Tiptoft slipped as silently as a thief into Athelstan's house, quietly announcing that he was here to act as Athelstan's courier.

'Sir John gave me my orders,' his voice was hardly above a whisper, 'and what the Lord High Coroner decides is my duty to follow.'

'Don't worry, I will have work for you,' Athelstan retorted. 'But first, you can be my escort.' The friar took his cloak from its peg on the wall. 'We shall visit The Candle-Flame. They left the house, two men-at-arms trailing behind as the friar and his green-garbed escort disappeared into the warren of Southwark's alleyways. Athelstan walked purposefully, head down, cowl pulled over, especially when he passed The Piebald, where all the great and the good of the ward met to discuss matters. Everyone was an expert with a story to tell and, of course, like attracts like. A wandering *chanteur* had also decided to exploit the occasion and set up his pitch outside the main door of tavern. He stood on a barrel, his powerful voice describing how 'the corpse of Ymir the frost giant' had led to the creation of heaven and earth. How Ymir's blood provided the seasonal lakes; the soil came from the corpse's flesh; the mountains from his massive bones; whilst the stone and gravel originated from the dead giant's shattered molars. He concluded how the first two humans had been fashioned out of pieces of driftwood washed up on the shores of Asgard. Athelstan paused to listen to some of this. It reminded him of the poem *Beowulf*, whilst he was always fascinated by how these professional storytellers always appeared when news was being hotly discussed. Was it simply, the friar wondered, that once people have an appetite to listen it had to be satisfied? Athelstan plucked at the sleeve of his escort and they moved on, pushing their way through the now crowded streets. The usual shifting shoal of the denizens of the seedy slums and tumbling tenements were out, busy on their usual trade of selling what they had filched and keen for fresh mischief. Athelstan noticed how the *chanteur* now had rivals. Thibault's assault on The Candle-Flame was clearly well known and the wandering gossipers were all offering dramatic accounts of 'Southwark's Great Battle'. Once they reached the tavern, however, Athelstan could detect little sign of the recent ambuscade. He met Thorne and his wife in the Dark Parlour, still empty as the Angelus bell had not yet summoned in the local traders and tinkers.

'Brother Athelstan?' Thorne wiped his hands on a napkin, which he passed to his wife. 'What do you want now?'

'You keep a journal of who stays here, who hires a chamber,' Athelstan waved a hand, 'and so on. I think you do.' He smiled. 'Mistress Eleanor, I understand you keep records as skilled as any chancery clerk?'

'Of course,' Thorne declared. 'I will show you.' He brought the ledger and Athelstan took it over to the window seat to study the entries. He leafed through the pages and soon found what he was looking for.

'It is as I thought,' he murmured. He rose, handed the ledger back and informed the taverner that he wanted to wander around The Candle-Flame so he could acquaint himself a little more closely. Thorne agreed and offered some refreshment. Athelstan refused and led his small escort out into the Palisade. All the remnants of the burning had been removed. The only scar was a stretch of blackened, ash-strewn earth where the execution stake had stood. Athelstan strode on. He pushed open the door to the Barbican and crossed to where he believed the inferno had been deliberately started. He calculated the size of the searing scorch mark against the wall. Athelstan stood staring; in his mind's eye he imagined the assassin slipping into the Barbican with sacks of oil. His assailant split the skins, dousing the cot beds and other furniture, then a flame would be thrown. Of course, before this happened, the assassin secured the trapdoor with bolts from below, thus trapping him on the upper storey. Athelstan shivered at what might have happened and shook his head at Tiptoft's questions.

'This is a seat of murder,' he whispered. 'And I have seen

enough.' Athelstan led his escort back outside. He walked
across the Palisade and paused to visualize what the assassin
must have seen on the night those two archers were murdered.
Satisfied, the friar returned to the tavern. He walked up the
stairs and inspected the loft chambers on the topmost storey.
He noticed in one gallery the narrow bed chambers overlooking
the stableyard and Athelstan, who had entered one room, realized he had a clear view of where Lascelles had been standing
the morning Beowulf had loosed that crossbow bolt. The friar
opened the small horn-covered door window. He leaned out,
pretending to be a bowman and, once again, tried to recall
those who had been with him in the stableyard below.
Afterwards Athelstan went down to the gallery where Scrope
had his chamber; both that and the one opposite were open,
being cleaned by maids and slatterns. Athelstan inspected each
room carefully before scrutinizing the bolt and lock on the
door to Scrope's chamber. He noted what he wanted as well
as the staircase at the near end of the gallery, which would
provide swift escape to the floor above. Athelstan, his mind
now buzzing like a beehive as he confessed to Tiptoft, thanked
Mine Host and made his way back to St Erconwald's. Two
relic-sellers tried to pester them, and Athelstan recalled the
relics described in Scrope's *vademecum* on Glastonbury. As
soon as he was back in his own house, Athelstan studied the
pilgrim's guide.

'*Sancta spina*,' he breathed, 'and, talking of holy things
. . .' Athelstan left and visited the church to have words with
Pike and Watkin. They seemed as happy as Bonaventure before
a fire. Benedicta and the rest had brought hot food as well as
a small tun of ale. Looking around the church, Athelstan was
amused at how pious his parishioners and others had become.
Usually at this hour, the nave would lie empty. Now people
wandered about inspecting statues, shrines and the chantry
chapel. Visitors clustered around the ankerhold, whilst another
group, escorted by the Hangman, seemed fascinated by the
different wall paintings. Athelstan smiled to himself. Watkin
and Pike were being closely watched by both friend and foe.
Leaving the church, he asked Benedicta to take Tiptoft and the
men-at-arms to The Piebald to break their fast, then begged

her to buy supplies for his own house. He asked her to spread the word that he was not to be disturbed; ordinary parish business would have to wait. After that Athelstan retreated into himself, locking himself away, chatting now and again with Benedicta and Tipftoft, whom he despatched into the city with sealed letters for Sir John and other individuals. For the rest, Athelstan sat at his kitchen table testing the hypotheses he had constructed: four strands, each of them quite separate and distinct but all intertwined around two different clasps, the season and the place. Eventually he received replies, all despatched in confidence, from the city. Athelstan's conviction that he was following the right path strengthened. He sent a letter to Sir Robert Paston, closeted against his will at The Candle-Flame. He instructed Tiptoft to deliver the letter, wait for a reply and spend the time making certain discreet enquiries amongst the servants. Athelstan, brooding on what might happen, became concerned that those whom he wanted kept at The Candle-Flame might slip away, so he petitioned Cranston to have a ring of steel placed around the tavern and two war barges stand off the quayside close to it.

Naturally this quickening of events attracted the attention of Thibault, whose spies kept a rigorous watch over St Erconwald's. The Master of Secrets sent Albinus, a sinister-looking mailed clerk and Lascelles' apparent successor, to make enquiries, which Athelstan deftly deflected. The two friars, Roger and Marcel, also objected, pleading benefit of clergy, the rights of Holy Mother Church and the pressure of important business. Athelstan replied that what he needed them for was the unmasking of murder and the restoration of justice; this was their God-given duty as much as his. Painstakingly, Athelstan continued to build his case. He spent three days on it before despatching Tiptoft late in the afternoon to ask Sir John Cranston to join him in sharing one of Merryleg's finest creations. Cranston arrived to find Athelstan's kitchen scrubbed clean, the platters, knives, horn-spoons, jugs and mazers glimmering in the light. Athelstan served freshly minced beef pie, a fine Bordeaux, pots of vegetables and sugared almonds to add, as he teased Sir John, a little sweetness. He reported how the two sanctuary men now lived

in the lap of luxury, being better served than My Lord of
Gaunt in his palace at the Savoy. Only when the friar fell
silent did Cranston lean across and squeeze his arm.

'What have you discovered?' the coroner asked.

'I cannot tell you, Sir John, not yet. It's not because I don't
trust you. I need you to listen and I need you to judge. You
will sit and hear the case I prosecute. Now, I have little
knowledge of the law,' Athelstan paused. 'Sir John, what
powers do you have, I mean, as a judge?' Cranston sipped at
his wine.

'Well, I am Lord High Coroner, a justice of the peace—'

'You have the power of *oyer et terminer*, to hear and decide?'
Cranston screwed his eyes up.

'I can, in times of great danger to the Crown, the realm and
the community, assume certain powers and listen to pleas of
the Crown.'

'I would like you to do that.'

'It will mean going to Thibault . . . Oh, no.' Cranston paused
at the look on Athelstan's face. 'You mean Gaunt?' Again the
look.

'Oh, sweet God in heaven,' Cranston whispered, 'the young
king himself?'

'Go to him tonight, Sir John, where he shelters at the Savoy.
Beg him for my sake to commission you as the king's own
justiciar in the wards of Southwark with special power to sit,
listen, judge and condemn at a special session to be held in
The Candle-Flame tavern.'

'When?'

'At the very latest the day after tomorrow.'

'But why, Athelstan?'

'Sir John, I swear, you will sit and have to judge heinous
offences: treason, murder, theft, blackmail and horrid
conspiracy. If these cases were referred to King's Bench or
an ordinary assize, certain people would flee and escape true
justice. Others, because of cruel threats against them, risk
being adjudged guilty as those who practice such cruelty.
Thibault would interfere. He is secretive but also a bully
boy. I want justice, Sir John, not revenge.'

'In which case . . .' Cranston lurched to his feet.

'Sir John?' Athelstan also rose. He went across to his chancery satchel and took out a roll of pure cream vellum, delicately sealed with red wax and tied with a scarlet ribbon. Athelstan handed this to Cranston.

'When you meet His Grace the king and go down on one knee, beg him to accept this humble petition from his loyal and true subject, Brother Athelstan, Dominican priest of St Erconwald's.'

The coroner weighed this in his hand. 'Little friar?'

'Please, Sir John.'

oOoOo

PART FIVE

'Mainpernor': surety for someone under arrest.

'Know ye now, Richard, by the grace of God, King of England, Scotland and France, Lord of Ireland, Duke of Aquitaine has appointed his faithful subject, Sir John Cranston, Lord High Coroner of London to be his own justiciar in all the wards of the king's borough of Southwark and those shires south of the Thames. He has, at our own pleasure and with full royal licence, power to hear, determine and to decide on all cases brought before him by Athelstan, Dominican priest of St Erconwald's in the above mentioned borough.' The royal herald, standing on a stool outside the entrance of The Candle-Flame, cleared his throat. He lowered the proclamation and stared at the two squires garbed in the gorgeous blue, scarlet and gold tabard of the royal household. Each of these stood either side of the herald holding a royal standard and were fighting to keep these steady against the buffeting breeze. Once satisfied they were, the herald continued.

'The said Sir John Cranston has the power of axe, tumbril, pillory and gallows both immediate and without appeal. Know ye too . . .' The herald's powerful voice continued to roll out the list of dire penalties imposed against anyone who tried to impede or obstruct. Such powers were being emphasized by the tavern being ringed by troops of the royal household, men-at-arms and archers under the personal command of King Richard's tutor, Sir Simon Burley, Knight Banneret of the royal chamber. Athelstan nudged Cranston and they entered the sweet-smelling Dark Parlour. All the furniture had been swept to one side except for a trestle table with a candelabra strategically placed to create pools of light around the insignia of the court: a bronze crucifix on its stand; a leather-bound Book of the Gospels close to where those summoned would sit; Cranston's commission bearing the seals of the royal chancery and his sword on one side of the manuscript; a small but cruel-edged flail on the other. At the end of the table Athelstan had laid out his writing materials: parchment, quill pens, ink horn, knife, pumice stone and sander. He had also arranged for a small crossbow to be primed and placed near at hand. Before the trestle table, now termed the 'Royal Bench', were three high-backed chairs for those who had been summoned to answer. The windows of the Dark Parlour were shuttered. Once in session the doors would be closed and guarded. No one would be admitted without Cranston's permission. Master Thorne had objected but Athelstan had assured him that any monies lost would be reimbursed by the royal exchequer. The taverner was given a brief, succinct lecture by Cranston on the rights of the Crown, how no one was to interfere with the administration of royal justice, how the tavern was to be sealed and secured by soldiers, whilst the herald and his entourage would signify the king's own presence.

Athelstan took his place on the chancery stool whilst Cranston sat on the cushioned judgement chair. The coroner looked every inch the royal justiciar with his black felt cap and ermined scarlet robe. Cranston had ensured the side table would be used to hold the refreshment he might need but not now. Athelstan was impatient to begin. After their supper meeting Athelstan had spent an agonizing day waiting for the king's response and, when it came, it was fulsome and direct. The king had also enclosed a personal letter to Athelstan as well as a sealed chancery roll. Athelstan had put these into his writing satchel. For the moment he had obtained what he wanted. The justiciar court would sit the following morning.

'Sir John,' Athelstan sharpened the quill pen, 'we are ready. We will use Tiptoft as our court officer.' Athelstan picked up the small hand bell and rang it. When Tiptoft appeared, Athelstan told him to bring in Sir Robert Paston, waiting with his family in the buttery. The merchant manor lord bustled in all red-faced, protesting volubly until Cranston roared at him to shut up and sit down. Athelstan rose, took the Book of the Gospels and thrust it into Paston's hands. He made him repeat the words of the oath, warning him that a failure to plead an answer was a felony which could be dealt with in the press yard of Newgate prison; Paston would be stretched out on the cobbles, a heavy door placed on him, then increasingly powerful weights dropped on top of that. He also warned him how perjury could mean that final journey in the death cart to the gallows at Tyburn or Smithfield. Athelstan accepted he was being dramatic but he had to hide all compassion in order to establish the truth and the sooner the better.

'Let us move swiftly to the heart of this matter,' Athelstan declared, taking his seat. 'Let us grasp the substance and ignore the shadows. You, Sir Robert, are a merchant, a manor lord, the widowed father of Martha, whom I suspect you love dearly; she in turn is deeply smitten with William Foulkes, a trained clerk, a skilled scribe and, I suspect, like your daughter, a fervent member of the Lollard coven, a disciple of Master John Wycliffe. Foulkes is very discreet. He has hardly spoken during my searches but keeps his own counsel and stays well out of my way. An educated man, Master William does not so much fear me but my order, who act, God forgive them, as the Inquisition of Holy Mother Church.'

'I . . .' Paston stuttered.

'Please,' Athelstan replied. 'For all I know, Sir Robert, you too may be a Lollard, but I don't want to know and I don't really care. I am not here to debate religious belief. I am not too sure what true heresy is but I am aware of the temptations of the flesh. You, Sir Robert, are a regular visitor to The Golden Oliphant, well known for the Mistress of the Moppets and her midnight ladies. I know of your games there. Please.' Athelstan ignored Paston's attempt to interrupt. 'You are also the owner of a handsome cog, *The Five Wounds*. You carry on a legitimate trade exporting wool and importing wine and other goods, all according to the law, except, of course, for those weapons purchased in Flanders, where the red-coloured oxhide roundel shields are popular. These are, of course, to escape the hawk-eye of the harbour masters, brought in piecemeal by ships of other nations. You have an agreement with their captains: you visit these and transport the weapons back on a barge to the armament store on board your own cog. You buy these weapons, bring them into London and put them at the disposal of the Upright Men. Hush now!' Athelstan insisted. 'As I said, these weapons are stored deep in the hold of your cog. They remain hidden until you are ready to send the wine and the other goods you have imported to different parts of Southwark and the city. I am sure your customers and clients are manifold: taverns, alehouses, hospitals, the mansions of the wealthy – all of course, in turn, provide excellent hiding places . . .'

'But the tavern masters, the merchants of the city, would have no dealings with the Upright Men and the Earthworms.'

'You do,' Athelstan retorted. 'Sir Robert, we know more than you think. Most prosperous Londoners are taking protection against the evil day. Moreover, what I describe is not difficult to organize. I suspect it's the servants, the retainers, the tapsters, the scullions and slatterns, the workmen and the labourers who are personally involved, whilst their masters look the other way. If such secret weapon stores were ever discovered, everyone would throw their hands in the air and declare they had no knowledge of what was happening. In addition, the Upright Men are very cunning. The more places they have to store weapons, the more they can scatter them around and the less obvious it will be. Coghill, master of *The Five Wounds*, tried to pass off the weapons I saw in the hold of your cog as the armaments to be found on any fighting merchantman. In fact, they are part of a secret hoard. The Upright Men and their Earthworms have, I wager, a myriad of such hidden caches all over this city and elsewhere. When they plan an attack such as the recent one in Cheapside, the summons goes out. I suspect they would have appeared whatever happened that day; they were fortunate in that a group of Thibault's retainers presented themselves. I suggest the Earthworms have a routine which is orderly as any monk's horarium: ponies housed in the countless stables across London are prepared, disguises are donned and weapons taken up, all swiftly carried out along that warren of needle-thin alleyways stretching either side of Cheapside. The Earthworms converge, attack then retreat. They have made their mark.

They have demonstrated how they can come and go as they wish. Once over, their mounts are left at the stables, masks are removed and weapons returned to their hiding place.' Athelstan shrugged. 'Of course, such locations can be discovered but it's like trying to stop the rain by catching its drops. New hiding stores are found, and so it continues.' Athelstan pointed a finger at Paston. 'Of course, the Upright Men value you because you provide a service which is quite exceptional.'

'I am sorry,' Paston mumbled, scratching the side of his face. 'I don't understand . . .'

'First, you hide weapons as well as transport them into the city along with your barrels of wine and crates of goods. More importantly, you import them. After all, where can the Upright Men purchase weapons in England without provoking the sharp interest of a royal official or one of Thibault's legion of spies? You buy them and bring all this weaponry into the heart of London.' Athelstan paused. He sensed Paston would not deny the charges but he wanted a full confession so he and Cranston could dig further.

'Why should I,' Paston tried one protest, 'a manor lord, a shire knight and a member of the Commons—?'

'Why indeed?' Cranston leaned forward then looked quizzically at Athelstan.

'Because the Upright Men are the same as you and I, Sir John. They are also privy to Sir Robert's secret pleasures at The Golden Oliphant. More importantly, amongst their own ranks are members of the Lollard sect. The Upright Men have enough evidence to indict Sir Robert's daughter and her beloved William for heresy. Marsen and Mauclerc were hunting for the same knowledge. They found something out about you and the Mistress of the Moppets but perhaps they sensed there was more. Do you remember Marsen baiting you about your own daughter here in the Dark Parlour? That salacious remark about Martha being sent to him? He was hinting at your secret life at The Golden Oliphant, whether your daughter knew about it or, perhaps, that she was involved in much more serious matters. Oh, yes,' Athelstan nodded, 'Marsen was a demon incarnate, a vicious, very dangerous man. If he could, he would have destroyed you and your family.' The manor lord now sat face in his hands and began to sob. Cranston looked at Athelstan, who just shook his head and put a finger to his lips.

'We are ruined anyway.' Paston took his hands away. 'I could be indicted for treason, even heresy. My lands and goods will be seized, my daughter and her beloved taken up for questioning.'

'Sir Robert, I assure you I am not here for your destruction. Such fear is not necessary, so compose yourself. Have you written the account I asked for? Did you keep it confidential to yourself?'

'Yes, every word.' Paston dug into his wallet, took out a scroll and handed it over. 'I dictated this to William Foulkes. I would trust him with my life.'

'And what did Foulkes say?'

'Like myself, on reflection he thought it very strange. I mean, Brother, it is. Once you start recalling this conversation or that.'

'I am grateful,' Athelstan murmured. He undid the scroll and read the neat clerkly hand. He was correct. Foulkes was an excellent clerk and the report provided chapter and verse – it more than confirmed Athelstan's suspicions on another matter. He read and re-read it until he was satisfied, then glanced up.

'You may stay, Sir Robert. I am now going to question your daughter and Master Foulkes. Rest assured I saw you separately; it would have been unjust to let her know about The Golden Oliphant.' Paston took a deep breath and sank down into his chair. Athelstan picked up the bell and rang it. Tiptoft, accompanied by Sir Simon Burley, came into the Dark Parlour.

'Sir Simon, all those summoned are being kept separate and closely guarded?'

'Yes, Sir John.'

'Very good. Master Tiptoft, bring Martha Paston and William Foulkes here. Sir Robert will be staying also.'

'And you have sent a messenger to St Erconwald's asking for that person to present himself here?' Athelstan asked.

'I have.'

'When he arrives I want him kept hooded and masked alone in some chamber; no one is to see him.'

Burley nodded his agreement. A short while later Tiptoft ushered Martha and Foulkes into the Dark Parlour. Looking highly nervous, they took the chairs either side of Sir Robert. Athelstan noticed how both young people were very soberly garbed in dark-brown robes. He wondered if the Lollards adopted their own distinctive dress: dark, unassuming clothing with little or no concession to frippery or fashion.

'Mistress Martha, Master William. Let me be brief and blunt. I know where Sir Robert was on the night of the murder. He was in the gallery above, restless about his own concerns, although I would hazard that he was also worried about you. On that same night both of you were preparing to leave with Mooncalf because both of you and the ostler are members of the Lollard sect. You were planning to go to one of your conventicles, though I suspect something much more serious happened. Didn't it? No, no,' Athelstan raised a hand, 'please don't protest. I remember the first time we met in the small refectory. I gave a blessing which as Lollards you could not acknowledge. Martha, you wear no religious insignia, nor do you, Master William. Lollards are as hot against such practices as they are against priests. You seem to tolerate my presence rather than welcome it. I also noticed the rather strange signage between yourself and Mooncalf. I am sure the Lollards, like every sect, have their own tokens so members can identify themselves to each other. I also watched you as poor Sparwell died. Why were you there? I don't think you are the sort of people to watch a man burn to death. You were present as witnesses, to offer some comfort and consolation, to demonstrate that he was not alone. You watched that horrible scene with profound sadness. I assure you, I too gave Sparwell what comfort I could. Sir John here did better: a goblet of drugged wine put Sparwell into a sleep close to death.' Foulkes held Athelstan's stare but Martha bowed her head, now and again quickly dabbing at her eyes. 'You later returned to collect what little remained of your comrade – shards of bones, shrivelled, blackened flesh. You wanted to provide a holy and decent burial performed secretly either in a London churchyard or some village cemetery when you returned home. I am sure, though it will not be necessary, that a search of your chambers would reveal a funeral urn as well as documents, handbills and prayer books – enough evidence to prove your Lollardy.' Athelstan tried to hide his compassion, though his heart went out to these two poor innocents stumbling towards a death as gruesome and horrific as Sparwell's.

'I will not lie,' Foulkes declared.

'I deliberately did not make you swear,' Athelstan murmured. 'Moreover, I am not too sure whether a Lollard would take such an oath or recognize its validity. I also wish to be kind. And believe me,' Athelstan rose and walked round the table and, standing behind Foulkes, stretched out his own hand to touch the Book of the Gospel. 'I swear by the living God,' Athelstan declared, 'I mean you no harm.' He withdrew his hand. 'I cannot say the same for your ostler friend, Master Mooncalf.'

'What do you mean?' Martha asked, all flustered.

'You know about him, don't you?' Foulkes asked, turning in his chair to face Athelstan, who'd now returned to his own seat. 'You know?' he repeated.'

'Yes, I do.'

'What?' Cranston barked.

'Sparwell was not denounced by an enemy,' Athelstan replied. 'I doubt if that poor tailor had any. He was betrayed by a traitor at the heart of the Lollard conventicle here in London. I believe that Judas to be Mooncalf. He went to the shriving pew at St Mary-le-Bow and gave Sparwell's name, trade and house to a priest. This priest did not hear it in confession so he had no choice but to pass such information on to the Bishop of London's curia. Mooncalf tried to remain anonymous, though the priest clearly recalls a coarse voice and the stench of the stableyard. Mooncalf would fit such a description. Now, on the evening the murders took place, he didn't take you to a meeting of the conventicle but to some lonely place outside this tavern. I am correct?'

'Yes,' Foulkes replied, ignoring Martha's cry of protest. 'I am committed to the truth. Mooncalf houses a wicked spirit. He informed us that he had denounced Sparwell and, unless we paid him good silver, he would betray us and others.'

'Did he make a similar threat to Sparwell?' Cranston asked.

'No, he did not.' Athelstan answered the coroner's question. 'Master Foulkes is correct. Mooncalf is possessed by a nasty spirit. Sparwell was the innocent lamb of sacrifice. He was both a warning and proof of what Mooncalf could do, that his threats, his blackmail, were potent and real. Yes, Master Foulkes?'

The clerk nodded his head.

'Many a man,' Cranston asked quietly, 'would have killed Mooncalf on the spot. He was a villain who not only threatened you but your beloved as well.'

'The Lollards are not like that, are they?' Athelstan offered. 'They are quietists. They reject violence of any sort.'

'Yes, we are,' Foulkes agreed. 'I once served as a cross-bowman. I saw service in Brabant, where my mother comes from. I have killed and seen killing. I confess,' he hurried on, 'when Mooncalf made his threat my hand fell to . . .' Foulkes smiled thinly, 'where my dagger should have been.'

'But Mooncalf had prepared for that, hadn't he?' Athelstan asked.

'Yes,' Foulkes admitted. 'He certainly had. He informed us how he had invested good silver in drawing up a bill of indictment which he had lodged with a notable serjeant of law at the Inns Court. He assured us that if anything happened to him, Mooncalf, the lawyer would immediately send the bill of indictment to the Bishop of London's curia. He told us that we each had to make a payment and he would never raise the matter again. He gave us until the end of this month. If we had not paid by St David's Day, he would denounce us as he had Sparwell.' Foulkes shrugged and stared at Sir Robert, who had sat through the questioning, hands on the table, staring down at the Book of the Gospels.

'Mooncalf,' Foulkes added slowly, 'said we would have to make a third payment for Sir Robert, not for any heresy but for lechery.'

'I confess,' Sir Robert raised a hand, 'that neither my

daughter nor Master William told me any of this directly, though I suspected.'

'Did Marsen know?' Cranston asked.

'I cannot say and I don't really care,' Sir Robert whispered. He lifted his head. 'My daughter thinks I may be responsible for his murder and that of the others.' He turned to face his daughter. 'You said as much with your eyes . . .' His voice trailed off and he sat as if deaf to his daughter's heated denials.

'You are Lollards,' Athelstan declared. 'You face harassment and persecution. Now tell me something. Whom do you fear, I mean, apart from the likes of Mooncalf?'

'The Bishop of London.'

'What about the Papal Inquisitor? Have you or your conventicle had any dealings with him?'

'No we have not. We raised this matter with Mooncalf. He simply replied that the Inquisitor meant nothing to him.' Foulkes spread his hands. 'What will happen to us?'

'Wait and see,' Athelstan retorted, 'for we have not finished.' He summoned Tiptoft and asked him to bring Mooncalf from where he had been detained in one of the loft chambers. A short while later the sweaty-faced ostler was pushed into the room. Mooncalf was all a-tremble as Athelstan indicated he sit on the stool at the other end of the table facing him. The friar then rose, picked up the Book of the Gospels and walked round, placing it before the terrified ostler. Athelstan demanded that Mooncalf put his hand on the book and repeat the oath he administered. The ostler did so in a harsh, stuttering voice. Once he had finished, Athelstan put the book back and returned to place his hand on Mooncalf's shoulder. The ostler was trembling so much he couldn't sit still.

'Sir John.' The friar winked at Cranston. 'What is the punishment for a blackmailer convicted on at least three or four counts?'

'Strangling.' Cranston's blunt reply rang through the chamber. 'Strangling on a special gibbet. However, according to ancient custom, blackmail ranks with heresy so it can mean hanging over a slow-burning fire.' Mooncalf moaned a long, drawn-out sound which came from the heart.

'You are a blackmailer,' Athelstan continued remorselessly.

'Three of your planned victims sit close by. Death, however, draws near. It stretches out its cold, skeletal fingers to seize you by the nape of your neck.' Athelstan moved his own hand accordingly. 'You are going to die, Mooncalf, just as horribly as Sparwell, whose innocent soul you sent for judgement.' Athelstan walked back to his own place. He warned Cranston with his eyes to let the silence deepen. They needed Mooncalf. If he cooperated, Cranston would inflict just punishment. 'You want to escape the rigours of the law?' Athelstan eventually asked. Mooncalf, half-choking, grunted his assent. 'Master Foulkes, you too want to assist me?'

'Of course,' the clerk replied.

'Good.' Athelstan rose and took a piece of parchment from his chancery satchel. 'You and Mooncalf will be taken to a private chamber. You will ask him the questions listed here. You will carefully write his responses. Mooncalf, I want the truth. Nothing more, nothing less. No additions or subtractions, just honest and accurate replies to very simple questions. Do you understand?' Mooncalf nodded, rubbing his hands together and peering nervously over his shoulder. Athelstan summoned Tiptoft and Sir Simon, giving them strict instructions how the Pastons should be kept under close guard. Foulkes and Mooncalf were to be given a separate chamber and the clerk furnished with all the writing necessaries he would require.

Once the door closed behind them all, Cranston rose, stretched and walked across to the side table. He filled a goblet with the sweet white wine and, at Athelstan's request, half a cup for the friar.

'Very good.' Cranston smacked his lips. 'I must remember that. The Piebald holds wine as good as its ale.' The coroner drank again. 'So the Pastons have nothing to do with Marsen's murder?' he asked.

'All things are still possible, Sir John. Until we have a full confession nothing is certain. I have certainly made mistakes.'

'Such as?'

'Foulkes is a learned scribe, a clerk from the schools . . .'

'And a former crossbowman? A possible suspect, like Beowulf?'

'Precisely, Sir John. Foulkes may now be a Lollard but,'

Athelstan laughed sharply, 'in my brief and sheltered life I have met priests, monks and friars who have killed, killed and killed again. The old proverb is true: "The cowl does not make the monk nor the tonsure the saint", which brings us to our next guest, Brother Marcel.'

The Inquisitor was full of himself as he strode into the Dark Parlour. Even from where he sat Athelstan could smell the perfumed oil rubbed into Marcel's smooth, shaven face. His robes were spotless, the strapped sandals a gleaming oaken brown. Athelstan offered him the Book of Gospels but he pushed it away, quoting certain clauses from canon law. Both the coroner and friar had met similar clerical recalcitrance before.

'Shall we, Sir John?' Athelstan turned to Cranston.

'Whatever you wish, Brother Athelstan.'

'What?' Marcel pushed his hands up the sleeves of his gown.

'Brother Marcel, I am going to have you arrested on a charge of high treason. You will be taken to Newgate Prison or the Tower, perhaps the latter. It contains a chamber called "Little Ease" dug beneath the level of the river so it sometimes floods. Rats swarm there. You will be held in such a place – what's the Norman French for it? Ah, yes: *Sous peine dure et forte* – punishment strong and hard. Of course, our order will argue for your release but the Dominican Minster General, not to mention Father Provincial and Prior Anslem at Blackfriars will find themselves in a veritable quandary.'

'What do you mean?' Marcel had now lost a great deal of his arrogance.

'Well, our order will argue all sorts of things. They will appeal to the Archbishop of Canterbury, Lord Sudbury, not to mention the Holy Father and sundry others amongst the great and noble. However, the allegations being levelled are those involving crimes against the English Crown, and they are not brought by some troublemaker but no lesser person than Sir John Cranston, Lord High Coroner of London, the king's own justiciar south of the Thames, and also a fellow Dominican, Brother Athelstan of Southwark. Oh, I am sure that eventually some satisfactory conclusion will be reached. Nevertheless, that could take months, even years, whilst you are left to float in the filth and foul stink of "Little Ease".' Athelstan paused. 'For the love of God, man, take the oath and let's have done with this business. You were given a task and failed. Logic dictates you have to answer. Years ago we clashed in the schools, we engaged in fierce debate – we shall do so again.'

'Take the oath,' Cranston snapped, 'or I will send for the guard.' Marcel had recovered his composure, drawing deep breaths, a faint smile as if he conceded he had panicked and made a mistake but that could soon be rectified. He placed his hand on the Book of the Gospels and repeated the words as Athelstan dictated the oath. Afterwards the Inquisitor sniffed and pushed back the chair so he could stretch his legs.

'I will dispense with the usual courtesies, Brother. You came to this kingdom as a Papal Inquisitor. Oh, I am sure,' Athelstan waved a hand, 'that the Holy Father has furnished you with all the necessary documentation. Indeed, my discoveries will come as a great surprise to him. I would even say a nasty shock. Brother Marcel, you are not just a Papal Inquisitor or a Dominican friar but the most secret emissary of Oliver de Clisson, High Constable of France. You were given privy instructions from him to discover and report on the strength and extent of this kingdom's naval power, particularly along the Thames and in the city of London.' Athelstan paused as Marcel sprang to his feet.

'How dare you!' the Inquisitor thundered. Athelstan clapped his hands as if applauding a mummer's play.

'Very good, Brother. There is nothing more engaging than outraged innocence when it's false.' Athelstan's smile faded. 'This is not some debating hall but a court of law. You must not forget the "Little Ease", where no one except the rats will be entertained by your false outbursts of hurt innocence. So sit down and let me continue.'

'Sit down!' Cranston roared. 'I am growing tired of this, Brother Marcel. Time is passing and we are very busy. If you are innocent, prove it, then dine with me, but you are not leaving this chamber until we have the truth. Or, if you wish, you can leave for the Tower.' The Inquisitor slumped back in his chair.

'You were also sent,' Athelstan continued, 'to discover as much as possible about the growing unrest in and around London. In addition you were told to seek out some military post which could be an advantage to any invading fleet. As we all know, Brother Marcel, England has lost its war in France. Our king is only a child; his self-proclaimed Regent is despised by both lords and commons. The peasants and the poor seethe with discontent. Tax collectors and others move across the shires like some pack of rapacious beasts. Our exchequer is empty. No wonder the French perceive a marvellous opportunity to bring war, fire and sword to this kingdom. To let us, God forgive us, experience the same destruction our armies wreaked in France, to teach us a lesson we shall never forget.' Athelstan sipped from his goblet. Marcel was now quiet and attentive. 'Good.' Athelstan breathed in. 'You, Marcel, are of Gascon parentage but, like many of your countrymen, you have come to resent any alliance with England. You see yourself as French through and through and you wish to prove that. You are a master of the University of Paris. I'm sure Monseigneur Clisson secretly approached you and your present mandate would only be a matter of manipulation. The papal curia has a good number of French cardinals. You have a praiseworthy reputation as a theologian and debater. You are of keen mind and sharp of wit, personable, charming and, of course, utterly ruthless in your quest. You were confirmed as Papal Inquisitor to England but, in truth, you are a French spy.'

'Brother Athelstan,' Marcel wetted his lips, 'what you say, well,' he shrugged elegantly, 'most of what you say could be the truth. But where is the evidence for your last claim?'

'First,' Athelstan countered, 'you arrive in England. I have made careful enquiries at Blackfriars. You spent little time at our mother house, whilst you made it very clear to me from the outset that you would not lodge in the Dominican parish of St Erconwald's. Consequently, instead of staying in one place, you move along the south bank of the Thames, a marvellous opportunity to scrutinize and assess the strength of English shipping. You take very careful note of various craft, the different fortifications and defences, anything which may be

of use to Monseigneur Clisson in Paris. You lodge at St Mary
Overy, a fact I shall return to, before moving here to The
Candle-Flame. This tavern is an ideal watching place; its
desolate Palisade and the towering Barbican would be of great
use should a French fleet breach our river defences and sail
as far as they can up the Thames, which is of course to London
Bridge, a mere walk away. The Candle-Flame would be ideal
for an invasion force to pitch camp. The French could launch
attacks across the river against the city, assault the Tower,
seize the bridge . . .'

   'Proof! Evidence!' Marcel shouted, yet beneath the pretended
outrage Athelstan sensed a deeply agitated soul, wary and
watchful.

   'You move to The Candle-Flame because of its location,
but also because Sir Robert Paston resides here during his
attendance at the Commons,' Athelstan declared. 'Paston is
an excellent quarry. Bitter, disillusioned and a publicly
vowed opponent of John of Gaunt, Paston is also an authority
on English shipping. You have marked Paston down whilst,
at the same time, you are moving through Southwark, a
hotbed of unrest and intrigue. Sir John here believes that
we friars are the only people who can move through the
slums, which lie only an arrow flight from where we now
sit. You take advantage of that. You visited my parish and
learnt all you could about the Upright Men, the Great
Community of the Realm, the coming revolt, but, above all,
you strike up conversations with the Pastons, Sir Robert in
particular. You feed his vanity, not that he needs much
prompting. Sir Robert holds forth, yielding all kinds of
information about English shipping.' Athelstan took another
sip of wine. 'Do you remember the afternoon I escaped from
the fire in the Barbican? I first climbed to the top of that
tower. You were there, provided with a spectacular view of
the ships, ports, quaysides and defences on both the north
and south bank of the river. Even better, Sir Robert was
holding forth, an excellent guide, a true source of sound
information. In truth, you had a man who could have been
Admiral of the Eastern Fleet providing you, a French spy,
with your heart's desire. To everyone else, you just appeared

to be a friar, a visitor to these shores asking innocent questions, perhaps developing an interest in shipping. To all appearances you are a Papal Inquisitor, not an expert on cogs of war or river defences. I remember when I escaped from the fire, you were preparing to meet Sir Robert yet again over supper. I suggest by the time that supper was finished you knew as much about English shipping as Master Thibault or any member of the king's council.' Athelstan held up a scroll. 'I asked Sir Robert to draw a report on what you and he discussed; only then, in the cold light of listing items, did Sir Robert become suspicious. He has confessed that quite deftly and cunningly you always brought the conversation back to caravels, hulkes, cogs of war and the state of English defences, be it the ships at the Tower quayside or those patrolling the estuary. I recall you at St Erconwald's. You were examining a war painting; you lectured Crim, our altar boy, on the difference between a cog and a caravel.'

'I enjoy looking at ships and talking about them,' Marcel countered. 'I have done so since I was a boy. We all have our interests. You, I understand, are fascinated by the stars.'

'No, Brother Marcel, your interest isn't shipping, your interest is in spying. Let me continue. On the night of the murders at The Candle-Flame you were lodged at St Mary Overy. Earlier that day Ruat, a Hainault sailor and your emissary, or at least one of them, to Constable Clisson, came here.' Athelstan glanced up. Marcel started plucking at his robe. Athelstan hid his quiet satisfaction; he had gambled, and would do so again, that Marcel knew nothing about the attack on Ruat, his brutal murder and Thibault's seizure of that most incriminating document.

'Ostensibly Ruat had been visiting the Shrine of the Virgin of the Narrow Seas; in fact, he visited St Mary Overy to collect this.' He pushed Thibault's documents towards the Papal Inquisitor. Marcel took one look, desperate to hide his agitation. 'You gave Ruat a comprehensive report on shipping and the naval defences along the Thames. You also gave him a purse of silver. By chance Ruat came here to celebrate his good fortune. He drank, became merry and hurried across the river to his ship berthed at Queenhithe. Unfortunately, within a short distance of that vessel, Ruat was assaulted, robbed and killed, his corpse thrown into the river. The perpetrators were caught and hanged out of hand. Ruat's dead body was dragged from the Thames. Your report to Clisson was found on him, waterlogged but still decipherable.'

'It was not mine. I don't know . . .'

'It's obvious that Ruat's death and Thibault's discovery remained unknown to you. You thought Ruat was safely despatched back across the Narrow Seas. Nor did you realize that, later that same day, a drinking dirge was held in Ruat's memory here at The Candle-Flame.'

Marcel stared back, his shock obvious.

'As for proof,' Athelstan pressed on, 'well, we could compare your handwriting with that of the report. I am sure there is a very strong resemblance.'

'Nonsense!'

'Oh, there is more than just handwriting. At the end of this document,' Athelstan kept his tone conversational, 'there is a sentence. Thibault deciphered and translated it as "I reside at The Candle-Flame, 16 February",' Athelstan shrugged, 'the same evening the murders took place here. Thibault, however, was incorrect. The manuscript was water-stained. Your use of a cipher and the usual abbreviations of a trained chancery clerk make its study more difficult. Thibault thought you wrote *resideo* – I reside; in actual fact you use the future tense, *residebo* – I shall reside – a simple, understandable mistake. Thibault also overlooked another word, because it was faded and abbreviated, the Latin word *post* – after. Once we correct this sentence it reads, "I shall reside at The Candle-Flame after 16 February." I investigated this with Mine Host. I have closely inspected the tavern ledger. You, Marcel, are the only person who, days earlier, hired a chamber for after 16 February. You hired a very comfortable one. You wanted to make sure that you would be well housed and fed.' Athelstan paused. 'I can show you the ledger?' Marcel simply waved a hand. 'There is more. You are supposed to be a Papal Inquisitor, that's the proclaimed reason for your arrival in this kingdom. By your own admission you have a special interest in the Lollard sect. However, when I ask Lollards about you, including one imprisoned and condemned to death in the Bocardo, they make no mention of you. I am sure, and I can check this, that Master Thibault must have told you about Sparwell. What a splendid opportunity to find out more. You could have visited him.' Athelstan paused. 'Indeed,' he smiled, 'if you had, Blanchard would have met you. He would have been prepared for the imposter which led to two prisoners escaping and the keeper himself and some of his turnkeys being brutally slaughtered.'

'I heard about that,' Marcel snapped. 'Such men should be rigorously punished.'

'That's not your concern,' Athelstan declared. 'My point is that you have shown no real interest in the Lollards. That's not just my opinion but that of the Bishop of London's curia. Of course, you believed no one would dare challenge a Papal Inquisitor going about his business. My question is very simple. What business? According to all the evidence it is English shipping rather than English heresy. Finally,' Athelstan glanced down as if he was studying a document, when in fact he was quietly praying that Marcel would step into the trap, 'what you also don't know is that Master William Foulkes once served in Brabant as a crossbowman. On the afternoon Ruat came here to celebrate in the Dark Parlour, he struck up a friendship with Foulkes, whom he regarded as a Brabantine, an ally of Hainault. Ruat informed Foulkes how you had given him the silver—'

'Ruat couldn't have . . .' Marcel stopped his outburst and closed his eyes, a gesture of defeat. Athelstan sat watching the flame on the nearest candle burn away another ring. He allowed the silence to deepen, broken by a knock at the door. Sir Simon Burley came in. The knight placed a sheaf of documents before Athelstan and left just as quietly.

'You were going to say, Brother Marcel, how Ruat could not possibly know because you met him deep in the shadows of St Mary Overy. Yes? But who would know the truth about that except you?' Athelstan stared down at the documents, sifting through them quickly. 'We have ransacked your chamber and been through your chancery satchel. No, please spare us your protests. And what do we find? What looks like an innocent list

of ships, including Sir Oliver Beresford's great new war cog
out of Yarmouth now berthed at Baynard Castle. So . . .'
Athelstan gestured at Marcel.

'I admit,' Marcel waved his hands, 'that in the interest of a
lasting peace between England and France, I decided to take
careful note of England's naval strength whilst here on papal
business. My motive was to discourage the French from any
hostile action.' He paused at Cranston's snorting laughter. 'I
appeal to a higher court. I plead benefit of clergy. I demand
that as a subject of the king of France I be returned safely to
that kingdom or to one of its officers here in England. Finally,
I am a Dominican—'

'You are a spy!' Cranston broke in. 'You will be detained
as such until His Grace, Richard King of England, Ireland,
Scotland and France,' the coroner emphasized the last word,
'decides what to do. Brother Athelstan?'

The friar summoned Tiptoft, who brought back Sir Simon
and a military escort. Cranston gestured that the Papal
Inquisitor should go with them. Once their footsteps in the
gallery outside faded, Cranston and Athelstan left the table
and quickly ate some of the food the friar had bought together
with white wine in a sealed jug, a gift from The Piebald.

'The mills of God, eh, little friar?'

'Yes, Sir John. The mills of God are grinding slowly but
surely. Nevertheless, deep in my heart, nothing we do in
this chamber will fully restore God's justice or his harmony.
All we can do is deal with mortal sin and its malignant
consequences.' Athelstan finished his food then washed his
hands and face at the *lavarium*. Cranston also prepared
himself, leaving the chamber for the garderobe. Once he
returned, Athelstan asked Thibault to fetch Brother Roger.

oOoOo

The Franciscan sauntered in as if attending a colloquium, a
friendly debate in some refectory. He blithely took the oath
and sat with an amused smile on his face as if rather surprised
at the proceedings.

'*Ic waes lytel?*' Athelstan asked.

'When I was little,' Brother Roger translated. 'My friend, I did not know you were skilled in the Saxon tongue.'

'I am not but you certainly are. You are Roger Godwinson, that's your family name. You claim descent from the ancient royal Saxon family displaced by William the Norman.'

'Roger Godwinson,' the Franciscan agreed, becoming more wary.

'A scholar of the Saxon tongue as we have just proved and you have admitted,' Athelstan replied. 'A man recognized in his own order, by the ancients who taught him at Greyfriars, as a scholar deeply immersed in the study of all things Saxon. A man who, by common recollection, studied the poem *Beowulf* and could quote it line by line. Indeed, time and again, ever since we met, you have unwittingly quoted verses from that poem.'

The Franciscan raised his eyebrows.

'Three examples will suffice,' Athelstan replied, 'though I could quote others. First, when the Earthworms attacked us in Cheapside you made a unique reference to fighting as long as the World's Candle shines, a phrase quoted directly from Beowulf. Secondly, after I escaped from the inferno in the Barbican, you talked about your fear of fire and how each man nursed his own special fear within him. You also joked about how I had escaped from the Dragon's breath. Again, direct quotations from Beowulf. Finally, when we first met, you referred to "this fierce hostility, this murderous lust between men", a phrase which can also be found in your favourite poem.'

'So I quote lines from an ancient poem,' the friar laughingly replied. 'There is no crime in that.'

'A Franciscan,' Athelstan pressed the point, 'who also travels the shires around London begging alms, one who was always in close vicinity when Beowulf, that secret assassin, attacked Master Thibault's minions.'

'You are accusing me of being Beowulf. You are, aren't you?'

'Yes, I am. Let me lay my indictment against you.' Athelstan emphasized his points on his fingers. 'First, you are very proud of your Saxon heritage. I have proved this and you have admitted it. Secondly, as a novice at Greyfriars you won a reputation of being steeped in your heritage as well as proving yourself to be a scholar in both the tongue and literature of the Saxon people. I understand that.' Athelstan tapped his chest. 'My own family also claims descent from the ancient earls, hence my own name which, as you know, is also that of a great Saxon king. I have proved this and you have admitted as much. Thirdly, even in conversation you make reference to your Saxon heritage and, in particular, that great epic *Beowulf.* Indeed,' Athelstan smiled, 'you know more about Erconwald, the great Saxon saint, than I do. You are undoubtedly a fervent student of all things Saxon, including their sermons, which often quote those ominous words from the prophet Daniel about God numbering, weighing in the balance and being found wanting. Only a scholar, albeit a very arrogant one, could quote such a phrase in its original tongue. Fourthly, you have a licence to beg for your order in and around London. You move in a circuit from place to place residing where you wish . . .'

'You have proved that and I admit it.' Friar Roger mockingly echoed Athelstan's phrase. 'But tell me, where is the wrong in that?'

'Fifthly,' Athelstan moved inexorably on, 'every time one of Thibault's minions is attacked you are close by on your so-called begging circuit. Indeed, I believe Marsen, despite his wickedness, was also a man of sharp wit; he was growing increasingly suspicious about you. He once made reference that he knew someone was following him but that he would take care of it in his own way. Marsen was also a killer. He would know how difficult it was to challenge you; after all, you are a priest, a Fransiscan. I believe that one day, and that day would have come sooner than you think, Marsen would have tried to murder you. Indeed,' Athelstan pointed at the Franciscan, 'I openly concede that what I say here is garbled. Marsen, deep in his cups, once referred to Beowulf then to slaying the Wolf of Guttio. Why should he say that? He was in fact referring to St Francis of Assisi who in his life tamed the savage Wolf of Gubbio. Marsen, or his listener, in this case a prostitute, mismatched the words. St Francis took care of the ravenous Wolf of Gubbio. Marsen would take care of his Wolf of Gubbio, which mistakenly became Guttio, a worldly friar, very much a wolf in sheep's clothing – a skilled assassin. Marsen was parodying a story which, in its original, exemplifies all the idealism of the Franciscan Order. Furthermore,' Athelstan tapped the manuscripts in front of him, 'Sir John provided me with a list of places and times when Beowulf was attacked. I also asked Father Guardian at Greyfriars to send me an extract from the alms rolls, a true record of what monies you collected, where and when. Friar Roger, there is virtual concordance between the places where such attacks occurred and your whereabouts.' Athelstan stared at the Franciscan. Brother Roger was now more attentive and not so supercilious. *You are all the same*, Athelstan reflected. Murderers are steeped in sin which is always rooted in a deep pride. You truly believe you are superior to everyone else. You think you have a God-given right to judge, condemn and execute as you think fit.'

'I believe Athelstan has proved his point,' Cranston observed, 'but whether you admit to it or not . . .?'

'Who do you think you are?' Athelstan decided to taunt his opponent. 'Some great Saxon hero defending the poor with your sly, furtive attacks, arrows whipping out of the darkness? The real Beowulf didn't do that. He confronted the monsters, met them face-to-face in heroic combat.'

Friar Roger just sat, lip jutting out. He glanced swiftly at Athelstan and gently shook his head.

'The same happened during Marsen's journey to The Candle-Flame: he was attacked at Leveret Copse. According to your Father Guardian you were close by. You lodged at this tavern to plot fresh mischief. You planned to strike on the morning of the seventeenth of February. The previous evening you entered the stables and placed miniature caltrops under the saddles of both Marsen and Mauclerc's horses. The next morning they would hoist themselves in the saddle, ready for another day's wickedness. They would drive the caltrops into their horses' backs. The animals would rear in agony and both men would be thrown, at least injured, and so rendered suitable targets for you and your crossbow. In the end your plot was overtaken by another more deadly. Nevertheless, a more important target presented itself when Lascelles unexpectedly arrived here.'

'You cannot prove that. I was preparing to leave for the city.'

'Seventhly,' Athelstan pressed on like a lawyer before King's Bench, 'I know from my enquiries that Lascelles arrived here cloaked and cowled. No one was expecting him. Only when he reached here did he pull back his cowl, reveal himself and begin an argument about whether the tavern gates should be closed or not.'

'Which means?'

'Listen now,' Athelstan urged. 'I had met you earlier. You were all ready to leave. Consequently when Lascelles arrived you acted swiftly. You slipped out into the street and gave that beggar boy the hastily scribbled note and a coin. You then returned. Like the professional assassin you are, you know all there is about The Candle-Flame: the different galleries, empty chambers and lonely vantage points. Beneath your cloak you carry an arbalest and a quiver of bolts. You tried to kill Lascelles but failed because of me. Now, I recall vividly who was in the yard that morning when the attack took place. You certainly weren't!'

Friar Roger simply stared back.

'Thorne was talking to Mooncalf. The Pastons and William Foulkes were closeted together in the Dark Parlour both before and after the attack. Ronseval was also in the yard. The only person missing was you.' Athelstan moved the parchment before him. 'You came down later and, as an act of impudence, asked to join Lascelles' escort into the city. Later, when you visited St Erconwald's, I mistakenly made reference to Pike and Watkin being involved with the Upright Men. I saw you cultivate them when you visited St Erconwald's. I have questioned them. They distinctly recall you asking both where they lived; in fact, they invited you to their houses. This is my ninth charge against you. You used that knowledge to provoke that conflict here at The Candle-Flame. You knew where Pike and Watkin lived. You are a friar, popular with the people and certainly on good terms with those leading lights amongst the

Upright Men, Watkin and Pike. Once twilight had fallen, you slipped along to their houses dressed in a simple robe and hood and delivered those messages about Marsen's treasure still lying here at The Candle-Flame. All you had to do was wait for them to leave for their muster. You knew they would. The Upright Men would be delighted to steal such wealth from Master Thibault. Only then do you send that letter to the Guildhall and bring about the confrontation. The Upright Men disappear but Thibault and Lascelles remain. Of course, everyone in the tavern is alarmed. Once again, you choose your vantage point, strike and kill at least one of your intended victims.' Athelstan fell silent, tapping the table with his fingers. 'Brother Roger, let me weave all this together. Your Saxon heritage, your absorption with the epic *Beowulf*, your constant quotations from it, your presence close in time and place to all the assaults, successful or not, against Thibault's minions and Marsen's veiled allegations against you. Then your presence in The Candle-Flame when those saddles were primed so the horses would rear and throw their riders. Your whereabouts when Lascelles was attacked in the stableyard and, again, after the Earthworms occupied The Candle-Flame. Your knowledge of Pike and Watkin being placed amongst the Upright Men as well as where they lived. Finally, and I admit only I know this but cannot reveal all as I have not yet finished, the elimination of other possible suspects leaving only you. Of course,' Athelstan gestured towards the door, 'a search is now being carried out in your chamber and all your possessions.'

'Sit down!' Cranston bellowed as the Franciscan sprang to his feet. 'Sit down,' the coroner repeated, 'or I will have you chained. What does it matter, Brother Roger, the case weighs heavily against you. If all this was submitted to a jury they would, I assure you, return a true bill of indictment for murder, treason and a litany of other felonies.'

'I am a Franciscan!' Friar Roger shouted back. 'My order works with and for the poor. I am a true son of the soil. I wander the shires of this kingdom and see the lords of the soil bully, harass and exploit the humble. So yes, I am like Beowulf: I fight monsters, I slay them.'

'No one gave you that right,' Athelstan countered.

'I will not confess to you what I did or why,' Brother Roger sneered. 'I plead benefit of clergy. More importantly, I quote the constitutions of my order accepted by Holy Mother Church and the Crown of England that I can only be questioned, tried and, if found guilty, convicted by my own Minister General in full chapter at our mother house in Assisi. I appeal to that process. I will not, shall not say any more.'

'Nor shall you,' Athelstan retorted. 'You, Brother Roger, are a killer, an assassin. You are not the son of the Poor Man of Assisi, the great St Francis, but the offspring of Cain. You are as arrogant as the Lord Satan, full of false pride at your heritage. You decided not to pray or administer to the poor but act as their so-called, self-proclaimed champion in slaughtering those you, and only you, consider worthy of death. You have made yourself your own idol, turned yourself into a graven image of God himself.' Athelstan rang the hand bell. 'Think, Brother, think long and hard. Do not be so proud or confident. Remember the words of the psalm: "Put not your trust in Egypt, nor your confidence in the war chariots of Pharaoh or the swift horses of Syria. God's power is the truth." Athelstan slammed the bell down, rose and walked away as Cranston supervised the Franciscan's arrest, instructing Burley that Brother Roger be chained and kept under close watch. The door had hardly closed when a ferocious knocking brought Athelstan back. Tiptoft stood there with William Foulkes.

'He has something for you,' the messenger declared. Foulkes handed over the small scrolls detailing Athelstan's questions and Mooncalf's answers. Athelstan swiftly read the latter and smiled. He had what he needed.

'Ask Mine Host,' he declared, 'to bring us some wine.' A short while later Thorne, aproned and carrying a tray, came into the chamber. He put the tray down on the side table. Athelstan walked to the door and opened it. He had warned Tiptoft before and felt reassured at the crossbowmen, all wearing the royal livery, quietly taking up their position outside. Athelstan sketched a blessing in their direction and walked back to Thorne, who was tutting under his breath at the food and wine Athelstan had brought from The Piebald. Cranston stood looking rather perplexed, though the coroner

sensed danger and his right hand now rested on the silver-
hilted dagger in its sheath beneath his cloak. Athelstan clapped
the taverner on his shoulder.

'Take off your apron, Master Simon,' he urged, 'and there
is no need for this either.' He plucked the dagger from the
taverner's belt, threw it on the floor and kicked it away.

Thorne raised his big, muscular hands. 'Brother Athelstan,
what is this?' he protested. 'Why do you bring wine and food
to my tavern?'

'I don't want to be poisoned,' Athelstan retorted. 'I don't
want to be sent into that sleep close to death. Sit down, Master
Thorne. Take the oath, for your very life is to be challenged.
You are a true brother of the man we have just questioned.
Like him you have murdered and snatched the souls of others
out of this life and hurled them unprepared into the eternal
dark.'

Thorne staggered back, his hand clawing for where his
dagger should have been, but Cranston had slid behind him
and the coroner's razor-edged sword brushed the side of his
neck.

'Sit down, Thorne!' Athelstan almost pushed the taverner
into the chair in front of the table. 'Simon Thorne.' Athelstan
took his seat as Cranston, hiding his own surprise, went to sit
opposite the accused.

'Simon Thorne,' the friar repeated, 'I formally accuse you
of murder on many counts.'

'This is not true!' Thorne made to rise.

'I wouldn't leave that chair.' Cranston leaned across the
table, his podgy finger jabbing. 'You must not leave that chair.
You will remain silent or I shall order the guards to bind and
gag you.' Cranston tapped the hilt of his sword, its blade
pointing towards Thorne. The taverner slumped back. Athelstan
studied the accused's hard, muscular face, the pock-marked
skin drawn tight, the slightly bulbous eyes bright with cunning
and fear. The taverner was sweating, his breath heavy. Now and
again his thick fingers would scratch at his black, wiry hair.
Athelstan recalled their first meeting. He quietly marvelled at
how so many individuals could hide their true soul, the *karpos*,
as he called it, the dominant spirit which could shift, hide and

lurk for a lifetime yet rarely manifest its true self. Athelstan
had plotted this carefully. Once he had eliminated others, logic
and evidence pointed to this guilty taverner. Athelstan had
been anxious lest Thorne discover that he was suspected. Flight
from the law was common enough. Men disappear never to
be seen again. Thorne might lose his tavern, but he would take
with him the stolen treasure from where Athelstan suspected
he had hidden it and flee to any part of the kingdom or beyond.

'Master Thorne, you are a taverner. I know very little of
your previous life. I understand you fought in France. You
were a captain of hobelars. Now, Sir John, correct me if I am
wrong, but a hobelar is a man-at-arms and a bowman? Not
just one of the levy but skilled and seasoned. Hobelars are
often used as scouts or despatched under the cover of dark to
kill enemy sentries before a night attack is launched.'

Thorne just glanced away.

'You know that to be true,' Cranston remarked quietly. 'You
have as much experience in war as I have.'

'I simply say that,' Athelstan declared, 'to demonstrate that
you, Thorne, have killed, albeit the king's enemies. I suspect you
were very good at it. You amassed considerable wealth from
the war in France. Your first wife dies and you marry again.
You invest in this tavern. Of course, you wonder sometimes,
more often than not, whether it was such a prosperous venture.
London seethes with unrest. When the Great Community of
the Realm raises the black banner of anarchy, I truly believe
that Southwark will burn. Oh, you make payments to the
Upright Men and you also curry favour with Master Thibault,
but you know that that can't save The Candle-Flame from
devastation. Now, your wife Eleanor is the daughter of a
tavern keeper who owns the The Silver Harp on the Canterbury
road. Last summer the assassin Beowulf successfully attacked
and killed Justice Folevile, one of Thibault's horde of tax
collectors. Of course, families meet and mingle. You must
have heard about such an attack and, I suspect, the seeds
of the heinous murders committed here were sown: a plot
to seize a treasure which would be your surety in the time
of trouble.'

'You are very much mistaken,' Thorne spluttered. 'I . . .'

'I shall prove I am not,' Athelstan replied. 'Marsen arrived here with his treasure chest. He was a most unsavoury character, Mauclerc not much better. You leave them to their own devices. Mooncalf serves the food whilst you visit occasionally. We know the reason why and I shall return to that later. In the main, you act the busy taverner who resents having to pay court to the likes of Master Thibault, as well as contribute just as secretly to the Upright Men. You hate them both but, as I've said, you have your own devious plan to escape the coming fury. Undoubtedly I could summon your father-in-law from The Silver Harp on the Canterbury road. I would place him on oath. I am certain that he will agree with me that he provided you with a very detailed description, at your insistence, of the crossbow bolts used to kill Folevile and others. I am more than certain that he would have repeated those mocking verses taken from the prophet Daniel. A search of your muniments will reveal a copy. I could ask why a taverner has written down such verses.'

'There is no law against that!' Thorne retorted. 'True, I have heard the verses before. I find them compelling, like many lines from the scriptures. I, too, am a scholar, Brother Athelstan, learned in my horn-book. I have read the scriptures, I understand Latin. Certain verses, as I have said, appeal to me.'

'Oh, I am sure they do.' Athelstan smiled. 'Such as "By their fruits ye shall know them". But to return to my indictment. On the night of the murders, you pretended to be concerned about a possible intruder in the stables.'

'But there was one!' Thorne beat against the table, hastily withdrawing his hand as Cranston's fingers fell to the sword lying close to him.

'Oh, I know there was an intruder. However, on that particular evening, you used that as an excuse, a pretence to explain your absence from your own bed. Master Thorne, I shall be swift. You had planned well and your motive was the oldest of sins – pure greed. You must have seen the heavy exchequer coffer during your visits to Marsen. You observed how he loved to throw back the lid to glory at the gold and silver heaped within. There was no need for any keys. Marsen thought he was safe. He had a guard of six veteran archers and he was locked and secured in the formidable Barbican. You did see the gold and silver, didn't you?' Thorne grudgingly nodded his head. 'Such a sight would only whet your appetite and hone your greed. Under the cover of darkness you took a stout cask of your famous ale from the cellar. You pulled back the bung and poured in a very powerful sleeping potion. You walked across the Palisade and stopped before the campfire. Two of the archers were there but, of course, Hugh of Hornsey was missing. You would know that, wouldn't you? Because you keep everything under close watch, yes, Master Thorne?' The taverner, now more wary than angry, simply stared back. 'Hornsey and Ronseval were lovers. You knew that because they had lodged in your tavern before. I have inspected your chamber ledger; your wife is very methodical. The last time they were here was during the festivities at Christmas. Of course, they stayed in separate chambers, but that was only a pretence. They had to protect themselves against being discovered, public humiliation and execution. I shall return to both these victims of your murderous heart. On the evening in question, however, you offer cheer to those two archers. They are cold, tired and of course they would love to sample your tastiest ale, which I am sure is markedly better than what the niggardly Marsen bought for them. Moreover,' Athelstan gestured to his right, 'I made discreet enquiries with your cook. I understand that on the night of the murders you helped him prepare the dishes for Marsen and his comitatus. He recalled you making the capon highly spiced and very strong, which of course only deepened their thirst. You fill their blackjacks and wait. They drink and soon lapse into sleep. I suspect the potion was very strong and would soon have an effect. You then take the tankards and empty what is left of the tainted ale on to the ground. You use the common ale the archers have brought out with them to clean those tankards as well as remove any trace of the sleeping draught.

'Juice of the poppy?' Cranston asked.

'Perhaps,' Athelstan replied. 'You have some here, Master Thorne?' Again the only reply was that hard, unblinking glare. You tried to murder me, Athelstan thought. You are quite prepared to watch me burn a horrible death simply to conceal your own dire, wicked acts. I was to be silenced so you could hide your host of mortal sins.

'Brother?' Cranston asked.

'*Quieta non movere, quieta non movere*,' Athelstan declared, 'let sleeping dogs lie.' I recall seeing a bear fast asleep on a corner in Southwark. Its owner claimed the animal had been given a sleeping draught. On other occasions my cat Bonaventure, who drank my ale, lay fast asleep on the hearth and, at the other extreme, Sparwell lurched in that execution barrel bereft of all consciousness. Such images made me recall this tavern's great pig, the boar Pedro the Cruel, falling fast asleep outside its sty on a freezing winter night. Pedro, I suspect, is a benevolent animal but still a very greedy one, with a snout for any titbit left lying about, including all the drugged ale you poured out of the tankards used by those archers. On reflection, I concluded, that could be the only explanation for a pig who loves its comfort not to return to sleep in its sty on such a night.' Athelstan sipped from his own goblet. 'Of course, unlike poison, a sleeping potion leaves no visible effect. Even the rats in the Guildhall dungeon would just creep back into their holes to sleep. So let us return to the Palisade, shrouded in an icy darkness. You leave the archers sleeping and move to the Barbican.'

'What if Hornsey had returned?' Thorne, his lower lip trembling, gestured with his hand.

'Quite understandable: he would have found two guards asleep. He would probably welcome that and go back to his lover, Ronseval. Oh no, that didn't pose any danger. The only real threat to you, Master Thorne, was someone actually finding you in the Barbican when the murders were taking place, though that would be nigh impossible because you were going to seal yourself in. Even afterwards, if someone had stopped you on the Palisade, it wouldn't be proof enough. After all, you are the tavern master here.' Athelstan breathed in deeply. 'Oh no, what you plotted and planned was very devious. You arrive at the Barbican and the guards in the lower chamber welcome you; after all, you are the genial Mine Host making sure everyone is comfortable. You brought that tun of your special ale. You insist on sharing it out before climbing up into the storey above. Again, Marsen and Mauclerc cordially greet you. They like that, someone dancing attendance on them, eager to please. You are their host, a man who has to report to Master Thibault. You carry a gift and they are certainly deep in their cups. Of course, the exchequer chest lies open as you suspected it would be. Marsen had insisted that Hornsey unclasp the third lock – he and Mauclerc have unfastened the other two. I suspect even if it had been locked, once you had dealt with your victims you would have just forced the locks, but Marsen's glorying in his greed made your task all the easier. You measure out the ale containing that powerful sleeping draught. You are serving a refreshing drink to men and women who have eaten your highly spiced capon, which would only sharpen their thirst. You tried to claim Marsen wouldn't want cheap ale – he didn't, but a tankard of your best is another matter. Toasts are exchanged and, within a very short while, your victims are deep in a drugged sleep. You then move swiftly. You leave the Barbican and bring in the hooked ladder as well as a small crossbow and quiver of bolts you've hidden close by. You also move a barrow or cart from that tangle of conveyances beneath the tarpaulin to stand just beneath the window. Once inside, you lock and bolt the main door and carry the ladder to the upper chamber and continue your plan. In both chambers you make it look as if the most violent conflict had occurred. Indeed, you will make people wonder if there was one attacker involved or more. You confuse matters even more by drawing the weapons of your sleeping victims and placing them nearby. You ensure that the blades rasp together in case they are closely scrutinized.' Athelstan gathered himself as he approached the black heart of this matter. 'God forgive you,' he whispered. 'You then carry out dreadful murder in different ways, inflicting on each victim a mortal wound. Tax collectors, archers and whores, every single soul in that Barbican you slaughter without mercy.' Athelstan sat staring at the accused. 'Now you must cover your sin, you make sure the tankards in both chambers are clean. You pour the tainted drink into the great water bucket on the *lavarium*. You swill out those tankards and use the ordinary ale to refill them. Of course, once I'd left, you made sure that the bucket of dirty water was taken and poured into the river. You've achieved what you wanted – all traces of any sleeping potion are removed. The taunting verses about being numbered and weighed in the balance, purportedly the words of Beowulf, are pinned to the inside of the window shutter.'

'And the money?' Thorne broke in. 'How was I supposed to—'

'I wondered about that, Master Thorne, I really did. It was far too dangerous to carry a clinking sack across the Palisade and into the tavern. For a while I suspected you concealed it in the piggery or somewhere along the Palisade, but that would be highly dangerous. You suspected Thibault and others might come hunting for the lost treasure. If it was found outside the Barbican, somewhere in your tavern or the land around it, suspicion would naturally fall on you. So I concluded that the treasure is still in the Barbican.'

'Nonsense! The fire . . .' Thorne fell quiet, almost squirming in the chair.

'Oh, Master Thorne, what did you just nearly say? That you wouldn't hide your plunder in a place you tried to burn?'

'You are tricking me. You trip me up with words.'

'No, Thorne, you stumble over your own lies. You started that fire. I saw the scorch marks against the wall where it began. I smelt the oil. I asked myself then who could so easily bring oil into the Barbican?'

'Someone coming in from the river. Many people wander here, trespassers on tavern land. Anyone of these could have brought in the oil.'

'But you did realize that the fire was deliberately started by oil being poured?' Athelstan asked.

'Well, yes.'

'But on the afternoon when the fire occurred, when I escaped and came here into the Dark Parlour, you claimed it must have been an accident. '

'Yes, yes, of course.'

'But even then, as owner of the Barbican, you must have wondered what caused a fire to rage so violently.' Thorne just glared back. 'Anyway,' Athelstan continued serenely, 'you must have searched the Barbican after the fire and, like me, smelt the oil?'

'Yes.'

'And you, the owner, must have realized that there was no oil in the Barbican to begin with. I certainly didn't see any. It must have been specially brought in, so the fire was no accident but an attempt to murder me.' Thorne just blinked, wetting his lips.

'In which case,' Athelstan spread his hands, 'why didn't you inform me, send an urgent message to St Erconwald's or to Sir John at the Guildhall? After all, you did assure me it was probably an accident, then you discovered that the opposite was the case.'

'I am sorry, I made a mistake.' Thorne blinked. 'I am not too sure whether I really did know it was oil.'

'Master Thorne, your attempt to murder me was a terrible mistake. You didn't think it through, or perhaps you did but wagered I would never survive to question you. I will go back to the beginning. You must have gone into the Barbican to satisfy your own curiosity about why your property had been burnt. In fact, you did more than that; a great deal of the wreckage had been removed.'

'I hired la-labourers,' Thorne stammered.

'Which labourers?' Cranston roared as the realization dawned on the coroner that the accused had almost murdered his beloved Athelstan. 'Which labourers, Thorne, and I want every detail!'

'I forget, I forget,' Thorne mumbled. He sat, head down, and, when he glanced up, Athelstan caught the man's sheer desperation. 'Brother Athelstan, Sir John, I am confused. If I, as you allege, stole Marsen's treasure and hid it in the Barbican, where, according you, it still remains hidden, then why should I deliberately start a fire in the same place?'

'Oh, for many reasons. Never mind my murder, you deliberately made the Barbican a ruin, derelict, a place of little use to anyone. After the fire, who would go there? Which is why you insisted on clearing the wreckage yourself. You didn't bring in any labourers, Mooncalf has informed me of that and Mooncalf would dare not lie to me. Oh, before the fire you allowed the likes of Paston and Brother Marcel to climb to the top of the tower to view the river.' Athelstan pulled a face. 'To try and stop them would have created suspicion, but of course,' Athelstan lowered his voice, 'I was different. You resented my snooping, my prying and, above all, me going anywhere near the Barbican, where the gold and silver you stole, held in a leather sack, has been pushed deep into that latrine, the ancient sewer beneath the garderobe.'

'But the fire?'

'The fire did not reach it. The bag is thrust down deep in a pit, sunk amongst the most filthy refuse. No one would think of searching for it there, especially now after the Barbican has been reduced to a ruin. Time would pass and, when all was quiet and memories faded, you would dig deep and remove what you had stolen.' Athelstan stared at the taverner, who now kept glancing over his shoulder at the door. The friar had wondered if Eleanor Thorne was implicated but he concluded that she was not, which is why Thorne had told her the tale about searching for the intruder in the stables. However, did Eleanor herself secretly suspect her husband?

'No one will come here, Master Thorne,' Athelstan declared softly. 'We have no need, as yet, to question your wife, so let us return to the Barbican the night you committed these murders. All your victims lay dead; both chambers left in chaos, the proclamation has been pinned, the gold and silver hidden away. Now you prepare to leave. You ensure that you have everything with you – you return to the lower chamber to check for the final time. The door is locked and bolted. You take the ladder into the upper storey, you secure the trapdoor and move swiftly. All lights are doused as you prepare to leave through the window.' Athelstan held up a hand at a knocking at the door. He rose, crossed and opened it. Burley stood there holding a crossbow, three small quarrels and a wristguard. The knight put the quarrels and wristguard on the floor and held up the arbalest.

'Found in Friar Roger's chamber,' he declared. 'But very clever, look.' The knight banneret swiftly unpinned the apparatus on the crossbow: the hand-drawn chord and the studs which held everything in place, the metal groove and release clasps could all be taken off. Burley did this swiftly and

Athelstan smiled. The hand-held arbalest was no longer a deadly weapon but a Tau, the symbol beloved of the Franciscan order: a T-shaped cross which took its name from the Greek letter 'Tau', the symbol used by St Francis Assisi to sign his letters.

'It can be assembled very swiftly,' Burley explained, 'and then just as speedily be stripped of all its war-like paraphernalia.'

'And the quarrels?'

'Found in his chamber. Again very cunning. All three can be taken apart, watch.' Burley picked up one of the quarrels, removed the metal clasp with the miniature stiffened feathers which served as its flight, then the barbed steel tip. 'All three were kept separate,' Burley explained, 'and unless you knew what you were looking for, it would be very difficult to realize that hidden amongst clothing, manuscripts, beads and other items, were these different pieces which, when brought together, would form a deadly hand-held arbalest and crossbow bolts.' Athelstan took the flight and studied it carefully. He was certain that a similar bolt or quarrel had killed Thibault's henchman. He recalled leaning over Lascelles to administer the last rites; the crossbow quarrels were the same and, more importantly, that could be proved. Lascelles' corpse had been removed for burial; the quarrels, as the law laid down, would be stored away as evidence. It would be enough to despatch Brother Roger to the gallows, if he had not been a cleric.

'Brother?' Athelstan looked up at Burley's lean, saturnine face.

'You told me,' the knight banneret declared, 'to search his possessions but to forget that he was a friar and more probably a very skilled assassin. Everything we found we laid out on the floor of the chamber. It was like a puzzle, deciding which pieces would go together. I suspect when he travelled, as he was apparently preparing to do, the weapon would be dismantled. At other times, and it's only a hand-held one, the arbalest would be readied, primed and hidden away.'

Athelstan thanked Burley, instructed him to keep the evidence safe and returned to the Dark Parlour. Thorne sat staring moodily into the goblet of white wine Cranston had poured for him. The coroner slouched stock-still in his judgement chair, watching the taverner as closely as a terrier would a rat hole.

'You said I left by a ladder from the window,' Thorne protested, 'but that was locked from within and we have no ladder long enough . . .'

'Silence, Master Thorne. This is how matters proceeded. You went up into the upper storey, locking the trapdoor from that side. You doused the candles and opened the shutters. Before you entered the Barbican you wheeled a handcart beneath the window. You dropped the ladder down on to the barrow; the hooks at either end of the ladder are secured on the sill which runs beneath the window. In fact, as I shall prove, the way you went down is the same way you later went up – that was an essential part of your plan.' Athelstan stared down at the notes he had made. 'You climbed out. You pull the inner shutter back; you slammed it shut to bring the hook down on the other side. Whether it did or not, I admit, is debatable because in the end it's all pretence. The inner shutter looked sealed. You also closed the horn-covered window by simply loosening the horn and slipping your hand through to bring down the latch. You then repair the horn as well as you can before closing the outer shutters. Again the hooks could have swung down into their clasps just by the force of it being closed. If it did, all to the good. Whatever happened, for someone staring up through the murk with no light within and certainly none without, that window would appear sealed and locked as the main door of the Barbican. More importantly,' Athelstan stared at the taverner, 'you only had one person to convince.'

'Who was that?'

'You know full well. The ostler Mooncalf, who would go out to rouse them, stare up through the darkness and, full of panic, hasten back to raise the alarm. I shall come to that. You came down the ladder, the arbalest hooked on the war belt beneath your cloak. The night is pitch black. The Palisade stretched desolate, you are its owner, you know every inch of the ground. You move the barrow and ladder back to the nearby tangle of carts and other items stored under that tarpaulin. You then hurry across to the campfire. The archers lie fast asleep. What you have fed them would take hours to fade; anyone who did wander out would only see two very tired men who'd drank too much. In a few heartbeats you changed that. You primed your crossbow and loosed the killing shaft at close quarters into the heart of each of your victims. You return to the tavern and, in some narrow chamber, you would inspect yourself, hide your weapons, clean your boots. Oh,' Athelstan held up his hand, 'other matters. First, you are a very greedy man, Thorne, avaricious to the bone. You plundered the purses of your victims, stole every coin they owned. I suspect this lies with the rest. Secondly, you filched some of Mauclerc's documents, his scribbles about what he'd discovered during his travels and stay at The Candle-Flame. You took care of these documents, burning them here in the tavern after you'd returned. You wanted everything to be safe!'

'But Hugh of Hornsey?'

'Really, Master Taverner? What could Hornsey say? That he had abandoned his post to meet his male lover? He'd either have to tell the truth or be swiftly cast as the killer – possibly both. You know what ensued. Hornsey returned and did what you, I and Sir John would expect – he panicked and fled. At first Hornsey was bound by terror; only later did he begin to reflect. Whatever happened, in your eyes, Hornsey was still dangerous. He had wandered round the Palisade. God knows what he might have glimpsed, which is why you killed both him and Ronseval.'

'I didn't—'

'Let me finish. You returned to the tavern and your bed. Sure enough, early the next morning, Mooncalf raised the alarm. You were expecting him. You get up and go out to the Barbican. What happened then was crucial to your plan. You wanted to create the impression that the Barbican was totally sealed from within, both its door and window shutters. You make great play that the window is too high for any tavern ladder. Everyone is bustling around. You ask for a cart and ladder to be brought and up you climb. You prise open, or pretend to, the shutters and door window. Any suspicious indicator that they were loosed already is now removed. Once satisfied, you declare you are too bulky to enter. In fact, you are not, but you have accomplished your essential task. Mooncalf can now be used as the first witness to the horrors within. He climbs in, opens the door and you sweep in with the fresh opportunity to ensure you have not overlooked anything. Now,' Athelstan picked up a scroll and let it drop, 'Mooncalf has been terrified by me, and rightly so. I asked him, on his life, to reply to certain questions. He certainly recalls how you directed him to that tangle of carts and barrows under their canvas sheeting. He distinctly remembers you asking for the items which could be found there.' Athelstan pulled a face. 'I do wonder how you could be so precise on a freezing cold February dawn, that both cart and ladder are stored away there? Anyway, you climb that ladder. Mooncalf cannot say if the shutters were sealed, though, on reflection, he reports how you seemed to open them rather swiftly and made little attempt to climb inside. Again, I concede, I may be too suspicious.' Athelstan paused and stared down at his sheet of vellum where he had constructed all these questions. 'You see, Master Thorne, for the life of me, I cannot understand why you didn't enter. Thanks to you, I stood in that window trying to escape the flames. There is plenty of space. Why didn't you go in? You are a former soldier accustomed to danger?' Thorne refused to reply. 'After all, this is your Barbican, your tavern? Important guests have been beset by grave danger; two of their guards lie dead and no one appears to be alive in that tower? You have climbed a shaky ladder, perched perilously at the top, painstakingly opened shutters and windows yet you make no real attempt to enter? Mooncalf was certain of that. I would have gone in even if it was just to satisfy my own curiosity. Finally, and Mooncalf is very direct on this, you do not peer inside, nor do you call out. Why? That was the logical thing to do but of course you know there will be no answer, not from the horrors which lurk in the darkness.'

Thorne was now deeply agitated; sweat drops coursed down his face, his breathing was laboured and he found it difficult to sit still.

'At the time,' Athelstan continued, 'you considered opening the Barbican as the most difficult problem you had to face.

However, nothing in this vale of tears runs smoothly – certainly not murder.' Athelstan pointed at the ceiling. 'Physician Scrope had his own deep grievances against Marsen and, by mere coincidence, he was out on the Palisade that same night. We know that by the mud on his belongings. He certainly carried a lantern, so you must have glimpsed him. I cannot say whether he saw you, though he certainly entertained his own suspicions. He left us proof of that; anyway, only God knows what Scrope was trying to achieve but he certainly went out that night and for that alone he had to die.' Athelstan rubbed his hands together. 'What we see, hear and feel,' the friar got to his feet, 'is very strange. When it happens can be very different to what we later reflect upon. What we dismiss as ordinary or innocent can, in time, emerge as exceptional or even sinister. Scrope was a highly intelligent man. He went out that night full of hatred for Marsen and, as I have said, God knows what he came across. The dead archers? The sealed Barbican? Some dark shadow flitting through the night? In the end, he paid for it with his life and I will show you how.' Athelstan walked to the door, opened it and ordered four of the royal crossbowmen to take Thorne under close guard up to the middle gallery. Once ready, they made their way to the stairs. Eleanor Thorne came out of the kitchen, face all stricken. She glimpsed what was happening and sank to her knees with the most heart-rending scream. The woman knelt, hands to her face, rocking backwards and forwards, refusing to be comforted by the slatterns and scullions around her. Thorne tried to break through the cordon of soldiers but was roughly pulled back and pushed up the stairs. Potboys and servants, all wide-eyed and open-mouthed at the grim spectacle unfolding before them, hastily scattered out of the way. They reached the chamber where Scrope had lodged. Athelstan ordered this to be unlocked as well as the one directly opposite. Once he had arranged things as he wished, Athelstan entered the empty chamber facing Scrope's. He took the long pole from its two supports in the aumbry.

'If I stand here within the doorway and lean forward,' Athelstan did so using the pole to bang on the door of Scrope's former chamber, 'that was the knocking heard on the morning of Scrope's murder, though no one was seen in the gallery.

Master Thorne,' Athelstan pointed at the taverner held securely by the crossbow men, 'you did that. You unlocked this chamber and used it to lure Scrope to his death. You knocked on his door with this pole which you later left when you fled. Scrope first used the eyelet but saw no one. By then you'd swiftly closed the door to this chamber. Scrope walked away. Again the knocking. Scrope, already agitated and holding his *vademecum*, the pilgrim book on Glastonbury, hastens back. He opens the door and sees you standing here, hidden in the threshold of this chamber with an arbalest primed and ready. You are swifter than he. You loose and the quarrel strikes Scrope here.' Athelstan tapped himself high in the chest. 'Scrope staggers back. He is dying but the full shock of the attack has not yet had its effect. Scrope hastily closed the door, locking and bolting it. I later detected faint stains of dried blood on both lock and bolt. Scrope finally slumps to the floor. I cannot say if he meant this or it was just an act of chance, or perhaps divine providence, but Scrope died with the *vademecum* open on the page which lists the famous lists of Glastonbury. Amongst them, the *Spina Sacra*.'

'The Holy Thorn,' Cranston whispered. 'A play on our taverner's name.'

'I think so but,' Athelstan spread his hands, 'the actual details I cannot say. Perhaps Scrope had enjoyed the pun before. I suspect he deliberately opened it on that page during those last few heartbeats of his life.'

'Impossible!' Thorne protested. Nonetheless, Athelstan could see the sheer desperation in the taverner's eyes only deepened by the shrill cries of his wife which rang chillingly through the tavern.

'If Scrope was struck he would have died instantly . . .'

'Come now, Master Thorne,' Athelstan retorted. 'You have served in France and so have I and Sir John. Men, mortally wounded, may continue to act as if nothing had happened. Sometimes this can last as long as it would take to recite ten Aves. Some mortal wounds are instant; others afford a brief respite.'

'I've seen that,' one of the crossbowmen interjected. 'I've seen it on more than one occasion.'

'Even men who have lost a hand or arm,' another added.

'And so have I,' Athelstan declared, 'very recently. Lascelles received a crossbow bolt here, high in the chest. He still continued to walk forward almost unaware of his wound. Only a second crossbow bolt which struck him deep in his head brought him down. Physician Scrope, clutching that document, certainly had enough time to turn a key, draw a bolt and fumble for a page before collapsing. The poor man didn't realize he was dying, so intent was he on protecting himself against further attack and trying to leave some sign as to whom his assailant had been. Finally,' Athelstan pointed to the chamber opposite Scrope's, 'on the morning in question you had to unlock that: you used it as your murder place then hastily locked it again and,' he gestured at the nearby stairs, 'hurried up those, along the gallery above then down to act all busy in the taproom. Only you, Master Taverner, had the means to do that, no one else.' Athelstan breathed in deeply. 'Sir John, we are finished here.'

Cranston closed the doors to both chambers and ordered Thorne to be taken back to the Dark Parlour. Once again they had to pass Mistress Eleanor, who could only stretch out her arms and cry pityingly. Thorne's deepening agitation was so intense that when they entered the Dark Parlour, Sir John ordered the taverner to be bound, whilst two of the crossbow men, with weapons primed, were ordered to stay with them.

'Ronseval was killed just as swiftly,' Athelstan continued, retaking his seat, 'once you had lured him to his death. Some of this I cannot prove; I admit it is only conjecture, though it's logical. Ronseval and Hornsey trusted you. I have demonstrated why. Now, on the night of the murders, Hornsey saw something, or guessed something but then fled. No one knows what he told Ronseval but the very fact that Hornsey had been out on the Palisade meant that he had to die and so had his lover. Ronseval, the sensitive but terrified troubadour, was easy prey. He was searching for his lover. You – Thorne – promised to help. You told him to pack all his possessions, slip out of the tavern and meet you along that lonely stretch of the Thames. Ronseval did so, walking causally towards you, only to receive his death wound.'

'I was elsewhere the night he was killed!' Thorne yelled.

'Who informed you he was killed at night?' Athelstan countered. 'Where were you that night? You did leave the tavern. I want the times, the places and witnesses.'

Thorne kept his head down. Athelstan rose to his feet. 'Sir John, excuse me. I need to fetch something.' The friar pointed at the two crossbowmen. 'Whilst I am gone you are to allow no one into this room except me.' Cranston grunted; the two guards nodded in agreement. 'Only me,' the friar repeated and left. Cranston, mystified, glared at the door then shifted his gaze to Thorne. The coroner was convinced, as would any jury before King's Bench, that Thorne was guilty of the most malicious murder. He was also a traitor because those he had slain were Crown officials, whilst the treasure had been stolen from the king. If that was the case, Thorne would be condemned to a most terrifying death here at the scene of his crimes. An execution platform would be set up in the Palisade. The Southwark Carnifex, together with his assistants, would carry out all the horrors of the legal punishment for treason. Thorne would be dragged on a hurdle from the Bocardo. He would be stripped, his body carefully painted to indicate where the executioner would plunge his knife. He would be half-hanged before being slit from throat to crotch, his belly opened, his entrails plucked out and burnt before his still-seeing eyes . . . Cranston's reverie was broken by an insistent rapping at the door. He gestured at one of the crossbow men to answer it. The soldier pulled down the eyelet, grunted and swung the door open. Cranston glanced up. He immediately wondered why Athelstan had drawn his cowl over his head, then stared in disbelief as the cowl was pushed back to reveal the smiling face of one of the guards outside.

'What on earth . . .' Cranston roared. The crossbowmen were now laughing.

'Peace, Sir John,' Athelstan declared as he swept back into the room. Thorne, who had watched all this, just slumped in defeat. Athelstan thanked the guard and once the door closed behind him, retook his seat.

'I have just demonstrated how Hornsey, a veteran soldier, a cunning man, was killed. He took sanctuary in St Erconwald's. He thought he would be safe there. Perhaps his close proximity to me was a silent threat to you, Thorne. He sat in the mercy enclave. I retired to my house and the night wore on. Hornsey had no reason to leave and believed he was safe. He hears a knock on the door, leading from the sacristy to God's Acre. He goes to answer, pulls back the eyelet and sees a Dominican standing there, head down, cowl pulled over, which is understandable as the night was very cold. Hornsey makes a most hideous mistake. He thinks it's me. He draws the bolt, opens the door and you release the crossbow bolt, which sends him staggering back to collapse in the sacristy. You then flee. I've said this before and I will say it again: friars can walk the streets of Southwark in safety,' Athelstan smiled grimly, 'and in the dark I suppose we are like cats – one looks very much like another. Nobody would accost you.'

'And where did I get the robe?' Thorne sneered.

'Oh, my learned colleague Brother Marcel unwittingly supplied it. A most fastidious man, Marcel insisted on changing his robes at least once a day. He sent the used one to your wash house. I saw your washer woman and she commented on it. You and Marcel are of the same build and size.' Athelstan rose. He walked behind Thorne, bent down and whispered in his ear. 'You are guilty, Master Thorne. I have established a burden of proof which you cannot answer. You will be condemned to the most gruesome death, but not before Thibault has racked and twisted your body with the most terrible torture. Suspicion will fall on your wife; she too might be questioned. You will be adjudged a traitor. Consequently, even if she is innocent, Mistress Eleanor will lose everything because all your property will be forfeit to the Crown.' Athelstan straightened up before leaning down again. 'I invite you to make a full confession. Reveal the whereabouts of the treasure, which, in fact, I know already; confess and express your sorrow. I will ensure a priest shrives you, whilst the Hangman of Rochester, whom I have brought secretly to this tavern, will carry out sentence immediately. The Hangman is most skilled. You would not strangle but die instantly.' Athelstan turned and walked away. 'The choice is yours. I suggest you make haste because it's only a matter of time before Master Thibault interferes. Sir John, tell me, what I offer is both legitimate and judicial?'

'I am the king's justiciar,' Cranston replied, holding Athelstan's gaze. 'I have the power to hear and decide. I have authority to carry out, in the king's own name, the sentence of death be it now or on some appointed day. I can also exercise mercy in the manner of that death. I believe we have said enough.' Cranston snapped his fingers. 'Have the prisoner taken down to the cellar. Keep a close watch on him.' Cranston pointed to the hour candle glowing on its stand under a broad copper cap. 'By the time the flame reaches midway to the next ring, you, Master Thorne, must decide or it will be decided for you.' The prisoner was dragged to his feet. He tried to resist, until one of the soldiers punched him hard in the stomach and dragged him groaning from the room.

'I hope he confesses,' Athelstan murmured. 'I pray that he does. He murdered twelve people, Sir John, and all for the sake of filthy greed. The love of money is indeed the root of all evil. If he confesses . . .' Athelstan took a deep breath.

'The tavern sign can be his gallows,' Cranston declared. 'It stretches high and strong. We will use the same ladder he did to enter the Barbican.'

'I'd best inform the Hangman, he is also a skilled clerk.' Athelstan left. Cranston gestured at the two crossbowmen to follow and sat staring at the empty chairs in front of him. Thorne certainly deserved his death but he wondered what Athelstan would do with the others. The coroner dozed for a short while. Now and again he would stir and peer at the hour candle, its flame burning merrily away. Athelstan returned. He spoke to people waiting in the gallery outside and closed the door.

'Sir John,' Athelstan walked slowly towards the table. 'I am going to ask you for an indulgence regarding the Pastons.'

The coroner chewed the corner of his lip. 'In theory, Brother . . .'

'In practice, Sir John, Paston is a good man. He has told the truth and he is guilty of no more than many of his kind

in this city. I do not want to see him become the object of
Gaunt's vindictiveness.' Athelstan kept his face composed. He
knew nothing would persuade Cranston more than a dig at the
self-proclaimed Regent.

'His daughter, Martha, and William the clerk are deeply in
love. They were of great help to us.'

Cranston waved a hand. 'As you wish, little friar.'

Athelstan went back, opened the door and ushered Paston,
his daughter and Foulkes into the chamber. Once they had
taken their seats Athelstan went to stand beside Cranston.

'Please.' He smiled. 'I beg you not to look so anxious.
Master William, I thank you for your help as I do you, Sir
Robert. Now this is what Sir John and I have decided. Sir
Robert, I want you to clear the hold of *The Five Wounds* of
all weapons. You will move your ship to another harbour.
You will return to Surrey and resign your post as a member
of the Commons. You will not become embroiled in politics
and cease forthwith your attacks on His Grace the Regent.
You will not return to this city unless it is with the special
permission of Sir John here and only to do business. Master
William, Mistress Martha, you too will not enter this city
which is so dangerous for you.' Athelstan lowered his voice.
'Go home,' he urged. 'Marry each other, love each other.
Steer clear of all danger. Keep what you believe in the secrecy
of the heart.' The relief on Sir Robert's face was obvious.
Foulkes looked at Martha, who nodded her agreement.

'Sir Robert, I suggest you make to leave very, very swiftly.'

'Don't worry,' Paston got to his feet, 'everything is packed
already, Brother. I know what is going to happen here. A special
commission of oyer and terminer invariably ends in blood . . .'

'True, true,' Cranston murmured, 'and Master Thibault will
be here very soon.'

The coroner rose and clasped Sir Robert's hand and that of
his daughter and Foulkes. Athelstan did likewise. He sketched
a blessing over them and noticed with relief that Martha and
William crossed themselves. They had hardly left the chamber
when there was a rap on the door and the Hangman of
Rochester walked in holding a piece of parchment, which he
handed to Athelstan.

'God knows what happened here, Brother, but Thorne has made a full confession.' The Hangman fought to keep the surprise out of his voice. 'He murdered twelve people, he stole the gold . . .'

'Did he say where it is?' Cranston asked.

'No, Sir John.' The Hangman clawed at his long, yellowish hair. 'He just said that Brother Athelstan would know where it is.' The Hangman's skeletal face creased into the smile. 'I suppose he didn't trust me. Thorne is a broken man, all juddering and trembling. He cries like a baby. He wishes to see his wife and be shriven by a priest.'

'Let Mistress Eleanor see him then ask Brother Marcel to hear his confession – swiftly, mind you. Tell Marcel to issue a general absolution.'

'And execution?'

Cranston repeated what he told Athelstan earlier.

The Hangman nodded. 'I will arrange it.'

'Do so quickly,' Athelstan urged. 'Before Thibault arrives.' The Hangman left. Athelstan asked to be alone. Sir John clapped him on the shoulder and murmured something about supervising the arrangements. The coroner sheathed his sword, finished his wine and quietly left. Athelstan bolted the door and went to kneel beside the table. He leaned back, eyes closed, as he murmured the *'De Profundis'* and the *'Miserere Mei.'* All was resolved, he thought, yet lives had been shattered, souls despatched to judgement and the storm was still raging. Evil was like a seed, Athelstan thought: it took root and erupted into a wild, malignant tangle. Taverner Thorne probably regretted spending the profits of war on The Candle-Flame and decided to recoup his losses in a most sinister way. He had planned and plotted well but totally underestimated the souls around him, filled with their own private passions, be it Sir Robert Paston's dabbling in power, Physician Scrope's desire for vengeance or the highly illicit relationship between Ronseval and Hornsey. Now he was to pay the price. For a while Athelstan made himself relax, thumbing his Ave beads as he prayed for the souls of the departed and for Thorne's, who would soon be brought to judgement. He dozed until roused by Cranston, his beaver hat pulled down, cloak tied tightly around him.

'You'd best come, Athelstan,' he declared quietly. 'War barges have been glimpsed on the river. Thibault is probably on his way. We are ready. I have brought Mooncalf with me.' The coroner shouted an order and two crossbowmen, escorting an ashen-faced, trembling Mooncalf came into the passageway.

'What should we do with him, Brother?' Cranston whispered. Athelstan walked forward and grasped the ostler's white, unshaven face between his hands.

'Master Mooncalf,' he whispered, 'you are about to witness the grisly end of a malefactor. Unless you are more prudent and more prayerful, one day you will make the same journey. So tell me now, who is the serjeant-at-law holding your letter denouncing the Pastons?'

'Master Ravenscott,' the ostler replied swiftly, eyes almost bulging with terror. 'Master Jacob Ravenscott. He lodges at The Hoop of Heaven near the Inns of Court.'

'I know it well,' Cranston declared. 'And, as an officer of the law, I will collect that letter and burn it. So, Brother, what shall we do with Mooncalf? Hang him?'

'No, no.' Athelstan still held the ostler's face. He gently squeezed his hands. 'Listen to me, Mooncalf, and listen well. We shall collect your letter and burn it. If I ever hear that you have troubled the Pastons again, I will have you hanged as high as heaven. You will watch your master suffer just sentence, after which you will pack your possessions and never be seen in London or Southwark again. If you are, my good friend, Sir John Cranston, will issue warrants for your arrest. Do you understand me? I make no idle threats but a vow as sacred as any taken in church. Do you understand?' Athelstan took his hands away.

'Yes, Brother!' If Mooncalf hadn't been held by the crossbowmen the ostler would have collapsed in nervous prostration.

'Bring him with us,' Athelstan ordered. Stepping round the ostler and his guard, Athelstan followed the coroner out into the front of the tavern. A small crowd had assembled, servants and slatterns. Eleanor Thorne was being led away by one of the maids, her heart-rending sobs almost muffled by the blankets thrown around her. The Hangman of Rochester had prepared well. The tavern sign had been removed from its hooks and a thick rope with a noose at the end hung down. Against the signpost leaned a ladder; the Hangman had climbed this and sat legs dangling either side of the projecting branch. The execution area was surrounded by crossbowmen. Thorne appeared. Athelstan was relieved that a sack had been pulled over the taverner's head. He could see the effect of the man's laboured breathing. Thorne, hands bound behind his back, was taken to the foot of the ladder. Cranston, in a powerful voice, briefly proclaimed the name of the condemned man, his heinous crimes and how he deserved death. Thorne was immediately pushed up the ladder by the crossbowmen, who thrust him as high as the Hangman instructed, before turning him round. The Hangman leaned forward, shortened the rope and placed the noose over the condemned man's head, tying the knot expertly just behind his right ear. The Hangman issued another instruction and the crossbowmen pushed the gasping Thorne further up the rungs. Once he was ready, the Hangman gestured at the crossbowmen to go down. He lifted his hand.

'On my sign!' he shouted. For a few heartbeats nothing could be heard except the gasps and moans of the condemned man. The sacking over his face was blowing out as he fought for his last breath. The Hangman's gloved hand dropped. The ladder was twisted. Thorne, hands still tied behind his back, dropped like a stone. Athelstan closed his eyes as he heard the awful crack as the condemned man's neck broke. He murmured the requiem, opened his eyes and stared at that grim sight. Thorne's corpse swayed slightly. Athelstan sketched a blessing. At least Thorne had died in the twinkling of an eye. He had not choked as others did, sometimes for as long as it would take to say a rosary, whilst the taverner had escaped the full horrors inflicted by a traitor's death.

'Let him hang for an hour,' Cranston proclaimed, 'then cut him down. Let Mistress Eleanor have his corpse. Brother Athelstan?' Cranston took the little friar by the elbow and steered him away. Sir John had witnessed many executions, but he could tell by the friar's pale face that Athelstan was deeply agitated.

'Come on, Brother,' Cranston whispered. 'We will share a

goblet of Bordeaux and what is left of the food whilst we await the arrival of Master Thibault.'

Cranston was correct. They had scarcely poured the wine when Sir Simon Burley announced that the war barges had reached the nearby quayside and Master Thibault could be glimpsed crossing the Palisade. When questioned, the knight banneret assured Cranston that the Pastons had left almost immediately, whilst Mooncalf, almost a gibbering idiot after what he had witnessed, was hastily collecting his paltry possessions, determined at putting as much distance between himself and the 'Terrible Sir John'. Burley also assured Cranston that the two friars were safely guarded in their respective chambers.

A short while later Thibault, accompanied by his new henchman Albinus, strode into the Dark Parlour. Athelstan lowered his head to hide his smile. Thibault was taking no chances. Both he and his henchman carried kite-shaped shields for protection and both wore long coats of chainmail, which fell beneath the knee. Thibault pushed both helmet and shield into Albinus' hands, nodded at Cranston and Athelstan then sat down in the judgement chair, peeling off his leather gauntlets.

'I've seen the corpse. I understand the Pastons have left and the guards are laughing at the antics of an ostler who is so terrified he's soiled himself. A Franciscan priest lies under arrest, likewise a Dominican. In God's name, Sir John, Brother Athelstan, what has happened here?'

Athelstan told him. He had anticipated this so he chose his words carefully. He made little reference to the Pastons except that Sir Robert now believed he should withdraw from public life in all its aspects. He would reside quietly in his manor, tending his lands and supervising his trade across the Narrow Seas. Thibault seemed slightly amused by this; he grinned over his shoulder at Albinus, a strange-looking man with snow-white hair and reddish skin, his icy-blue eyes ringed by pink.

'My Lord of Gaunt will be very pleased,' Thibault murmured, 'to see the back of Sir Robert both literally and metaphorically. And the creature Mooncalf?'

'He shouldn't have meddled where he did,' Athelstan

retorted. 'Now he has seen the error of his ways, I suspect he will be leaving Southwark to seek employment in a tavern just south of the Scottish march.'

Thibault nodded and glanced down. Athelstan had noticed he had done the same when he described the treachery of Marcel and the murderous nature of Brother Roger. Athelstan recognized that gesture. Thibault, despite his innocent-looking face, was quietly seething with fury. The Master of Secrets breathed in deeply through his nose and brought his head back. Athelstan flinched at the fury raging in those eyes.

'Brother Marcel will be sent back to France.' Thibault played with his gauntlet. 'His Grace the king will despatch a letter to the Holy Father and copy it to the Minister General of your order, Athelstan. He will demand that Brother Marcel be rigorously punished on bread and water for two years in some stinking monastery out in the wilds where he can learn true poverty, humility and obedience. I don't think our Holy Father will need much persuading when he discovers that his own Inquisitor was being used as a French spy in this kingdom. The papacy needs English gold and support. As for Friar Roger,' Thibault stared past Athelstan as if he was watching something else, 'I will personally ensure that he is escorted back to Assisi. One of my sea captains, Eudo Tallifer, a kinsman of my henchman Albinus, will supervise his passage.'

'Eudo Tallifer?' Cranston asked. 'The privateer, once a pirate off Goodwin Sands?'

'And now the Crown's most loyal subject,' Thibault retorted. 'His ship, *The Dapifer* is due to sail tomorrow.' Thibault glowered knowingly over his shoulder at Albinus. 'I am sure,' he added caustically, 'the Franciscan will be most royally welcome aboard. As for the rest, Thorne is now past judgement. I presume his wife is innocent and that he submitted a full confession? The felon escaped the penalty for treason and so his property cannot be forfeited. I will offer Widow Thorne a reasonable price; she can rejoin her kinsman on the Canterbury road. Now we come to the crux of this matter.' Athelstan gestured at the door. 'You trust Albinus?' he asked.

'With my life.'

'You will find Marsen's treasure,' Athelstan retorted, 'hidden deep beneath the garderobe in the Barbican. An ancient sewer runs there.' Athelstan pointed to his papers still strewn across the table. 'Thorne confessed as much before he died.' Thibault clicked his fingers and pointed at the door.

'Take two trusted guards,' he ordered Albinus. 'Seize whatever tools you need. I want every penny of that treasure.'

Once the henchman had left Thibault sat drumming his fingers on the table. 'There is more, Brother Athelstan?'

'You know there is, Master Thibault.' Athelstan drew a scroll of white parchment from the pocket of his gown. 'This is a charter issued by the king granting full and complete pardon, without any reservation, to Watkin the dung collector and Pike the ditcher now in sanctuary at St Erconwald's in Southwark. A full pardon, Master Thibault! Indeed, both men are under royal protection and brought within the king's love.'

Thibault spread his hands.

'You must have seen copies,' Athelstan continued, 'on roll in the Chancery, the Exchequer and King's Bench?'

'His Grace the king thinks highly of you, Brother Athelstan.'

'And I have the same high regard for His Grace.'

'Your parishioners are safe.' Thibault shrugged. 'What does it matter if two more rogues are welcomed back by their kith and kin?'

'In which case,' Athelstan got to his feet, Cranston likewise. The friar had reached the door when Thibault called his name. He turned; the Master of Secrets beckoned him back.

'Sir John, I implore your kindness. I would like a word alone with Brother Athelstan.' Cranston pulled a face and left. Athelstan walked back to the table and stood staring down at Thibault, who put his face in his hands, rubbing his forehead with the tips of his fingers. He took his hands away. Athelstan was surprised at the tears brimming in the eyes of this hard-souled man.

'Brother Athelstan, you did good service. Very good service. You and Sir John. I assure you both the king and His Grace, My Lord of Gaunt, will be appraised of it.'

Athelstan sketched a bow. Thibault pushed back the chair and rose. Resting his hands on the table top he leaned across; the usual sly, sardonic look had disappeared. 'Brother Athelstan,

I have a great favour to ask. The Day of the Great Slaughter is fast closing upon us. The strongholds will fall and London will be riven by revolt.'

'And?'

'When that day of wrath arrives, I will send my daughter Isabella to you. I want your promise that she will be kept safe, unharmed. She will carry a letter giving you precise details of what I would like to be done should I not survive that terrible day.'

'She would be safe in the Tower or sanctuary at Westminster Abbey?'

'No, Brother Athelstan. You will be her tower, her sanctuary, her church. Just give me your promise. For God's sake, Brother, she is only a child. You know what will happen to her if she falls into the hands of the mob.' He extended a hand. 'Please?' he urged. 'I am begging.' Athelstan clasped it. Thibault relaxed and stepped back. 'Thank you.'

'Sir John is waiting,' Athelstan declared. 'And I am sure my parish is brimming with excitement.' He sketched a blessing in Thibault's direction. 'You have my word. Believe me, Master Thibault, you are correct. The time of great tribulation will soon be upon us.'